Delicious Heat: Bangers Tavern Romance 3

Sadira Stone

Delicious Heat

♥

Cupid has lousy timing.

After kicking her cheating husband to the curb, nurse Anna Khoury discovers she's pregnant. When Bangers Tavern's hunky chef makes heart eyes at her, she dismisses that delicious thrill as the last thing she needs. Single motherhood will take all her strength and focus. Anna's battered heart can't take another blow.

Chef Diego Vargas is aiming higher than burgers and tater tots. His dream—his own food truck, the Empanada Angel, but he'll need his family's support to pull it off. Meeting Anna leaves him thunderstruck, even though his attraction to her threatens all his plans. Call it fate, call him crazy, but he's determined to prove he's in it for keeps.

With a belligerent ex-husband and two overprotective families set on breaking them up, Anna and Diego will need more than red-hot passion to pull them through. His career and her baby's future are on the line.

Come back to Bangers Tavern for a spicy tale of forbidden love that will warm your heart...and other parts...and make you hungry for empanadas!

Copyright

♥

Contents

1. Chapter One: Surprise!   1

2. Chapter Two: Flakey Empanadas   10

3. Chapter Three: Tots for an Angel   17

4. Chapter Four: Slaying a Dragon   25

5. Chapter Five: Probably a Bad Idea   38

6. Chapter Six: Mistletoe Magic   47

7. Chapter Seven: Busted   57

8. Chapter Eight: Blueberry   65

9. Chapter Nine: Olive   72

10. Chapter Ten: A Kiss, Interrupted   79

11. Chapter Eleven: Serving Brock   93

12. Chapter Twelve: Valentine's Showdown   105

13. Chapter Thirteen: Et Tu, Hermana?   112

14. Chapter Fourteen: An Interloper   122

15. Chapter Fifteen: Kafta and Kisses   129

16. Chapter Sixteen: Abuelita Concedes   143

17. Chapter Seventeen: Brock Strikes Back 150

18. Chapter Eighteen: Meatballs and Bad Luck 163

19. Chapter Nineteen: Betrayal Served Hot and Cold 171

20. Chapter Twenty: Love, Interrupted 184

21. Chapter Twenty-One: Abuelita Up and Down 193

22. Chapter Twenty-Two: Sweet Success and Dirty Tricks 201

23. Chapter Twenty-Three: Make Up, Lock Up 208

24. Chapter Twenty-Four: Diego on Ice 218

25. Chapter Twenty-Five: Lost and Found 229

26. Chapter Twenty-Six: Almost Sorry 240

27. Chapter Twenty-Seven: Empanada Angel 246

28. Epilogue: Ellie's Debut 257

29. Saint Patrick's Day Cocktails from Bangers Tavern 263

Acknowledgments 264

About the Author 265

Also By Sadira Stone 266

Chapter One: Surprise!

♥

"I swear to God, Anna, she's just a work friend."

Anna Khoury Spencer's hands shook too hard to unfasten the buckles of her nursing clogs, so she kicked them across the foyer, gave her spluttering husband a stiff-armed shove, and marched to their bedroom.

Clutching his perfect golden hair, Brock trailed after. "Kristi flirts with everyone at work. It doesn't mean anything."

Jaw clenched, Anna ignored him. She needed time to think. Space, too, as far as possible from her cheating, lying, scum-sucking, soon-to-be-ex. Then again, why should she leave? He caused this mess—let him pay the price. She snatched up the gym bag he'd dropped in the corner and stuffed it with the contents of his underwear drawer.

"Come on, be reasonable." Brock clutched her shoulder.

She swatted him like the loathsome bug he was and stomped to the closet where she yanked garments from hangers and flung them onto the bed.

A Seattle Seahawks jersey landed on Brock's outspread arm. He pitched it onto the floor. "Damn it, Banana—"

She whirled and stabbed a finger into his chest. "Don't you dare call me that, you...you...lying weasel breath!"

His eyes narrowed to slits. "Now just a goddamn minute. This is a simple misunderstanding. You're overreacting."

If looks could kill, her glare would've reduced him to ash. "Elena saw you."

"Who the fuck is Elena?"

"Elena from the clinic." You'd think her so-called husband would remember the work friends she talked about daily. She sure as heck remembered all the times he'd mentioned Kristi, his boss's new receptionist. Kristi did this, Kristi said that, Kristi is so funny...

Jaw clenched, she crammed the last of his socks into the bag. "You've met her several times. She's my best friend, for frick's sake, and she saw you and Kristi kissing outside the Pita Palace."

Brock's face flushed an even deeper shade of maroon. If he kept it up, he'd pop like a tick. "Elena is lying."

She pulled her phone from her pocket, tapped the screen, and shoved it in his face. "Then explain this."

As the incriminating video unwound, his jaw dropped lower and lower.

"Did you really think you could kiss your girlfriend on the street in front of the hospital where I freakin' work and no one would notice you?"

For a moment, he just gaped like a startled goldfish. Then his pale brows lowered. "No way. It's gotta be one of those deep fakes. People can manipulate videos and—"

"Shut up." She pulled a suitcase from beneath the bed and crammed his clothing inside. "You know what can't be manipulated? Me."

"But baby, I love you!" He flapped limp hands.

"Right. Love." Straightening, she planted her fists on her hips. "Is that why you forgot my birthday and our anniversary this year?"

"Baby, I—"

"Is that why you pick a fight over every stupid little thing?"

"But you get so—"

She swept a hand over the pile of his discarded gym clothes in the corner. "Is that why you leave a mess around the house and make snide comments about how your mom always kept things neat as a pin?"

"Well, she—"

"Ya know what, baby?" She spat the last word like venom. "Ever since we came back from our honeymoon, you've been waving big ol' red flags in my face, and I've been ignoring them. Well, I'm done. Good luck to you. I hope you and Kristi are very happy together."

"Anna, you don't mean that."

"You're right. I actually hope you'll both be effin' miserable." She sucked in a deep breath and straightened her shoulders. "I'm filing for divorce."

By the next morning, Anna had memorized every crack in the bedroom ceiling. Odd, though, she didn't feel sad so much as—she wiggled deeper under the covers, trying to put a name to this slippery feeling. Was it, could it be... relief?

She rolled toward Brock's side of the bed. He probably spent the night at his parents' house. She could almost smell the fluffy pancakes Deborah Spencer would cook to comfort her poor baby. For a moment, Anna wondered what sort of lies Brock would tell his family about their break-up, then decided she didn't give a flying fig.

With a groan, she pushed to her feet, trudged to the bathroom, and huffed a laugh at her bedraggled reflection. Hair snarled from tossing and turning, eyes puffy from crying, nose and upper lip raw from blowing her nose. Her stomach was off too—not surprising. One look at her and Dr. Zakariya, her boss, would send her home. But home alone was the last place she wanted to be. She needed the normalcy of work, the familiar surroundings and sense of purpose. Yesterday's bombshell was too much to digest all at once. First step, lawyer up. Second step, tell her family. No, she'd tell her sister Charlie first. Dad would absolutely freak.

On autopilot, she dug in the bathroom drawer for her birth control pills. "What's the point?" she asked her reflection. Not likely she'd have anything to do with a penis for a long, long time. Still, the pills helped with her painful periods. "Let's see, today is..." She squinted at the tiny print. "Tuesday?"

Her heart stuttered. The packet slipped from her fingers.

Yesterday was Thursday. She was a hundred thousand percent sure because she'd skipped her Thursday night yoga class to rush home and confront Brock. And her period should have started last Sunday.

Pulse galloping, she searched her memory. How long ago had she made the error? Swallowing her pill each morning was as automatic as brushing her teeth. And yet, she'd clearly screwed up sometime this month.

"Think, think." She rapped her skull with her knuckles. She and Brock hadn't had sex in ages, except...

Her stomach plummeted like a runaway elevator.

Two weeks ago. Or was it three? A post-argument cuddle had led to a quick tumble that left her unsatisfied. She remembered lying beside him as he snored, too tired and sad to bother bringing herself off. Lately, she was always so tired...

Wide-eyed, she goggled at her reflection. "It can't be."

"I'm going on break," Anna sang out in a tight, squeaky voice as she trotted past the clinic's toy-decked Christmas tree. Past the busy lobby, in a restroom far from her colleagues' prying eyes, she pulled out the pregnancy test she'd bought on her way to work. The irony twisted her gut as she unwrapped the package—through caution and good luck, she'd reached the age of twenty-nine without ever having to pee on a little plastic stick. Still, she knew the drill. What she didn't know was how to keep from shaking to pieces during the three minutes' waiting time.

"It's just stress," she muttered, pacing the tiny, tiled room. "No one's cycle is perfectly regular."

Sure, she wanted children—eventually. Someday. She'd promised herself to wait until she was at least thirty, and the shakier things got with Brock, the farther back she shoved the starting line. Besides, she had plenty of time.

Here at the clinic, she met lots of women who had their first children well into their thirties. Forties, even.

But pregnancy now meant facing some hard choices— go it alone? Chain herself to a man who'd never, ever love her the way she deserved to be loved? What kind of environment was that for a child? What kind of role model would she be if she endured eighteen more years of Brock's neglect and disrespect?

Down, down, down her thoughts spiraled until her phone timer finally dinged. Wincing, she lifted the plastic test stick and peered into the little window. Two pink lines, clear and sharp.

Clutching her heart, she collapsed against the wall and slowly slid to the floor.

The streetlamps beside her apartment building illuminated swirling snowflakes as Anna tossed her hastily packed bags into the back of her elderly Subaru, slammed the hatch, and peeled out of the parking lot.

"Corksucking ash wipe," she shouted to no one in particular as she rolled up Sixth Avenue past restaurants, weed dispensaries, vintage clothing shops, and Bangers Tavern, the bar where her sister Charlie worked. Shop windows glittered with merry Christmas lights as if mocking her fury.

"Scum-licking motherfudger!" Not even twenty-four hours into their separation, Brock strolled back into their apartment as if he'd only gone to the store. Seems he figured her rage would fizzle overnight. "Like I'd ever forgive you, you flipping cheater!"

Since taking the job at the pediatric clinic, she'd trained herself not to curse aloud, but Brock's smarmy "Now, let's be reasonable" had her itching to spew the filthiest words imaginable. What would that accomplish, though? Like it or not, he was the father of her child. The lawyer she talked with today warned her to keep her head on straight and button her lip when interacting with him. Already, she dreaded their first meeting with the divorce mediator next month.

Correction—what she dreaded most was telling him about the baby. Because faced with his oily smirk, she just couldn't force the words out.

At the traffic light, she let her head thunk onto the steering wheel. *How did my life get this screwed up?*

Sleet pelted her windshield as she turned onto her dad's street. In the darkness of a December evening, most of the block blinked with holiday cheer, a hodge-podge of Christmas lights and inflatable characters. But not Dad's house since he was under doctor's orders to rest and elevate his broken leg.

She jammed her key into the lock and flung the door open to find him sprawled on his recliner, watching boisterous sports dudes argue on TV. He looked up and wiggled the bare toes poking out of his cast. "Hey, Anna-Boo. How's my girl?"

Grinding her teeth, she surveyed the mess—wrappers and soda cans everywhere. One had even rolled under the tacky aluminum Christmas tree. Still in his pajamas, her formerly sharp-dressed father clearly hadn't shaved in days. Probably hadn't bathed, either.

Her stomach roiled at the scent of garlicky meat wafting from the kitchen.

"Your sister made meatloaf. It's not your mama's kibbeh, but it ain't bad. Saved you a plate." Dad never let an opportunity go by to remind his daughters of Mama's cooking. But Mama had been gone for years now, and neither daughter had the interest nor the time to reproduce those time-consuming Lebanese delicacies.

"I'm not hungry." She hung up her scarf and coat, then marched down the hall toward her childhood bedroom, currently occupied by her older sister Charlie who came back from Portland to help care for Dad.

She had five seconds tops before tears spilled down her cheeks, and she didn't need Dad to witness her breakdown. She and Charlie didn't always see eye to eye, but at least Anna could count on her older sister to take a twenty-first century view of her dilemma.

Anna rapped on the door, then flung it open so hard it banged against the wall. Halfway through pulling a sweater over her head, Charlie jumped and squeaked.

"It's me." Anna slumped against the wall and waited while her sister extricated her long hair from the turtleneck.

"Anna, what's wrong?"

She opened and closed her mouth several times before spitting out, "I'm pregnant."

Charlie tilted her head. "Are you happy about that?"

"Fuck no!" There were no little kids around, and she just didn't have the strength to hold back anymore. Flopping onto her childhood bed, Anna curled up, her face to the wall as her despair burbled out in messy, snotty sobs.

The mattress dipped, and Charlie's soft hand rubbed soothing circles on her back. "Does Brock know?"

She shook her head. "I asked him to clear out for a few days. But he came back, and I was so mad I just, I couldn't —"

"Hey now, take a breath. I don't have to be at work for another hour. Why don't you start at the beginning?"

"He cheated, Char." She swiped her runny nose with her sleeve. "You were right about him. Shoulda listened to you."

Charlie rubbed Anna's shoulder. "Somehow, this doesn't feel like the time for an 'I told you so.'"

Pulling her knees to her chest, Anna sighed. "Might as well take all my medicine at once. Back then, I thought you were just jealous. Turns out, he really is a total sleaze, just like you said. And I let him play me like a saxophone. No, a sax is too sophisticated. What's a really stupid instrument? A kazoo?"

Admitting the truth hurt like an unmedicated root canal, but it was high time she faced reality. And reality painted her as a big, honkin' fool.

Pretty, polished, and polite, Boyfriend Brock said all the right things, brought her flowers and little gifts "just because," listened sympathetically when she spilled her guts about Mom's early death from cancer, work woes, Charlie's feud with Dad, all of it. Until he became Husband Brock and dropped the act.

One night stood out in her memory. All dressed up for a promised date night, she found him sprawled on the couch. "Ban-Anna," he'd drawled without looking up from the stupid game on his stupid tablet, "give it a rest. We're married now. You can't expect me to keep spoiling you like a girlfriend."

Anna clutched a pillow to her face and sobbed.

"Oh, hon. I'm so sorry." Charlie wrapped her in a tight hug. "Are you going to keep the baby?"

All afternoon, she'd chewed on that very question. The timing of this pregnancy couldn't be worse. Freshly separated, her heart shredded by Brock's betrayal, how on earth was she going to handle single motherhood? A quick medical procedure was all that stood between her and a fresh start. Later, when the dust settled, she could think about finding someone new, maybe even having a baby on her own.

Except this baby was here now. As much as the idea of co-parenting with Brock turned her stomach, ending this pregnancy just felt—wrong. Deep in her gut, she knew she wanted this child.

Anna wiped her tear-slicked cheeks and faced her sister. "I'm keeping the baby."

"Okay." Charlie squeezed Anna's shoulders and fixed her with an intense gaze. "But if you change your mind later, that's fine too. Whatever happens, we're on your side."

"We?"

"Me and Dad."

A shiver tightened Anna's skin. Despite her sister's optimism, she dreaded telling her father. With his old-school ideas about family, he'd push her to get back together with Brock.

The clomp, clomp of Dad's crutches pulled them both upright. He stood in the doorway, worry etched across his baggy, bristly face. "What happened, Anna-boo?"

Anna laced her fingers with Charlie's before facing him. "Dad, it's over between Brock and me. It's been bad for a long time, and I can't take it anymore."

Dad hobbled to the other bed and dropped down with a grunt. Rumpling his thick black brows, he leaned his elbows onto his knees. "Look, kiddo, all couples fight.

Brock loves you. And it's Christmas. Time for forgiveness, right?"

"Loves me?" She could almost feel the cartoon steam shooting out her ears as she sprang to her feet. "He cheated on me, Dad. Should I forgive him and live with a cheater who'll do it again and again? Is that the kind of life you want for me? For your grandchild?"

Dad's scowl dissolved into wide-eyed wonder. "Grandchild?"

Anna nodded and clasped Charlie's hand.

A wide grin bloomed across his face. "Holy Christmas. Me, a grandpa. I was starting to wonder if it was ever gonna happen." His gaze met hers, and his smile flattened. "You want me to kick that zabre's ass, baby girl?"

She leaned onto Charlie's shoulder and sighed. "No, but I have to tell him about the baby. He has a right to know." She rubbed her belly absently. Funny how, only a few hours after getting the news, it felt natural to hold herself there, as if reassuring her tiny passenger they were going to be okay.

Charlie squeezed her hand. "You want to tell him alone, or you want some company?"

Anna fixed her with a watery gaze. "Could you come?"

Dad pounded the mattress with his fist. "Hell yeah, we'll come. Charlie, call your boss. You're gonna be late tonight."

Chapter Two: Flakey Empanadas

♥

"Get the doorbell, Abuelita?" His arms loaded with empanadas he baked for their family's Sunday gathering, Diego Vargas shivered on his parents' ice-slicked stoop. Laughter and loud conversation drifted through the closed door.

His tiny grandmother poked the doorbell with her knuckly finger. "Come on, quit yapping in there." When no one answered, she pushed the Christmas wreath aside and rapped on the brass knocker like an impatient little woodpecker.

Footsteps approached. "Keep your pants on, jeesh!" His sister Elena threw the door open, dressed in pastel scrubs. "Sorry, Abuelita. We're all in the kitchen."

"And they say I'm going deaf." She bustled inside and squinted at her eldest granddaughter. "Why are you dressed for work?"

"Taking an extra shift this afternoon. Oscar's growing like a weed, and kids' clothes are so expensive."

Abuelita tisked and dug into her purse. "You work too hard. Why don't you just ask your parents for a little help?"

"And endure another judgy lecture? No thanks." His sister jutted her chin, but she didn't push away the folded bills Abuelita pressed into her hand.

Elena shot him a sheepish glance. No need to razz her about it, though. With the money she earned from her neighborhood catering, Abuelita could well afford to spoil her grandchildren and great-grandchildren.

As if nothing had happened, Abuelita snapped, "Help your brother, gordita. Those trays are heavy."

Diego winced. His oldest sister had long ago lost her childhood pudge, but their family clung mercilessly to labels. Elena, "the practical one," had an emotional streak the family ignored. Their brother Jorge was "the athletic one," though he hadn't played sports since blowing out his knee in college. Anita was "the pretty one," though Elena had long since caught up in that department. And Diego, the youngest sibling, was forever "the flakey one" in his family's eyes.

He followed Elena into the kitchen and set down his tray of empanadas before pecking his mom on both cheeks.

"Don't be stingy, guapo." She enfolded him in a squishy hug, then held him at arm's length and gave him a head-to-toe inspection. "You forgot to shave."

He stroked his jaw. "Stubble is stylish, Ma."

She snorted. "Either grow it out or shave it off. This scruffy stuff makes you look disreputable."

"Ma, I work in a kitchen. No one sees me." Besides, his almost-beard countered his natural babyface. At twenty-eight, he still got carded in bars. Every. Single. Time.

"Tío D!" A thigh-high blur of dark hair and pinwheeling arms streaked toward him.

"Oof!" He pretended to reel under the impact, then scooped up Elena's son and flung him high overhead. "Oscar, you're getting so heavy! How old are you now, twenty?"

The tot squealed as Diego spun him around.

Jorge's youngest girl stomped up, hands on hips. "Tío D, don't be silly. Oscar is four." She thumped her chest. "I'm six. Mari is eight." She pointed to her solemn, skinny sister.

"Thanks for the reminder." He ruffled his niece's hair. "I was never very good at math."

Little Nita crossed her arms. "Math is important. STEM girls rule the world. Pew pew!" She sprinted away, firing her forefinger ray gun at the Christmas tree.

"Hi, Unc." Mari waggled her fingers before trailing after her little sister.

Diego's father sidled into the kitchen, smooched Abuelita's cheek, and reached for an empanada. "Baking again, Mama?" He took a bite and wiped crumbs from his mustache.

"These are your son's creation." Beaming, Abuelita patted Diego's arm. "He's got a real knack for flavors, this one."

Diego couldn't help puffing out his chest. "Sweet potato and rosemary crust filled with ground turkey, kale, garlic and sage."

Dad huffed. "Not very authentic."

Abuelita clucked her tongue. "It's fusion cuisine, Antonio. Get with the program."

Mama motioned them toward the table. "Enough squabbling. Enchiladas are getting cold."

Diego took his seat between Oscar's highchair and his two nieces. Entertaining the littles kept the critical spotlight off him. Besides, they were fun.

"I want a Hot Pocket," little Anita demanded.

Diego passed the empanadas.

"Hang on." His sister-in-law raised her finger. "You know what these are called. Say it right."

Anita huffed. "Em Pa Na Da. Por favor."

He nudged a cut-glass serving dish closer. "You want some cranberry salsa with that?"

His niece wrinkled her nose. "Is it spicy?"

"Just a little."

She lifted her chin. "I can take it. I'm brave."

His empanadas and salsa made the rounds to oohs and ahhs. Decision made—he'd add this one to his future menu.

Conversation among the adults shifted to his brother Jorge's recent promotion to manager of his auto-parts store. Diego gripped his silverware tightly. Here it comes.

"How about you, Flake Meister?" Jorge aimed a sharp-toothed smile at Diego. "Still slinging tater tots?"

"Don't call him that." Dad didn't even look up from his plate.

"Your baby brother has exciting plans." Abuelita's dark eyes sparkled. "Tell them, kiddo."

His bite of enchilada stuck in his throat. He hadn't planned to tell his family about the food truck until he was much closer to launch date.

His brother flashed a cheesy grin—literally, since a strand of cheese dangled from his lip. "Let me guess. You're gonna sell tater tots door to door."

Diego silently mouthed every Spanish curse he knew. Most of them he'd learned from his grandmother, not that he'd ever rat her out.

It wasn't his fault his first freelance ideas had fallen flatter than a bad souffle. There was the tailgate catering fiasco when a rented grill refused to light, leaving him with forty pounds of spoiled chicken. And the posole debacle when his promised helpers didn't show. Time and again, his attempts at breaking into the Tacoma food scene went down in flames or up in smoke due to crappy equipment, poor planning, or flaky helpers. He learned from each experience—but try telling that to his family.

This time would be different. He'd spent the past few years learning everything he could about the food truck business. He'd saved enough from his Bangers job to buy the Airstream, and he was slowly refurbishing the interior. One baby step at a time, he was inching closer to his dream.

Rising with the empty casserole in hand, Mama fixed him with a stern look. "I wish you'd apply for that position in the hospital kitchen. It's a nice, practical job."

Abuelita scoffed. "How's he going use his creativity in a hospital kitchen? Dress up the vanilla pudding?"

Mama raised her chin. "He could become a registered dietician."

Diego huffed a sigh. Here he was, a grown-ass man with a responsible job, a healthy savings account, and his family still talked about him as if he wasn't even there.

He pushed his chair back. "Ma. Ma. MA."

The squabbling stopped.

"I don't want to work in a hospital. I don't want to go back to school. I want to be a chef." He brushed crumbs from his shirt. "I am a chef."

"That's right, corazón." Abuelita added. "And your food truck is going to be a knockout."

"Food truck?" his youngest sister Luisita finally piped up. "You mean the old Airstream in Abuelita's backyard? I thought that was your man cave."

"He doesn't need a man cave. He's got a big room at my place." Abuelita lifted a forkful of enchilada. "Our place."

Like sports fans doing The Wave, a collective eye roll made its way around the table—excluding Diego, who noticed, Abuelita, who didn't, and the little ones, giggling over the cheese dangling from their great grandmother's chin.

After dinner, Abuelita and the kids adjourned to the living room to watch Peppa Pig while the rest of the adults moved to the kitchen. Loaded down with dirty dishes, Diego was the last to join them.

"It's not fair to Diego," Jorge crossed his arms and leaned on the counter.

Since when did you ever care about fairness? "What's not fair?"

All eyes swiveled to him, but no one spoke. Their scrutiny itched like a scratchy holiday sweater.

Finally, Mama broke the silence. "We don't like the idea of you taking care of Maricela. A young man like you should be finding a place of his own."

Here they went again. Since Abuelo's death three years ago, the fam whispered about putting Abuelita in an assisted living facility. Which was totally stupid. She was doing just fine where she was, still running her informal catering business, still meeting with her girlfriends to play poker and giggle over homemade sangria. He'd learned the hard way how sharp those old gals still were. Bunch of card sharks disguised as sweet old ladies.

He straightened his shoulders. "I like living with Abuelita. Her house has plenty of room for the two of us, and I enjoy her company. She's teaching me lots about cooking, too."

Jorge snorted. "Why did you go to cooking school if you could just learn from your grandma?"

Dad smacked his elder son's shoulder. "Be respectful when you talk about my mother." He turned to Diego. "Seriously, son, isn't it time you moved out on your own? Maybe find a nice girlfriend? It's been—" He glanced at his wife. "How long now?"

This again. Mama and Pops thought marriage and babies were the key to happiness. And they were still pining for Carolina, his culinary school girlfriend who moved to Seattle two years ago. He missed her sometimes, but his life was here. Especially since living rent-free with Abuelita allowed him to save up the capital he'd need for his food truck.

"Look." He faced his family. "Finding a girlfriend is not a priority right now, but if I meet someone, I'm sure Abuelita will welcome her with open arms." He leaned through the kitchen doorway and called, "Isn't that right, 'Lita?"

She looked up from the Lego castle she and the great-grands were building. "What's that, corazón?"

"You got no problem with me bringing home a girlfriend, right?"

She beamed. "Of course not. Is what's-her-name coming over?"

"No ma'am. She's still in Seattle."

"Pity. Tell her I said hello."

"See?" Mama said with a sniff. "She can't even remember your girlfriend's name. She's slipping."

He threw up his hands. "For fu—for goodness' sake, Ma. How many people has she met in her lifetime? And Caro is not my girlfriend. In fact, she's engaged."

Mama rushed over to enfold him in a hug. "Oh, baby, I had such hopes for your two. You'd make beautiful babies together."

"Who said anything about babies?"

She clucked like the puffy hen she resembled. "You're so good with your nieces and nephews. You'd make a wonderful dad."

All this smother-love was giving him a headache. "Look. I'm fine. Abuelita's fine. Remember what Abuelo always said—If it ain't broke, don't fix it." He pointed toward the living room. "We're not broke, neither of us. Just let us be."

He stalked into the living room. He'd rather spend his Sunday family time with the generations who weren't bent on giving him a whole-life makeover. "Let's see that castle."

Little Oscar held up a clump of Legos. "This is the dragon. He's hungry. He wants Hot Pockets. Rwaor!"

"Well then, let's get cooking. Pass the dough, please."

When the Play-doh empanadas were "baked," the dragon fed, and the castle destroyed by pillow bombs,

Diego and Abuelita helped clean up the mess, distributed hugs all around, and pulled on their coats.

"Diego, wait." Elena trotted out from the kitchen, a dish towel in her damp hands. "Listen, you know you're my favorite brother, right?"

"What do you want?"

She pasted on a wide, phony smile. "A friend from work needs help moving on Saturday. Caught her husband cheating, and now the bastard refuses to move out. A bunch of us from work are gonna pack up her stuff. Should only take a few hours."

He wrinkled his nose. "I was going to work on the Airstream."

"Pleeease, Gogo? She's a good friend, and she's in a really tough spot. It would mean a lot if you could help out."

Working in a metal trailer during a cold snap or toting boxes for Elena's friend? Neither sounded particularly appealing, but the second option would earn his sister's gratitude.

"Okay, I'll help."

"Thanks! You're the best." She smooched his cheek. "You'll like my friend. She's really cute."

Always with the matchmaking. Even Elena was in on it now. You'd think, as a single mom, she'd be on his side of this fight.

When Elena went back into the kitchen, Abuelita patted Diego's shoulder. "I'm proud of you, putting family first. You'll make a great papá someday.

"Thanks, 'Lita, but I'll stick with being a tío for now. Less pressure."

Chapter Three: Tots for an Angel

♥

"Baby, ya yo me something, something, sabes que yo te something." Diego warbled along with the music on his ear buds as he slapped thinly sliced chicken breast onto the grill and sprinkled it with his smoky spice blend.

At the fryer, his assistant chef Shelby grumbled, "At least learn the words."

"I will. Someday." He danced over to the cooler and pulled out slices of pepper bacon.

Charlie, Bangers Tavern's newest server, popped through the swinging kitchen doors. "Sorry, Diego, customer changed her order. Can you sub a bacon-mushroom-Swiss burger for the chef's salad?"

Diego saluted. "On it. Who comes to Bangers for a salad, anyway?"

"Right?" Charlie scooped a few tater tots from the warming tray. "So good," she moaned with her mouth full.

Diego didn't bother hiding his proud grin. When he first took over as head chef, Bangers' tots came in two options: cheese or no cheese. Now, his creatively topped tots drew customers from all over Tacoma and beyond. Still, there's only so much you can do with fried potatoes.

"Hey, Charlie, wanna try my experiment?" With his spatula, he gestured to a tray of empanadas.

She plucked one up and took a bite. "Wow! What is this? Spinach and—"

"Manchego cheese and pine nuts."

She chewed thoughtfully, then pursed her lips. "And something sweet?"

"Golden raisins. From a Spanish tapas recipe. Weird combo, but it works, right?"

"Delicioso." She kissed her fingertips. "I don't get why you're still single. Handsome and talented. I'm surprised some hungry customer hasn't snapped you up."

Shelby snorted. "It's his singing. Dude can't carry a tune in a bucket."

"You love it," he teased back. "I see you dancing along when you think I'm not watching."

"Pfft." Shelby slid a lettuce, tomato, and pickled-onion garnish onto the plate, then filled a paper tray with tots. She leveled a sly glance at Charlie. "You're single too, right?"

Charlie raised both palms and backed away. "No, no, no. I am most definitely not on the market."

"Too bad." Shelby tilted her head in Diego's direction. "Got a sister?"

A shadow flickered across Charlie's face. "Yeah. She's not on the market either."

"Enough with the matchmaking, Shel." Diego plated the burger. "Someone's gonna sic H.R. on you."

"What? She knows I'm just kidding."

Dawn O'Malley, their boss, slammed through the kitchen doors. "Goddamn sonfoabitch on a stick!" Glowering, she crossed her arms over her Seahawks hoodie, then sniffed the air. "Empanadas again?"

"Con espinacas a la Catalana." Diego slid one into a paper tray and handed it over.

Dawn bit into the pastry with a growl. As she chewed, her expression slowly relaxed from furious to flat.

Diego exchanged worried looks with Shelby and Charlie. The boss was clearly chewing on more than pastry. "Anything I can do?" he asked.

"Nah. I need you in here. And I can't send Charlie again because of their stupid dress code." She snatched another empanada from the tray and chomped with a vengeance. "You're wasting your talents here."

Diego hated to see his mentor so upset. Normally, she was a champ at shrugging off all the pain-in-the-ass obstacles that befell the bar. Whatever was squashing her mood, it must be bad.

He nudged her with his shoulder. "C'mon, Mama Dawn. Tell us. Let us help."

"It's that snooty new place across the street. Defiance Brasserie. They're copying us again. Last week, we did latke tots for Hanukkah, right? The very next day, guess what they're serving? All-you-can-eat latkes. And tonight, they're doing karaoke."

Charlie scowled. "Sunday is our night! Isn't that against the rules?"

"There are rules for karaoke?" he asked.

"All members of the Sixth Avenue Business Association agree not to run the same promotion on the same night. It's unfair competition." Dawn chewed her lip. "If I could prove it, I could sic SABA on them."

Charlie snatched her phone from her apron pocket. "You need a spy. And I know just the person to ask." She tapped her screen and put the phone to her ear. "Hey, Anna. Feel like taking a break?" She quickly outlined her plan then ended the call. "I knew she'd bite. My sister's stuck at home with our dad."

"How's Jack's leg?" Dawn asked.

"It's not going to get better if he doesn't follow doctor's orders and stay off it. Anyway, she'll dress up and check out the competition. We'll have our answer in an hour or so." She loaded the burger order onto her tray and sailed through the swinging doors.

With a sigh, Diego watched her go. Too bad, really. Thick, wavy hair, bright dark eyes, snarky smile—no denying Charlie was a beauty, yet he didn't feel the tiniest spark with her. Since his breakup with Caro, he really hadn't sparked with anyone. What was wrong with him?

Dawn poked her head into the kitchen again near closing time. "Diego, I need a super-deluxe tots plate to go, pronto." She waggled her eyebrows. "Our spy did an excellent job."

When the tots were crispy and golden, Diego layered on the toppings: shredded extra-sharp Tillamook cheddar, crumbled pepper bacon, paper-thin slices of green onion, garlicky sauteed mushrooms, pickled sweet-hot pepper slices, sour cream, and a drizzle of his house-made spicy ketchup. Heart attack on a plate. He hoped Charlie's sister was hungry. Was she as pretty as Charlie?

He smoothed his apron, blotted his sweaty forehead, and told Shelby, "Be right back."

At the bar, he found bartenders Kiara and River, along with all three servers, huddled around a brunette knockout in a curve-skimming red dress.

She glanced up. Their gazes met and held. Everything else slowed down.

Those last few steps to the bar felt like being towed through honey. Her espresso-dark eyes widened, sparkling under the Christmas lights. Her plump lips parted. Her chest rose and fell.

She's a goddess.

He set the tots before her, removed his cap, and scrubbed a hand through his squashed hair. She echoed the gesture, winding a chestnut curl around her slender fingers.

Abuelita had told him the story of when she and Abuelo first met. "It was like a golden rope wrapped around my heart and pulled me to him. It holds us together still."

At the time, he'd laughed off her hyperbole. But now, in this electric moment, Diego understood exactly what she meant.

"Hi." The angel murmured, her voice low and musical like a cello. "Did you make these?"

Dumbstruck by her beauty, he could only nod.

She lifted a tot to her lips, inhaled the steam rolling off it, and sighed.

He thanked the kitchen gods for the apron hiding his erection.

She took a bite, then her head lolled back on a groan. "Soooo good."

Charlie narrowed her eyes and moved closer to her sister, bristling with protective vibes. Couldn't blame her.

He'd do the same if someone was eyeing his little sister like a tasty snack.

Say something, idiot! He cleared his throat. "They go really well with the Port Angeles Amber." He hooked a thumb over his shoulder toward the beer taps.

Her gaze dropped, and the corner of her mouth hitched up in a shy half-smile. "Wish I could try it, but I'm pregnant."

No ring on her left hand, but a pale indentation where one had recently been. Divorced? Please let her be single. Please, please, please.

"Oh. Well then, enjoy, Miss..."

"Anna." Though it didn't seem possible, her wide smile made her even more beautiful.

Flushed and breathless, he backed toward the kitchen and bonked into something soft.

"Watch where you're going, Romeo." With a chuckle, Dawn grasped his shoulders, spun him around, and sent him on his way with a gentle shove.

What are you doing? his common sense shrieked. She's pregnant! But he allowed himself a final glance over his shoulder. Anna popped another tot into her lush mouth and winked. Waggling his fingers, he pushed through the swinging doors then collapsed against the wall, clutching his heart.

"Whatsa matter with you?" Shelby asked with a snort.

He closed his eyes and heaved a happy sigh. "I just met the woman I'm going to marry."

"Ow, what's that for?" Anna winced and rubbed the spot where Charlie punched her arm.

"Are you out of your freakin' mind? Flirting with Diego?"

"Diego." She rolled his name on her tongue. "Diego what?"

"Vargas." Scowling, Charlie leaned in close and lowered her voice. "He's a sweet guy. He doesn't need to get swept up in your mess."

"Diego Vargas. What a beautiful name." With a sigh, she fastened the lid on her to-go box of heavenly tater tots. "Don't worry, I have no intention of sweeping him up. It's just—I really needed this. I'd almost forgotten what it feels like to have a cute guy notice me. I should borrow your clothes more often."

"You should get your own clothes," Charlie grumbled. "You'll have to anyway, pretty soon."

"True." She fingered the neckline of Charlie's knit dress. "Wonder if I could find something like this in a maternity dress. Très sexy."

Polishing a beer glass, the girl bartender leaned in closer. "Diego sure thought so. Never seen him blush like that."

Charlie huffed. "Yeah, well some guys have a fetish for pregnant women. Never took Diego for a perv."

Anna poked her sister. "Judgmental, much?"

Could the cute chef have a pregnancy kink? She pressed her mental rewind button. There was a definite spark before she dropped the big P bomb. No way had she imagined the sudden widening of his eyes, the way his plump lips parted, the way he froze in place holding the steaming takeout box like a sacred offering.

With a sigh, Anna shrugged off the pointless question. Her love life was on hold for at least the next few years. "Well, I'd better get back to Dad. I'll share these tots with him."

Charlie snorted. "What happened to the nutrition police? Last week you bit my head off when I gave him Pringles."

"These are too good to let them go to waste. I wonder what else Diego can cook?"

Charlie's boss sauntered over and flashed a wry grin. "Seems the Khoury girls are burning through my staff. You got any more sisters back home, Charlie?"

"Just us two." Anna hopped down from her barstool. "Thanks for the tots, ma'am." She patted Charlie's arm. "And thanks for the adventure. It was fun playing spy. I hope you guys kick that snooty bar's butt." She headed out, hips swaying as she tottered on Charlie's sky-high heels.

Back at home—well, Dad's home—she reluctantly changed into soft pajamas and gathered her hair into a topknot. "Bye, sexy Anna," she told her reflection. "Hope to see you again sometime." She reheated the tots, then scraped half the pile onto a plate for Dad.

"Thanks, doll." He speared a tot and stuffed it into his mouth. "Holy cats, that's good. Where'd you get these?"

"Charlie's work."

Dad's bushy eyebrows lowered. "What's a pregnant lady doing in a dive bar?"

"Drinking orange juice, Dad. And helping my sister."

"You're serving beers now? Aren't they paying you enough at the hospital?"

"Got a new side hustle as a spy."

Dad scowled as he chewed. "A bar ain't no place for a pregnant lady. Even a nice bar like Dawn's."

"You know Dawn?"

"Ain't seen her for a while, but yeah. And don't change the subject. You gotta think about your baby now, not booze and fellas."

Anna huffed a lock of hair from her forehead. "I wasn't drinking, for cripes sake! I'm not gonna do anything to hurt my child. And who said anything about fellas?"

He shoveled in more tots and talked around them. "Pretty girl like you is gonna attract attention, especially dressed up in you sister's hoochie mama clothes."

He'd been so supportive the other night. When did Neanderthal Dad take over? "Most of my clothes are still at the apartment, so I borrowed Charlie's dress. I wouldn't expect you to understand, but a woman needs to be admired now and then."

He pushed his empty dish aside and scrunched down in his recliner. "Like I said, you're a mom now. Your time for that is through."

Heat flushed through her body and pushed her to her feet. "My God, Dad, what century are you living in?" She snatched up his empty dish and stalked to the kitchen.

"Controlling, chauvinistic jerk face," she grumbled under the clatter of dishes. Charlie had complained about this side of Dad for years, but Anna always assumed her sister was exaggerating. No wonder Charlie moved out as soon as she started college. Living with Dad and his opinions would only worsen her stress, and that couldn't be good for her or the baby. As soon as he got his walking cast in January, she'd find somewhere else to live. Better start looking now.

Chapter Four: Slaying a Dragon

♥

The herbal scent of roasting poblano chiles perfumed Abuelita's kitchen, and holiday salsa music blasted from her satellite radio. Using her tongs like castanets, she clacked along to the beat while she waited for the chiles to reach the perfect char. Meanwhile, Diego divided the chilled dough into equal portions, dancing from counter to table and back.

"Look at you wiggle, mi luz." Abuelita snatched a chile from the broiler and popped it into a paper bag to steam. "A person might think you had good news. Something you're not telling me?"

"Just enjoying cooking with you." His cheeks heated at the half-truth. Diego had always been terrible at keeping secrets, especially from the woman who practically raised him. While his parents worked and his older siblings played sports, little Diego spent his after-school hours helping Abuelita prepare the empanadas, tamales, and pasteles she sold in the neighborhood. Culinary school taught him to be a restaurant chef, but Abuelita taught him to cook with soul.

"What's next, 'Lita?"

"Use those young muscles to roll out the dough."

As he rolled the last piece of dough into a perfect circle, Abuelita tottered over to inspect his handiwork. "Good job." She patted his arm. "So, spill it, hijo. What's got you all lit up like Christmas?"

"Just the holiday spirit," he lied. Though he enjoyed Christmas as much as the next overworked millennial, it was the beautiful woman he met last night who inspired his big, goofy grin. Tonight he'd ask Charlie to pass his number to Anna, the dark-eyed beauty whose name he'd been singing under his breath all day.

What was he thinking, crushing on a pregnant woman? Okay, a beautiful pregnant woman, one whose gaze filled his chest with champagne bubbles and shooting stars, but still. Asking her out was just the kind of flakey, irresponsible decision his family was always giving him shit for. But he hadn't sparked like this since his first crush in middle school. That had to mean something, right?

Abuelita poked his arm with her crooked finger. "Don't lie to your grandmother. The angels are listening." With her tongs, she pointed to the shelf above the window, laden with ceramic angel knickknacks.

"Okay, okay. I met somebody last night at the bar. Nothing will come of it, but I just—" He trailed off on a sigh. "I felt something, you know? It was...surprising."

"Good news." She squeezed his biceps. "A handsome young man like you shouldn't be spending all his time with his grandmother or holed up in a greasy bar kitchen."

"Why does everyone keep saying that? I like Bangers, and the customers love my cooking."

Abuelita sucked her teeth. "Tater tots. You can do better."

"I will. But Bangers is perfect for now." No other cooking job was likely to offer such reasonable hours, five to ten, perfect for working around his days with Abuelita.

"Bullshit," his grandmother coughed into her fist.

"Abuelita!" He couldn't help laughing. "Aren't you worried about the angels?"

"I'll pray for forgiveness. And you told me this bar job was just for a few years, to get experience. How long has it been now?"

"Not so long." Five years. Most chefs would have moved on by now—except for Alice, the semi-retired cook who covered Bangers' smaller lunch crowd. The Lunch Lady, they called her. Her cooking was okay but lacked personality, in his not-so-humble opinion.

"Pfft." Abuelita ladled garlicky black beans into the cumin-scented sweet potatoes. "When will that food truck of yours be ready?"

"Maybe by summer." He was saving big bucks by remodeling the kitchen using reconditioned parts, but six months in, the food truck was only half finished.

She added paper-thin green onion slices into the filling mixture. "Good. And how long until you open a real restaurant?"

He pushed a damp curl off his forehead. "There'll be time for that after, you know…"

"After I'm dead?" Abuelita planted her fists on her hips. "My mother lived to be ninety-six, and my Abuelita made it to a hundred and two." She poked his chest with her crooked finger. "If you use me as an excuse to delay your dreams, I'll kick you out on your behind. Lo entiendes?"

"Yes, ma'am." He trudged across the kitchen to make an egg wash for the pastry.

"If those food trucker people on TV can do it, so can you." She shook her wooden spoon, spattering them both with orange mash. "So, did you ask her out?"

"Who?"

"The pretty girl, of course." A mischievous grin pleated her cheeks. "The one who has you dancing in my kitchen."

"Not yet." How do you even ask out a pregnant woman? Hi there. Wanna go shopping for baby clothes? Hell, she'd probably turn him down. But he had to try, or he'd never get any peace, judging by last night's tossing and turning. Besides, plenty of guys fell for women who already had kids. Was this so different?

"None of this pokey stuff." Abuelita prodded him with a gnarled finger. "You ask her out."

"Why are you being so pushy about it?" He got to work peeling charred skin off the roasted chiles.

Abuelita tilted her chin toward her angel figurines. "Because when heaven bops you on the head, you better listen."

"Okay, okay, I will. Maybe Saturday." In fact, a daytime coffee date would be perfect. After all, she had every reason to be suspicious of some strange guy asking her out, especially in her condition. But coffee was just coffee, right? Just an hour or two to chat, no pressure. Do pregnant women drink coffee? Maybe tea...

He scooped filling into the first empanada shell, then dropped the spoon and smacked his forehead. He'd promised to help Elena's friend move on Saturday. Sunday was out of the question—the Vargas family gathering was sacrosanct. And he was scheduled to work every night this week. Damn, damn, damn.

Rocker-girl anthems blasted through Anna's soon-to-be-former apartment, courtesy of Elena's 'Good riddance Brock' playlist. While the rest of her work friends packed her belongings and loaded them onto the rental truck, Anna pulled her bestie into the bedroom for a very important, very private conversation. Besides, no one could help her navigate this bumpy road ahead better than Elena, a single mom who juggled child rearing and work like a boss.

Three times in the past week she'd tried to tell Elena her big news, but someone or something always interrupted —a five-year-old patient who vomited into a potted plant, the records clerk's birthday cupcakes, and multiple deliveries of cheesy gifts from Brock. Flowers, balloons, a gift basket of Dollar Store bath bombs. After three years of marriage, you'd think he'd remember such things gave her a rash. It's like the guy never even met her.

"What's the big secret?" Elena asked once Anna shut the door.

Anna shifted from foot to foot. No reason to be nervous. If anyone would understand her dilemma, Elena would. She had divorced her loser husband two years ago and was doing fine. In fact, her little Oscar was a happy, healthy kid who lit up every room he entered. Still, telling her somehow made the situation feel far too real.

Anna drew a deep breath. "Okay. Here goes. Shit."

Elena chuckled. "Must be a big deal if you're cursing."

"It is. I'm pregnant."

Elena's eyes widened and her cheeks twitched, caught somewhere between a grin and a grimace. "It's Brock's?"

Anna glared. "He's the cheater, not me."

"Sure. Of course. I'm sorry. It's just—wow." She raked her fingers through her curls. "And you're sure it's over between you two?"

"One thousand percent sure."

"Okay then." She grasped Anna's shoulders. "You're not alone in this. You got me and your family, and there's a single parents' support group at the hospital. And you'll want to sign up for the on-site daycare ASAP. Like, yesterday. Unless—" She tilted her head. "Are you gonna stop work for a while?"

"I don't see how I can." Anna's hand settled below her navel. "Providing for this little one is on me now."

"What about Brock?"

She snorted. "I'm sure he'll contribute something, but it's gonna be a fight. He keeps insisting he doesn't want a divorce. Shoulda thought about that before he bounced into bed with his boss's secretary."

Elena pulled her in for a tight hug. "You got this, Anna. You're a strong, smart woman. Fuck that loser." She released her. "Who else knows?"

"Just my family and you. I'll tell Doctor Z and the work crew next week." Her chest rose and fell on a shaky sigh. "I'm dreading it. I'm already poor dumped Anna. Now I'm gonna be poor, dumped, preggo Anna."

"Hey." Elena gripped Anna's chin and lifted it until Anna met her gaze. "You've got nothing to be ashamed of. This mess isn't your fault, and you've got lots of people who care about you. Let them help."

"Yeah—you're right." Anna gave her friend's arm a playful punch. "Thanks to you, I've got a house full of helpers."

"Let's put 'em to work." Elena linked her arm through Anna's. Limp with relief, Anna let herself be towed back into the action.

Under Elena's and Charlie's direction, the crew divided to tackle each room. Someone called for pizza, and soon the apartment took on a party atmosphere. At least, that's what Anna kept telling herself, trying to put a positive spin on the dismantling of her old life.

"How about this lamp?" Elena asked.

Anna chewed her lip, fighting to concentrate—hard to do with questions flying at her from every direction and the sharp rrrrrrrip of moving tape. And—the cherry on top of the poop sundae—morning sickness was kicking her right in the gut.

"You look green. I'll get some crackers." Elena set down the lamp and strode to the kitchen, where Aunt Hala, Dad's sister, had taken charge of packing the dishes.

Anna sank into a chair and rubbed her throbbing temples. At least Dad's not so subtle threats convinced Brock to spend the day elsewhere. But her weasely ex still found a way to screw up her plans. In the spirit of fairness, she'd asked him to mark his belongings so nothing of his would get packed. His response—bright orange sticky notes with "Brock's. Don't touch" on just about everything, including expensive items she bought with her money, since at Brock's insistence they'd never mixed funds. Others were gifts from her friends and family, and she'd be damned if she'd let him have those either.

Jojo Williams, the ginormous but gentle phlebotomist from her clinic, pointed to a wingback chair. "This one too, Anna? It's got one of those orange stickers."

Anna's lip curled. "Are you effin' kidding me? That was my grandmother's."

"Your ex is a real piece of work, ain't he?" Smirking, he hefted the chair and headed for the front door, where he barked a laugh. "Cookie! What you doin' here, man?" His bulky body blocked her view of the newcomer.

"My sister bent my arm. Said her friend needed help."

Something about that voice set Anna's scalp to tingling. Deep and rich with just a touch of roughness. She flipped through her memory files—had she met any of her work friends' brothers?

Jojo stepped aside and waved the newcomer through. "The more the merrier. Hey, Anna, meet Diego."

Before her stood the guy from Charlie's bar, the heart-fluttering chef with curly hair and sparkling eyes, the king of the tater tots. Even in faded jeans and a Bangers Tavern hoodie with sleeves pushed up to his elbows, he was every bit as delectable as she remembered. Incredible! A week of silent pining brought him right to her door. Well, her ex-door. Judging by his open-mouth stare, he was equally astonished to see her.

She sprang to her feet, just as Elena returned from the kitchen with a sleeve of saltines and a can of ginger ale. "You're here! Gogo, meet my friend Anna. Anna, this is my brother Diego."

Elena's brother? Now that she saw them side by side, the resemblance was hard to miss—same olive complexion, curly espresso-brown hair, and flashing dark eyes. Both had sharp jaws and full lips. Even the perplexed tilt of their heads was the same as they gawked at each other and then at Anna.

Uh oh. Elena knows something's up.

"Gogo?" Jojo snorted.

Diego's gaze fell to his beat-up Chucks.

Elena gave her brother's shoulder a playful punch. "When he was little, he couldn't pronounce his own name. All he could say was Gogo, so that's what we called him."

Diego rolled his eyes and grimaced. "Thanks, gordita."

"Now, now, we're not here to fight. We're here to help Anna." Elena pressed the crackers into Anna's hands. "You sit. Diego, help Jojo carry furniture to the U-Haul."

Diego shot Anna a look she couldn't quite decipher before following Jojo out the door. With his rumpled brow and crinkled eyes, he looked almost...disappointed?

"Anna?" Charlie beckoned from the hallway. "Wanna give the bedroom a final check?"

A visual sweep revealed nothing left behind, no trace of her in this room where she and Brock slept side by side for three years. Blinking hard, she tugged the comforter back into place. She'd been a giddy new bride when she bought it, full of stupid hope. Stroking its satiny surface, she pushed back the desire to wrap herself up in memories of a safer, happier time. But there was no going back, no happiness left in this bed, this apartment, this sham of a marriage.

Charlie's hand fell on her shoulder, warm and steadying. "You want to take this?"

"No." Anna gave her a grim smile. "There's nothing I need here."

She turned her back on the empty room and returned to the living room where Diego was taping a box shut. He'd shed his hoodie to reveal a snug black T-shirt that hugged his broad shoulders. The shift of his muscles was mesmerizing.

She cleared her throat. "Thanks for coming, Diego."

He jolted upright, eyes wide for a split second. "Oh. Uh. Hi." He rubbed the back of his neck with his free hand. "Must be hard, moving right before Christmas."

She stepped closer and lowered her voice. "So, you're Elena's brother. Small world, eh?"

"I hope you don't mind me coming." A wash of pink painted his cheekbones.

"Why would I mind?"

Again with the shoe inspection.

"I asked Charlie to give you my number and you didn't call, so..." He finally met her eye and gave her a half-smile that pinched her right in the feels. "I understand. You've got a lot going on in your life. I just hoped we could maybe grab a coffee or something."

"Charlie never said anything." She glanced around. There she was, the traitor, shoving books into a box. "Charlie? C'mere a minute."

Charlie caught her eye and froze, clutching a cookbook to her chest like a shield. "What's up?"

"Come here and find out." Grumbling under her breath, she added, "You sock-munching skunk."

Shuffling like a second grader summoned to the principal's office, Charlie approached. "Hi, Diego. Thanks for coming."

"Glad to help. Any friend of Elena's is a friend of mine." He took a step back, then another. Smart guy.

Anna jutted her chin. "Why didn't you pass on Diego's message?"

Charlie couldn't look more guilty if she tried. "Can we talk about this in private?"

"No," she snapped. Nothing got her back up faster than being treated like a child. "Why don't you want me to talk to him?"

Diego side-stepped away. "I'll just, uh, give you two some privacy."

Anna lowered her voice and poked Charlie's shoulder. "That poor, sweet guy thought I turned him down. Why would you let him think that?"

"Look, Anna-boo—"

"Don't start that crap. I'm twenty-nine, not two."

"It's just—Diego is a super-sweet guy—"

"—who knows I'm pregnant and still wants to see me. What gives you the right to interfere?"

"I'm just trying to protect you."

Anna shut her eyes and silently counted to five. "I know you mean well, but for God's sake—" She blinked back threatening tears. Dang pregnancy hormones. "Can't you understand how wonderful it is to have a cute guy notice me after years of being treated like a piece of furniture? I'm not going to fall in love with your chef friend. I'm not going to drag him into my divorce drama, but don't I deserve a little fun?"

Charlie exhaled through pursed lips. "Okay. For the record, I think this is a bad idea, but I'll give you his number."

"I'll get it myself." She turned toward the kitchen and bonked right into her soon-to-be-ex mother-in-law. "Gah!"

In all the bustle and noise, Anna hadn't even noticed her arrival.

Deborah Spencer pulled herself up to her full height and glared down her knife-sharp nose. "Why are you doing this, Anna? Haven't you caused us all enough trouble?" Her tone dripped with scorn.

Anna could only blink, too astonished to form words.

Charlie, on the other hand, had no such blockage. She planted her fists on her hips and lifted her chin. "What the hell is your problem?"

A saccharine smile wreathed Deborah's face. "Charlotte. I haven't seen you since the wedding. How are you, dear?"

"Why are you here, Mrs. Spencer?"

"To make sure this silly twit doesn't steal my son's family heirlooms."

Anna waved toward the curio cabinet filled with Hummel figurines. "Don't worry. Your tchotchkes are safe."

Though Deborah knew Anna loathed the cutesy things, she sent one every Christmas. And anniversary. And Valentine's Day. Perhaps they were meant to take the place of gifts from Brock.

Deborah gave Charlie a dismissive finger flick. "Grow up, Anna. Men wander. It's in their nature. But Brock loves you. You're carrying his child. It's time to put your petty grudge aside and think of what's best for the baby."

"Petty?" She hadn't meant it to come out as a shriek. "Your son cheated on me, and you call that petty?"

Helpers gathered, encircling them. Thank God Dad hadn't come, or he'd probably swing his crutch at Deborah's perfectly coiffed head.

One male voice rose above the mutters and whispers. "Ma'am?"

Deborah leveled an icy gaze at Diego, who'd pushed through the circle of onlookers. Amazing—he hardly knew Anna, yet there he stood, facing down the dragon lady as if placating a hysterical child, his palms up, his voice gentle. "Ma'am, you need to go. You're upsetting Anna, and that's not good for the baby."

"Who the devil are you?" Deborah asked with a frosted pink sneer.

"Just a friend. Listen, put yourself in Anna's shoes. This situation is not her fault."

Finally registering the ring of astonished faces, Deborah betrayed just the tiniest waver in her icy voice. "I'm trying to stop her from wrecking her family."

"Brock already—" Anna spluttered, but Diego halted her outburst with a gentle squeeze of her arm. I've got this, his steady gaze promised. I'll protect you.

Flabbergasted, she could only let him have his say.

He turned back to Deborah. "My sister, she went through something similar. Her ex's parents refused to admit he did anything wrong. Now my nephew hardly ever sees them." He rested his fingertips lightly on Deborah's arm. "And that's a damn shame. Grandparents and grandkids, they share a special bond. You want that with your grandchild, right?"

Deborah's gaze slid to Anna, then away. "Of course I do."

"Then maybe back up, take a breath, and let Anna and your son figure this out."

Anna's tight chest loosened and filled with warmth. This near stranger stepped into an ugly spat and diffused it, just like that. Was he some kind of guardian angel?

Deborah crossed her arms and huffed. "Neither of them has the maturity to handle this."

Aunt Hala stepped forward, a note of sympathy in her smile. "And yet, my dear, we must let them. I'm Anna's aunt. Come, I'll walk you to your car." As she passed, she flashed Diego a thumbs-up.

When the two older women left, a collective exhale whooshed through the room.

Elena wrapped her arms around Diego and squeezed him in a tight hug. "Gogo the peacemaker. Thanks for helping my friend. You're the best."

"Oof." He extricated himself and backed away while Elena and Charlie fussed over Anna.

Gradually, her hammering heartbeat slowed. Thank God she'd been surrounded by friends and family, a cushion against Deborah's fury. She'd never understand what made a woman like her tick—and she didn't care to. Still, Deborah was her child's grandmother, divorce or no. Hopefully, she'd take Diego's warning to heart.

Not holding my breath.

A moment later, when the crowd dispersed and the packing resumed, Diego approached and set down the carton he was carrying. "You okay, Anna?"

Smoothing her sweater, she sucked in a deep breath. "I am. Thank you." She pulled her phone from her pocket and handed it to him.

He tilted his head like an adorable, confused puppy.

"Your number?"

Despite the icy wind whistling through the open door, Diego's slow-blooming smile warmed Anna right to her toes.

A few hours later, when the last of her belongings had been packed into the rental truck, Elena pulled Anna aside. "Listen, you aren't seriously going to date my baby brother, are you?"

Charlie hovered nearby, no doubt eavesdropping as she shoved tape and scissors into a shopping bag.

All righty then, two birds with one stone.

"Elena, you've been a good friend to me. The best." She squeezed her friend's arm. "And I was a good friend to you when you were going through your divorce, right?"

Elena nodded slowly, her gaze wary.

"But here's the thing." She moved to the couch and patted the seat beside her. "I don't think you could possibly understand how frustrating it is to be an adult but have your sister still treat you like the baby of the family. It's like we can never prove ourselves, no matter how well we handle our grown-up business."

"But you can't—"

"I know, you're looking out for Diego because you love him. But maybe you could try trusting him. And me too. Because Diego knows I'm pregnant, he knows I'm in the middle of a messy divorce, and he still wants to have coffee with me." She raised her voice and glanced over her shoulder. "Just coffee. Not wild, juicy sex."

With a noisy sigh, Charlie gave up the pretense of minding her own business and perched on the arm of the couch. "Sure didn't look like he had his mind on just coffee."

"Hey," Elena interjected with a scowl, "my brother's a gentleman. He would never pressure Anna to do something inappropriate."

"Exactly." Anna shot them each a sharp look. "By the way, what's appropriate is up to me and Diego, not you two. And you can rest assured, I'm not looking for a romance, not until I've put all this mess behind me. So don't interfere, okay?"

Grumbles and eye rolls from both sides.

"Thank you." She hugged them each in turn. "And thank you for all your help today. I couldn't have handled this without you."

As she drove home, she replayed the afternoon in her mind. Wiped out by all the drama, she also felt a certain relief. Let Brock have the bland apartment. Already, the real estate agent she'd contacted on Monday had sent her info on several promising rentals. She'd find a new home for herself and her baby, close enough to the Khoury clan to call for help when she needed it, but far enough to give her and the little one a fresh start. She rubbed her belly as she steered through the slushy streets. "You and me, kiddo. We're gonna be okay."

She imagined chasing a giggling toddler through a sunny, toy-strewn backyard while a fluffy dog romped in circles around them, until a dark-haired man whistled from the back door. "Dinner's ready." In his hand, a steaming platter of tater tots.

Shoot, shoot, shoot. She thunked her fist on the dash. Get out of my head, Diego. Giving him her number was probably a mistake. He was entirely too cute and kind, and already she was spinning pointless fantasies when she should be focusing on the task at hand—the many tasks at hand—a steep, jagged mountain of tasks.

Diego's sad-puppy expression floated into focus. Despite Charlie's gatekeeping, he stayed to help her move and even stood up to her ice queen mother-in-law. What an amazing guy.

Just a coffee. A little conversation. No big deal.

Clinging to that comfortable lie, she steered toward home. Well, home for now.

Chapter Five: Probably a Bad Idea

♥

Halfway through dusting his grandmother's guardian angels, Diego nearly fell off the ladder when Elena slammed the back door and stormed into the kitchen.

Fists clenched, she glared up at him. "Gogo, have you lost your freakin' mind?"

Abuelita bustled in from the bathroom, her hands encased in dripping purple dish gloves. "What's wrong? Elena, are you trying to break your brother's neck?"

Elena's jaw muscles bulged as she glared up at him.

Clucking her tongue, Abuelita peeled off her gloves and dropped them in the kitchen sink. "Nice of you to drive me to mass this morning, Gordita, since your brother has an appointment."

When their grandmother bustled out of the room, Elena hissed, "An appointment? Is that what you told her?"

"I told her I was meeting someone for coffee. Which happens to be the truth." Diego resumed his chore, carefully dusting around wings, haloes, and other heavenly accoutrements.

"Gogo, you can't."

"And why not?" He whisked away a cobweb.

"Because she's pregnant!"

He shrugged. "I know. She told me."

Elena grabbed his leg in a vise-tight grip. "And she's still married."

Another shrug. "Not for long."

Of course, that bit bothered him, but all he was doing at this point was getting to know Anna a little better—over coffee, for Chrissakes. He wasn't shopping for engagement rings.

Elena poked his leg. "The last thing Anna needs is some flakey dreamer who's just gonna let her down."

He winced at her well-placed stab. Of all his siblings, Elena was the one he could usually count on to take his side. Looks like this time, she cared more about protecting her friend. Her lack of trust was a painful surprise. Then again, she'd been acting weird lately, secretive.

"Hypocritical, much?" he shot back, keeping his voice low. "You're a single mom, you're divorced, and you're definitely seeing someone."

Elena's eyes narrowed to slits. "Who says I am?"

"Last Sunday you snuck out of family dinner three times to check your phone. Don't tell me that was for work."

"That was for none of your damn business, baby bro. Besides, I'm divorced, not divorcing."

He rolled his eyes. "Again, just going out for coffee. I'm not gonna molest your friend over cappuccinos."

Abuelita returned, wrapped up in her winter coat and carrying her purse. "What on earth are you two squabbling about?"

Diego and Elena exchanged a volley of pointed glances. Finally, Elena pasted on a phony smile. "I was just checking out your angels, Abuelita. Who's this one again?" She pointed to a winged figure holding a staff and a fish.

Abuelita chuckled. "Archangel Raphael. Watches over nurses, travelers, young people, and lovers."

Diego gave the figurine an extra polish. If he sent up a silent prayer for heavenly aid, that was strictly between him and Raphael.

Abuelita pulled on her good leather gloves. "I don't want to be late for church. Father Pete always notices." She waggled her fingers at Diego. "See you after church, hijo. Don't forget to pack the tamales in extra foil."

"Will do, 'Lita." He snapped a salute.

On her way out, Elena stabbed a finger in his direction and mouthed, "We're not done with this."

When the front door closed, Diego swiped a palm down his sweaty face. Would his sister rat him out in front of the whole family over Sunday dinner? He was used to barbs from Jorge and clueless comments from Luisita, if his eldest sister abandoned him, he'd only have Abuelita on his side, and no one in the family listened to her.

He climbed down from the ladder on shaky legs and splashed cold water on his face. Hopefully, he'd have time to get to know Anna before the bomb dropped. No reason to stir up family drama unless their connection turned out to be worth the strife.

He was 99.9 percent sure she was totally worth it.

This late in December, there was no escaping the Christmas music, but at least the playlist at Blackbeard Coffee had a hipster edge—more saxophone than jingle bells. Arriving ten minutes early for his coffee date with Anna, Diego ordered a gingerbread latte and claimed a window table with a good view of the entrance. Outside, holiday shoppers bustled up and down Sixth Avenue, laughing and chatting despite the gray sky and swirling snowfall. He checked his phone, half-expecting a text filled with polite excuses. Who could blame her? This really was a weird situation.

The more he ruminated on his sister's tirade, the more trouble he had justifying his desire to meet Anna here—or anywhere.

He sipped his sweet, spicy drink. Does everything need a justification? Can't some things just be?

In the Coolidge Middle School sports field across the street, three kids were scraping up the meager snowfall to make a snowman. A big, scruffy dog bounded in circles around them. Snow was a rare treat for Tacoma kids. Would his own kids get the chance to build snowmen?

"Hi, Diego."

Anna's soft, alto voice yanked him upright. There she stood, close enough to touch, wrapped in a woolen cape that sparkled with melting snow. Her chocolate curls tumbled beneath a fuzzy red beanie, and her cheeks bloomed pink. Holding his gaze, she nibbled her lip.

His heart skipped a beat, then slammed into overdrive.

"Hi!" Wincing at his own dorky enthusiasm, he popped from his seat. "You came."

"Of course." Her smile held just a hint of snark. "I mean, you did slay a dragon for me. What kind of damsel would I be if I didn't grant your request?"

Beautiful and brave and funny. The points in her favor kept piling up. "Here." He pulled out a chair for her. "Let me get you something to drink. What's your pleasure? Are you hungry?"

Chuckling, she unwound her cape and draped it over the seat. "You know, I'm only one month along, and already I'm sick of people telling me to have a seat while they fetch me things."

"Fair enough, but the knight's code says I must offer you refreshment. You know, a cup of mead, a haunch of— what did people eat in days of yore?"

She tipped her head back and laughed, her smile bunching her cheeks into glowing pink apples. God, he wanted to take a bite. "Okay then, Sir Knight. How about a decaf chai and a muffin?"

"What flavor dost thou prefer?"

"Surprise me." She pointed to his seat. "I'll guard your steed."

His heart thumped in a giddy rhythm as he made his way to the counter. She thinks I'm funny. She's so beautiful. I'm totally going to marry her.

Shaking off his goofy giddiness, he placed his order and returned a moment later with her drink and two muffins. "Banana-blueberry and lemon-poppyseed. Take your pick."

More sexy lip nibbling. "How could I possibly choose?"

Back he trotted to the counter to fetch a knife. Once he loaded her plate with half of each muffin, he sipped his lukewarm latte and fought the urge to stare. "So, how long have you known my sister?"

"Since I came to work at the clinic. Five years, I guess."

"And she never mentioned me?"

"Sure." She wiped crumbs from her lips. "She said you're a chef in a bar and the adorable baby of the family." Her cheeks pinked again. "We have that in common."

"I don't know about me, but you certainly are adorable."

"Gah." She nudged him under the table with her foot. "I meant we're both the youngest."

"Yeah, Charlie didn't seem too pleased when we first met. Guess she's protective."

"Bossy older sisters, right?" Anna's gaze slid away. For a long, silent moment, she fiddled with her napkin, folding the corner into a point. Finally, she looked up, her lips pressed in a tight, straight line. "I don't get it."

"Don't get what?"

"Why did you stand up to Deborah?"

How to explain something he didn't fully understand? "Everyone else was just gawking. I know how her type operates—shock and awe, so no one challenges them. Except you." He remembered the jut of Anna's jaw as she faced down the venomous older woman. "You looked ready to rip her head off."

"I was." Her gazed dropped to her napkin again. "I'm grateful you spoke up, though. Dealing with my ex will be hard enough. No need to go to war over his mom's passive-aggressive bull caca."

"Caca?" He spluttered into his napkin.

She ducked her head. "It's a habit from work. My first week at the clinic, a five-year-old bit me, and I dropped an F bomb. My boss chewed me a new one. Since then, I've trained myself not to curse." She gave a dry little chuckle. "Not even when I caught my ex cheating."

"So, ah—" He fiddled with his napkin. "He's definitely your ex?"

Her jaw set, she gave a curt nod. "Absolutely, one hundred percent, total has-been."

"Good." Thank God! "I mean, it must be tough. How long were you together?"

"Five years in all. He—" She huffed and took a sip of her chai. "Sorry. They say the worst thing you can do on a first date is talk about your ex. Not that this is a date. I just meant..." With a groan, she dropped her head into her hands.

He reached across the table and gently grasped her wrist. "Tell you what, let's call it a pre-date."

"A what?"

"We're just feeling things out."

Her gaze drifted to his hand on her wrist, and he realized he was rubbing circles there with his thumb.

He yanked his hand back. "Sorry. Didn't mean to be creepy." Nothing for it but honesty. "It's hard to explain, but I feel—drawn to you. I mean, you're pretty and all, but there's more to it." Ah, but how to explain the inexplicable? "My grandmother, she believes angels communicate with us through signs."

"Like that angel in your bar?"

"Sorry, what?"

"The carved angel on top of the shelves that hold the booze."

How had he never noticed that? "Sure. Like that one. Anyway, when I first saw you, it felt—important, I guess. Like I was supposed to meet you. So—" He spread his hands, palms up. "Here I am. Just a guy, sitting in front of a girl, hoping she'll maybe go out with him sometime."

Her eyes narrowed. "And it doesn't bother you that I'm pregnant?"

"Nope." Another thing he couldn't explain—most young, single guys would probably sprint away from a woman, no matter how enticing, once they found out she was expecting. But he'd chewed on that question ever since meeting Anna two weeks ago, and it still wasn't enough to kill his infatuation. It wasn't like he had some weird pregnancy fetish, it just—didn't matter.

"Why don't I believe you?"

The way she wrinkled her nose plucked his heartstrings like a guitar. He gulped a deep breath. This might be his only shot. "Look, I like kids. Hope to have some myself one day. So if I meet a woman I like, why should the fact that she has a kid drive me away?"

"Hmmf." More napkin twisting. "To hear my divorced friends tell it, guys run for the hills as soon as they hear you're a mom."

"None of your single mom friends are dating?"

She held his gaze, appraising. "Are you fishing for details about Elena? 'Cause I promised her I wouldn't tell."

"Nope." Elena would confess in her own good time. She always did.

Anna gazed out the window at the kids pelting each other with snowballs. "You and I are connected by a lot of threads. Your sister, my sister, Jojo, the clinic, the bar. Odd that I never met you until now."

"Well, I don't come out of Bangers' kitchen very often." Taking a chance, he set his hand on the table, palm up. "I'm so glad I did."

First one side of her mouth crept up, then the other. "Me too." She nestled her hand in his. Happy sparks danced up his arm as she held his gaze for a sweet, slo-mo moment. "Elena says you're building a food truck?"

"Shit," he muttered, releasing her and raking his fingers hand through his hair.

"Sorry?"

"I mean, shoot."

Her laughter tinkled like wind chimes. "You can curse in front of me. Hell, I'm a real potty-mouth in my head. See? I said hell." She leaned across the table, hand poised. "You got crumbs in your hair."

Her slender fingers brushed his forehead, triggering shivers of pleasure. At this rate, he'd be sporting an inappropriate boner in no time. Not the best strategy for convincing her of his honorable intentions.

He yanked his focus back to their conversation. "It's just, I don't want people at work to know yet. About the food truck. Actually, it's an Airstream trailer."

"Even cooler." She made a lip zipping gesture. "I won't tell Charlie. What will you serve?"

"Empanadas, to start with. It's the perfect portable dish, right? I'll do traditional fillings, plus fusion ones—meat, veggie, even dessert."

"Sounds delish. But why keep it a secret? Everyone loves food trucks."

"Well, if I can make a go of it, I'll have to leave Bangers."

"Ah. That'll be hard, won't it? Charlie loves working there."

"Yeah, we're like family. But eventually, I'll have to strike out on my own."

"I'm sure your boss will understand." She finished her last bite of muffin, leaving no crumbs for him to brush from her cheek. Too bad.

She reached for her purse, signaling the end of their time together.

Now or never. "Can I ask you something?"

"Sure." Her open, honest gaze gave him the courage he needed.

"Why did you come? Here, I mean. With me."

"Umm...you asked me?"

"Do you always do what people ask you to?"

"Hell no." Her lashes lowered as she laid her hand over his, a soft touch that thrilled him right to his marrow. "It's great to have someone interested in me as a person. I mean, if you were just looking for a hookup, you wouldn't pick a pregnant woman." She tilted her head and squinted. "Unless you're one of those guys with a pregnancy kink?"

"No. Definitely not."

Misunderstanding his sharp tone, she pulled back.

He rushed to correct her. "I mean, your being pregnant doesn't turn me on, but it doesn't turn me off either." He swiped his hand down his roasting face. "I'm screwing this up, aren't I?"

"No. You're doing fine." She lifted her bag onto the table. "This was—surprising. Thank you."

Don't go! "Maybe I could help move you into your new place."

"I've gotta find one first. Right now, Charlie and I are sharing our childhood room at Dad's house. Funny how much it's shrunk over the years."

Should he tell her he lived with his Abuelita? Some people would assume he was a loser with no ambition. Better keep that to himself for now.

"Well, call me anytime." He flexed his biceps. "Your trusty knight is at your service."

"Will you bring tater tots?" Her smile sparkled and sang. "'Cause that's your secret weapon."

"Wait till you try my empanadas."

Her flirty glance reduced him to jelly. "How could I possibly resist? Tell you what—call me after the holidays."

"I will." He struggled to keep a cool façade through his manic inner happy dance. "And if you come into the bar before then, come back to the kitchen. I'll sneak you some tots."

"That, Sir Knight, is an offer I can't refuse." She scraped her chair back. "Thanks for the coffee. I have to get home —but this was fun." Her smile twinkled as she wrapped up in her cloak thingy. "You're fun. Crazy, to involve yourself in my mess, but fun."

"The best bits are always messy." He rose and took her hand. "Merry Christmas, Anna."

She scanned the room, then rose on her toes and pressed a kiss to his cheek. "Merry Christmas, Diego."

Off she went with a sweep of her cape, like some medieval lady fair, into the hustle-bustle of Sixth Ave. Down he sank into his chair, boneless and buzzy and grinning like a kid whose Christmas wish had been granted. Because it had.

Chapter Six: Mistletoe Magic

♥

"Be honest now. Is this cute or obnoxious?" Charlie tapped her phone, and belly dance music warbled from the tinny speaker.

Seated on her narrow twin bed, Anna shimmied her shoulders to the lively drumbeat. "It's weird, but catchy. You can definitely tell it's Jingle Bells."

Their mom's old belly dance LPs and CDs yielded nothing Christmas-y enough for Charlie's performance tomorrow night at Bangers' Christmas party, but an hour of online rabbit-hole diving yielded this cute number as well as a twangy "Oh Christmas Tree" played on flute, drums, and Qanun, a Middle Eastern zither. Perfect.

Aunt Hala knocked on the open door and bustled inside, her arms full of sparkly stuff and red chiffon. "Finally found it." She laid her bundle on the bed and smoothed out the voluminous skirt. "Ten layers, this thing has. Took me forever to sew." Her eyes held a misty sheen. "Your mama's was green, perfect for her blond hair. I'll never forget that recital. Your dad just about had a heart attack at the sight of his sister and his wife wiggling in these costumes. So much—what do you kids call it now?" She lifted a rhinestone-encrusted hip belt. "Bling, right?"

"You still dance, Aunt Hala?" Anna asked.

"Sure. I take classes downtown." Hala executed a complicated hip shimmy. "You should come with me sometime. Belly dance is good exercise for pregnant ladies."

Anna handed the jeweled bra top to her sister. "I'll go if Charlie will."

Charlie huffed. "Why bother? I'll be back in Portland by the time classes start after the holidays."

"Oh." A sudden tightness squeezed Anna's chest. Charlie's arrival three weeks ago had been a godsend. Dad's car accident coinciding with the death spiral of her marriage—it would all be too much without her sister's help. She knew Charlie missed her "real life" in Portland— God knows she grumbled about it enough—but Anna wasn't ready to let her go yet.

Hala folded her arms and regarded her oldest niece. "Seems to me you could stay a little longer, maybe help your sister get settled."

It was as if her aunt could read her mind, but Anna hadn't shared the good news she received this afternoon —good news that might fall flat if Charlie left.

"So." Hala clasped Charlie's shoulders. "Make sure you take lots of photos. It'll be good to see my old costume dancing again."

"I'll take pictures," Anna volunteered.

"You just want to visit Diego," Charlie muttered as she fastened the fringed belt around her hips, then gave it a shake, making the beaded fringe and silver coins swish.

"Diego?" their sharp-eared aunt asked. "Who's he?"

"Just the chef at Bangers," Charlie told her with a smirk. "Anna's in love with his tater tots."

How did Charlie make that sound so dirty?

"Oh well." Hala patted Anna's cheek. "You're eating for two now. Tomorrow, I'll bring you a nice fattoush. You need your veggies."

Hala hugged them both and left to look in on her injured brother. As soon as the door clicked shut, Anna pitched a pillow at Charlie's head.

"Ow. What was that for?"

"Ratting me out to Hala," Anna grumbled. "I'm not in love with Diego, for frick's sake. It was just a coffee date."

"So, you're not gonna see him again?"

"I didn't say that. Just don't make more of it than it is, okay? There's no reason I shouldn't talk to a nice guy."

"I can think of a couple of reasons why you shouldn't." She wrapped the veil around her shoulders and examined her reflection. "Besides, rebound relationships never work out."

"Oh really." Anna planted her fists on her hips. "Didn't you just break up with Marvin? And now you're sniffing after that bartender guy."

"Neither of us is expecting a baby. Or still technically married."

Why was her sister being such a pain? Right now, she needed Charlie's support more than ever. But, as Mom always said, you catch more flies with honey than vinegar —so she wiped the scowl from her face and fetched Mom's old sewing basket, a souvenir of happier times. "You'll look great in Hala's costume. Try it on before you go. It might need some alterations."

Charlie gave her a long, appraising look before stripping off her T-shirt and jeans and slipping into the sparkly bedlah.

"I'll reinforce these bra hooks, maybe make the belt a little looser." She smiled up at Charlie. "Funny. Looks-wise, the only thing we got from Mom is her wide hips."

"Child-bearing hips," Charlie said with a snort. "Lucky you."

"You still don't want kids?" Anna marked the hooks' new position with pins.

"Doesn't seem likely. Guess I'll just be the cool aunt."

Now or never. Anna set down the pincushion. "Charlie, I know you want to get back to Portland, but—"

"Correction. I am getting back to Portland. ASAP."

"Oh. Okay." Anna sank onto her bed and slumped, staring at her stocking feet.

"Hey, I'm sorry." Charlie peeled off the costume then sat beside Anna. "What were you going to ask me?"

"Doesn't matter." Anna stared at her fingers, knotted in her lap.

"C'mon." Charlie squeezed her shoulder. "If you don't tell me, I'll imagine the worst."

"It's just—I found this cute little house, over on North Seventh. Three bedrooms, two baths, fenced yard, quiet street. Perfect for a family." She swiped at her damp eyes. "Sorry. Pregnancy hormones."

"Sounds perfect."

"It is. And I could afford it if I had a roommate." She fixed Charlie with a pleading expression.

"What about your nurse friends?"

"They're all either married and settled, or single and not interested in sharing space with a noisy newborn."

"Ah. That's too bad." Charlie rose and pulled on her work clothes, then fluffed her hair in the mirror. She caught Anna's eye, and her jaw dropped. "Oh. Holy shit. You're asking me to stay?"

Anna kneaded her pillow in her lap. "Tacoma's so much cheaper than Portland. You said you were squashed in your apartment, and your roommates are slobs. If you shared with me, you'd have so much more space. And you could do your freelance work from here."

"But my clients are all there. Except—" Charlie's gaze slid to the door, and she nibbled her lip.

"Except what?" Anna clung to that morsel of hope with a white-knuckled grip.

Still evading her gaze, Charlie asked, "When do you have to decide?"

"The landlady gave me until the twenty-sixth. She had other applicants, but she's a retired nurse, so—" Anna's lips lifted in a sheepish grin. "You gotta take the little advantages you can get, right?"

Charlie drifted to the door. "I have to go. I'll be late for work. But I'll think about it."

Anna jumped up, threw her arms around her sister, and squeezed her tight. "Think real hard, okay?"

Anna stepped into Bangers Tavern a little before nine and plunged into the mob of rowdy customers in tacky holiday sweaters. Christmas music blared, nearly drowning out the roar of conversation and laughter. Overhead, holiday lights twinkled and paper snowflakes fluttered. Typical

Bangers, the dozen artificial Christmas trees were decorated in sports-themed bling.

She spotted Charlie sliding like a sparkly eel through the teeming crowd, heading toward the pool tables. Of course, Diego would be in the kitchen cranking out tater tots at warp speed. The tempting odor of fried potatoes wafted above notes of beer, booze, and bodies. Funny, she'd never thought that scent would make her heart go pitter-pat.

Jojo looked up from his stool at the entrance. "Anna! How's it going?"

"Not bad." She jiggled the tote bag she'd packed with safety pins, needle and thread, and fashion tape. "I'm here to help Charlie get ready for her act."

He stamped her hand, then handed her a coupon. "Get yourself a drink on the house. She'll swing by the bar soon."

She maneuvered past guffawing frat boys, tattooed locals, and dressed-to-the-nines couples from Gig Harbor slumming it on the Ave. At the bar, she stepped between a pair of women flirting with the hunky bartender, the one Charlie alternately swooned over and sparred with.

"Hey, it's Anna, right? Charlie's baby sis?" River pushed his golden hair back with one hand and flashed a brilliant smile. Charlie is toast. Good news, actually—the harder she fell for this guy, the more likely she was to stay in Tacoma.

"Hi, River." She handed him her drink coupon. "Got a holiday mocktail on the menu?"

"Let's see what I can whip up." He set a cocktail shaker on the bar and poured in cranberry juice, orange juice, apple juice, and a squirt of syrup. "My house-made gingerbread spice blend." He shook up the ingredients, poured them into a tall, ice-filled glass, and topped it up with ginger ale. "Let's see—need a fancy garnish for my future sister-in-law."

"Confident, aren't you?"

"Charlie calls me cocky." He added a skewer of sugared cranberries, an orange wedge, and a sprig of mint. "In truth, I'm too stuck on her to quit. Even if she thinks I'm a weasel."

"Well, I'm on your side." She sipped the delicious fruity concoction. "Say, Diego asked me to say hi next time I'm here. Do you think I could...?"

"Say no more." He straightened and called out, "Going on my break."

"River, are you effin' kidding me?" the girl bartender moaned. "We're swamped."

He clapped the skinny barback's shoulder. "Eddie's got it handled. I'll be back in ten."

Drink in hand, Anna followed River to the back hallway, where he poked his head through a pair of swinging doors. "Visitor."

His back to them, Diego flipped burgers and chicken breasts on the grill, his hips swaying to the music on his headphones. Dressed in a paper chef's cap and a canvas apron over a snug black T-shirt and dark jeans, he moved as gracefully as a panther. "Ay, corazón," he warbled. "Cómo me duele la vida sin ti."

"Awful, ain't he?" A stocky young cook emptied tater tots from a fry basket. "You here for him or me?"

Anna inclined her head toward Diego.

The girl fiddled with the pompom on her Santa hat, her gaze bright with curiosity.

"Shelby, meet Anna. Take care of her, okay?" River squeezed Anna's shoulder and left her there.

"Oh, this is gonna be fun." The cook beckoned, then crept up behind Diego, still oblivious as he danced from griddle to cooler. Shelby tugged Anna into his path. Holding a dish of sliced onions, he pivoted—and nearly dumped them down Anna's front.

"Anna!" His goggle-eyed expression relaxed into a glowing smile. "Hey. You came."

Onion fumes or no, standing so close to Diego filled her chest with a delicious buzzing sensation. Her chin came right to his collar bone, the perfect height for a hug. A friendly hug, that is. Nothing untoward. Nothing sexy. Nope—just friends.

Could he hear her heart's riotous pounding? She shuffled her feet, painfully self-conscious. "I hope it's okay, me being back here."

"Of course." His gaze roamed down her body and back to her face. "You look lovely. Are you spying again?"

She brushed her fingers over the low-cut, fuzzy red sweater she'd mooched from her sister's closet. "I'm here to help Charlie. She's performing soon."

"Sorry—gotta flip these." He pulled a metal stool up to the central island. "Have a seat."

Shelby set a paper tray of tots in front of Anna, then busied herself slicing tomatoes.

Anna nibbled her snack while Diego plated three sandwich orders and set them beneath a warming lamp. The server with long pigtails sailed in, gave Anna a curious glance as she loaded them onto her tray, and sailed back out.

"So." Diego spread his hands wide. "Welcome to my realm. You've met my trusty squire, Shelby?"

Shelby pitched a tater tot at his head.

He snatched it out of the air and popped it into his mouth. "See? She adores me."

His coworker snorted. "What time's your dad's thing?"

"Oh, right." He pulled his phone from his pocket. "Any minute now. You ready?"

Shelby saluted with her spatula.

"There was trouble with tonight's program," Diego told Anna, "so my dad's mariachi band volunteered to perform."

"With a little prodding from you?"

He lifted one shoulder. "Dawn, our boss, fell off a ladder hanging Christmas decorations. Banged her head pretty good. No one could make sense of her notes for tonight's party, so we all pitched in to find entertainment. You'd be surprised how many people will work for tater tots and beer."

A blast of trumpets rang out from the bar. Grabbing Anna's hand, Diego pulled her to an empty spot beside the bar.

He's holding my hand! Charlie would give her hell later. And yet, she couldn't quite force herself to relinquish his cozy warmth.

Eight men in black suits trimmed with silver braid and shiny buttons wove through the crowd, playing an up-tempo rendition of "Deck the Halls" on violin, trumpet, and guitar.

Diego pointed with his free hand. "There's my dad."

A handsome, barrel-chested trumpeter with salt and pepper hair and his son's sparkling eyes mounted the low stage. The others arranged themselves around him in a semi-circle as they finished the song. Mr. Vargas bowed with a flourish of his snow-dusted sombrero before launching into the next song, sung to the tune of Jingle Bells. Diego sang along with the chorus.

Anna leaned against his shoulder to be heard over the music. "You have a great voice. You should join the band."

"Pssht. I don't have a musical bone in my body."

"Not true. I saw you shaking your musical bones in the kitchen."

"Did you, now?" His smile was playful, but something a little sharper sparkled in his eyes.

Oh my God, I'm flirting like a shameless, horny hussy. She'd read that pregnancy could amp up a woman's libido, but not until the second trimester, right?

Still holding his hand, she eased a half-step away. "I bet Christmas is fun with your family."

"It is. I help my Abuelita make a mountain of tamales, and Mom makes a turkey and all the American sides. How about your family?"

"My Aunt Hala makes a ton of Lebanese food. Her kibbeh is to die for. And Uncle Fred makes deep-fried turkey."

"Maybe you can help me work up a Lebanese filling for my empanadas." He nudged her with his elbow. "I'll name it after you. Anna's Mediterranean magic."

She giggled into his shoulder.

"No good, huh? Anna's desert delight?"

The band launched into "Feliz Navidad," and they joined the noisy chorus.

"Muchisimas gracias," Mr. Vargas called out from the stage, his trumpet raised high.

Diego sighed and squeezed her hand. "I'd better go. I promised to feed these guys."

"And I'm supposed to meet Charlie in the break room."

"I'll show you the way." With a gentle touch on the small of her back, he guided her down the hallway.

Passing with a brimming ice bucket, the skinny barback lifted his chin. "Look up, guys." A sprig of mistletoe dangling above the restroom doors.

"For cripes' sake, Eddie," Diego grumbled, but he didn't look at all displeased.

"It's tradition, man." Eddie waggled his eyebrows before continuing on his way.

Eyeing the greenery, Anna debated and dithered. What a perfect excuse to satisfy her curiosity and claim a no-strings kiss. But Charlie might see them, or someone might tell Charlie, or...

Diego gently gripped her elbows and pulled her closer. "Christmas is all about tradition, right?"

For a thrilling, breathless moment, he hovered there, his softly parted lips an inch from hers. Impossible to wrench her eyes from that luscious mouth, so tempting, so close. His breath fanned across her skin. Her heart hammered.

And then he pressed a tender kiss to her forehead. "Merry Christmas, Anna."

Not enough. Throwing caution to the tater-tot scented wind, she rose on her toes and brushed her lips against his.

Just the barest touch, soft and warm, just the tiniest moan rumbled from the broad, firm chest beneath her palm. And yet, that simple gesture lifted the lid from her tightly clamped control, letting in fresh air and sunshine and a rush of delicious possibility. Heady stuff.

She took a deep breath and stepped back. "Gotta go help Charlie. Merry Christmas, Diego."

Grinning and flushed, he wobbled in place. "I'll call you."

"Please do."

"Break room's that way."

"Okay."

Like teenagers reluctant to hang up the phone, they inched toward their respective destinations, holding eye contact as long as possible.

"Thanks for coming to see me."

"Thanks for the tots."

"I hope you have a great Christmas."

"You too."

Finally, Shelby's arm shot through the swinging doors and yanked Diego into the kitchen. "Get your ass back to work, lover boy."

Laughing, he called, "Bye, Anna."

"Bye." Resting her back against the wall, she splayed her hand over her heart. Maybe it was the general holiday merriment, or some kind of magical seasoning on those tater tots, but this friendly connection was quickly blooming into a full-blown crush. Which was a huge mistake, considering the morass of complications her life had become.

On a deep inhale, Anna shook off the fairy dust and went back to help Charlie with her costume.

Chapter Seven: Busted

♥

"Piñata, piñata," Diego's nieces and nephew chanted as they tugged on his sleeves. Since their family's Christmas Eve feast was held at Abuelita's house, he'd been tasked with hanging the piñata from the back porch roof, sheltered from the steady icy drizzle. His dad gave him grief for buying a sneering Grinch piñata instead of the traditional tasseled star, but that's what little Oscar asked for, and Christmas is for kids, right?

Elena took charge of wrestling the littles into their winter coats while Abuelita poured mugs of hot chocolate spiced with cinnamon. Mama added a generous glug of tequila to Diego's mug before nudging him toward the door. "Good practice for your own kids. Papa tells me you were holding hands with a pretty girl last night."

He hid his panic behind a tongue-scorching gulp of hot chocolate. Sure, he'd held hands with Anna all through Dad's performance, but the old man had seemed too focused on his performance to notice. Stupid, stupid, stupid.

"Pretty girl?" Elena's gaze was sharper than Abuelita's best knife.

Dad joined them in the kitchen, tugging on his parka. "Rosa, this damn zipper is stuck again."

"Let me." Diego grabbed a bar of soap from the sink. "This'll loosen it up."

Abuelita emerged from the hallway, wrapped from chest to nose in a fuzzy scarf. "So, who was this pretty girl?"

He caught her eye and gave his head a sharp shake, but it was too late. Dad grunted as the zipper finally slid up. "About Elena's age. So tall." He held his hand to his jaw. "Dark hair. Looking at Diego with gaga eyes."

Elena's jaw dropped, then snapped shut with an audible click.

Diego dodged the eye daggers she was throwing. "The kids are waiting. Let's go smash the Grinch."

By the time the hideous piñata finally scattered sweets across the porch, everyone seemed to have forgotten about Diego's indiscretion. Laughing and stomping the cold from their feet, they trooped back inside the house. Time for presents—which meant he was off the hook. Diego shed his coat and headed toward the living room, where the littles were already handing out gifts.

"Hang on, Gogo." Elena snagged his arm in a vice-tight grip. "You were holding hands with Anna, weren't you?"

"One of your nurse friends, Elenita?" Abuelita asked, her voice saccharine sweet.

Mama barreled into the kitchen in search of scissors. Grinning, she elbowed Diego. "I'm glad to hear you're dating again." She turned to Elena. "Tell me, is this Anna a nice girl?"

Diego and Elena exchanged a silent volley of sharp glances.

Abuelita pulled a pair of scissors from the drawer. "Of course she's a nice girl. Our Diego has a good head on his shoulders. He wouldn't fall for a floozy."

Elena straightened. "Anna's good people. But she's—"

"Elena." Diego stamped his foot—not the best way to convey maturity, why would his sister pick this moment to drop this bomb? "It's Christmas. The kids are waiting."

With a final glare, Elena stalked into the living room. Everyone followed. Abuelita took Diego's arm for support she didn't need—and gave him a good pinch as they walked. "What the devil was that, mijo?"

"I'll tell you later." He would have to confess eventually if he continued to see Anna. But for now, he'd keep their secret. After all, nothing had happened. Just a little handholding and an innocent kiss under the mistletoe.

Okay, maybe his head hadn't stopped spinning since last night, but that was nobody's business.

As soon as he squeezed onto the sofa, little Oscar dropped a package in his lap. "This is for you, Tío. From me and Mama."

He ripped open the paper to reveal a pair of socks printed all over with tan pastries and "I love empanadas." He clutched them to his heart. "They're just what I always wanted. Thank you so much."

Elena rolled her eyes but held her tongue.

An hour later, the living room looked like someone had set off a wrapping-paper bomb, the kids' pajamas were dusted with buñuelo crumbs, and it was time to go.

"Mass starts at ten tomorrow. No excuses," Mama reminded everyone as they bundled their gifts, leftovers, and sleepy kids into their respective cars. Hugs and kisses all around, and finally Diego and Abuelita were alone in blessed peace and quiet.

He collapsed beside her on the sofa and smooched her cheek. "What a great Christmas, 'Lita. Thank you. I'll clean up all this in the morning."

"Don't thank me." She patted his knee. "You did most of the work. Now tell me about this pretty girl."

With a groan, he folded over and hid his red-hot face in his palms.

She rubbed his back. "Don't be afraid, kiddo. I'm on your side."

He peered up at her—so cute in her new fuzzy scarf, her wispy white hair held back with the jingle-bell headband Oscar gifted her. To an outsider, she looked harmless, but there was no escaping her X-ray vision.

"You're not going to like it."

"Try me."

"Okay." He pushed up and faced her. "Anna is Elena's nurse friend. She's very pretty, and funny, and smart. And when I first saw her, the heavens opened up and the angels sang. I know that sounds like some silly cartoon, but I swear, it was magical."

Abuelita's smile was misty as she patted his hand. "Just like me and my Alberto. Go on."

He squeezed his eyes shut. Just get it over with. "She's pregnant."

No response from Abuelita. Absolute silence.

He opened one eye. Tapping her pursed lips with her forefinger, she looked—disappointed, he supposed.

Finally, she released a sigh. "You gonna do the right thing?"

He blinked at her in confusion. "Oh." He raised both palms. "No, see, the baby's not mine."

Her eyes widened. "Whose is it?"

"Her husband's."

Abuelita's jaw dropped, and he quickly corrected himself. "Her ex-husband's. They're getting divorced."

Her head thunked back against the sparkly Christmas pillows. "Diego. My darling boy. You can't."

Defiance flared in his chest. "I know it sounds crazy, but she's so much more than her circumstances. 'Lita, she's—"

"Going to break your heart." She fixed him with a baleful gaze. "Your tender heart is a gift, Gogo, but it could be your downfall. This girl, she's in a terrible place right now. Raising a baby on your own is hard. Just ask Elena." She clasped his hand. "Your new friend probably sees you as a lifeline. But corazón, what if she goes back to her husband?"

"She'd never do that. He cheated on her."

She shook her head. "Maybe she won't, maybe she will. It's never as simple as it looks, and no matter what she decides, she and that man are family." She squeezed his hand tight. "You can't break up a family."

The inside of his chest crumbled, remnants of hope dropping like ash. "I won't, I swear. If she makes that choice, I'll step aside. But she needs a friend—and so do I."

Shaking her head, Abuelita pushed to her feet. "You're fooling yourself. But some life lessons must be learned the hard way."

She shuffled to her room, and Diego stayed alone on the couch, staring unfocused at the winking Christmas lights. The longer he let his thoughts spin, the more he felt the sickening truth—his grandmother was probably right. But a stubborn kernel of determination refused to be extinguished. He and Anna had a connection, damn it, something deep and bright and true. He wasn't ready to give up hope.

"C'mon, Dad, we're gonna be late." Anna shifted the heavy sack of gifts to her hip and tapped her booted foot on the foyer tiles.

The clomp, clomp of Dad's crutches sounded from the back hallway. At this rate, Aunt Hala and Uncle Fred would probably start Christmas dinner without them.

Charlie burst through the front door, pink-cheeked and breathless. "Salad's in the trunk, wine in the back seat. Feels like I'm forgetting something." She trotted toward the kitchen, the jingle bells on her ponytail holder ringing in rhythm with her steps. On the way, she hollered, "Dad, for Chrissakes, get a move on."

More clomping and grumbling, but still no Dad.

Charlie returned clutching a tin of Christmas cookies. "I swear, I'm gonna drag him out by his Santa suspenders."

Scowling into the hallway mirror, Anna fiddled with her Christmas wreath pin that wouldn't stay lit. "At least he's dressing up again." Dad's slovenly habits since the car crash made her worry that he might be seriously depressed, but he'd spent the morning trying on nice shirts and kitschy holiday ties. Good to see him more like his old, pre-injury self.

"Here, take this." Charlie handed off the cookie tin and strode down the hallway toward Dad's room.

"For Pete's sake." Anna grumbled at her reflection. Being late always wound her nerves up tight, but this was good training for dragging a pokey toddler out the door. That would be—she rubbed her stomach—just two years from now. Amazing.

The doorbell rang. Neighbors? Sometimes Mrs. Fong next door brought baked goodies. Sweet lady, she'd looked in on their little family every holiday season since they lost Mom.

A barrage of ding-dongs assaulted her ears. Someone was leaning on the darn button. Rude.

She set down her packages, opened the door, and came face to face with a giant plushy Santa.

Holy flaming poopballs. One of the hands holding the toy aloft bore a familiar gold band—the one he whined about wearing because it hurt his knuckle.

"What do you want, Brock?"

Her ex set down his tacky offering. New jacket, expensive-looking. Probably cashmere. No doubt Deborah was spoiling her poor, abandoned baby boy. Or maybe he wanted to be snazzy for Christmas dinner with his new girlfriend.

Brock's lip curled. "Merry Christmas to you too, Anna."

Saint Nick, give me strength. "I told you, no more gifts."

"It's not for you, it's for the baby." He set the ugly plushy at his feet.

"Who won't be born until August. Have you worked on the parenting plan? We're supposed to bring that to our mediation appointment."

Brock flinched as if she'd socked him. Which would be very satisfying, but...Christmas. No violence.

He crossed his arms. "There's no need for mediation because we're not getting divorced. Now, can I please come in? It's freezing out here."

Boiling. Anna rubbed her middle. That life coach whose blog she read over this morning's decaf said you should identify emotions as sensations in your body. Right now, her solar plexus was burbling with frustration and rage. But she could ride it out. She was a grown woman with common sense and self-control and—

Brock reached for her hand. She yanked it back. So much for Zen.

He shoved his hands into his pockets. "Look, I get it. Your pride is hurt, and you want to hurt me in return. The way you found out about Kristi, that was..." His gaze drifted skyward, as if searching for his next line.

"Shitty. It was shitty, Brock." She'd be damned if she would make this any easier for him.

"Yeah, okay, that's fair. I made a mistake. A big one."

She nodded. "Huge. Ginormous."

"But we can get past it. I'll give her up if you'll just come back."

"You will? As in you haven't yet?"

He staggered back a step. Two or three more and he'd tumble down the porch steps. She'd love to see that.

"Listen," he continued, "all couples fight. But marriage takes hard work and sacrifice and, uh—"

She held up her palm. "I'm not interested in the speech your mom wrote for you."

His nostrils flared. "For fuck's sake, Anna, it's been two weeks. Aren't you ready to make up yet? I'll go to counseling. I'll let you monitor my phone. Whatever." When she only glared, his voice grew shrill. "It's Christmas. Can't you forgive me for our child's sake?"

She glared icicles at her red-faced ex. How had she ever thought him handsome?

He threw up his hands. "You want to hurt me back, Anna? Living with my mom sucks, and I can't afford the apartment without your salary. So yeah, I'm hurting. Are you happy now?"

"No." Surprisingly, her voice came out steady and calm. That life coach would be proud. "I wouldn't say I'm happy, but I can see a path forward. You took a wrong turn, Brock, and that changed everything for both of us." She gave a dry chuckle. "In a weird way, I'm grateful. You opened my eyes to how awful our marriage was, and I finally realized I deserve better. So does our child."

He widened his stance. "Our child deserves two parents."

"And she'll have them. Stepparents too, most likely. Nowadays, that's totally normal. She won't be the only kid in her class with divorced parents."

He glared for a long, tense moment before grinding out, "Look, I had my reasons. You're not blameless."

Her jaw dropped. "Oh, you're gonna pin this on me?"

"You were always tired. It felt like you cared more about your job than about us."

The boiling in her gut rose to volcanic proportions. "Says the man who couldn't be bothered to—" She gulped a breath of icy winter air, then another. Slowly, the lava subsided. "I'm not having this conversation with you. It's not just the cheating. Your behavior over the past three years proves that my happiness was always your lowest priority. I'm better off without you."

Brock shook his head. "I can't accept that. You're a good person, Anna. How can you be so selfish?"

Rapid clomps heralded Dad's arrival. He loomed behind her, his breath hot on her cheek. "Selfish? You calling my baby girl selfish when you dipped your wick in some floozy's inkwell?"

She placed her hand on his arm. "Dad, I got this."

"No." Dad planted his crutch's rubber tip in Brock's chest. "It's Christmas. Family's waiting. I'm not gonna let this turd-for-brains ruin our holiday."

Brock staggered back under the force of Dad's shove and grabbed the porch railing. "I won't sign the papers, Anna. You'll change your mind. You don't want to be a single mom. You're too kind-hearted to do that to your child." He whirled away and stalked back to his car.

With a growl, Dad lunged.

Anna barred the doorway with her arm. "No, Dad. He's taken up enough of our time. The family's waiting. Let's go enjoy our Christmas."

Chapter Eight: Blueberry

♥

They say the true measure of friendship is whether they'll help you move. Of course, Charlie's new boyfriend River volunteered to help Anna and Charlie unpack their new home. But he had ulterior motives—convincing Charlie he wasn't some flakey rich boy toying with her affections. Secretly, Anna suspected they would have a new roommate soon.

So yeah, no surprise to see River's motorcycle in their driveway on that frigid January morning. But Anna never expected to find the whole Bangers Tavern crew on their front porch.

"Surprise!" Rosie, the blue-haired one, threw a handful of confetti into the icy wind before stepping into the living room, now piled high with moving cartons. On the way in, she smooched Anna's cheek. "Happy new house, Anna."

Lana, the one with the long pigtails, hefted a takeout coffee box and grinned. "Unpacking fuel."

Next came Eddie, the skinny barback, and River, each lugging a toolbox. Kiara, the girl bartender, and Shelby, Diego's snarky assistant, carried six-packs of soda and beer. Bringing up the rear, scruffy and adorable in a Bangers hoodie and stained jeans, Diego held a tray covered with a kitchen towel. When he lifted a corner, savory-scented steam billowed out. "Breakfast empanadas." His sweet smile made Anna's insides tickle in the best possible way.

Calm down, Miss Horny Pants. He's here to help, not to flirt. Besides, he's Charlie's friend too.

As she set up the food and drinks on the kitchen counter, Anna asked Charlie, "Aren't we supposed to provide the refreshments?"

"Pshaw." Kiara waved away her objection. "Think of it as a housewarming gift."

River snagged an empanada, chomped, and moaned. "Awesome. What's in here?"

Diego's aw-shucks grin could've lit the room. "Just the usual stuff: eggs, chorizo, potatoes, peppers. Try the avocado salsa." He removed the lid from a glass bowl. "Jojo's got a training appointment this morning. He'll be along as soon as he finishes torturing his client. And Dawn sends her regrets—bad back."

After a quick breakfast, they all got to work. No one would let Anna lift anything, which was ridiculous considering she wasn't even showing yet, so she reluctantly accepted her role as director of traffic and arbiter of furniture placement. Each time Diego passed, his flirty glances refreshed her memory of their kiss under the mistletoe—a foolish, impulsive gesture she couldn't force herself to regret.

If anyone noticed their playful vibe, they didn't comment. Charlie was too focused on unpacking her computer gear—and squeezing River's butt.

Dad arrived later that morning and, after scarfing up the last of the empanadas, started bossing everyone around. A few hours in, he limped into the living room and leaned on his cane. "Habibti, River's taking me to the hardware store. I need a couple parts to fix your drippy tub." He leaned closer and whispered, "Smart of your sister to find a fella who's handy."

Lucky Charlie, Dad liked her new boyfriend. Not much chance he'd approve of Diego—not that he was anything close to Anna's boyfriend. But still.

Dad bellowed, "Yo, Domingo. You need anything from the hardware store?"

"Dad," Anna hissed. "His name is Diego."

Diego poked his head through the kitchen doorway, a power screwdriver in his hand. "I'm good. Just need someone to hold the ceiling lamp while I screw it in place."

Anna popped up from the sofa. "I'll help."

Dad's caterpillar eyebrows scrunched. "You don't need to be climbing no ladders."

"For cripes' sake, Dad, I'm only seven weeks pregnant. The baby's the size of a blueberry." Ignoring her father's protests, she moved to the kitchen, where Diego leaned over the table, fiddling with the new light fixture. Before she had the chance to drink in his broad, muscular back and firm behind, he turned and flashed a lopsided grin. "Dad's a little over-protective, eh?

"He's ridiculous. It's not like I'm about to give birth." She patted her still-flat stomach. "I won't even start to show for another six weeks."

A twinge of foreboding pinched her. Would Diego's interest diminish when her middle started expanding? She almost wished she hadn't told him about the baby. But no, that would be dishonest. She could never do that— especially to such a decent guy.

Diego unfolded a second stepladder. "When a man cares about a woman, he wants to protect her. It's an instinct."

"Is that why you're here?" The words popped out quicker than her brain could engage. Horrified, she clapped a hand over her mouth.

His grin widened. "Something like that. If you and Blueberry will hold the cover in place, I'll screw it in."

Stretching both arms overhead caused her boxy sweater to ride up. Before mounting his ladder, Diego paused and spoke to her exposed midriff. "Hang in there, little one. We'll have your house fixed up in no time." His breath tickled her bare skin.

Could he be any sweeter? Biting her lip, she focused on the new, brass-rimmed ceiling lamp. "Gotta admit," she told him, "I worry about you messing around with naked wires."

"How do you think I got this curly hair?" He reached past her to tighten a bolt. Happy sparks of pleasure shimmied down her spine when his muscular forearm brushed her cheek.

It's just pregnancy hormones, she reminded herself.

"Actually," Diego continued, "my dad's an electrician."

"That must come in handy for your food truck."

He snorted, a disturbingly sexy sound. "His help comes with endless lectures about how I should be doing something more practical. No thanks." He leaned behind her to tighten a screw, the awkward posture pressing his chest against her side. "Besides, so far I've found what I need on YouTube."

Bracketed by his arms like some weird, vertical game of Twister, Anna didn't know which way to turn. She huffed a shaky breath.

"You okay? I could get someone else to hold this."

"No, no. I'm fine." She swallowed a lump in her throat. "I'd love to see it sometime."

"My food truck?" He chuckled, a low, rumbly sound that made her lady parts very, very happy. "Kinda feels like the universe is nudging me to hurry up and finish it."

"How so?"

"My family knows about it now, so I've gotta to prove I can make it a success." His eyebrows flicked up. "Besides, you work days, and I work nights. Pretty hard to get to know you if I can only see you on Saturdays."

"What about Sundays?"

"Family dinner." He dropped his gaze, and his smile slipped. "I like you, Anna. But a Vargas family meal is a lot to handle."

An awkward silence descended. Of course he wouldn't want to bring his pregnant girlfriend to meet his family. Not that she was his girlfriend. Not by any stretch of the imagination. Shut up, brain.

"Shall we try it?" she chirped like some over-caffeinated sparrow.

He blinked rapidly. "Try what?"

"The light, silly."

"Oh, right. Of course." They both climbed down. Diego beat a drumroll on the counter while Anna flipped the switch. Bright, warm light flooded the kitchen.

"Tah dah!" Diego bowed with a flourish of his hand.

Her arms twitched with a sudden urge to hug him. Wrestling control, she gave him a huge smile instead. "Just beautiful. Thanks so much, Diego. I'll love cooking in here, with all this wonderful light."

Stuffing his hands into his pockets, he shuffled closer and stared down at their toes, just inches apart. "Listen, Anna. I don't want to give you the wrong impression. I'd love you to meet my family. It's just—" He looked up and sighed. "Two of them already know you're pregnant."

"Two?"

"Elena and my Abuelita. She pried it out of me on Christmas Eve. Needless to say, they think I'm crazy."

"You probably are."

"Maybe. But here I am." He held her gaze for a long, heavy moment. Then the corners of his mouth quirked, breaking the tension that held her immobile. "Anyway, when my food truck launches, I'll focus on the breakfast and lunch crowds. If you're still interested, we'll be able to spend more time together." His fingertips skated down her arm. "You, me, and the blueberry."

This was madness. By the time the baby arrived, Diego would be long gone. Still, she had to ask. "When do you think it'll be ready?"

"Summertime. Maybe sooner." He glanced at her belly. "When's the baby due?"

"End of August."

"Cool." What was going on behind those warm dark eyes of his?

A deep voice boomed from the living room. "Diego. Where you at?"

"Jojo," he muttered, then called, "In here."

The giant strode into the room. "Oh, shit. Am I interrupting something?"

Stepping back from Diego's powerful gravity, Anna pasted on a phony smile. "Why would you think that?" She stood on tiptoe and pecked Jojo's cheek. "Thanks so much for coming."

He winked at Diego. "Well, Lana's here, so..."

Diego socked his arm. "When are you going to finally ask her out?"

"All in good time, my man. All in good time."

Speak of Jojo's devil, Lana poked her head into the kitchen. "Hi, guys. Anna, Charlie needs you."

With a wistful backward glance at Diego, Anna followed Lana to the front room.

"Ya know," Lana remarked, "you and Charlie really look alike."

That's what most people said, but Anna didn't see it. A little taller and curvier, Charlie was much more confident and flirtatious. Speaking of flirting— "Seems like Jojo has a crush on you."

Lana rolled her eyes. "Why do people keep saying that? He just likes to tease me. Doesn't mean anything."

"If you say so." Anna sat on the couch beside Charlie, who was unpacking knickknacks from her Portland apartment. "Hey, I remember this lumpy ashtray. Didn't you make this for Jaddi?"

"Yeah. In kindergarten, I think. I miss him." Gone for ten years now, their dad's father was a sweet, gentle man with huge, strong hands and a playful smile.

Anna sighed. "If he were here, what would he think of this?" She waved a hand to take in the mess of boxes, paper plates dusted with empanada crumbs, and laughter coming from the kitchen.

Charlie shrugged. "He was from another time. He'd probably come after your Brock with his hunting rifle."

"Not my Brock anymore, thank God. Though I'd love to see that. He'd probably piss his pants." With a sigh, she dug into the open carton. "Men, right?"

Charlie squeezed Anna's knee. "The good ones try to help, in their clumsy way."

"Like River. Can't believe how well he gets on with Dad. Of course, he's totally courting you." Anna narrowed her eyes. "You're going to ask him to move in, aren't you?"

"Well, Diego's totally courting you. Which is a terrible idea, by the way." Charlie reached into the box, then straightened. "How would you feel about that?"

"About what?" She fought to keep her breath even and her tone nonchalant. She wasn't ready to defend this weird flirtation with Diego, but she wasn't ready to give it up either. Maybe this was a stupid idea, maybe she'd have to listen to another big-sister I told you so, but right now, the thrill she felt whenever Diego smiled at her was the shining star twinkling above her murky days. Anyway, he'd forget her soon enough. Why not bask in his attention a little longer?

Charlie poked Anna's shoulder. "River. Moving in. What do you think?"

"Honestly, all this change at once is knocking me on my ass. Let's give ourselves a few months with just the two of us before we add another roommate, okay?"

"Deal. Same goes for you and Diego."

"Who said anything about Diego?"

"You." Charlie tickled her ribs. "In your sleep last night. And the night before, and—"

"Did not, you lying liar." Anna swatted her hands away. Holy crap on a cracker. Anna had been a sleep-talker since earliest childhood, and they'd shared their tiny childhood bedroom for the past month. Good thing she'd have her own room now, before she spilled any more secrets with her nighttime blabbing.

She pushed up from the couch. "I'm going to help Lana and Rosie." As she made her way to the garage, she chewed her lip. Was Diego really courting her? Not many guys would go to such lengths to help a woman they weren't even having sex with.

But we could be. The flash in his eyes, the dreamy promise in his smile were ample proof of his interest. For just a moment, she let herself imagine the steamy possibilities. Her growing library of books and websites agreed sex during pregnancy was usually safe, and the fizzy, sparkly feeling that filled her gut every time he looked her way—wow. Her body was voting one hundred percent for jumping Diego's hunky bones. But the idea of letting a guy get that close so soon after Brock's betrayal, not to mention the tiny passenger she was carrying—

She gave herself a wet-puppy shake and moved into the garage. Better to focus on moving cartons than on Diego's distracting charms.

Chapter Nine: Olive

♥

A half hour before his shift, Diego huddled in a booth with Eddie over a plate of tots. He'd never seen the soft-spoken barback this animated. Eyes bright, Eddie tapped his open notebook with his pen like a one-handed drummer. "So, your business plan starts with an overview. What's your purpose?"

"Um, to sell empanadas?"

"Nope." More tapping. "You're raising money for the development of your food truck. To do that, you've gotta show a detailed forecast of your financials over the first three years. I assume you're going for a loan."

"Couldn't I just do a Kickstarter?"

"Maybe. What do your investors get in return?"

"Empanadas."

With a groan, Eddie dropped the pen and massaged his temples.

Diego spread his hands palms up. "Look, that's why I'm talking to you, Mr. Business Major."

"Let's take a different tack. What kind of research have you been doing?"

"Well, I watch that Food Truck Race show with my Abuelita."

Eddie gave a disgusted grunt. "Reality TV? Really?"

"Just teasing you, man. I joined the Washington State Food Truck Association, and I talk to every food truck owner I meet." Most were surprisingly helpful, and a few even gave him tips for best parking spots to catch the breakfast and lunch crowds.

"And how close are you to opening?"

"I'm about halfway done installing the kitchen. I figure maybe July."

The Airstream hadn't been maintained with the love she deserved, but her bones were excellent. When he spotted her at the fairgrounds with a For Sale sign in her window, it was love at first sight—kind of like when he met Anna.

Rosie wandered to their table and peered over Eddie's shoulder as she tied on her apron. "Working on your future bar, Eddie?"

"No, Diego's food truck."

Her eyebrows shot up. "You're leaving us, Diego?"

"Ssssh!" He glanced around the still-empty bar. No sign of the boss yet. "I don't want Dawn to know until I'm ready to launch."

Rosie and Eddie exchanged a dubious look.

"Don't worry, I'll give her plenty of notice. I'll even train my replacement. But until then, I need this job."

"And we need you." Rosie leaned down and pecked his cheek, giving them both a view of her abundant, tattooed cleavage. Eddie's face went beet red.

"Scoot over." She slid onto the bench beside Eddie, who bit his lip. They were so cute together—bubbly, curvy Rosie with her bright blue hair, and skinny, taciturn Eddie. Did she even notice how gaga Eddie was for her?

She propped her chin on her interlaced fingers. "What's the name of your truck?"

"Empanada Angel." Hopefully, his grandmother's celestial helpers would watch over him.

"Good name," she said. "Charlie could help you set up your website. She did a great job with my online tattoo portfolio."

Eddie nudged her with his elbow. "Maybe you could help Diego with a logo?"

"Hmm." She tapped her pursed lips. "Angels and empanadas. Lemme think on that."

He flashed a grateful grin. Who better to draw his logo than their resident tattoo artist?

"You three cooking up schemes over here?" Wiping her hands on a bar towel, Dawn sauntered over, her eyes narrowed.

Absorbed in their conversation, Diego hadn't noticed her approach. "Shoot, is it time?" He popped out of the booth.

"What's tonight's special?" Dawn asked, chalk marker in hand.

"Greek burger with pickled onions, Kalamata olive tapenade, and feta."

"And the tots?"

"Also Greek, with garlic, tomato, cucumber, red onion, olives, and tzatziki."

She clapped him on the shoulder. "Kiddo, you're a genius with flavors. What would I do without you?"

Guilt pinched him hard.

The front door swung open, letting in a blast of wind.

"Evening, miss." Dawn called.

"Hi, Ms. O'Malley. I'm just dropping this off for my sister."

Diego spun at the sound of the familiar voice. "Anna! Hi!"

He hadn't seen her since a few weeks back when he helped her and Charlie move into their new place. He'd tried a few flirty texts, but his skill with the written word left a helluva lot to be desired, judging by her noncommittal responses. And suddenly, here she was, looking right at him with those huge dark eyes and nibbling her plump lower lip. Even in a puffer coat and scrubs, with her glossy hair scraped back in a ponytail, she made his mouth water and his heart race.

Anna held out a shopping bag. "Charlie's hung up with a website client in Gig Harbor. She sends her apologies for running late. I brought her work shoes, so she won't have to stop at home first."

Dawn took the bag. "How's that baby treating you?"

Patting her middle, Anna chuckled. "For a person the size of an olive, she sure makes her opinions known. Seems she doesn't like the smell of fish, or broccoli, or perfume."

"Haven't seen your old man since before Christmas." Dawn patted Anna's shoulder. "Tell him to come in sometime. We'll shoot the shit about the old days."

"I will." Twisting her knit scarf, Anna glanced at Diego.

He seethed with impatience. Go back to your office, Dawn. His telepathy ray seemed to be on the fritz, though, because the boss just doffed her Seahawks cap and massaged her scalp. "When I first met your dad, he and your mom were newlyweds. Cutest couple—big blonde farm girl and little Lebanese stallion. Bangers was an English-style pub back then, and I was bartender." Her gaze focused somewhere far away. "Now I own the bar, and Jack's gonna be a grandpa. Time goes so fast." With a sigh, she started toward her office, calling over her shoulder, "Diego, get this young lady something to eat. Gotta nourish the next generation."

"Will do, boss." He beckoned to Anna. "Keep me company in the kitchen?"

She followed him through the swinging doors. "Whew. Warm in here."

"Let me." He helped her out of her coat. "Cute outfit. I'll bet the kids love those ducks on your shirt."

She climbed onto the stool he offered and stretched out her feet to display flowered clogs. "I'm such a fashionista. Admit it, these reduce you to a quivering blob of lust, right?"

He bit his knuckle and groaned. "How did you know about my orthopedic footwear fetish?" Truth be told, hearing the word "lust" on her lips was enough to send his thoughts zooming to the not-suitable-for-work zone. "So, what'll it be? Tonight's special is a Greek burger and garlic tots."

"Yes, please." The way she wiggled on her seat made him picture her wiggling on his...

None of that. Focus. He pulled a burger from the fridge and slapped it on the grill.

"Where's your partner?"

"It's Shelby's night off." He flipped the burger. "Is your little olive okay with onions?"

"Absolutely."

"Garlic?"

"Bring it."

"Olive tapenade?"

Anna slapped her hands to her cheeks in mock horror. "Mashed olives? Diego, how could you?"

He dipped a spoon in his olive and sun-dried tomato tapenade and held it to her mouth. She held his gaze as her soft pink lips closed delicately around the morsel. Then her eyes closed, and her fingers fluttered to the delicate V where her collar bones met. Her soft moan brought his dick to full attention.

Note to self—cook for Anna as often as possible.

A devilish smile bloomed across her lovely face. "What Olive doesn't know won't hurt her."

"Smart mom." He slathered her feta-studded burger with tapenade, topped it with a dollop of tzatziki, and filled the rest of the plate with garlic tots.

Watching Anna eat was his new favorite thing. Each groan of pleasure echoed between his thighs as she attacked her dinner with enthusiasm bordering on feral.

Licking tzatziki from her thumb, she glanced up and caught him gawking. "Oh, jeez, I must look like a pig."

He shook his head. "A pig could never be so pretty." Or hot.

She ducked her chin and giggled. "You're trying to seduce me and Olive with your cooking superpowers, aren't you?"

"Drat." He smacked the counter. "You've discovered my evil plan."

The kitchen terminal pinged and spat out an order. Reluctantly, Diego turned back to his griddle.

After demolishing her meal, Anna carried her plate to the dish sink.

"Hey, you don't have to—"

She waved off his protest. "You cook, I clean. That's the rule."

"Not in here, angel." He took the plate from her hands. "My kitchen. My rules."

"Bossy, aren't you?" But she grinned all the same as she shrugged into her coat.

He searched his lust-addled brain for a reason to keep her here a bit longer. "So, uh, you need any more work on your new house?"

"Nah. The house is great, thanks to you and River. I've got plenty of time to set up the baby's room." She huffed a laugh. "Still feels weird to say that."

"I'd be glad to help," he exclaimed a little too loudly. Calm down. Don't be a pushy weirdo. "I mean with painting. Or whatever."

Lana bustled in to collect her order and snapped her head in a double take. 'Hey, Anna. You working here now?"

"No. Just mooching."

"You should give it a try. We're always short-handed on Friday and Saturday nights. Tips are good." She lifted her tray in a graceful swoop and sailed through the swinging doors.

Anna chuckled. "Just what you all need. A pregnant waitress."

Diego started his next order. "How are you feeling? If that's not too personal to ask."

She patted her belly. "Full. Tired. Confused."

"About?"

"You." Tilting her head, she regarded him as if he were a puzzle she was determined to solve. "You're sweet, and talented, and so cute it almost hurts to look at you. Why waste your time with my big ol' mountain of baggage?"

He slapped another burger on the grill. Easier to say this if he wasn't looking into those sharp, dark eyes. "I see it as an investment."

"How so?"

"In your shoes, I wouldn't be quick to trust a guy. It's on me to prove myself."

"With tater tots and home repairs?"

"Whatever gives me a chance to spend time with you."

"No." Her sharp tone spun him around. "I like you, Diego, but I don't want to be in your debt."

His heart deflated like a leaky balloon. "I understand." He didn't. None of this made sense, but he'd hoped—

Her soft hand gripped his arm. "You've gotta let me help you too."

"I, uh...what?"

"A good relationship is balanced, not one-sided. How about if I help you with your foo—" She clapped a hand over her mouth and glanced over her shoulder. "Sorry, I mean with your secret project."

"You want to help me fix up the Airstream?"

"Absolutely. My dad would never let Charlie and me touch his tools. I'll need to know how to fix things around the house, right? You won't always want to come running when something breaks down."

I will if you let me. "Tell you what. It's supposed to be sunny this weekend. Why don't you come by around ten? We can work for a while, and then I'll make you lunch."

She shook her head. "You can teach me a recipe. Like, let me be your assistant." Her grin turned sheepish. "I never really learned to cook beyond the basics, and I'm going to have to feed Olive, so..."

"Deal."

The doors swung open, and Charlie charged in, her thick ponytail bouncing as she gaped at Anna then Diego. "Here you are. What's going on?"

"Nothing." Anna slid off her stool and pulled on her coat. "I brought your shoes, and Diego gave me dinner. You should try the Greek burger. It's amazing."

While Charlie glared, Anna gave him a finger-waggle. "See you Saturday. Text me the address, okay?"

Would she have kissed his cheek again if her sister wasn't there? Or maybe even his mouth? Ever since their encounter under the mistletoe, he'd craved her soft lips like a camel craves water. Maybe Saturday...

Biting his lip, he turned back to his grill. No doubt about it, Anna Khoury was full of delightful surprises.

Chapter Ten: A Kiss, Interrupted

♥

Clutching her coat tighter, Anna followed the narrow brick path around the side of Diego's cute brick house. The wooden gate swung open at her touch, revealing a garden all wrapped up for winter. Straw-covered flowerbeds held garden statuary and whimsical figures on metal stakes—mostly angels. On a cement pad beside the detached garage sat a small Airstream trailer, its aluminum hull gleaming. A portion of the exterior wall stood raised like an awning above a service window. The whir of power tools punctuated the salsa music playing inside.

Rapping on the windowpane got no response, so she tried the door handle. Stepping through, she found Diego bent over a boxy contraption on the metal counter. The sight of his muscular ass, cupped by worn jeans and swaying to the music, brought back a phrase from her high school Spanish classes—¡Dios mío!

She waited until he set down his drill before tapping his shoulder.

"Anna, hey." His brilliant smile nearly knocked her over.

She lifted a takeout bag. "I brought doughnuts."

"Awesome. Thanks." He made a sweeping gesture. "Welcome to Empanada Angel."

She spun to take it all in—shiny metal walls, cushy rubber floor mats, and bright fluorescent lights that chased away the winter gloom. The trailer's nose held a multi-basin sink, and a deep-fat fryer took up the other end.

"Looks like you're almost ready to launch."

"Far from it." He unwrapped the doughnuts and offered her first choice before chomping into a chocolate Long John. Mesmerized by the movement of his strong jaw and plump, chocolate-smeared lips, Anna felt her cheeks flush.

He wiped his lips on his sleeve. "Okay, the tour. Found this baby when I took Abuelita to a swap meet at the Puyallup fairgrounds. She was a gourmet doughnut wagon back then with a For Sale sign in her window. I made an offer, and...voilà."

He pointed to the fryer. "For fried empanadas. I'm installing a convection oven for the baked ones. Cooler for salad here." He pointed to a built-in metal bin with a lid. "Mexican sodas and other bottled drinks here, coffee there."

"Pretty small menu, isn't it?" She leaned against the counter and wiggled her icy toes in her boots.

Diego leaned beside her, the press of his hip against hers a delectable distraction. "In the past I tried to do too many things at once and gave up too quickly when it didn't work out. This time, I'm going deep and taking my time."

He was talking about his business, of course, but his words echoed between her thighs.

She scooted away, putting a few inches of safety between them. "So, you've tried food trucks before?"

"No, catering, mostly. Didn't spend enough time planning for what could go wrong. This time, I want to do one thing really well before expanding."

"To what, your own restaurant?"

"Someday." His eyes glittered with excitement. "Pan-Latin fusion cuisine. So I'll start with fusion empanadas."

Pushing up from the counter, she broke his hypnotic gaze. "How can I help?"

For the next hour she held his flashlight and handed him tools while he explained the wiring, safety precautions, and other technical things she didn't quite follow because she was spellbound by the sexy rumble of his voice, the way his hair curled behind his ears, and the woodsy-spicy scent wafting from his body. As she leaned in to illuminate a particularly tricky spot, the side of her breast brushed his arm, igniting a shower of invisible sparks.

When the oven's installation was complete, Diego stepped back. "Last step, test run. Drumroll, please."

She drummed her fingers on the metal counter while he flipped switches and turned dials. Bouncing on his toes, he whispered, "Come on, baby. Get hot for me."

Anna's poor, tantalized pussy throbbed as she imagined other scenarios where he might whisper those very words. Risking spontaneous combustion, she wound her arm through his. "You can do it, little oven."

The temperature readout climbed slowly...a hundred degrees, a hundred and fifty, two hundred...

Diego pressed his hand to the oven door, then beamed. "It's working! We did it!" He pressed a kiss to her temple, and her knees went all wobbly.

"Hey, you okay?" His gaze raked her from head to toe. Not that he'd find the cause of her distress unless he undressed her. Which she was not going to ask him to do. At least, not today.

"I'm fine. Just hungry, I guess. All this talk of empanadas —"

"Well then, you're in luck." He slid his arm around her waist and led her outside. "My Abuelita's off to the casino with her church ladies, so we have the kitchen to ourselves. Ready for your first cooking lesson?"

As soon as he opened the back door, the rich scent of meat and spices floated out. Now her stomach was rumbling for real. And what an interesting, colorful kitchen! Sunny yellow tiles covered the counters and backsplash, and angel figurines in every style imaginable clustered on high shelves.

"What a pretty room." She did a slow turn to take in the heavenly host. "Your grandma's quite the collector."

"Oh yeah." He took her coat and hung it from a hook by the back door. "She could tell you the history of each one. This guy's my favorite, though." He pointed to a wooden carving of a monk holding a metal grid. "San Lorenzo. He was grilled to death, so he's the patron saint of cooks."

"Gruesome." The very idea was enough to squash her inappropriate lust.

After they washed their hands, he pulled two baking trays from the fridge. "I prepped these shells this morning. We've got two fillings—ropa vieja on the traditional side, and hoisin chicken with shiitake mushrooms on the fusion side." He lifted the lid from the first of two slow cookers on the counter, and she nearly swooned from the tantalizing scent.

"Flank steak, chiles, herbs, olives, carrots. This one goes in the whole wheat pastry. And this," He lifted the second lid and wafted chicken-scented steam her way, "goes in the scallion pastry."

"You cook like this every weekend?"

"Sunday is family dinner at my parents' place. My little nephew and nieces love my Hot Pockets—that's what they call them." He shrugged sheepishly. "And I am trying to impress you."

"Mission accomplished." She wasn't sure which she craved more, his cooking or his delicious smile.

He chuckled. "Don't be so quick to judge. You haven't tasted these yet."

Working side by side, he showed her how to fill the pastry rounds, seal them with egg wash, and crimp the edges to form perfect half-moons. "More egg wash on top to make them shiny, and into the oven they go." But instead of switching on the kitchen's double oven, he held out her coat.

"Let's go test the Airstream's oven. Two birds with one stone." He waggled his eyebrows. "Three, actually, since I get to spend time with you in close quarters."

She pulled on her coat and followed him outside. It made zero sense that this sweet, hunky guy was fixated on her, and she had no doubt it wouldn't last, but for now, her ego purred like a well-fed kitten.

Back in the Airstream, the heavenly scent of pastry and savory fillings soon filled the air. Diego pulled a stool from beneath the counter and offered Anna a seat. "Mexican soda while we wait? I've got tamarind, fruit punch, and guava."

"Guava, please."

He opened one for himself. "So, does Charlie know you're here?"

"She was still in bed with River when I left. I swear, we need to install soundproofing. Those two kept me up half the night." Of course, their giggles and moans had sent her thoughts spiraling toward Diego.

He clucked his tongue. "Older siblings, right? Full of double standards." The way he rubbed his stubbled jaw made her itch to do the same. "Elena's been giving me the stink eye since she found out I'm spending time with you, but she has a kid too, and I know she's seeing someone. She only gets shifty-eyed when she's trying to keep a secret."

A pang of regret pinched Anna's gut. Back around Thanksgiving, Elena confessed she'd met someone new, but didn't reveal his identity and swore Anna to secrecy. "I want to be sure before my family finds out. They're on my ass to partner up with someone, anyone, and give Oscar a new dad."

Of course, Anna would keep her promise, even though Elena had been avoiding her ever since moving day and always begged off when Anna asked to meet up after work. It hurt. A lot.

She heaved a sigh. "Yeah. Elena's pissed at me too. We used to go to lunch together almost every day, but lately she's always busy."

"Listen." Diego scuffed his boots on the rubber mat. "I have a million questions, and the answers are probably none of my business. So if I cross a boundary, just tell me, okay?"

She searched his gaze and found only kindness and curiosity. Funny how Diego stepped in to fill his sister's shoes in that respect. And right now, she craved a sympathetic friend even more than she craved his delectable body.

"Go ahead. I'll do my best to answer."

"Right." He looked down at his feet, then into her face. After a very distracting lip nibble, he reached for her hand. "Is there any chance you and your ex will get back together?"

Good thing she'd set down her soda, or she'd have sprayed him with sugary fizz.

"No. Absolutely not." She smoothed the sharpness from her tone. "Some women can forgive infidelity, but I never will. And with everything else that happened—well, let's just say I was the world champion red-flag ignorer. I've learned my lesson. I deserve better."

She didn't realize she'd clenched her fist until he gently stroked her white knuckles. "You do. You deserve the best."

"For someone who doesn't really know me, you sound awfully sure about that."

"I'm enjoying getting to know you. It'll take time, and that's okay. We've got plenty of time, right?"

The corners of her mouth twitched upward. "I'm not going anywhere."

"Me neither." With gentle kneading motions and feathery strokes, he loosened not just her fists but her tightly wound nerves.

Leaning on the counter, he gently pulled her closer until his legs bracketed hers while he rubbed circles on the sensitive inside of her wrist. "So, you're getting divorced for sure?"

"One thousand percent sure. It'll take a while, though. Brock's dragging his feet."

"He wants you back?"

Such a weird feeling, unpacking her ugly baggage while Diego's gentle touch soothed the sting. "He says he does, but it's just hurt pride. There's no way I'm bringing up my child in a home where I'm treated like trash. I can't let the baby grow up thinking that kind of relationship is normal."

"The thing is, this guy—what's his name, anyway?"

"My ex? Brock."

His lip curled. "Yupster name. Anyway, he's Olive's dad, and you two will always be connected. I just want you to know up front I respect that, and I won't interfere."

She chewed on his statement for a long moment while the oven ticked and Diego's broad chest rose and fell, rose and fell. Trusting him was sooo tempting, but...

"Diego, you seem pretty darn close to perfect. And you know what they say about things that are too good to be true."

Dropping his gaze to the floor, he huffed a laugh. "I'm miles away from perfect. Just ask Elena. The whole family calls me flakey, and falling for a pregnant woman damn sure won't change their minds." Releasing her, he sighed. "Not so long ago, if I ran up against an obstacle, I'd just give up and try something else. Now, I'm determined to stick it out." He tapped the counter. "Both with this old girl, and with you, if you'll let me. It's worth a try, don't you think?"

Her cheeks heated as she reached for his hand. "Yeah, I do. Think it's worth a try, I mean. And I won't waste our time together carping about my ex."

"Carp away, angel. That's what friends are for. Sometimes, a person's gotta vent, before too much steam builds up and busts the pipes." Chuckling, her rubbed the back of his neck. "Yeah, I'm a poet. Plumbing metaphors slay the ladies, right? Speaking of vent." He flipped a switch on the wall, and a fan set in the ceiling hummed to life. "You can always vent to me, Anna. Call me, text me, cry on my shoulder. I'm at your disposal." He opened his arms and gifted her a smile that promised so many things—understanding, patience, maybe even...No, way too soon to think about that.

No matter how sweet his words, how soft his gaze, she couldn't allow herself to hope for too much. This was just a passing flirtation. A tiny crush. Soon, she'd be big as a house and he'd move on to someone less encumbered, less complicated.

Diego spread his arms wider. "You just gonna leave me hanging?"

Damn it, she could no more resist him than she could defy gravity. She stepped into his embrace, and his arms closed around her, warm and comforting. For a long, sweet moment, they nestled together, quiet and safe.

Maybe all those guardian angels were trying to tell her something.

Rocking her slowly, Diego murmured into her hair, "Anna, I want you. But I realize this is a weird situation, and I'll wait until you feel comfortable trusting me. Or until you tell me to get lost." Pulling back, he cupped her cheek in his broad, warm hand. "I hope it's the first one."

His bottomless dark eyes held her pinned. With exquisite slowness, they came together, lips brushing feather light. And then the sexiest moan in the history of moans rumbled from his chest, as his embrace tightened.

Breathless, she slid her fingers into his soft, thick hair.

He teased her lips with gentle nibbles until she opened to him. His tongue stroked hers in languid slides, unhurried, soft...but her body responded with a rush of heat and a growing pressure between her thighs. She needed more. Now.

Gripping the front of his down jacket, she tugged until the snaps opened with firecracker pops, then yanked her own coat open and pressed her body against his. Another rough moan vibrated through his chest, teasing her nipples to stiff points. The pressure of his erection against her belly unleashed an avalanche of lust that short-circuited her brain and lit up her nerves like the Northern lights.

I should stop. He's kissing away my sanity. But her body demanded just a moment more, and another, and another...

The oven pinged.

Chuckling, Diego released her. "I'm, uh—well, I won't say I'm sorry, because that would be a lie." He scrubbed his hand through his curls, mussing them delectably. "But maybe we should take a breath. After all, there are three people involved in this decision."

"I don't give a damn what Brock thinks."

He laid his palm below her navel. "I was talking about Olive."

Emotions chased each other round and round her fluttery stomach. Did Diego regret kissing her? His dreamy expression suggested otherwise.

She'd never felt a kiss flare this hot and fast—but trusting her body's urges might be stupid right now, especially with her chaotic hormones drowning out the voice of common sense.

Deep breath. "Okay." She snugged her coat tighter. "For the record, my vote is for more kissing, but Olive wants empanadas."

He pulled on oven mitts and removed the trays from the oven. Beautiful, golden, and fragrant, the pastries won the argument.

His head still spinning, Diego locked up the trailer before carrying the tray of steaming empanadas back to the house. That kiss— If the oven timer hadn't dinged, would they have christened his mobile kitchen with a feverish fuck on the counter? He'd never be able to look at that shiny metal surface again without imagining Anna there, her fingers stroking his hair, her breasts crushed to his chest, her pleading whimpers...

Last night, he lay awake for hours pondering how to convey his overwhelming infatuation without scaring her off. When the crucial moment came, he was far too bamboozled by her presence, her openness and trust, and all his rehearsed lines dried up, leaving just the unvarnished truth. Never in his life had honesty paid off this well.

Still, he was playing the long game. Time to take a breath.

Back in Abuelita's kitchen, he pulled out a chair for Anna, then fetched her a glass of sparkling water with a slice of lime.

She beamed as he fussed over her. "I could get used to this."

I hope you do. He slid one of each pastry onto her plate, then pulled a metal bowl from the fridge. "I'll serve something like this with the empanadas." He plated two portions of chopped salad: iceberg and romaine lettuce, diced radishes, red onion, carrots, jicama, and cilantro. "Tell me what you think of the dressing. Too sweet? Too sharp? Too spicy?"

She tasted a forkful. "Amazing. What makes it so creamy?"

"Avocado."

"Mmmm." Anna took another bite. "You could get rich on this alone."

He straddled a chair backward, leaned his folded arms on top, and watched the sexy way she flicked her tongue to capture a smear of dressing from her cheek.

She froze with her fork in the air. "Feeling a little self-conscious here."

"Sorry. Don't mean to be creepy. It's just—you're so sexy when you're enjoying your food."

She tapped her lips with her forefinger. "Note to self—when flirting with a chef, make lots of num-num noises."

"We're suckers for that." A twinge of alarm pinged in his chest. "Hey, you're not flirting with other chefs, are you?"

"Only you, Diego." She nibbled her plush lower lip. God, she was killing him with all these sexy, unconscious gestures. "Which empanada should I try first?"

A familiar bang sounded from the front of the house, catapulting Diego from his seat. Abuelita had a bad habit of slamming the front door open when she was irritated. Amazing how such a tiny old lady could make such a big dent in the drywall.

"'Scuze me." He bolted into the living room to intercept her. She was pissed all right. The sparkly muffler wound up to her nose hid her scowl, but her penciled-on eyebrows were scrunched tight.

Well, shit. So much for flirting over empanadas—not gonna happen with Abuelita looking on.

He helped his grandmother out of her fake fur coat. "I thought you were at the casino today."

"Bus broke down. Maldito company kept us waiting on the side of the highway for two hours. Finally, Father Polanski sent the church vans to bring us home." She threw her hands up, imploring the heavens. "Twenty-nine stranded seniors and no bathroom!" She stomped toward the kitchen. "I need lunch. And a stiff drink."

He sprinted after her. "'Lita, wait."

Too late. She halted in the doorway, fists on her hips. Still at the table, a bug-eyed Anna froze with her fork halfway to her lips.

"Hmph." Abuelita turned to Diego. "Your pregnant girlfriend?"

"She's umm—" What the hell should he call her? "Abuelita, this is Anna Khoury. Anna, this is my grandmother, Maricela Vargas."

Anna stood and wiped her hands on her jeans. Lips pinched together, she crossed the room and extended a trembling hand. "Pleased to see you again, Mrs. Vargas. We met at Elena's baby shower." When Abuelita only stared, Anna added, "You have a lovely kitchen."

"Cut the crap, honey." Tilting her head, Abuelita scrutinized Anna's middle. "You're not showing yet."

Overcome by an urge to defend Anna, Diego blurted, "She's only two months along. The baby's as big as..." Both women swiveled to gawk at him. "An olive."

A flush prickled his skin as he stared down at his shoes.

Finally, his grandmother broke the silence. "Gogo seems very involved in your pregnancy." Crossing her arms, she squinted up at Anna. "Tell me, why are you after my boy?"

Anna's panicked gaze darted from Abuelita's scowling face to his roasting one. "I'm not after anything but his friendship." It was like watching a shopkeeper lower the shutters, the way the light dimmed in her expression, her voice, her posture. "I'm intruding. I should go."

"No," Diego snapped.

"No," Abuelita said at the same moment, softening her tone. "Please stay. And forgive a cranky old woman. I had a crappy morning. No reason to take it out on you." She patted Diego's arm. "Or you, Gogo. Now, what's for lunch? I'm famished." She bustled to the cupboard and, standing on tiptoe, pulled out a plate.

Diego searched Anna's wide-eyed expression. Was she horrified? Would she flee?

Her chest rose and fell, then she gave him a wobbly smile.

He quickly set another place for Abuelita and pulled his chair between the two women. "Okay then. Today we're sampling my first batch of empanadas baked in the Airstream. Anna helped."

"Did she, now?" She stabbed her chicken empanada with her fork. "You like to cook, Anna?"

"Actually, I'm not much of a cook, but I'd like to get better." She squared her shoulders and looked Abuelita right in the eye. "For the baby's sake."

Well then, Anna wasn't afraid to take on his overprotective grandmother. Good. She'd need that strength when she met the rest of his family.

Abuelita brushed crumbs from her chin. "Excellent." Did she mean the pastry, Anna's cooking ambitions, or her spunk? "So, you're Elena's friend?"

He caught the uncertainty in Anna's expression, a quick inhale, a flicker of her eyelids. "We're work friends, yes."

"Then you know she's been through something similar. Though our little Oscar is four now, and she's still not dating." She bit into her first empanada. "About time she got back on the horse, if you ask me."

Diego opened his mouth to protest, but Anna gave her head a sharp shake.

Abuelita appeared to be focused on her plate, but her lips quirked up. Clever old bird, this was a test. Her smile widened. "Having your first child is a life-changing experience, no matter the circumstances. I'm glad you have a friend like Diego to help you."

Baffled by his grandmother's change of heart, he decided to roll with it. "Friends can be like family too, you know. If I ever needed help, my friends from Bangers would come running, no questions asked."

Abuelita gave a little snort. "Even after you quit?"

"Absolutely." I hope so. Time will tell.

Anna nudged him under the table with her foot. "I'm sure they would. After all, they came to help me move just because I'm Charlie's sister."

"She's one of our servers," Diego prompted.

"I know." Abuelita poked his arm with her fork. "I may be old, but I'm still sharp." She turned to Anna. "Diego talks about his work friends all the time."

He nodded. "They won't dump me when I leave. I have faith in them."

Anna placed her hand atop his. "You've gotta have faith in people."

Their gazes met and held. The ticking of Abuelita's angel wall clock slowed down. The air grew heavy, still, golden.

Breaking the spell, Abuelita leaned onto the table and fixed Anna with a gentle look. "Don't you worry, honey.

Elena will come around. She's just protective of her baby brother."

Diego cleared the table while Abuelita asked Anna about her family. To his delight, they were soon laughing over easy banter. He hadn't prepared a dessert, but Abuelita insisted Anna try her leftover tres leches cake, then thoughtfully adjourned to her room for a nap, but not without a parting comment.

"Diego, you invite this young lady to Sunday dinner."

Anna's eyes widened. "Actually, I have a family thing tomorrow."

Abuelita patted her hand. "I don't blame you, honey. A Vargas family dinner is like a three-ring circus. But I hope you'll join us soon. It was a pleasure to meet you." She shuffled off to her room.

Diego chuckled as he carried dishes to the sink. "You were lying, weren't you? She always knows. It's her grandma superpower."

"Thanks for the warning. Actually, my family thing is filling out forms for my lawyer. I'm officially filing for divorce on Monday. I thought it would be easier. And faster."

"The wheels of justice turn slowly, eh?" He walked her to the door, helped her into her coat, then leaned against the frame when she stepped onto the porch. "Hey, I hope I didn't come on too strong. You know, back there in the Airstream."

She tucked her chin, an endearing gesture that made him want to lift it and kiss her silly. "What happened back there was totally mutual. I'm a little embarrassed, but I'm not sorry." She raised her soft, dark gaze to his and gifted him a crooked smile. It took every atom of willpower he had not to pull her back inside.

"However—"

He braced himself.

"I think I'd better get through this next bit before we spend any more time groping in your kitchen. Can I call you in a few weeks?"

"Sure." Disappointment weighted his chest as he backed away. Still, if patience is what it took to win her, he'd be as patient as a mountain. "I'll look forward to it. And if you need anything before then, think of me, okay?"

Her gaze raked him from head to toe. "Oh, I'll be thinking of you, Diego." With a final, flirty glance over her shoulder, she walked back to her car.

He'd always heard falling in love gives you butterflies in your stomach. For Diego, it was more like fireflies, buzzing and blinking as they danced along his nerves. He closed the door, leaned his forehead on the cool glass pane, and whispered, "I'll be thinking of you too."

Chapter Eleven: Serving Brock

♥

The courthouse clerk tapped Anna's paperwork into a neat pile. "That'll do it. Just pay the filing fee, hon, and you're all set to serve your divorce papers on your husband."

Anna's hand shook as she paid her ticket to freedom. Well, her bridge toll on the way to freedom, anyway. Marching into the courthouse this morning felt like a daring victory, a raised middle finger to Brock and his shrewish mother and everyone else who thought Anna's happiness didn't matter.

She snatched the documents. "It's gonna feel so good so shove these in Brock's face."

"Oh no, doll." The clerk raised a warning finger. "You can't serve him. It's gotta be someone who's not a party to the suit."

Crap on a cracker. She must've missed that part. To be fair, her divorce lawyer talked lightning-fast, and Anna found it hard to concentrate while daydreaming about Brock's reaction. She'd really wanted to see the look on his face when she served him his righteous comeuppance. So much for her plan.

"Who can serve him, then?"

"You can hire a professional process server, but most people have a friend or family member do it."

"What if he won't take the papers?"

"Just keep trying." The clerk leaned onto her elbow. "I could tell you some hilarious stories—sending someone in disguise to deliver the papers, ambushing the person in church, hiding divorce papers in a box of chocolates. Sometimes you gotta get creative."

Anna scrunched her lips to one side. Brock might be an ass, but he was no dummy. Six weeks after their split, he was still fighting the divorce. She'd blocked his number, so no more pleading texts, but the delivery of tacky gifts to her work and Dad's house continued. His last peace offering, a giant teddy bear, she'd donated to the Tacoma Rescue Mission after removing the "I'm sorry" balloon tied to its pudgy arm. Since then, a few maudlin greeting cards, a half-dead peace lily, and several pounds of drugstore chocolates. Yuck. At least he hadn't showed up to pester her in person.

"How long do I have to serve the papers?"

"Sixty days, hon'. After that, you'll have to come back and get a new divorce petition." The clerk patted Anna's hand. "But you seem like a smart cookie. You'll figure it out."

Who could she rope into serving him? She'd need someone with a sharp eye who could relate every delicious detail.

Elena was the first person who came to mind. Normally, her friend would jump at the chance. But nowadays, all she got from Elena was avoidance and excuses. It would have to be Charlie. The sooner she served these divorce papers, the sooner she could rebuild her life.

Later that evening, Anna and Charlie huddled in the Furniture World parking lot while Anna tried to calm her frantic breathing. This runaway panic was ridiculous—all she had to do was sit behind the wheel and wait.

"You ready?"

Charlie interlaced her fingers and cracked her knuckles. "Let's do this."

They only had a short window between the end of Anna's shift and the beginning of Charlie's to catch Brock at work.

Before their breakup, Brock's schedule ran like clockwork—leave work at six, hit the gym, then trail home at—well, the closer to the day he got caught, the longer his "workouts" ran, even though his pasty body never got any bulkier. Seems the only muscle doing any heavy lifting was the one he kept in his undies.

Charlie glanced at the dashboard clock. "Five-thirty. Think he'll still be on the showroom floor?"

"Unless he's in back smooching with Kristi." Anna handed her the divorce petition, folded into an oversize greeting card. "Now remember, just hand him the papers and say, 'Anna asked me to give you this.' After he takes them, tell him it's court papers for the divorce."

"Very sneaky and underhanded. I approve." Charlie tucked the card inside her bomber jacket and strode toward the store.

While she waited, Anna fidgeted with her keys and watched tiny blobs of sleet patter on the windshield. Just a few minutes more, and this first step toward freedom would be behind her. Thank heavens she had such an understanding sister. Despite their childhood squabbles, grown-up Charlie had Anna's back when it really counted.

Fifteen minutes later, still no Charlie. Anna wiggled in her seat, sure if she had to wait one minute more, she'd burst right out of her skin.

Twenty minutes later, Charlie trudged across the parking lot, opened the passenger door, and plopped into her seat.

"All done?"

With a sigh, Charlie set the envelope on the center console. "Sorry, sis. No go."

"What do you mean? Wasn't he there?"

"I'm sure I spotted him over by the dining sets. I looked away for just a second to pull out the envelope, and when I looked up, he was gone."

"Did you ask for him?"

"Yeah, at the rear counter, just like you said. The girl at the register called for him on the intercom, then this blonde chick flew out from the office. Said Brock had left for the day."

"Big boobs, lash extensions?"

Charlie nodded. "Lousy liar, too. Her big ol' bug eyes kept sliding to where she just came from."

"Damn, damn, damn." Anna pounded the dash. "Kristi's covering for him."

"Easy now." Charlie patted Anna's knee. "No need to break out the bad words. We'll catch him yet."

A nauseating headache bloomed behind Anna's forehead. "Brock must've recognized you."

"Hmph." Charlie tapped her pursed lips. "Bet his lawyer warned him to avoid any friends of yours carrying papers."

Anna's sigh emptied her lungs. "Thanks for trying. I'll just hire a process server." Not that she could afford the extra expense, what with all the baby gear she had to buy.

Charlie twisted to face her. "C'mon, now. Where's the fun in that? I'll wear a disguise next time."

The sound of screeching tires drew Anna's focus. A blood-red Camaro peeled out of the lot and disappeared into the rush-hour traffic. "That's him."

"Let's go."

Anna cranked her little Ford to life and zipped after him, but by the time she found a gap in traffic, he was already two lights ahead of them. Soon, he veered right and out of sight.

"He's heading home."

"We'll catch him there." Charlie smirked. "Make a big ol' stink with tons of witnesses."

Anna giggled at the thought of her nosy former neighbors poking their heads out to witness the drama on the second floor. This time, she didn't mind giving them something to talk about.

Twenty minutes later, they pulled into a spot hidden by the dumpsters behind Brock's building. Charlie hopped out. "C'mon. You can hide behind a potted plant. Might as well enjoy the show."

Charlie pulled her hood over her face and wove between the cars, crouching low. Anna followed, feeling like an extra in a TV cop drama. They tiptoed up the stairs but found Brock's windows dark. Anna crouched behind the neighbor's potted juniper and watched as Charlie rang the bell, careful to keep her face averted. No answer. She banged on the door and called in a gruff voice, "Mr.

Spenser, it's Carla from the office. We got a report of a gas leak."

Nothing.

Charlie whispered, "You sure he's here?"

Anna crept to the railing, then smacked her forehead. Brock's parking space was empty. Where the fudge could he be hiding? At the gym? She drummed her fingers on the railing. Of course. Where else could he be?

Beckoning to Charlie, she trotted down the stairs.

"I've gotta be at Bangers soon. Where are we going?"

"Mama's house."

A pair of colorful flags embroidered with tulips fluttered from Deborah Spencer's porch—not that any blooms had poked their heads through the winter mud yet. No sign of Brock's Camaro, but it could be in the garage. In fact, Deborah's Lexus sat in the driveway, because of course she'd give her parking spot to her precious baby boy.

"God, I do not like that woman," Charlie grumbled as she unbuckled her seatbelt. "Just being on her property gives me the creeps."

Anna rolled up the legal papers like a baton and passed them to her sister. "Think how much fun it'll be to see her face when you slap these into Brock's hand."

"He's onto us by now. I'll bet he's hiding in his car."

"Just one more try, okay?" When Charlie gave her a skeptical glance, Anna added, "Pleeease?"

"All right, all right." Charlie slammed her car door and strode up the walkway, clutching the papers. She knocked on the door. No answer, but the curtains twitched. Anna lowered her window and watched Charlie press the doorbell again, then tap her foot as she waited a minute, two minutes, three... No response except barking from Deborah's little schnauzer.

I smell a weasel.

Charlie rang again, leaning on the bell good and hard. "I know you're in there, Brock. Open up."

Nothing but frantic yapping.

The neighbor opened her door and leaned out. "Nobody's home." With her smug smirk and crossed arms, she reminded Anna of a fairytale troll guarding a bridge.

"Then why's Deborah's car here?" Anna hollered.

Hostile Neighbor Lady shrugged. "Took an Uber, I guess."

"Right." She didn't bother wiping up the sarcasm from her tone. Clearly, she wasn't going to accomplish the mission today, not with Brock's army of female excuse makers protecting him.

Brock was crouching behind his mommy's curtains—Anna just knew it. As she cranked the steering wheel in a U-turn, she grumbled, "Shit on a flaming stick."

Charlie chuckled. "Wow. That's very un-Anna of you."

"Now he'll be on the lookout for both of us. I'll have to get someone else to serve him."

"Probably for the best. Hire a pro."

"Yeah, I'll call someone tomorrow."

Charlie pulled into their driveway. "Well, I gotta get to work." She brightened. "Hey, why not ask Diego to do it?"

Anna gaped. "Weren't you the one who told me not to drag him into my divorce drama?"

"Seems a bit late for that now."

Anna watched Charlie's car zoom away before fishing her phone out of her bag. She got as far as pulling up Diego's number. He'd do it—she was certain. But the mature thing to do was leave this task to a professional process server. She'd have to be content with imagining Brock's face when he realized he'd been caught.

She'd seen that look before. It wasn't pretty. Let it go.

She stuffed the phone back into her bag and went inside for a night of well-earned relaxation—a bubble bath, a pizza, and brainless TV.

She was emerging from the tub when her phone screen lit up with a new message. Another sweet, flirty text from Diego would go a long way toward soothing the day's disappointment. She toweled off and poked the screen to life.

A text from an unfamiliar number.

Quit bugging my mom. No divorce. We're a family now. You have to forgive me for our baby's sake.

Anna's hands shook as she blocked the number. She smacked the phone down on the counter, tilted her dripping head to the ceiling, and roared.

Then she called Diego.

Diego pulled into Anna's driveway a little before ten, having bribed Shelby to close for him. No big deal on a Monday night—food orders had slowed to a trickle an hour ago. Eager to fix whatever made Anna's voice so wobbly, he'd packed up a half-dozen of this week's empanadas, filled with fire-roasted poblanos, cheese, and caramelized onions with chipotle yogurt dipping sauce, along with an order of loaded tots, in case the empanadas proved too spicy. The books he hid under his bed said most pregnant women couldn't tolerate spicy food, but Anna seemed to crave it.

She answered his knock dressed in faded yoga pants and a fuzzy sweater that hugged her curves—and just the tiniest hint of a baby bump? Hard to be sure. Her hair hung loose and messy around her shoulders as if she'd just awakened from a nap. Refreshingly real, freakin' adorable, and painfully sexy. Count on Anna to hit all the bases.

"Evening." He lifted the paper bag. "I brought a snack for you and Olive."

"Kumquat." She raised those huge mahogany eyes, heaved a sigh, and spread her arms wide.

Yesss. He stepped into her embrace. The top of her head nestled against his cheek, and her lush softness pressed to him from chest to—well, to parts he'd better not focus on right now. She'd asked for time to—how had she put it? —sort out her mess, or something like that. So he just cuddled her close and waited.

Finally, she released him and gave him a weary smile. "Thanks for coming."

"Hey, I told you—anytime you need me, all you have to do is ask." He lifted his offering. "Hungry?"

"Always." She beckoned him to the kitchen where she fetched plates and silverware while he set out their feast. She dug in, punctuating healthy bites with sexy moans that made his hands itch to stray to her knee, her thigh... He clenched his napkin and fork tight.

"You gonna tell me what's got you so upset?"

Her gaze slid down to her lap.

"I'm glad you called. But on the phone, you sounded kinda—"

"Emotional. I know." Raking her fingers into her hair, she arched back in her seat, causing her sweater to hug her full breasts. Face, man. Look at her face.

"I shouldn't have called you. Lately my emotions are so —volatile, I guess. It's a pregnancy thing."

"So I've read." At her wide-eyed glance he corrected himself. "I mean, my sister was like that when she was pregnant and—"

A wide smile bloomed across her crumb-dusted face. "You've been reading up on pregnancy?"

His cheeks heated. "Well, yeah."

She reached across the table and took his hand. "That's so sweet. But this time, it wasn't just pregnancy hormones setting me off. Got a text from my ex."

"Want me to off him?" He was only half kidding.

"Don't give me ideas. Anyway, I shouldn't have called you. In fact, you're the last person I should get involved in this mess."

"Anna." He squeezed her hand and leaned closer. "If I can help, I absolutely want to. I'm your friend, remember? I'd like to be more than that, but I'm trying to respect your boundaries." He scrubbed his free hand down his face. "Listen to me sounding like Dr. Phil."

"You watch Dr. Phil?"

"My Abuelita does." And admitting he sometimes joined her was not the way to impress Anna. "The point is, I want to help. What can I do?"

"Just let me vent, I guess." Still clutching his hand, she raised it to her lip and kissed his palm. A thrill zapped down his spine, right to his cock. "You're a good man, Diego. If I weren't pregnant..."

"Pregnant looks good on you." He chuckled. "I hope that doesn't make me sound like a perv. Now please, tell me what's troubling you."

Her huge sigh lifted her chest. "Okay, so today I filed for divorce."

He bit back a grin. Now was not the time for a victory dance.

"And I tried to serve the divorce papers on Brock. I mean, Charlie tried. He must've recognized her because he evaded us twice, and then he sent me this." She tapped her phone's screen and slid it across the table.

As he read, heat rose from his chest to the roots of his hair. How dare this bastard talk to Anna that way—as if she had no choice in her own future? He set the phone down carefully and reined in his impulse to smash something—preferably that loser's face.

"Let me do it."

Her jaw worked. Her nose scrunched. Her eyes narrowed. Then she snatched the phone back. "No, I can't ask you to do that. I'll hire a process server."

"You're not asking me, angel. I'm asking you. Whether we end up together or not, it would give me so much satisfaction to remove this obstacle from your path."

But her face remained screwed up tight, so he added, "This Burk guy doesn't know what I look like, so I can sneak up on him."

That did the trick. She dropped the scowl and even giggled a tiny bit. "It's Brock."

"Just tell me where to find him. I'll take care of it tomorrow."

"He's the floor manager at Furniture World, over on Union."

"I know the place. Dad bought a recliner there. What's he look like?"

"Ugh." She scraped back her chair and trudged to the hallway. Drawers banged. A moment later she returned holding a wedding photo. "I was waiting for the next full moon to burn these."

Diego took the photo and held it tenderly. "You were a beautiful bride." Of course, you say that to every bride, but she really was—in a figure-skimming lace gown, her chestnut curls swept up and held with some kind of pearl crown thingy, her dark eyes sparkling as she gazed up at a guy who looked like the photo included in a picture frame. Blond. Pointy. Smug smile. He knew damn well he'd won the grand prize—and he had no intention of treating her right. Asshole.

"Right. Give me the papers. I'll handle it."

He couldn't quite explain the urgency crackling along his nerves. Of course, he wanted Anna for himself. But damn it, she had the right to live her life on her terms, no matter which guy she chose or didn't choose. And being shackled to a douchebag like Brock sure as hell wasn't good for baby Kumquat.

Anna nibbled a cuticle. "If Elena finds out, she'll never speak to me again."

"She won't find out. I promise."

How he was going to keep that promise, he had no idea.

The next morning, dressed in his dad's baggy electrician coveralls, a ballcap pulled low over his eyes, and carrying a clipboard, Diego strode into Furniture World.

A cute young woman clicked toward him on high heels. "Can I help you, sir?"

Was this the one Brock cheated on Anna with? He forced his lips into an easy smile. "Got a work order for the floor manager."

"He's right over there." She pointed toward the sofas and recliners, where a dude with shiny blond hair and tight slacks flashed a cheesy smile at a busty blonde woman.

Adopting his dad's bowlegged gait, Diego ambled over. "'Scuze me, chief. Lookin' for the boss. Mr. Spenser, I think his name is."

The douche waffle puffed out his chest. Tall, good-looking in a bland way, like a model in a catalog for cheap clothing. "Yeah, that's me. What can I do you for?"

Ugh. Hard to imagine Anna married to this smarmy loser.

"Got a work order." He held out a manila envelope.

Brock eyed the Vargas Electric logo on Diego's chest. "Maintenance is Frank's domain."

Diego shrugged. "Boss said give this to you." He shoved the papers at Brock's shiny tie.

"All right, all right. No need to get pushy." Brock snatched them with a huff.

Diego couldn't contain his victorious grin any longer. "Much obliged, chief. By the way, those are your divorce papers. You've been served." He tipped the brim of his cap.

Brock's face flushed a deep pink. "You fuckin' lied to me."

The woman he'd been talking to slapped her hand to her mouth and backed away, stumbling into an ugly recliner couch.

Brock threw the envelope to the floor and advanced, fists and jaw clenched. "I told Anna, there's no way I'm divorcing her. We're having a baby, for fuck's sake."

The blonde gasped, her bug-eyed stare darting from Brock to Diego. She spun on her heel and fled, dodging overstuffed couches and recliners.

"Kristi, wait. I—" Brock raked his fingers into his hair and snarled at the ceiling. "Now look what you did, motherfucker." He drew his fist back, telegraphing his intentions from a mile away, then threw a clumsy punch that Diego easily dodged. Brock lost his balance and smacked a blocky entertainment center. Cradling his bruised hand, he hopped and howled, drawing the attention of everyone in the place, including an older dude in a suit heading their way.

Please let that be his boss.

Diego snapped a salute and, despite his better angel's protests, fired off a parting shot. "You screwed up, dude. Take your medicine like a man and let her go."

He turned his back and strolled toward the entrance, ignoring Brock's shouted curses.

"Hey, Vargas. How's it going man?" The cheerful greeting snapped Diego's head up. A vaguely familiar guy around his age strode toward him, his hand outstretched. "You working for your old man now?"

"Sorry, I—what?"

The guy pointed to his Furniture World nametag. "It's me, Carlo DiPaolo, from Saint Anthony's. We went to youth camp together, remember? You had the hots for my cousin Rita."

"Oh, yeah." Diego remembered Rita well enough. She'd given him his first blow job on the last night of camp. "I, uh, gotta jet. Got another appointment. Good to see you, man."

He threw a nervous glance over his shoulder and spotted Brock barreling toward them, bellowing, "I will end you, motherfucker."

The suited man clamped Brock's shoulder and spun him around, giving Diego a chance to escape.

Outside, he collapsed against the store's brick façade and gulped lungfuls of frigid air.

Stupid, stupid, stupid. Now it was only a matter of minutes until Brock found out who he was. One way or another, that cheating bastard would seek his revenge. Could he shield Anna from the blowback?

Chapter Twelve: Valentine's Showdown

♥

"Order up!" Diego tapped Lana's button on his screen, then zipped back to the grill. Dawn's Anti-Valentine's Day bash was a raving success, and the two specials he'd dreamed up flew out of the kitchen as fast as he and Shelby could cook them.

Shelby waved her kitchen towel in front of her flushed, round face. "Never thought I'd get sick of bacon smell, but this is ridiculous." She plunged another basket of Love Bites—bacon-wrapped jalapeño poppers— into the fryer.

Diego removed another tray of bacon hearts from the oven. Carefully shaped the night before, then came out thin and crispy, the perfect garnish for tonight's Heartbreaker Tots with cheesy artichoke dip. Leftover dip got slathered on burgers studded with more bacon. Not a great night for vegan guests, though he whipped up a batch of spicy cashew "queso" dip just in case.

"Dawn says bacon cures a broken heart." He dumped tots into a basket and nestled in a bubbling ramekin of dip.

"Damn right it does." Shelby plated an order of tots. "So, did your girlfriend like your Valentine's gift, or should I fry up more bacon?"

"I haven't heard yet."

In the two weeks since he handed Brock the divorce papers, he and Anna had traded dozens of texts, but no in-person visits, though not for lack of trying. Anna invited him to her favorite Thai place for an early Saturday dinner, but she caught a nasty stomach bug going around her clinic. On their second try, little Oscar fell off his scooter and ripped a toenail loose, so Diego had to cancel and ferry his nephew to the Emergency Room while Elena held the screaming tot in the back seat. Honestly, it felt like someone up there was conspiring against them.

Still, Anna kept in touch. Each time her number flashed on his phone screen, he lit up like a pinball machine. Her messages were sweet but far too brief. Knowing everything she was facing, he hesitated to push too hard. But how could he ignore Valentine's Day, especially since every contact deepened his certainty that Anna was The One? He scoured every shop on Sixth Avenue searching for the perfect token of his affection—not too corny, not too sexy, not too pushy. Finally, he settled for a beautiful flowering plant for her new house, a miniature orange tree with fragrant white blossoms that would later yield tiny edible fruit—the perfect metaphor for what he was cultivating with Anna. Or hoped to, anyway.

And the card—funny or mushy? Silly or serious? He finally chose a watercolor image of a couple walking hand in hand into a beachy sunset. A little on the nose, but the colors reminded him of Anna, bright and soothing at the same time. He filled three pages in his notebook with rough drafts before settling on the inscription:

Finding you was a gift from the angels.

Take a chance on us?

Heart thundering, he'd sealed the envelope and tucked it among the blossoms. The florist would have delivered it by now. All Diego could do was wait.

The kitchen doors swung open, and Charlie trotted in, her long ponytail bouncing. "It's a mob out there. Kiara sent me for more lemons." She grabbed a net of fruit from the cooler, then swung by the fry station and gave Shelby a side hug. "Lay some tots on me, doll? I'm famished."

Shelby scooped tots into two paper trays. "One for you, one for the bartenders. How they holdin' up without River?"

"Like champs. He'll be back from his fishing trip in a few days." She popped a tot into her mouth, then made hoot-owl noises around the steaming morsel. Sliding to the grill, she snatched a strip of bacon. "Hey, Diego, you coming on Saturday? We could use the extra hands to paint the baby's room."

"Wouldn't miss it." He passed her a cup of spicy artichoke dip. "Try this with your tots."

Charlie took a bite and moaned, though the sound didn't echo in his body like Anna's groans of pleasure. She pecked his cheek on her way out.

"Woah, hold up." Shelby gawked across the kitchen island. "Charlie's pregnant?"

"No. Her sister." He slapped another burger onto the grill.

Not one to give up so easily, Shelby scrunched her pierced eyebrows. "Isn't that the girl you like?"

"Yeah." Might as well admit it. His nosy assistant would figure it out soon enough.

Shelby's face lit up in slow motion. "Hoooooly shit, Diego, you're gonna be a daddy!" She squeezed him in a too-tight hug.

"Let. Go." He peeled her off his middle. "It's not my kid."

Her spiky hair bristling, Shelby gaped like an outraged baby bird. "She cheated on you?"

"No!" He flipped the burger and leaned hard with the spatula, forcing a loud sizzle. "Look, she was pregnant when we met, okay?" He plated the burger, set it under the warming lamp, tapped Lana's button again, then pulled his phone from his pocket. Three messages from Anna had arrived in quick succession. He must not have heard the ping over the roar of the ventilator fan.

The plant is so beautiful! Thanks. Xoxo
And the card! You made me cry. In a good way.
Coming to Bangers. See you after your shift?

His thumbs flew over the screen.

Yes please!!!

He nearly levitated when she sent a kissy-lips emoji.

Leaning on his shoulder, Shelby peered at his phone. "Man, you're a goner."

"Mind your business, Miss Nosy." He nudged her away.

The rest of the evening flew by in a hurricane of tots, bacon grease, and giddy anticipation. At quarter to ten, Dawn rang the ship's bell behind the bar and announced last call for food, triggering an avalanche of orders. A little past ten, Diego paused production long enough to text Anna about the delay.

No prob. Fun party out here.

Good sport, funny, patient, gorgeous... mentally ticking off Anna's many fine qualities, Diego attacked the remaining orders.

Fizzy with anticipation, Anna greeted Jojo at the door of Bangers Tavern, then stepped into the pink and red maelstrom. What a mess! Most of the paper hearts Charlie strung up before the party had been yanked down, and not a few had been made into paper airplanes. Charlie, Rosie, and Lana zipped through the crowd, their trays held high. Kiara and Eddie hustled behind the bar. Even grumpy old Gus, usually glued to a barstool, manned the beer taps.

After four years with Brock, going out on her own felt weird, like testing a new skill. Might as well enjoy it before the baby arrived. Still, joining the party felt a bit naughty, like she was getting away with something she shouldn't.

She scanned the crowd and spotted a free seat at the bar. Weaving and dodging, she made it across the room with minimal damage—just a minor beer spill on her coat and a few tater tots stuck to the soles of her boots.

"Hey there, cutie," Kiara greeted her. "You waiting on Charlie?"

"No, um—" Unsure which of the Bangers crew knew about her connection to Diego, she kept it vague. "Just, you know, ready to hate on Valentine's Day. And eat some tots."

"Gotcha. Want the special?"

"Yes, please. Got a mocktail tonight?"

"One broken heart slushy, coming up."

While Kiara loaded the blender with berries and crushed ice, Anna shed her coat and swiveled to watch the action. Up on stage, a customer was telling a story about a first date marred by a surprise allergic reaction to his date's lipstick. Years from now, would she and Diego reminisce about their first coffee date? Or did her packing-out party count as their first date? They'd already kissed twice. Time to arrange a real date, one that didn't involve cardboard boxes and packing tape. Somewhere private, where they could talk and—

"For fuck's sake," a familiar voice huffed. The woman to her left pulled back her hood and glared. "You're here to see my brother, aren't you?"

"Elena." Anna's mouth went dry. "Uh, hi. Good to see you."

Elena's tight expression made it clear she did not share Anna's opinion.

Kiara set down a frosty reddish-purple drink, her wary gaze darting from Anna to her former best friend. "Everything okay here?"

"Just fine," Anna said much too brightly. "Elena's my friend from work."

"Hmmph." Elena hunched over her drink.

"Okaaay." Pursing her lips, Kiara moved up the bar to help the next customer.

Anna reached out a tentative hand, then pulled it back. This shouldn't be so awkward. Not long ago, she and Elena shared everything—Elena's bad dates and single-parent woes, her own fights with Brock, funny stories from the clinic. And now, here they sat, Elena sullen and closed off, Anna unsure how to begin.

"Listen, Elena, I wish you'd talk to me."

She slowly turned her head and fixed Anna with a dead-eyed stare. "Why?"

"Because we're friends! Because we've shared so much, and now—" Her voice wobbled. "Now that I really need my best friend, you've shut me out."

"You want to be friends again? Promise you'll leave my brother alone."

"Why?" She knew the answers Elena would spit back in her face, but maybe she could shoot them down one by one.

Elena choked on her drink, spraying her pink cocktail onto the bar. "Are you seriously asking me why?"

Anna stiffened her spine. "Diego and I like each other. We have fun together. He sent me the coolest housewarming gift, a little orange tree, and—"

Elena rolled her eyes heavenward. "Great, now he's sending her flowers. What's next, baby clothes?"

"It's a plant, Elena, not a freakin' ring. He's a sweet guy, and—"

"Too sweet for his own good. And too naive to understand what he's getting into." Elena turned to face Anna, her stare flinty-hard. "Don't you get it? Your life has changed forever. Until they go to school, kids are total bloodsuckers. You won't have a moment to yourself."

Anna knew for a fact Elena and Diego's parents often babysat Oscar when he wasn't in their church's daycare, but now was not the time to contradict her.

"You're rushing my brother into a mess he's not prepared for. I know him, Anna. When it comes to relationships, he's as naïve as a baby, and I can't stand to see him get used. Not even by you."

"Used?" Chills and heat chased over her skin. "I'm not using him, I'm just—"

"Using him for your personal Mr. Fix-it. He moved you out. He moved you in. He's buying paint rollers to paint your kid's room." Her nostrils flared. "He should be spending his time on his food truck, on his future. If you cared about him, you'd let him go."

"You're wrong." Anna jutted her chin. If she couldn't save their friendship, at least she could set the record straight. "Diego and I aren't rushing into anything, but it looks like we're heading toward a relationship. I don't know what that'll look like when the baby comes, but I'm not turning down the chance at love just because the timing is bad." Now that she'd said it aloud, she felt the truth of it all the way to her bones.

"Love?" Elena snorted. "You hardly know him."

Anna raised her hands, palms out. "True. But we're getting to know each other, and so far, he seems pretty freakin' perfect. I don't get why he wants me when I come with so much baggage, but we're good together." She blinked back tears. "You've been my rock, Elena, and I've been yours. How can you just trash our friendship? You, of all people, should understand what I'm going through. I know you've been seeing someone."

Elena's head jerked back as if Anna had slapped her. "We're talking about my baby brother, not some guy I met on Tinder."

Anna fought to control the tremor in her voice. "Diego's not a baby anymore. You're the eldest, so you don't get how it hurts when family dismisses your dreams and desires because they think they know what's best for you."

Elena's eyebrows shot up. "Dreams and desires?" She stabbed a finger into Anna's chest. "That's a luxury you don't get anymore. Here's a preview of your future, cupcake—Work. Family. Rinse. Repeat. Over and over and fuckin' over. Diego deserves better. Get your head out of your ass and focus on your child."

Onlookers gawked as Anna backed away on wobbly legs. Elena turned and hunched over her drink—done with their argument, done with Anna. Her bitterness hung in the air like an acrid stink, leaving Anna shaken to her core.

"Anna?" Charlie's voice rang out from across the room.

Tears blurred her vision as Anna stumbled through the crowd, knocking into people in her haste to escape. She had to get out before she screamed or puked or dissolved into a helpless puddle of tears.

Her friendship with Elena was over.

Chapter Thirteen: Et Tu, Hermana?

♥

It was well past ten-thirty when Diego finally left the kitchen. Up on stage, the Worst Bad Date competition was underway. Hoots of laughter rang out as a customer finished her tale about sushi-induced food poisoning. The bar's decorations had been decimated—paper hearts with snarky sayings like You Wish and Not 4 U littered the floor, and customers bopped heart-shaped balloons from table to table like volleyballs.

He launched into the rowdy crowd in search of Anna, elbowing his way first to the bar, then up the low stairs to the pool and darts area, and finally to the front door. "Hey, Jojo, you seen Anna?"

"She shot outta here a few minutes ago. Looked upset. All red in the face."

What the...? "Did she say anything?"

Jojo rubbed his shiny shaved head. "Nope. I woulda gone after her, but a bunch of underage college kids were trying to sneak in."

"Shit." What could have upset Anna so much she'd leave without waiting for him? He checked his phone for a text. Nada.

Where'd you go? You okay? he typed.

Out of the corner of his eye he spotted Charlie sliding through the crowd, her drink-laden tray held high.

"Charlie. Wait up."

She wheeled on him, her expression sharp as a boning knife. "A little late, aren't you?"

"What the hell happened?"

She tilted her chin in the direction of the bar. "Ask your sister."

Sure enough, Elena perched on a barstool, her head in her hands. He barreled through the crowd.

"Hey." He poked her shoulder hard. "What did you do?"

She glanced up, her face red and blotchy, then pressed the heels of her hands against her tear-rimmed eyes. "I'm sorry, Gogo. I just—" She thumped a fist on the bar. "She told me about your Valentine's gift, and I lost my shit."

"What the hell does that mean?"

"I said some ugly things."

"Elena, why?"

Her only reply was a thin-lipped stare.

Pressure built inside his skull, hard and hot enough to crack bone. "It's just a plant. What the fuck is your problem?"

Kiara reached across the bar and gripped his wrist. "Diego. Lower your voice."

The room had gone quiet, and hundreds of eyeballs swiveled in their direction. His heart thudded to a standstill.

"Wanna see, Eddie?" Rosie's voice rang out through the mic.

Thank God. The crowd was gawking at the barback, not him.

Moving like a sleepwalker, Eddie stepped around the bar and stumbled toward the stage where Rosie stood, her skirt hitched up to reveal a new tattoo still covered in cling film. Eddie flung his arms around her middle and lifted her down. They kissed. The crowd cheered.

Maybe if I get a tattoo with Anna's name? He shook off that stupid thought and fixed his interfering sister with a death-ray glare. "Explain."

Closing her eyes, she drew a deep breath. "You've been avoiding me, so I came to talk to you. Anna showed up, all giddy like a high schooler with a crush." She strangled her cocktail napkin. "She's got no business dating in her condition. She needs to put her child first."

I need a drink, or I'm gonna say something that'll leave a scar. Kiara was busy shaking cocktails, and Eddie was still in a lip lock with Rosie, so he marched around the bar, filled a shot glass with rye, and scrawled an IOU on a napkin. He downed the shot, then grabbed Elena's jacket and yanked until their foreheads thunked together.

"Listen, Lena. I am a grown-ass man. I do not need you policing my love life. Neither does Anna. I thought you were her friend."

"I was," she whimpered.

"Wasn't she on your side when you went through your divorce?"

Elena nodded, her chin wobbling.

"And I know damn well you're seeing some guy. That makes you a Class A hypocrite."

"I'm not." Elena's words came out in a ragged whisper.

"We're family. Don't you dare lie to me."

"I need one of those." She pointed to his empty glass.

With a silent prayer for the strength not to throttle her, he poured another shot.

She gulped it down, closed her eyes, and shuddered. When she opened her eyes, they glittered with tears. "I thought we had a good thing, me and Justin. Last weekend, when Oscar was with his dad, we had our first overnight. I finally told him about Oscar." She hunched as if anticipating a blow. "He dumped me."

His angry stiffness melted as he clasped her hand in both of his. "Oh, Lena, I'm sorry."

She shook her head. "It's better this way. Oscar should be my focus now. He's too young for me to bring some guy around. He'd get attached, then we'd break up. I can't do that to him." She raised her trembling chin. "And that's what I told Anna. It's too hard to balance a man and a kid. Better if you don't even go there."

A red curtain dropped over Diego's vision. His sister was hurting, and he'd do almost anything to comfort her—anything except go along with this toxic bullshit.

He ground out his words through clenched jaws. "I'm sorry your boyfriend was an asshole, but I am not him. I would never abandon Anna when things get hard. And honestly, it hurts that you don't know me better."

He had to get to Anna, had to purge her doubts before they took root. He trotted back to the kitchen to make sure everything was safely shut down and put away, then grabbed his coat and sprinted for the exit.

Anna sat in her driveway, the only sound the tick, tick, tick of her car's cooling engine and the ragged rasp of her breath. Too exhausted to leave the car, too devastated to think, she hunched over her steering wheel as Elena's hateful tirade ran through her head in an endless, jumbled loop.

Bright lights flashed in her rear-view mirror, making her flinch. A slamming door, footsteps, then a soft tapping on the window. "Anna. Talk to me."

Of course Diego came to check on her. That's what perfect boyfriends do. But she didn't deserve one of those, according to her former best friend.

"Anna. C'mon. Please."

Eyes downcast, she shook her head.

"You want me to go?" His voice held such tenderness. Darn it to Helsinki and back, now she was going to cry. She hated crying. Some said a good cry was cathartic, but weeping only left her nauseated and blotchy. She swiped her eyes with her sleeve before gazing up at him.

Diego stooped over the car, palms and forehead against the glass, watching her with enormous, haunted eyes. "What do you want, Anna?"

She blinked hard, willing the tears away. Didn't work. "I don't know," she squeaked.

Diego gave her a heart-melting, crooked smile. "Well, I'm freezing my ass off out here. Any chance we could talk inside?"

"Unngh." She thunked her head back against the headrest and unlocked the passenger door. As he slid inside, she cranked up the engine, muttering, "Hope your ass isn't frostbitten."

"Wanna examine it?" He patted his hip. "You know, since you're a medical expert."

Pretty lame joke, but he was trying.

His smile flattened, and he clasped her knee. "Please, Anna, don't give up on me."

A tear slid down her cheek. She swiped it away, but another followed. "I take it you talked to Elena."

"More like tore her a new one." He wrapped her icy hand in his warm one. "She was wrong."

"Was she?"

"Completely." He kissed her knuckles. "No one but you gets to decide who belongs in your life."

She gently pulled her hand from his grip. "I don't want to lose my friend. I need her, especially now."

"If she's making you choose between us, then she's a being shitty friend."

A wry chuckle escaped her tight throat. "I can't disagree."

Diego leaned closer and cupped her cheek. The rough warmth of his palm felt so good against her skin. Taking comfort in the guy she was about to lose was beyond stupid, but she couldn't force herself to pull away.

"Look," he said, "Elena's hurting. Maybe, in some twisted way, she thinks she's saving you from the same pain. But you're not Elena, and I'm not the douche-waffle who dumped her."

She chuckled again. "Definitely not a douche-waffle."

"Thanks." He squeezed her hand. "She should've told that guy about Oscar from the start. Could've saved herself a lot of pain."

"I'm sure she had her reasons." Anna met his pleading gaze. "But is she really so different from me? She met a guy. They clicked, so she took a chance. Pretty much what I'm doing with you."

He brushed a strand of hair from her tear-sticky cheek. "You were honest with me from the start. And I'm not going to dump you because of Kumquat. In fact, I'm looking forward to meeting her."

"Lemon."

"Sorry?" He tilted his head like a confused puppy. Darn his cuteness.

"The baby's the size of a lemon now. And soon she'll be the size of a cantaloupe, then a watermelon. And I'll waddle like a tubby penguin." She laced her fingers through his. "Will you still want me then?"

"I will." He pressed his lips to her palm.

She fumbled in her pocket for a tissue to blot her runny nose. "Easy to say now, but Diego, I'm going to be a mom, and Lemon is going to be a person. A noisy, demanding, stinky little person who takes all my time and energy." Her voice broke. "And it's gonna hurt so damn much when you change your mind."

His arms enfolded her, pulling her tight against his chest. "I won't. I swear."

"Any woman with common sense would call me crazy for believing you," she murmured into the crook of his neck. Warm, strong, smelling of woodsy-spicy cologne and burger grease, his body offered shelter, support, pleasure —everything she needed and didn't dare believe she could have.

He pressed his forehead to hers. "I'm not rushing you, angel. Do I want you? Hell yeah. But I understand trusting me at this point in your life is a huge risk." He wound one of her curls around his finger. "It's a risk for me too. I do want kids, but I figured that would happen later, after I'd established my food truck, if not an actual restaurant. Falling for you means getting involved in a messy situation." He chuckled. "But hey, I'm a chef. I don't mind a mess. That's how you get the most delicious results."

Anna huffed. "It's such a double standard. Brock has a girlfriend, but I'm the bad guy for wanting someone to love me." She rubbed her stomach. "The baby's supposed to be enough."

"You don't stop being a woman because you're a mom." He pressed a soft kiss to her temple. "Anna, I can't explain why I feel this way. Anyone looking at this from the outside would call me crazy for wanting you. But what I feel with you is pure truth, and I'm not ready to let you go." He fixed her with a bottomless gaze. "Unless that's what you want."

She turned her face to the sky—well, the car's ceiling— and growled through a grimace. "It's so frickin' unfair. I want to believe God guides my steps, but why would he put the perfect guy in my path and then have everyone who loves warn me away from him?"

Diego's face brightened. "Perfect guy, huh?"

"Feels that way, but I can't trust my own instincts anymore. Pregnancy is scrambling my brain."

Chuckling, he lifted her hand to his lips and kissed her knuckles. "Listen to us, getting all Romeo and Juliet because someone put up an obstacle. We're strong and smart. We'll figure this out, you and me and Lemon."

Warmth bloomed in her chest at his sweet words. She leaned into him, tucking her head into the crook of his neck. "Wish I could believe that."

Stroking her arm, he cuddled her close—well, as close as they could get with the center console between them. "Once when I was little and frustrated over a school project, Abuelita said, 'mi amorcito, you don't have to swallow everything whole. You can take little nibbles, and eventually you'll discover you ate the whole thing, and it didn't choke you.'" He shrugged. "Something like that. It was one of her Spanish sayings, and my Spanish isn't very good."

Anna nuzzled him, enjoying the soft scrape of his scruff against her forehead. "Better than my Arabic. All I can say is sweetheart and a bunch of food words."

"What more do you need?" Cupping her jaw in both hands, he raised her gaze to his. "Anna, let's just admit this feeling makes no sense and all the sense in the world. Nibble it with me? I'll bet when we get to the center, we'll find something really sweet." His hopeful smile shone bright enough to light the darkness outside.

She couldn't help laughing. "Leave it to you to make an empanada metaphor."

"I was thinking more like pie. Or maybe those chocolate truffles. You like those?"

"Not so much." She pulled their linked hands to her heart. "But I like you, Diego. And I'm sick of being told what's best for me. It's high time I figured that out for myself."

"Yeah?" As he moved closer, his sparkling gaze fell to her lips.

"Yeah." And because blessed, stupid hope was stronger than fear, she kissed him.

At the soft press of his lips, it all fell away—the car around them, the icy wind, the worries and warnings and rules. With a whimper, she raked her fingers into his soft curls. It was cramped in her little car, and the center console kept their hips apart, but she claimed every inch of contact she could, pressing her chest to his, brushing his whiskered jaw with her thumbs. His velvet tongue danced around hers, sweet and slow at first, then hotter, more urgent. He grasped her down coat and pulled it open, the pop, pop, pop of the snaps loud in the cozy little space. His hands swept down her sides and lingered at the dip of her waist before rising again. When his thumbs brushed the outside curve of her breasts, a cascade of delicious shivers rushed through her body. Greedy for more, she arched into his touch and tunneled her hands beneath his coat.

"God, Anna," he growled against her lips, "I want you so much. It's like fire, when you touch me, trails of delicious heat on my skin and in my mind and—"

Too impatient for poetry, she claimed another searing kiss, then moaned when he finally cupped her breasts. Her nipples tightened under his palms. He pressed his hot, wet mouth to her throat, and her head lolled back on a moan. Her pulse fluttered beneath his tongue, a wild, fast beat. He stroked the curve of her belly, down toward the place she needed his touch more than she needed oxygen.

Inside her head, alarm bells clanged. Letting lust take the wheel was not the way to disprove Elena's accusations. For her own peace of mind, she had to prove she wanted Diego for himself, not for the favors he did her or his intoxicating touch.

She palmed his chest and pushed him back. "Okay, stop, stop, stop."

Immediately, he jerked his hands away and slammed back in his seat as if she'd just stomped the brakes. Which she had. *Drat my pesky conscience.*

She gripped the wheel and waited for her racing pulse to slow. After a tense, silent moment, she turned to him and confessed, "I should warn you I'm entering my second trimester."

"We're doing math now?" He drew in a deep breath. "Okay. What does that mean?"

Even in the low light, he had to see the flush heating her cheeks. "Well, I'll start to show. And with the increased blood flow to my breasts and—uh, lady bits—" She rolled her eyes. "Gah, this is so embarrassing."

His eyebrows rose. He looked—amused? "Is this the phase where pregnant ladies get horny?"

She socked his arm. "Have you been doing research?"

"I want to be supportive."

"And prepared." She clasped his hand. "That's good, actually. Wouldn't want you to think I'm always this out of control."

"Listen, it's one hundred percent okay with me if you want to let loose."

She glanced at the bulge in his lap. "I noticed."

He hid his embarrassed grin behind his hands.

"But tonight has been rough," she continued, "and I've got a lot to think about."

"Sure. Of course." He wiggled in his seat.

She felt like a rat for winding him up like this and then calling a halt, but she just didn't have the emotional bandwidth to continue. Sex with Diego would involve a lot more than happy underpants feelings. There'd be consequences, complications, strong emotions. She needed to prepare herself for the fallout.

She folded her hands in her lap. "Thanks for the beautiful plant. It's perfect for the table in the front window." Could I sound stiffer? "You still up for painting the baby's room on Saturday?"

"Wouldn't miss it for the world." He kissed the tip of her nose. "And now, my blue balls and I are gonna call it a night."

She stroked a fingertip along his jaw. "Next time, I won't start something I'm not prepared to finish."

"No rush, angel, no rush." He pecked her lips before boosting out of the car and limping back to his truck.

After he drove away, Anna climbed out of the car and let the night air cool her burning cheeks. "Should I sleep with him?" she asked the stars. "Feels like the worst outcome has already happened. What else could go wrong?"

Chapter Fourteen: An Interloper

♥

The scent of fresh paint mingled with the aroma of sweet and savory empanadas. Glad for another chance to impress Anna, Diego had risen at dawn to roll out dough and make fillings for their post-painting feast, now baking in Anna's oven: zucchini and corn empanadas with poblanos and mascarpone cheese, Chilean empanadas with spiced pork, olives, raisins, and hard cooked eggs—and for dessert, pumpkin-pie empanadas dusted with sugar and cinnamon.

A peek through the oven door revealed the pastry hadn't quite reached the golden shade of crisp, flakey perfection, so he reset the kitchen timer and headed back to the nursery, arriving just in time to hear Charlie exclaim, "God, that smells good. You sure you don't want Diego to move in?"

"Charlie, shush!" Anna hissed and shot him an apologetic grin.

Cheeks burning, he bent to gather paint-smeared rags.

It had taken him, River, and the sisters all morning and half the afternoon to paint the small office that would serve as the baby's nursery. The sunny yellow shade Anna chose gave the little space a warm glow, even on a gray Northwest winter day.

A soft touch fell on his back. "Hey." Anna nudged his foot with hers. "Sorry about that. Charlie's a little tipsy." With her toe, she poked a cluster of empty beer bottles—River's contribution to their painting party.

"Don't worry about it. I didn't expect an invite to move in." Not that he hadn't thought about it. All day, as they painted, he'd imagined how sweet it would be to share this cozy little house with Anna and Charlie—and probably with River too, judging by the way he and Charlie kept sneaking off to smooch.

Anna wiped a paint-spattered hand across her forehead. "Charlie and I agreed we'd give each other two months before inviting anyone else to move in, but River spends more nights here than he does at his place."

He pushed to his feet. "Well, it's been almost two months already. How do you feel about sharing your space with guys?"

"Guys plural?" She arched an eyebrow.

"I mean, you know, guys in general." Shut your stupid mouth, Vargas. He couldn't move in with Anna, even if she asked him. As soon as he vacated Abuelita's house, the fam would close in like hungry vultures, pressuring her to give up her beloved home.

Rising to his feet, he forced a breezy tone. "Empanadas are almost ready. Hope you're hungry."

"I'm always hungry these days." She patted her tiny baby bump. "Lemon thanks you for the empanadas."

He crouched and spoke to her navel. "Hope you like them, límoncita."

When Anna giggled and toyed with the hair at the back of his neck, he was sorely tempted to press a kiss to her belly, but that would definitely be overstepping. This wasn't his kid. Elena was right about one thing—he was getting sucked into Anna's situation, already thinking of himself as part of her little family. Best to remember that he wasn't.

He straightened as River and Charlie tumbled into the room. "Let's eat," Charlie exclaimed. "Tengo hombre."

Anna chucked a rag at her. "You just said 'I have man.' It's Tengo hambre."

"That's what I said. Besides, I do have a man." She wound her arms around River's middle. "A most excellent man."

Diego exchanged a look with River. "Better put her down for a nap before her shift."

River pulled her toward the kitchen. "He's right, babe. Can't have you showing up tipsy."

"Pffsht." She waved away his comment. "It's just the paint fumes."

"Yeah, right." Anna started a pot of coffee, and the four of them tucked into their early supper.

"These are empanadas are fantastic," River declared, rubbing his belly as he pushed back his chair. "When are you gonna tell Dawn about your food truck?"

"When I have a launch date. It'll take a few more months to get all my licenses and permits. I don't want to tell her too soon in case something goes wrong."

A sharp knock on the front door jerked them from their conversation.

Anna turned to Charlie. "You expecting someone?"

She shook her head.

"I'll get it." Diego pushed his chair back and trotted to the door, opening it to a tan, blond guy with a nose like a hatchet and squinty pale eyes. His stomach plummeted. Anna's ex.

The prick widened his stance and snarled, "Who the fuck are you?"

Brock didn't recognize him. Diego didn't know whether to be relieved or offended. Guess one Latino repair guy looks like another to you.

The hairs on Diego's nape bristled as he blocked the doorway with his body. "A friend of Anna's. Who the fuck are you?"

"Her husband." The jerk tried to shoulder his way through the doorway, but Diego stood his ground.

A soft hand curled around his biceps. "What do you want, Brock?"

"We need to talk." He glared at Anna's grip.

"You want to talk to him, Anna?" Diego asked over his shoulder.

She huffed a breath that tickled the back of his neck. "No. You don't get to barge in without notice. You want to talk, text me first, and we'll set up a time and place. How did you find me, anyway?"

Brock's mouth twisted into a sneer. "Your bright blue car kinda stands out, especially with all those stupid stickers on the back."

Anna stiffened. "You've been stalking me?"

Joining them in the doorway, River stood shoulder to shoulder with Diego, a protective barrier between Anna's ex and her new home. Diego's fists itched to punch the asshole's smug face, but it wasn't his place to do so—unless the loser made a move. Then he'd gladly bounce his skinny ass down the stairs.

Brock gave a dismissive tsk. "Get over yourself, Anna. My friend lives one block up. I was going over to watch football when I saw your car."

Diego snorted. "The Superbowl was two weeks ago." He set his hand on Anna's shoulder. "You want him gone?"

Anna raised her chin. "Let him dig himself deeper while I've got witnesses."

Brock's fists tightened at his sides. "I have every right to know where my child is going to live. This crappy old house is too small." He aimed a glare at Diego. "Especially if you're shacking up with your boyfriend. I got no reason to trust him."

Brock's face contorted, like he was working out a hard math problem in his head. "No." He backed up, stepping perilously close to the top step. "No way. This is the guy who gave me the divorce papers."

River snort-laughed into his fist.

Brock glared at Anna and stabbed a finger toward Diego's chest. "You been with this guy all along, haven't you? Kristi was just an excuse for you to dump me and move in with him."

"Now hold on just a goddamn minute." Diego stepped toe to toe with the slimeball. "Anna and I haven't—"

"Enough." Anna stepped between them and struck a superhero pose, chest out, fists on hips. "Brock, no one here owes you an explanation. You lost your right to have an opinion about my friends when you broke your vows."

God, she was hot when she got all bristly like this.

Brock dropped the tough guy act and whined, "But Banana, you're going to be a mom. You got no business hooking up with some guy—"

Cheeks blazing red, she poked his chest. "I told you not to call me that. And I haven't hooked up with anyone, not that it's any of your damn business." Another poke. "Are you telling me you're celibate now you're becoming a dad?"

Brock crossed his arms and glowered. "That's different."

"How?" She glared until her ex finally broke eye contact and took a step back.

Diego grinned in pride and amazement. Anna might be sweet and funny most of the time, but she blazed like a flamethrower when someone crossed her. She was going to make an excellent mom.

Brock ducked his head and raised his hands. "Fine. Okay. Can I just see the baby's room?"

"Not today. I'll text you when it's convenient." She started to shut the door, then swung it open again. "You want to prove you care about our child's welfare? Show up at the mediation appointment next month. And Brock, don't ever come over unannounced again." She flung the door closed and stood facing it for a long moment, shoulders heaving, fists clenched. Then she spun and threw her arms around Diego.

He stroked the tense muscles of her back. "You're a warrior, Anna."

"God, he makes me so mad," she grumbled into the crook of his neck. "How am I gonna co-parent with a turd like him?"

Charlie patted Anna's shoulder. "By defending your boundaries like a boss. Well done, sis."

Releasing Diego, Anna spun into her sister's embrace.

While the girls huddled on the couch, River tugged him aside and lowered his voice to a murmur. "I hate to leave them alone here with that asshole sniffing around."

Diego couldn't agree more, but he wasn't in a position to do anything about it.

Nibbling his lip, River glanced at the girls. "I've been dropping hints to Charlie about sharing this place, but she wants time to settle in with Anna first. I'd feel better if one of us was here full-time. But how do I suggest it without sounding like a sexist ass?"

Diego heaved a sigh. "All we can do is let them know we're here when they need us."

"I guess." River clapped Diego on the shoulder. "Something about the Khoury girls, eh? Sweet and snarky and stubborn. Makes you want to take care of them, not that they'd let you." He moved to the dining table and collected plates, using the clatter to cover their conversation. "The old man seems to like you. 'Course, he likes anyone who can fix things."

"We'll see how long that lasts when he finds out I'm serious about his pregnant daughter."

"Serious, huh?" River nudged his arm. "Pretty damn brave of you."

Diego moved back to the kitchen to clean up. A moment later, he looked up from the dishwasher to find Anna standing in the doorway, a crooked smile on her face. "You didn't have to do that."

He shrugged. "You were busy. I don't mind. But I do have to get to work soon."

"Oh. Right." She drummed her fingertips against her thigh. "Do you ever take a night off?"

"Not often, but I could. Especially Monday or Tuesday."

"Cool." She slid closer, and her gaze flicked up to his, then down as a blush tinged her cheeks. "How about Tuesday night?"

"I'll ask Dawn and Shelby tonight." Hooking his thumbs into her belt loops, he pulled her front to his. The warmth of her body felt amazing—cozy and sexy and addictive. "Where would you like to go?"

"Right here." Her fingertips toyed with the buttons on his shirt. "You've cooked for me—what, four times? Five? Time for me to feed you."

"I, uh..."

Her flirty smile slipped. "Unless you don't want to."

"Anna." He cupped her face in both hands. "Time alone with you is what I want more than...anything." Yeah, I'm a poet. Fortunately, she didn't seem to mind his clumsy words.

With her fingertip, she traced a swirl over his chest, ever-widening arcs of delicious sensation. "Whatever this is between us, it's going to get much more complicated soon. Before it does, I'd like the chance to, you know, explore."

If it weren't for her sister in the front room, he'd start exploring right now. Instead, he kissed her hand and backed away. "I'd better get going. I'll text you tonight."

"Please do. Hey—" She darted to the fridge and pulled a photo from beneath a Tacoma octopus magnet. "Before you go, meet Lemon."

He held the glossy black and white photo tenderly. The baby's body was hard to make out, but the delicate profile was unmistakable. Upturned nose, determined chin, just like its mama. A rush of emotion swamped him. Inside this beautiful, feisty woman, a tiny person was growing. A miracle.

"She's beautiful," he choked out, handing the photo back to Anna. "I can't wait to meet her."

Anna gave a low laugh. "We won't know if Lemon's a boy or girl for at least another month. But I think it's a girl. Just a hunch, you know?" Rising on her tiptoes, she pressed a soft kiss to his mouth. "Thanks for everything, Diego. I still think you're crazy to want to hang out with a pregnant woman, but I'm so glad you do."

Chapter Fifteen: Kafta and Kisses

♥

"Easy now, don't break my good mixing bowl."

Anna swiped a flour-dusted curl from her sticky forehead. "Sorry, Aunt Hala."

Hala hit the button on her food processor, filling the air with a loud roar and the sharp scent of onions. She dumped the minced veggies into a bowl, then faced her grumpy niece. "Darling, you know I respect your boundaries and all that, but you're stressing me out. Now, spill the beans."

"It's just Brock being Brock." Anna shook the water from a bunch of parsley with all the violence she'd like to apply to her ex-husband's neck. How dare he just show up and demand entrance to her home? And how dare he accuse her of sleeping with Diego? Even if she was strongly considering it—okay, pretty much planning on jumping his bones tonight—that decision came long after his decision to cheat with Kristi.

Still, she owed Hala an explanation for her murderous funk, especially because Hala cleared her Tuesday afternoon to help her prepare a proper dinner for Diego.

Anna filled a glass at the tap, gulped it down, and tried to force a light tone. "You know, nowadays people say spill the tea. Spill the beans is old-fashioned."

"Tea, beans, whatever. I'm gonna spill your brains if you don't stop bashing around my kitchen like a grumpy elephant."

"Okay, okay. Here goes." Anna clutched her blouse over her suddenly churning stomach.

Hala blanched. "Oh God, is something wrong with the baby?" Eyes wide, she forced Anna into a chair.

"No, no, the baby's fine. I'm just frustrated because Brock is giving me a hard time." And I'm falling hard for the most wonderful guy at the least wonderful moment.

Hala's rumpled forehead smoothed. "We didn't expect otherwise, right?"

"Yeah." Anna kicked off her work clogs and wiggled her toes. "But I'm dreading the next several months. I wish we could just sit down like sensible adults and work out a plan for the baby. Doesn't look like that's gonna happen. But he's been served his divorce papers, so the legal ball is rolling, and there's nothing Brock can do to stop it." Though he could delay it considerably, her lawyer warned. Anna tried not to dwell on that possibility.

Hala moved to the sink and filled the electric kettle. "I'll make you a nice, soothing tea." Rummaging in a cupboard jammed with tea cannisters and cartons, she called, "Is that why you're making this big feast? Celebrating with your girlfriends?"

"With a friend, yeah." After all, Diego was first and foremost her friend. A friend whose kindness made her feel warm and safe, whose deep, soul-delving gaze made her pulse flutter and her body tingle. A friend she hoped to get closer to tonight. As in skin-to-skin close—if she could relax enough to enjoy his company.

Hala set a steaming mug before her, then patted Anna's shoulder. "I remember how hungry I got when I was carrying your cousins. Your Uncle Fred used to joke he'd need a second job just to cover the grocery bill."

"Well, my friend has been very supportive, so I'd like to treat hi—uh, her—to a nice Lebanese meal." Anna nibbled her lip. Barely a lie, right?

Hala smiled. "Nothing like a good, homecooked dinner to soothe a broken heart. Especially if you have a handsome young man to share it with."

"Handsome young man?" she squeaked.

"Cut the crap, honey. I saw you and that chef boy making goo-goo eyes on moving day." She dumped parsley into the food processor and hit the button. The machine's growl covered Anna's groan.

"Listen," Hala said as she scraped the minced parsley into the bowl with the onions. "I think you're nuts for starting something in the romance department. But you're old enough to know what you're getting into. So is your young man—as long as you're telling him the whole story."

"He knows all the gory details." Anna massaged her aching forehead. "Ironic, isn't it, to meet the perfect guy now?"

Another shrug from Hala as she dumped raw ground beef and lamb into the food processor. "What's that saying? Man plans, God laughs. Maybe he's the one you were supposed to meet. You were in such a hurry to marry Brock. Your sister wasn't the only one who thought you should have waited."

Anna groaned. "I wish you had told me back then."

"We tried. You wouldn't listen." Hala added spices and the onions, fastened the lid, and ground the whole mess into a paste that would form the Kafta kebabs—one of the childhood favorites Anna craved lately. Maybe Lemon needed the extra protein.

Hala scraped the meat blend into a bowl and beckoned Anna over. "Come on, lazybones. You wanted to learn to make Kafta. Wet your hands."

Following Hala's example, Anna formed the meat glop into neat ovals and arranged them on a parchment-lined baking tray.

As they worked side by side, Hala nudged her. "Let me ask you something, darling. Are you one hundred percent sure?"

"About what?"

"Divorcing Brock. You're not just doing this because you met the new guy?"

Anna had been gnawing on that very question for the past forty-eight hours, examining it from every possible angle.

"Yeah, I'm sure. It's not about the new guy, it's about building a happy, healthy life for me and my baby." She dug her fingers into the goopy mass. "Besides, I can't keep the new guy."

"Why not?" Hala kept her sharp dark eyes on the kebabs she was forming—at twice Anna's speed.

"Just a hunch. He's so optimistic about us, but when I get huge, he'll change his mind. Besides, I can't build my future around depending on some guy. I need to be strong and independent." So no one can ever hurt me again the way Brock did.

"Darling girl." Hala wiped her hands on a paper towel, then grasped Anna's arms. "You can't have love without pain. The more you love, the more loss hurts."

Ugh. Why did truth have to be so heavy?

"Are you still hurting over Brock?"

"A little. Mostly, I'm just angry. Oh." A giggle burbled up. "I guess I didn't love him that much?"

"Maybe not."

"Right now, I miss our old apartment more than I miss Brock himself. I felt at home there, safe. I wish I could feel better about being single."

"Well." Hala squeezed her arms, then released her. "Some people can live a happy life without a partner. Others are happiest coupled. You've got to figure out which you are. Now, let's get to work on the Manakish."

While Anna kneaded the dough for flatbreads, she chewed on Hala's challenge. Despite not missing Brock himself one teensy, tiny bit, she definitely missed having a romantic partner—sweet little moments of connection, knowing someone's routine and flaws and quirks, watching the seasons change together, feeling comfortable and safe. Her new home with Charlie provided some of what she craved, but now that River had moved in, she couldn't help feeling like a third wheel. Witnessing their cozy way of moving through the day in tandem made her yearn for a partner of her own.

Too tempting, too easy to believe Diego could be that person. Besides, he had to look after his grandmother.

Right guy, wrong time.

Nibbling her lower lip, Anna took a last look around her kitchen. Pretty damn intimidating, cooking for a chef. Without Hala's expert help, she and Diego would be dining on rotisserie chicken and bagged salad, hardly fitting fare for a guy who tempted her with delicious empanadas. And delectable kisses.

Dinner first. Kissing later. A blast of spice-scented steam hit her when she opened the oven door to check the sizzling kafta. Ten minutes to go. She transferred the tabbouleh into a pretty cut-glass bowl, then arranged the za'atar-topped flatbreads on a baking tray.

They'd probably do a helluva lot more than kiss tonight if she didn't chicken out. It felt beyond weird driving across town to buy condoms, just in case things progressed that far. Normally, she shopped at the pharmacy inside the hospital, but there was no way she'd risk any of her work friends seeing her with a box of weenie beanies.

The doorbell rang seconds before the timer did.

"Shoot." Flapping her hands, she dithered between oven door and front door before dashing through the living room to let him in.

"Hi, Diego." She rose on tiptoe and pecked his lips.

Oh my frickin' gosh, you are so pretty.

He'd tamed his rowdy curls, and instead of his usual black T-shirt and jeans, he wore a soft maroon sweater and charcoal dress pants that hugged his muscular thighs. His eyes sparkled, his sexy smile sizzled, and for one heady moment she was tempted to forget about dinner and tug him straight to her bedroom.

"For you." He handed her a cellophane-wrapped bouquet. "Wow, something smells amazing."

"The kafta!" She dashed back to the kitchen, calling over her shoulder. "Sorry. Come in."

He shucked his coat and followed. "Kafka?"

"Kaf-ta." She pulled the sizzling kebabs from the oven. "Ground beef and lamb with onion, parsley, and Lebanese spices."

He took a deep sniff. "Smells amazing. What are these?"

"Manakish. Flatbread topped with olive oil and za'atar." She slid them into the oven to reheat.

"That's got sumac, right?"

She gave his arm a playful flick with her kitchen towel. "My aunt Hala would be impressed." Might as well admit the truth. "She kinda talked me through all this."

"Well then, here's to Aunt Hala." He pulled a bottle of wine from a paper bag. "We'll toast her with Safeway's finest."

Her hands flew to her belly. "Oh, I can't—"

He tapped the label. "It's alcohol free."

"Aww. How thoughtful." She smooched his cheek.

Looping his arm around her waist, he snugged her close. "I'm gonna need more than that, angel."

With a giggle, she yielded to his kiss, relishing his heat, the magic dance of his velvet tongue—until the toasty odor wafting from the oven took on a tinge of burnt.

"Yikes!" Squirming from his grasp, she grabbed potholders and whisked the flatbreads from the oven. "Well, these are mostly salvageable."

His hands settled on her hips. "Anna, for the pleasure of your company I'd swallow cardboard and call it delicious."

"Shoulda told me. I could have saved a lot of time."

"But since you went to all this trouble—" He slid the meat onto a platter while she arranged the flatbreads in a basket. "Thank you, Anna. I'm honored."

"Try it before you say that." She gave him a saucy hip-bump, then carried the platter into the dining room. While Diego lit the candles, she pulled up some soft R&B on her phone and connected to the speaker.

"Where do you want me?" He gestured to the chairs.

Pretty much everywhere. She took the chair closest to the kitchen. "Hostess sits here. Handsome guest sits wherever he pleases."

"Well then." He sat beside her, so close his foot nudged hers.

Keeping her composure through the meal was going to be tough. She lifted a skewer and slid the juicy kebab onto her plate, then pushed the platter toward him.

"Here." She passed the bowl of crumbled feta. "Try some of this on your meat." Why did that sound so dirty? "And the hummus is good too."

He lifted a forkful of meat to his lips and inhaled.

Anna's nerves jittered like a drumroll. What if he didn't like it?

Eyes closed, he chewed, then his head lolled back on a groan. "So. Damn. Good."

Thank you, Hala. With a triumphant grin, she tucked into her own plate of Mediterranean goodies.

"What are these spices?" he asked. "I taste cumin, coriander...is that cinnamon?"

"And allspice, mint, and Aleppo pepper."

"It's like meat perfume. Think your aunt would share her recipe? I'd name an empanada after her."

"Hala's kafta-panadas? She just might share for that honor." Oh, but then I'd have to introduce you. Once the rest of the family knew Anna was dating while pregnant and still technically married, the hummus would hit the fan. Change the subject stat.

"Try the manakish." She ripped a triangle from her flatbread and dipped it in the hummus.

Diego followed her example, flicking his tongue to capture stray sesame seeds. Heat pooled between her thighs. If he didn't stop those sexy moans of pleasure, she'd slide right out of her chair.

Focus on the food. "Hard to believe some people think it's rude to wipe up sauce with bread. I mean, that's what it's for, right?"

He chuckled. "Same deal in our house, but with tortillas. Mom serves them with everything—spaghetti, meatloaf, chicken."

Joking and laughing, they devoured their meal until only a few scraps remained. The fake wine wasn't bad, but it was Diego's easy smiles and playful touches that had Anna feeling tipsy by the time she pushed her chair back.

"Hope you saved room for dessert."

His dark eyes smoldered as he reached for her hand. The hypnotic brush of his thumb sent vibrations of pleasure straight to her core. Pretty clear what kind of dessert he had in mind. She craved more of his touch, but uncertainty held her back. As much as she wanted him, taking their flirtation to the next level was a huge risk. Monumental. Life-changing.

And then Usher started to croon from her Bluetooth speaker, all velvet seduction and breathy gasps, and her wall of reserve crumbled brick by brick.

Diego pulled her to her feet. "Let's take a breather before dessert. Dance with me?"

She nestled into his hold and let him sway her to the music. Resting her chin on his shoulder, she closed her eyes and breathed in his subtle woodsy-spicy scent—no burger grease tonight. He wove the fingers of his left hand through hers. His other hand drifted to the small of her back and gently snugged her closer. A firm ridge brushed against her belly before he quickly shifted away. "Sorry, angel," he murmured into her hair.

Lust whooshed through her, sparkling like the love child of an ocean wave and a magnum of champagne. Now or never. No matter the consequences, she couldn't let this perfect moment pass.

His gaze danced from her eyes to her lips, back and forth.

She slid her fingertips through the whisper-soft curls at his nape. "What do you say, Diego? Ready to make your life a helluva lot more complicated?"

He answered with a kiss—a soft press that quickly flared, heated and hungry. The slide of his tongue over hers matched the seductive swivel of his hips. Her heartbeat echoed the music's pulse. Waves of pleasure weakened her knees, knocking her off-balance as Diego tightened his hold and angled his mouth to delve deeper.

She broke free long enough to gasp, "Bedroom."

"Yes," he murmured, and backed into the dining hutch.

"This way." Sliding her fingers into his hip pockets, she steered him toward the hallway. Like giggling, kissing bumper cars, they collided with walls and furniture until they finally fell onto her bed.

Gathering her to his side, he pressed his forehead to hers, his hooded gaze so close she felt the brush of his thick lashes. Too late to pretend this magnetic pull was just second-trimester hormonal horniness. She didn't just want a man, she wanted this man, this sweet, patient, brave, gorgeous man whose hands skimmed over her body as if in worship.

"Beautiful Anna." He traced her collar bones with a fingertip, then with feather-light kisses. "I'm falling so hard for you."

Pinching her lips together, she bit back the words threatening to burst from her throat. Oh, Diego, I could love you. But this won't last. The truth was too dangerous, and she couldn't bring herself to lie to him.

In a shaky whisper, she told him, "Give me tonight. No pressure, no promises."

"Hey." He rose on one elbow, his dreamy expression sharpening. "We should have a conversation first. My feelings for you are—" He trailed off and wound a lock of her hair around his finger. "This is a big deal for me, Anna. Being with you means something. I'm not up for a one-night stand. So I've gotta know—what do you want from me?"

Your mouth on my skin, your hands in my hair, your cock so deep inside me... Closing her eyes, she counted her thundering heartbeats...seven, eight, nine. When she raised her lids, the truth tumbled out. "It's like I'm standing on a high cliff, and you're down below, arms wide open, ready to catch me. Everything inside me wants to jump, but I'm afraid to trust this feeling." Her voice caught. "Elena says I'm using you to get through a rough patch."

His fingertips skated over her cheek. "Are you? 'Cause I don't feel used."

"I'm not. I swear." She pulled him down for a deep, hot kiss that almost erased her doubts. Almost.

"I believe you." He nibbled her lower lip. "And I don't feel used. I feel honored."

Deftly he unbuttoned her blouse. She'd stuffed her expanding boobs into her sexiest lace bra, which became increasingly uncomfortable as the night wore on. Now, as his lips brushed over her hyper-sensitive skin, she was sure the thin cloth would burst if he touched her one...inch...lower.

His breath ghosting over her breasts made her nipples stiffen and tingle. "So lush. Can I take this off?"

"Please."

With a happy sigh, he released the front clasp and caressed her with hands, mouth, tongue, teeth, gentle at first, then rougher and more urgent. Each stroke and squeeze shot a zing of bright pleasure straight to her clit. If he kept this up, she'd come before he even touched her core.

Releasing her, he kissed his way down her belly. She tensed as he neared the swell of her baby bump. He swirled the tip of his nose around her navel, followed by the tip of his tongue. "Hello, Lemon." Chuckling against her skin, he hooked his fingertips into her waistband and tugged.

Inch by inch, he bared her, pressing kisses to her hipbones, her flanks, her thighs, everywhere but her pulsing center. Her pregnancy books spoke of this heightened sensitivity, but they'd understated the effect by miles. Breath held, she vibrated with each touch.

At long last, he slid her pants off her ankles, then knelt between her spread legs and pulled his shirt over his head.

His beauty stole her breath. Smooth, golden skin over defined pecs and belly dusted with dark hair. A sexy line trailed below his spiral-shaped navel. She longed to lick him there, to follow that happy trail down, down...

Holding her gaze, he unfastened his belt and shucked his pants, leaving only black boxer-briefs tented by an erection that made her mouth water and her pussy clench.

She reached for him, but he grasped her wrists and pressed her onto the bed, capturing her mouth for another deep kiss before sliding back down to grip her thighs. Spreading them, he kissed and nibbled the sensitive skin near her panties before sliding one long, clever finger beneath the elastic. He parted her folds, drawing the most delicious sensations—brilliant sparks and a throbbing, ecstatic ache.

"God, Diego, that feels so—" The language center of her brain shut down when he slid the fabric aside and licked her in firm, slow strokes.

"Mmm. So luscious," he murmured before treating her to a shower of rapid flicks that nearly levitated her off the bed.

Clutching his hair, she gasped, "I'm gonna come."

"That's the idea, angel." He spiraled his tongue round and round her clit until, all at once, the room fell away. Writhing, she cried out as shock waves of bliss shook her body.

Panting, dizzy, she slowly sank back to earth and opened her eyes to find Diego crouching above her, lips parted, face flushed, his thick erection already sheathed. "Anna, is this okay? I don't want to hurt you."

She hooked her leg around his back and pulled him down until his cock slid over her slick folds. "If you don't get inside me right now, I just might explode."

He kissed her, lowering onto his elbows so his chest pressed against hers, the wiry hairs tickling her nipples deliciously. His tongue probed her mouth in perfect rhythm with the fat head of his cock that nudged, nudged, nudged her entrance before slooooowly gliding inside. Inch by heavenly inch he filled her, the sweet sensation so overwhelming it brought tears to her eyes.

His breath heated her cheek as he rolled his hips in a smooth rhythm. Rocking up to meet each stroke, she surrendered control and doubt and just let herself feel. His hold on her tightened. His muscles tensed beneath her fingers. She murmured sweet nonsense into his ear, an endless stream of "Yes" and "Please" and "So Good."

Thrusting deep, he ground his pelvis against her clit, sparking jolts of pleasure. "I'm so close," he gasped. "Come with me, angel. Show me how to get you there."

She grasped his hand and pulled it down between their sweat-slicked bodies until his fingertips grazed her clit. "Two fingers, like this." She showed him how to glide his fingers in rhythm with his thrusts.

A smile of wonder lit his face as they undulated together. She held his gaze until she just couldn't any longer, ripped away by pleasure so intense it commanded all her focus. His breath grew shallow as he fucked her in short, fast digs, his muscular hips churning beneath her calves. Arching above her, face contorted with pleasure, he gasped her name with each thrust. Suddenly, his whole body stiffened. She felt his cock pulsing deep inside her right before a second climax crashed through her.

After, he shifted in some magic, yogic way so he lay with his heaving chest against her back, his cock still deep inside, one leg resting between hers. "Don't wanna squish Lemon." His fingertips traced soothing swirls over her breasts and belly. "God, I just want to stay here inside you." He gave a few slow, pussy-tingling thrusts. "But this condom's gotta go."

She stroked his arm. "Why don't you get tested so next time we don't need the condom?"

Cupping her jaw, he turned her to face his bright, eager gaze. "You mean it?"

She stroked his cheek. "I'm already pregnant, so why not enjoy each other fully while we can?"

Another delicious thrust from behind. He kissed her sweaty nape. "This is the start of something special, angel. Can you feel it?"

"I feel it."

Despite his comforting warmth, a chill slithered down her spine. No matter his intentions, once she was huge and unwieldy, cranky and uncomfortable, he wouldn't find her so appealing. And if he didn't leave by then, he surely would when she couldn't bear his touch on her sore, leaky breasts, or when their lovemaking was interrupted by a squalling infant. This sweet connection had an expiration date.

Still, she could enjoy him now, could relish his delectable body, his friendship, his sweet support while it lasted. And she'd be good to him—as good as she could be in her stressed, distracted state. Who knows, maybe someday, after the crazy baby years had passed, they could reconnect—if she could just keep her heart above water until then.

Diego returned from the bathroom with a towel for the mess and a dozen kisses for the crook of her neck. He spooned against her back with a contented sigh. Skin to skin, nestled in the safety of his embrace, she shoved her worries to the back burner. "Stay with me tonight?"

His fingers slid in swirls over her side and down her thigh. "Wish I could, but I can't leave Abuelita alone. She's eighty-seven, you know."

Anna's heart pinched. She'd been through the decline and death of her own grandparents, and those last years brought confusing behavior and outbursts of emotional venom. "Dementia?" she asked.

"Nothing so bad as that, but she sleepwalks sometimes. Or maybe she's just sneaking snacks and doesn't want to admit it. Still, if she got hurt and there was no one there to help..." The mattress shifted as he sat up.

Unwilling to let him go just yet, she cuddled his warm, broad back. "What happens when she can't be left alone while you're at work?"

Diego stiffened. "We'll figure it out when we get to that point. If we get to that point. Not all old people get dementia." He rose and gathered his discarded clothing.

Shit. Hot-button topic.

"Hey." She vaulted out of bed and closed the distance, wrapping her arms around him and laying her cheek on his shoulder. "I'm sorry. I didn't mean to suggest anything. Not my business, anyway."

Huffing a breath, he turned into her embrace. "You've got a lot of worries on your own plate. You don't need mine too." He rubbed circles on her back, but all the passion had gone out of his touch.

She laced her hands behind his neck and waited until he met her gaze. "Listen, I'm your friend. If I can help, I will."

"Thank you, angel." He gave her mouth a dry peck. "Sorry to ruin the mood. I hate this situation, but if I don't watch out for Abuelita, the fam will pack her off to an old folks' home. I'm afraid it'd kill her." His sigh lifted her hair. "She's done so much for all of us. She deserves to live her last years in the home she loves."

"What about Elena?"

"What about her?"

"Well, she's a nurse. She has a better understanding of elder issues than most people, right?"

"I suppose. If she weren't being such a bitch about us, I'd ask for her help." He quirked a wry grin. "Families, right?"

"There's no escaping family." Her hand strayed to her belly.

"I don't want to escape." He pressed a soft kiss to her forehead. "I just want everyone to get along."

She gave a dry laugh. "Let's wish for world peace while we're at it. Anyway." She pecked his lips. "Tonight was amazing. And I meant what I said about getting tested. I want to feel you bare inside me before I get all hippo-ish."

"Anna." He lifted her chin until she met his gaze. "I will always want you, no matter which size fruit you're carrying. You are beautiful and amazing, and I'm as gone for you as a man can go." He kissed the tip of her nose. "Next time, I'll see if one of Abuelita's friends can stay the night with her, okay?"

"Okay." They both dressed. Her arm around his waist, she walked him to the door, gave him a last, lingering kiss, and watched him drive off into the night. Something raw and needy inside her whimpered. She yearned to spend the night snuggled in Diego's arms. But that wasn't going to happen. Not his fault, not hers, just harsh reality. He was a good man, and he wouldn't abandon his grandmother. She could never ask him to.

As his truck's taillights disappeared around the corner, a tear trickled down her cheek.

"Stupid pregnancy hormones." She swiped it away.

Chapter Sixteen: Abuelita Concedes

♥

"Worthless, shit-sucking butt munch!" Diego threw his pliers to the Airstream's floor. They bounced on the industrial rubber mats —where's the satisfaction in that? He craved violence, or at least a satisfying loud noise, but he couldn't risk damaging his baby, so he settled for storming out into Abuelita's yard, slamming the trailer's door on his way. "Ugh." He sat on the step, his head in his hands.

"Niño, what's bothering you?" His Abuelita had the spookiest sense for when he was in distress. He hadn't heard her come out of the house and into the muddy yard. Typical Tacoma—yesterday they had glorious early-spring sunshine. Today: cold, gray drizzle. In flowered rainboots and an oversize fuzzy sweater atop her house dress, Abuelita sloshed across the yard holding two steaming mugs.

"It's the electrical system." He waved toward the mess behind him. "Everything was working fine last week. Now, it's all fu—Sorry, all messed up. I can't figure out where the fault is."

She handed him a mug, then settled in a lawn chair. "Chamomile tea to calm your nerves. Ginger for the stomach."

He sniffed the steam. "Something else in there?"

"Let an old lady have her secrets. Now drink up."

Sure enough, the herbal brew warmed his aching hands, sore from wrestling with bolts and screws, and loosened his tense muscles, if only a little.

"Electric problems, eh?" Abuelita tapped her pursed lips. "If only we knew someone who could help."

"You know I can't ask Dad."

"And why not? Family is for helping, Gogo."

"It should be." He knuckled his temples, trying to ease his stress headache. "But Dad's help always comes at a price."

She placed a gentle hand on his arm. "You want me to talk to him?"

"No!" He softened his tone. "No, I'll find a way. But thank you."

So far—or rather, as far as he knew, neither Elena nor his grandmother had blabbed to the family about Anna. Since his first tumble into her bed three weeks ago, their conflicting schedules mostly kept them apart. But they made the most of what little time they could carve out, and he guarded those stolen hours like the treasure they were—Saturdays together before his shift, sometimes right here in his trailer, sometimes relaxing at her house, sometimes exploring Tacoma together. Evenings he spent at Bangers, of course. The more shifts he worked, the more he could save for this aluminum-hulled money pit. At least a few times a week he'd meet Anna for lunch at the hospital. On the few occasions when they ran into Elena, she stalked past with a frozen expression. He wasn't too worried—she'd been a grudge-holder throughout her childhood, but she always thawed if you let her be long enough.

He finished his tea and pushed himself to his feet. The muscles in his back and shoulders grumbled from too much time spent hunched over the generator housing and breaker panel. Today's shift at Bangers was going to be rough.

He held out his arm to help Abuelita out of her seat, but she just fixed him with one of her bullshit-obliterating stares. "You need more money, don't you?

He did, but he hated to admit it. Despite his detailed plans and built-in financial cushion for emergencies, this food truck was gobbling money faster than he could earn it. Only a few hundred dollars remained in his Empanada Angel account.

"Ah." She tapped her forehead. "Too proud to ask your old Abuelita for help, eh?"

"You already do enough for me, 'Lita. You should spend your money on having fun with your friends."

"I do, but there's enough left over to invest in my grandson's business."

Sorely tempted, he bit his tongue. If things got truly dire, Abuelita was the one family member who wouldn't hold her help over his head. But making this work on his own was the whole damn point. He needed to prove to the family, and to himself, he was no longer Flakey Diego, the rash kid whose projects always crumbled. And he would do it, even if it took longer than planned.

Of course, the longer this took, the longer his work schedule would keep him away from Anna. How long would she wait? She deserved someone by her side, a steady partner to help with the baby, not someone who had to bolt from her bed after making love.

He cleared his throat, itchy under the awkwardness of this sensitive topic. He should have asked this weeks ago. "Um, 'Lita, I was wondering."

"Yes, mi corazón?"

"Do you think you might—I mean, could one of your friends, you know, spend the night sometime?"

"What for? A pajama party?" She cackled and slapped her knee.

"So I could maybe spend the whole night with Anna?"

Abuelita's brow furrowed. "You're getting serious with her, aren't you?"

"Yes, ma'am. Or maybe she could spend the night here?" His narrow bed was a poor substitute for Anna's wide, cushy one, and Abuelita would no doubt insert herself into their dinner conversation, but at least he could hold his love and watch out for his grandmother at the same time. Her sleepwalking was getting worse. Last night, he found her standing at the front door, muttering to herself. He'd guided her safely back to bed, but what if he hadn't been there? What if she'd stepped out into the cold, wet weather and wandered off?

Abuelita closed her eyes and sighed. "No."

His chest hollowed out. "No, what?"

She pushed to her feet. "No, I don't want her sleeping here. You're an adult, Diego, and I like Miss Anna, but this is my house, and I'm not comfortable facilitating your sexy times."

His jaw dropped. Where did she get language like that?

The corners of her lips twitched upward. "Don't look so surprised. I read the Facebook. I know the lingo." She patted his arm. "Tell you what. I still think you're crazy, both of you, but I'll ask around. A pajama party might be fun. And Diego—" She poked his chest. "I may be old, but I'm not helpless. I have a cell phone. And a house phone. You don't need to watch over me all night."

"Yeah, but if something happened."

She sniffed. "I raised four children and eight grandchildren. I can handle my business, thank you very much." She glanced at her wristwatch. "Now get a move on. You're going to be late for work."

"Shoot." Today's planning meeting for Bangers' St. Patrick's Day bash started in a half hour. He pecked her cheek, locked up the trailer, and dashed.

Anna jiggled from foot to foot on Diego's flower-trimmed porch. Stuck into a pot of pansies beside the door, an angel whirligig rattled in the stiff March wind. Banging sounds came from somewhere inside. Probably Diego in the kitchen.

Grinning like a middle-schooler with a crush, she clutched her package to her chest. Last night, he forgot his jacket at her house, giving her the perfect excuse to drop by on her way home from work. These past few weeks, he'd given her so much time and attention, despite his heavy workload, and she wanted to show her appreciation with more than words and kisses. This little treat was a start.

Footsteps approached. The door banged open. Where Diego's face should be, only air.

She glanced down. "Oh, hi Mrs. Vargas."

Wrapped in a stained floral apron, the old lady peered up at her with an odd, squinty expression.

"I was hoping to catch Diego before he left for work."

"I told you, honey, it's Maricela. Diego had an early meeting. Something about Saint Patrick's Day."

"Oh." Disappointment burst her bubble of anticipation. "Well, he forgot his jacket at my place. And I brought him a book we were talking about." She held out the plastic shopping bag.

Maricela tilted her head and raked Anna with a head-to-toe gaze. She must've passed inspection because the tiny woman stepped back and beckoned her inside. "Come. I was just making polvorones. We'll have tea."

Anna backed away. "Oh, I don't want to bother—"

"Nonsense. Come, come." She tottered away, leaving Anna no choice but to follow. The scent of butter and sugar and toasty baked goodies wafted from the back of the house. Anna stepped into the sunny, angel-decked kitchen and found the counters covered with rainbow-hued sugar cookies on cooling racks. No icing, just brightly colored dough baked to a sugar-dusted crackle.

"They're so pretty." She set her package on a free corner of the table. "I've never seen cookies this colorful."

"Sit, sit." Diego's grandmother patted the back of a chair, then fetched two mugs and switched on the electric kettle. "So, what did you bring my grandson?"

"Oh." So much for her surprise. She'd wanted to see the look on Diego's face as he paged through the stained, ragged cookbook. "It's a book of Lebanese recipes. My mom bought it when she was a new bride."

Abuelita's eyebrows rose, pleating her forehead like a paper fan. "Your Lebanese mama needed Lebanese recipes? Didn't she learn at home?"

Anna chuckled. "No, my blonde, German-American mom learned to cook Lebanese when she married my dad. She wanted to impress him—and her mother-in-law. My Aunt Hala said Mom cooked like she was native-born."

"Let's see." Maricela set a steaming mug of orange-scented tea before Anna. "I love old cookbooks." While Anna sipped tea and nibbled cookies in fire-engine red and sky blue, Maricela flipped through the pages. "Lots of stains, the mark of a well-loved cookbook. This is family history right here." She pierced Anna with a sharp gaze. "You must really care for Diego to let him borrow this."

Her heart squeezed. How much was safe to say?

Fortunately, the old lady didn't seem to expect further comment. She slid the book toward Anna. "Show me your favorite recipe."

"Hmm." Anna flipped through the pages. Just looking at the pictures brought back vivid sensory memories of threading slippery chunks of marinated meat onto wooden skewers, standing on a stepstool to stir dry spices in a skillet, Mom's gentle grip guiding her hand round and round. Mom's home was full of good food and love. She wanted that for her own child.

She pointed to a full-page illustration. "Probably this one, shish tawook. It's basically spiced chicken on a stick. When I was little, she'd make this for my birthday. Until—" Her voice wobbled, and she closed the book. "Sorry. We lost her when I was ten."

"Oh, honey." Maricela placed her gnarled hand atop Anna's and squeezed. There was strength there, despite her advanced years, and warmth too. "And now you're having a baby on your own. That's hard without your mama."

She cleared her throat against a sudden thickness. "It's okay. My dad's sister stepped in. She looks after Charlie and me like we're her own. She's a great cook too. She tried to teach me, but I never put in much effort."

"And now you're interested?" Maricela raised one painted-on eyebrow. "Or are you content to let Diego do all the cooking?"

"Oh, I—" She drew back, but the old lady's gaze held no malice, just an amused twinkle.

Maricela patted her hand before releasing it. "I'm just teasing. Besides, Diego loves to cook."

"It's kind of intimidating, cooking for a chef. He's very talented."

Maricela's penetrating stare made Anna itchy. "So. You and Diego."

Anna raised a shoulder and let it drop. "Doesn't make much sense, does it? I mean, from your point of view."

"No, it doesn't. But he seems happy." She cupped her hand to her mouth, though they were the only two people in the room. "Tell me, what do you think of this food truck business?"

"I think he'll be brilliant. He has such a passion for flavors, and he's so creative. The way he lights up when he talks about it, well—" Blushing, she dropped her gaze to her lap. "It's really cute."

"Hmmph." Maricela slurped her tea. "What does Elena think of this thing between you and Diego?"

Sly old fox, no doubt she already knew what Elena thought. Anna searched for tactful words, never her strong point. "Elena doesn't talk to me much anymore."

"Is that so?" She huffed through her nose. "Stubborn, that one. Always was. And proud. But she and Diego could usually see eye to eye. I'm sorry to hear that's not the case. Listen." Narrowing her eyes, she leaned in. "Let's not share this visit with Diego. He doesn't like it when family pokes into his business." She flashed a conspiratorial smile. "And I don't blame him. It's not a nice feeling, being underestimated. I'll just tell him you dropped off this book for him. Okay?"

"Um, sure?" She didn't like the idea of keeping secrets from Diego, but this tiny lie of omission couldn't hurt. Especially since his grandmother was showing surprising trust and candor. Nice to have at least one member of Diego's family on their side.

Maricela walked her to the door. "Nice visiting with you, honey." She squeezed Anna's arm. "I'm glad Diego has someone who believes in him. Besides me, of course." With a twinkling smile, she closed the door, leaving Anna blinking in surprise on the porch.

Had she just made an ally? Or had she just bared her vulnerable bits to a sneaky old lady with ulterior motives?

Either way, she'd learned a valuable lesson: never underestimate Maricela Vargas.

Chapter Seventeen: Brock Strikes Back

♥

"Now that's what I'm talking about." Jojo rubbed his hands together. "Gimme tots."

"Hold your horses," Shelby told him as she passed paper plates and napkins. "There's plenty for everyone if you don't hog it all."

Diego elbowed the huge bouncer aside and set down a tray of menu samples for Saint Patrick's Day. Just two days away, Bangers' party promised to draw one of the biggest crowds of the year.

Dawn dug in, helping herself to a scoop of tots, a paper cup of coleslaw, a quarter of a burger, and an empanada, which she examined with a squint. "What's this, Diego?"

Do or die time. He squared his shoulders and painted on his best salesman smile. "Thought it might be fun to add something new to the menu. Besides, it's Saint Patrick's themed." He shot River a help-me-out glance. They'd discussed his spiel last night, but his friend seemed too caught up inhaling tots to remember his lines.

Charlie shot Diego a wink as she reached for an empanada. "Ooo! These are the best." She dunked it in the dipping sauce, took a bite, and made exaggerated num-num noises. "So fricken good! What's inside?"

"Corned beef, potatoes, cabbage, onions, carrots, Worcestershire sauce. Very Irish, right?"

Charlie kicked River under the table.

"Right," he exclaimed. "And look, the sauce is green."

"Sour cream with horseradish, parsley, chives and dill." Diego slid a cup of sauce to Dawn. "What do you say, boss?"

Wrinkling her nose, Dawn surveyed her empanada-munching employees.

Lana flipped a long pigtail over her shoulder. "Fusion cuisine. I love it."

Rosie took a bite, threw her head back and groaned. Eddie flushed bright pink.

Even fussy Kiara, who eyed anything more complicated than tots with suspicion, chimed in. "Deeelish. We should totally offer these."

Charlie must've briefed them well.

Dawn drummed her fingers on the table. "Why do I get the feeling y'all are in cahoots?"

"Just try one, boss." River nudged her with his elbow. "They're really good. Besides, you let me try out new drink specials all the time. Why shouldn't Diego get to experiment?"

With an aggrieved sigh, Dawn took a bite and chewed so damn slowly, Diego nearly vibrated out of his seat with nerves. Trying out his empanadas on Bangers' customers would check one huge box on his food truck plan—market testing.

Finally, Dawn's crumb- and freckle-dusted face broke into a wide grin. "Well, I'll be damned. They do taste kinda Irish, don't they?" She leveled a don't-mess-with-me look at Diego. "We'll put them on the menu for Wednesday. But if they don't sell, no more empanadas."

"Got it, boss." He sagged into his seat, limp with relief. One step closer to his goal. Of course, the closer he got, the more pressing his need to break the news to Dawn— but that could wait, especially with his electrical system on the fritz. And getting his licenses and permits was taking for-freaking-ever. Maybe he should bring empanadas to City Hall.

Dusting crumbs from her hands, Dawn turned to River. "So, what's on the drink menu?"

"The usual—green beer, Irish whiskey, Baileys, Irish coffee, plus an Emerald Shake with marshmallow vodka, Pot o' Gold Jello shots with rainbow sprinkles, an Irish

Mule, and a Baileys Mint Martini. Rosie and I are making an illustrated list for the window."

"Sounds good. Print copies for the tables, too. Lana, how's the social media going?"

She flashed a thumbs up. "I put the bartenders' vids up on Saturday. And I got a close-up of Rosie's shamrock tattoo."

"Too close," Eddie grumbled.

Rosie nuzzled his neck. "You're the only one who gets to touch it."

"Window mural's almost done," Rosie said. "The slogan was Gus's idea—Get lucky at Bangers."

Speak of the devil, Dawn's grizzled business partner waddled in from the back room. "Just got off the phone with St. Brigid's. Sister Gladys will be here with her nun squad."

"Nuns in a bar?" Eddie tilted his head. "Isn't that counterproductive?"

"Nonsense." Dawn slapped her thigh. "The good sisters can drink any of y'all under the table. And their ol' Catholic guilt will help sell raffle tickets." She pointed. "Shelby and Kiara, you're in charge of hiding the shamrocks. I've got the raffle and the Irish trivia. Gus, you got the photo booth this time. And it's all hands on deck for judging the costume contest."

Charlie grabbed more tots. "Are we the only bar on the Ave doing costumes?"

"Far as I know." Dawn hooked a thumb over her shoulder. "Since that snooty bar across the street closed, everyone's been playing nice."

"What time does the band start?" Rosie asked.

Dawn checked her notes. "Eight, since it's a weeknight. Should be a foot-stompin' good time. Any question?"

None came, since everyone's mouths were stuffed with menu samples.

"Okee dokee." Dawn shut her folder. "Thanks for coming early, everyone. And don't forget to wear green."

"Even the chefs?" Shelby asked.

"Why not?" Dawn ruffled her assistant chef's spiky hair. "I swear, if I didn't need you in the kitchen, I'd put you in a Leprechaun costume."

As he made his way back to the kitchen, Diego felt a tap on his shoulder. Dawn's squinty expression sent a warning jolt down his spine.

She folded her arms and pursed her lips. "Empanadas, huh? Let's talk in my office."

Ruh-roh. He hid his panic behind a phony smile. "Sure thing, boss."

In her tiny, cramped office, Dawn sat at her desk and gave Diego an enigmatic smile. "Have a seat."

Gulping, he sank into a cracked vinyl armchair.

Dawn planted her elbows on the desk and tented her fingers. "When were you gonna tell me?"

Cold sweat prickled his brow. "Tell you what?"

"About your food truck?"

Caught. No way out but the truth. "I was going to tell you when I had a firm launch date. That might not be for a while."

Dawn's lips tightened as she regarded him though narrowed eyes.

His pulse cranked into overdrive. "Please don't fire me. I swear, I was gonna give you plenty of notice and train my replacement. Hell, I'll even help you find one. Or you could promote Shelby. She's got some great ideas, and—"

Dawn tipped her head back and laughed. "Cool your jets, kiddo. No one's getting fired. Wish you'd a told me first, though. We're family here. Family don't keep secrets."

Her words pinched his conscience hard. He'd been keeping a lot of secrets lately—and apparently, he wasn't very good at it.

"Who ratted me out?"

"Let's just say I like to keep my thumb on the pulse of my bar." Reaching across the desk, she patted his clenched hand. "Never thought you'd stay here forever, Diego. Don't get me wrong—I'd love to keep you. You're the best chef I've had in twenty-two years of running this place." She leaned back and laced her fingers behind her neck. "Whole bunch of my former employees have started their own businesses, and I'm proud of 'em, every single one." She slapped the arm of her chair. "So, tell me about this food truck of yours."

Twenty minutes later, Diego stumbled back to the kitchen on shaky legs. That went a million times better than he'd expected, but now he was under even more pressure. Dawn had every right to ask when he expected to leave, and he gave her his best guess: July first. Putting an actual date on his launch set a clock ticking in his brain. A very loud clock. Tick, tick, tick...

Back in the kitchen, during a lull between orders, he texted Anna:

Told the boss about my food truck. She didn't freak.

Her reply came swiftly.

Great news! See, all that worry for nothing.

"Oh, there's plenty more to worry about," he grumbled before typing **Up for a quick visit tonight?**

He needed to unload this tension, and nothing made him feel better than nestling in Anna's bed, spent and sleepy, talking into the night—well, until his midnight curfew.

Maybe July wasn't too soon to open his food truck. How about June? Plenty of business with the breakfast and lunch crowds, and he could have his evenings free to help Anna.

His head buzzing with to-do lists, he got back to work flipping burgers and dressing tots.

"Holy moly, what's goin' on here?" Leaning on his cane, Anna's dad pointed to the long line of customers outside Bangers Tavern, most of them in green outfits ranging from goofy to glamorous. Dad grumbled, "Dawn didn't mention no lines."

Seems he'd run into Charlie's boss in the produce aisle at Fred Meyer's, and she invited him to the St. Patrick's party. Anna tagged along to make sure he didn't do anything weird. Not that she'd miss Diego's empanada debut. This was a big night for her boyfriend.

Calling him that, even in her head, triggered a cascade of conflicting emotion—giddy delight, disbelief at her good fortune, and nagging guilt. Deep down, she knew it was a mistake to get this attached. Once the baby came, there'd be no more time for sweet snuggles, intimate suppers, Monday movie nights—just work, baby, work, baby, with every spare minute between spent on precious sleep. Soon, she'd have to sit Diego down for a serious talk about realistic expectations. But not tonight, not when he was so adorably excited over this milestone.

"Hey, Anna." Jojo beckoned from his bouncer's stool.

She groaned inwardly as Dad towed her past the line. "Comin' through. Crippled guy and a pregnant lady. Make way." Once inside, he bulldozed right up to the bar, nudging customers aside with his cane.

"Hey, Jack. What's your pleasure?" River gave him a handshake, then leaned across the bar to peck Anna's cheek.

Dad smacked the bar. "Gimme something green and strong."

"Gotcha." River reached for a tall glass. "And for Anna, how about a cucumber limeade?"

"Sounds delish."

"I'll tell Diego you're here."

She shot him a bug-eyed glare and jerked her head toward her dad.

"Because," River continued smoothly, "he'll want to make sure Charlie's family gets the best."

"Diego?" Dad asked as they searched for a seat. "Who's he?"

"The chef, Dad. You met him when we moved into our new place, remember? You kept calling him Domingo."

"Oh, the Mexican kid. Is he sweet on your sister too?"

"Just a friend, dad."

This was dancing dangerously close to the truth, but with a crowd like this, Diego would stay safely tucked away in the kitchen. Later, she'd text him about how amazing his empanadas were—because of course they'd be amazing. Maybe he could come over after his shift for some in-person praise. If he left Bangers promptly at ten, they'd have almost two hours of uninterrupted private time before he raced home to check on his grandmother.

Just two hours. She squeezed her eyes shut and breathed through a sharp sting of disappointment. Quit lamenting what you don't have. Celebrate what you do have. A sweet, attentive boyfriend with a tight schedule was a helluva lot better than a cheating husband.

"Look, those people are leaving." Her drink held high, Anna scooted through the crowd and claimed a tiny two-top table near the stage.

A moment later, Charlie stepped up. "Pops! Didn't expect to see you here tonight. Nice shamrock tie." She set down her drink-laden tray and pecked his cheek, then Anna's. "And you look smashing, baby sis."

Anna stroked the faux-fur collar of the green plaid jacket she'd picked up at Vintage Rapture, her favorite shop on Sixth Avenue. So what if she had to wear the jacket open over her baby bump?

"You guys want tots?" Charlie asked, "Or are you gonna try Diego's empanadas?" She waggled her eyebrows as she sing-songed those last two words.

"Burger and tots for me," Dad said.

Anna mouthed, "Empanadas."

With a knowing wink, Charlie lifted her tray and sailed into the crowd.

Dawn O'Malley stepped up to the microphone in an outfit so outrageous Anna couldn't hold back a giggle—green Doc Martens, snug green jeans cupping her wide hips, light-up shamrocks twinkling from a green satin vest over a T-shirt reading "Irish whiskey makes me frisky," green tinsel wound around her neck like a feather boa, and a green bowler hat atop her green-tipped dreadlocks.

"Erin go bragh!" she bellowed into the microphone. The crowd cheered and raised their glasses.

Dawn patted her tawny, freckle-dusted cheek. "Being a true Irish lass, Saint Patrick's Day is me favorite holiday."

She was probably aiming for an Irish accent, but she sounded more like a movie pirate.

Someone hollered, "Bullshit."

"Ain't you ever heard of the Black Irish?" Dawn flashed a teasing grin. "And watch your language in front of the good sisters. Where you at, Sister Mary-Agnes?"

"Yo!" A stout woman in a dark green pantsuit waved a roll of raffle tickets.

"That's a nun?" Dad grumbled. "Where's her habit thingy?"

Anna elbowed him. "Don't be a Neanderthal, Dad. Nuns can wear regular clothes."

Sister Mary-Agnes hopped up on stage and took the mic. "Top o' the evening, Bangers." Her Irish accent sounded one hundred percent real to Anna's ears. "And huge thanks to Ms. O'Malley for hostin' us tonight. We've got some lovely raffle baskets from local businesses." She winked and cupped a hand beside her mouth. "I've got my eye on that basket from Paradise Garden Dispensary."

A wave of gasps and giggles swept the room.

"What?" The nun blinked in mock innocence. "Their CBD cream does wonders for my arthritis." She held up her coil of tickets. "We got T-shirts, hoodies, caps, gift cards, all manner of good things from the fine merchants of Tacoma, so dig deep. All proceeds from tonight's raffle support Saint Benedict's free clinic and community medical outreach."

Dad obediently dug for his wallet. "You know Barney from my poker group? One of them nurse nuns visits his dad twice a week."

Dawn took the microphone back. "And don't forget, there's still plenty of shamrocks hidden around the bar. Each one is good for a free drink, so get to huntin', little leprechauns."

Dad hopped down from his stool and snatched up his cane. "I'm off to find my pot of gold."

While Anna scanned the noisy crowd, her stomach rumbled. "Chill out, Turnip. Empanadas are coming."

"Hey there, angel." A muscled arm set a plate before her.

"Diego!" she squeaked. "I didn't expect to see you tonight."

He gave her an adorable, crooked grin. "Charlie said you were here, so I'm taking my break. Tell me what you think of my Irish empanadas." He crouched and placed his hand on her belly. "Hope you like them too, Turnip."

"What the ever-lovin' fuck are you doing?"

The empanada in Anna's hand went flying. Dad had popped up at her elbow like some sneaky Lebanese ninja.

She would've toppled from her barstool if Diego hadn't thrown a steadying arm around her shoulders.

"Dad," she hissed, "watch your language around the nuns."

He waved a fistful of raffle tickets. "Thought I might win something nice for my pregnant daughter." His death-ray glare jerked from Diego's reddened face to his chest, where Anna clutched his T-shirt.

"You makin' a move on my baby girl, Domingo?"

"Dad, for frick's sake—"

Diego straightened but didn't release Anna's shoulder. "Yes, sir. I am." He searched her face, his expression solemn. "I'm crazy about her."

Dad spluttered, "But she's—"

"Still technically married. I know." Diego lifted one shoulder. "From your point of view, this probably makes no sense. But there it is." His grip on her shoulder softened into a caress.

Crap on a cracker. She'd hoped to delay telling Dad about Diego until the right moment—and the middle of a rowdy bar party was definitely not the right moment. Biting her lip, she gazed up at Diego.

His eyebrow flicked up, a silent invitation.

The brave, independent, confident woman she wanted to be would state the naked truth for all to hear— "Diego and I are together, and anyone who doesn't like it can kiss my patoot."

But Anna wasn't that brave yet. She needed her family's support—not just Charlie's, but Dad's, Aunt Hala's, Uncle Fred's, the cousins...

With a sigh, Diego released her shoulder. His hopeful expression flattened. "Well, then, I'd better get back to the kitchen."

"No, wait." Winding her arm through his, she snugged him to her side and faced her father. "Dad, Diego and I have been seeing each other. I like him. A lot." The pure relief on Diego's face fueled her courage. "It's a weird situation, but we'll figure it out."

A maroon flush rose from Dad's neck to his hairline. "The both of you ain't got the sense God gave mud." He swatted at Diego's arm. "Now let go of her. She's comin' home with me."

This stops now. "No, Dad. I'm a grown-ass woman, and I decide who I spend time with."

Dad threw up his hands. "Nice language. Is that your doing, Dee-ay-go?"

Fire flared in Anna's gut. "Don't you dare blame him."

Continuing to ignore her, Dad shoved a stubby finger in Diego's face. "Lemme tell you something, kid. This one has no judgment when it comes to men. First that turd-boy Brock, and now a fry cook. What kinda man butts his nose into—"

Charlie hurried to their table. "Shut it, Dad." She shouldered her way between the two men and grabbed Dad's pokey finger. "This is my workplace. You wanna yell, do it somewhere else."

Anna blinked in surprise. Lebanese ninjas everywhere. An eerie silence descended as dozens of eyeballs goggled at their family spat.

"Now, let's all settle down." With her thumbs hooked in her belt loops like a Wild West gunslinger, Dawn sauntered up to their table, her voice calm but her smile squeaky tight. She slung her arm around Dad's shoulders and spoke into his ear. "Jack, you're an old friend, so I'll cut you some slack. But this bellowing bull act ain't welcome in my bar. You hear me?"

The fight went out of Dad's face, and he hung his head. "Sorry, Dawn. I'm just trying to protect my daughter."

Dawn looked Anna up and down, then fixed Charlie with a flat stare. "I told you, I got no time for drama with my staff. And you." She leveled a glare at Diego. "You know better, son."

Charlie compressed her lips in a straight line and glared at the tabletop. Diego studied his shoes.

Anna squared her shoulders. "Please don't blame Charlie or Diego, Ms. O'Malley. This is my fault."

A shout from across the room broke their five-way staring match. "Holy shit, there's a bug in my tots!"

The accusation hit Diego like a cannonball to the chest. He kept an immaculate kitchen, always earning an A from the health inspector. He had to slam a lid on this complaint ASAP.

Charging into the crowd, he elbowed customers aside. Dawn's voice rang out behind him, "Diego, hold on," but he ignored her. His honor was on the line.

At the end of the bar, a skinny blond dude pointed at his plate of tots.

Brock.

It took every atom of Diego's self-control to keep his tone calm. "Problem with your food, buddy?"

Anna's ex wheeled on him, an oily sneer across his Ken doll face. Pinched between his thumb and forefinger dangled a huge cockroach.

Diego's stomach dropped. He'd never seen a single roach in Bangers' kitchen, much less one that size.

Behind him, Anna's voice rang out. "What the fudge are you trying to pull, Brock?"

Brock's eyes went wide with mock sincerity. "Just trying to protect these good people from unsanitary conditions." All around them, customers recoiled and poked gingerly at their own plates.

Diego's gut twisted hard. This asshole was trying to hurt him, but it was Dawn who would bear the brunt, all because of his mistimed crush.

Anna stepped between them. With a glare that could melt glass, she thrust her palm forward. "Give it here."

"Babe, no." Something like alarm flicked over the troublemaker's face as he closed his fist over the gross bug.

"Don't call me Babe." She raised her voice and turned to address the crowd. "My ex-husband is trying to pull some kind of sick joke."

Brock protested, "I swear to God, I found this in my plate."

Ignoring him, Anna continued to address the crowd. "See, I was married to this loser for three years, and not once in that time did he ever touch a bug. I had to squash them all because he's terrified of 'em." She ticked off on her fingers. "Spiders. Wasps. Bees. Once, he even ran from a moth."

"It landed in my hair," he protested, patting his blond waves with the hand hiding the bug. The roach fell to the floor. Brock lunged for it, but Anna stomped it with her cute little boot.

Diego gasped along with everyone else as Anna scooped up the totally non-squashed cockroach. "See?" She held it high overhead. "Plastic."

Diego didn't know whether to laugh or smash Brock's pointy nose. Before he had the chance to do either, a soft tut drew his attention.

Sister Mary-Agnes stood at his elbow, shaking her head. "Son, lying is a grave sin. Thou shalt not bear false witness against thy neighbor."

Brock flushed and stammered. "What about coveting thy neighbor's wife?" He stabbed a finger at Anna. "We're still married."

"Only because you keep stalling." She addressed the crowd. "He cheated on me with his secretary. What a cliché, right? And he didn't show up for our mediation appointment."

Titters and snorts broke out. A woman at the nearest table hooted. "Damn, this is better than Jerry Springer."

"Enough." Dawn stepped up, sounded more weary than pissed off. She pointed at Brock's chest. "You, get your ass out of my bar." Glancing over her shoulder at Sister Mary Agnes, she added, "Sorry, sister."

"No offense taken."

"But she—" Brock started.

Jojo stepped up, looming over the blond weasel. "Time to go, numbnuts. And take your plastic toy with you."

Anna tucked the creepy thing into her pocket. "I'll keep it."

"Lemme through, damn it." Anna's dad joined the fray, using his cane to part the mob of rubberneckers, then pointing it at Brock's middle. "You owe this young man an apology."

"Sorry," Brock grumbled, shoulders slumped. "It was just a joke." He slunk toward the exit.

Someone tossed a crumpled napkin as he passed. "Dick move, dude."

Someone else bounced a tater tot off Brock's retreating back.

"Jeez Louise." Dawn swiped a hand down her face. "Where the Khoury girls go, drama follows. Diego, back to the kitchen. Orders are backing up."

"One minute, boss." Beside him, Anna drooped like a melting ice cream cone. First her eyebrows fell, then corners of her mouth sank, then her shoulders sagged, then—

"I'm so sorry, Diego." She rested her forehead against his chest.

"Don't be." He rubbed slow circles on her back. "None of this was your fault."

"He's not done, you know. He'll keep making trouble for us both." The wobble in her voice tore his heart right down the middle. His work team needed him, but so did Anna. He ought to walk out, right now, scoop her up and take her home and hold her tight until she stopped shaking.

But what could an unemployed fry cook offer her? She needed someone steady, someone to pick up the slack when she got overwhelmed. And he couldn't do that.

"I can hear your wheels spinning," Anna muttered. She pecked his lips. "Call me when you're done, okay? We'll spin them together."

"Maybe we should take tonight off, angel. We're both upset after tonight's shit show—" He trailed off, waving toward the entrance.

"Is that what you want?" She gazed at him through watery eyes.

"No, but it's probably for the best." He kissed her forehead. "Sleep well, Anna." On legs of lead, he trudged back to his lonely, roach-free kitchen.

Chapter Eighteen: Meatballs and Bad Luck

♥

The next day, Anna found Dr. Zakariya at the clinic's reception desk, chatting over cupcakes with Dr. Jones. Three nurses also clustered around the treats, including Elena, who gave Anna a flat, cold stare then slowly turned her back and continued her conversation with their coworkers.

Forcing a chipper tone, Anna handed Dr. Z. a clipboard with forms for her signature. The boss scribbled her initials, then narrowed her eyes and peered into Anna's face. "You feeling all right, dear? Your eyes are puffy."

"I didn't sleep well last night. Heartburn." In truth, Anna's red eyes and aching head had far more to do with last night's cockroach debacle than with indigestion.

Such a sweet guy, patient and generous. The attachment she selfishly encouraged was bringing him nothing but bad luck. If she had a microgram of integrity, she'd break it off with him for his own good.

But she just couldn't force herself to make the call. Besides, you don't do something like this on the phone. He deserved a face-to-face discussion. He deserved a woman who didn't come with a trail of toxic mess. He deserved—

Dr. Z's cool hand touched her forehead. "No fever, but you seem a little out of it. Tomorrow's Friday. Maybe you should take a sick day, give yourself the weekend to recover."

"No, I—" She checked herself. Tomorrow she could meet with Diego, lay out all the reasons why they should cut the cord. And pray he'd talk her out of breaking up with him.

She squared her shoulders. "You're right. I will take a sick day. Thanks for understanding."

Laugh lines crinkled the corners of Dr. Z's dark eyes. "A wise woman knows her limits. Looks like you're pushing up against yours." She patted Anna's shoulder. "Being a single mom is tough. Don't be afraid to accept help when you need it. And don't be afraid to ask."

Relief flooded Anna as she left to pack up her things for the weekend.

"Anna, wait." Footsteps pattered behind her.

Sorely tempted to break into a run, she forced a counterfeit smile and turned.

Tala, the other single mom in the office, lowered her voice and gently gripped Anna's arm. "Oh, hon'. I'm so sorry. Friendship breakups are the worst. I hope you and Elena work it out." Her expression brightened. "Hey, the single parents' group starts in the cafeteria in half an hour. You should come."

"Will Elena be there?" And would this be one more door closed by her connection with Diego?

"Haven't seen her there in months. Come on." Tala patted her arm again. "You can sit with me."

Anna nibbled her lip. Perspective is what she desperately needed. And wisdom from single parents like Tala—especially since she'd lost her single-mom role model. "Okay. I'll go."

Tala's smile glowed with genuine warmth. "Excellent. See you there."

A half hour later, Anna entered the hospital cafeteria and spotted a group, mostly women, sitting around a long table near the hospital's meditation garden. Before joining them, she grabbed a decaf coffee and a pastry to give her nervous fingers something to fiddle with. As she approached, Tala rose and waved. Anna quickly scanned the group—no sign of Elena.

Tala pulled out an empty chair. "Okay, so everybody, this is Anna from my clinic."

"Hi, Anna."

"Welcome, hon'."

"Glad you could join us."

Tala made introductions. Anna recognized a few faces among the members who spanned the gamut from docs to nurses to lab techs and admin staff.

"This your first child, Anna?" Mike, a plump lab tech, asked.

She patted her belly. "Yeah. A badly timed surprise, I'm afraid. I split from my husband, and them—boom."

Sympathetic nods all around. Anna nibbled her snack and felt herself slowly relax as the friendly group chatted about babysitters, preschools, after-school programs, teething, colic, and kids' TV shows she'd never heard of. It was like being plunked down in a foreign language course after missing the first month of classes. Soon, she'd be fluent. The thought shook her to her toenails, but there was comfort in knowing this group was here to help.

"So, Anna, got any questions for us?" Tala asked. "We probably won't agree, but somewhere in this mess"—she gestured around the table—"you might find something useful."

"Um, actually—" Did she dare ask something so personal? Her Aunt Hala's voice sounded in her memory. "Fortune favors the brave." At the time, she'd been trying to talk Anna into trying out for the school play, but the same advice applied here.

She cradled her tummy. "I was wondering if any of you dated while you were pregnant."

Like toppling dominoes, all the smiles around the table slipped into scowls.

"Oooo, bad idea."

"Horrible."

"I had way too much on my plate."

"Wait until after the baby comes," an older nurse said.

"And you lose the baby weight," one of the docs added.

"I didn't even think about it until Liam was weaned," another said. "Who wants to date a woman with leaky tits?"

"Come on, y'all," Mike offered. "You're gonna give the poor woman a complex."

A tall, elegant doctor raised her eyebrow. "Would you date a pregnant woman, Mike?"

"Well, no, but—" He gave Anna a weak smile. "That doesn't mean nobody would."

Anna pushed her chair back. "It's okay. I asked my question, and you gave me honest answers. Thanks for that. I've got a pretty bad cold, so I'm going to head home." In reality, cold germs had nothing to do with the tears prickling her eyes and the sudden pounding in her head, but it was a harmless lie.

"See you next week?" someone asked.

"Sure." Hard to paste on a smile, after they just dumped a bucket of gloom on her head. "See you then."

Tala grabbed her coat and bag. "I'll walk you out."

As they passed into the corridor, Tala pulled her aside. "Listen, don't let their negativity get you down. I didn't date while I was pregnant, but my cousin did. It can work, sometimes."

"Is your cousin still with the guy?"

"With the girl. And yeah, they're married now."

That tiny flicker of hope was enough to keep the tears at bay as she made her way home. But it wasn't enough to keep them from falling as she typed out a message to Diego.

Taking tomorrow off. Can we meet? We need to talk.

As soon as Diego set the steaming pot of soup on Anna's kitchen counter, the waterworks started.

"Why are you so good to me? All I bring you is bad luck." Anna's plush lower lip protruded as she gazed up at Diego through tear-damp lashes.

He'd read about the volatile emotions of pregnancy. Time to tread with care.

Wrapping his arms around Anna, he swayed her to the soft patter of early spring drizzle against the windows. When her shoulders stopped shaking, he cupped her damp cheeks.

"Anna, meeting you was absolutely the luckiest, best thing that's happened to me since—" He searched his memory. "Since I bought the Airstream." Damnit, shoulda said since forever. I suck at poetry.

She dropped her head against his shoulder and snuffled. "Brock's just gonna keep making trouble for you, and I don't know how to stop him."

Diego didn't doubt it, but he swallowed his worries and focused on reassuring Anna. "He can't stop the divorce, Anna, and he can't keep us apart." He wiped away her tears with his thumbs, then nudged her into a chair. "I brought Abuelita's famous albóndigas soup, but I toned down the spice." He ladled steaming tomato broth into a bowl, then added four big meatballs, plus chunks of potato, carrot, and zucchini.

"Why not?" She sounded kind of disappointed.

"Why not what, angel?"

"I love spicy food."

"Oh." He rubbed the back of his neck. "I read that spicy food gives pregnant women heartburn, and—"

"Aww, Diego. You've been researching? That's sweet." She went to the fridge and pulled out a bottle of habanero sauce.

"All righty." He carried their brimming bowls to the table, then gave her a mock-stern glance. "You do like cilantro, don't you? Because if you don't, I'm gonna have to rethink this whole deal."

"I like cilantro fine." Her smile tickled him right behind the ribs. He made a mental note: Food and humor helped ease Anna's hard times.

"See? The worst is behind us. After the great cilantro controversy is settled, everything else is small potatoes." He showered a chiffonade of cilantro over their bowls, then added crumbled queso fresco before setting them on the table, along with small dishes of thinly sliced Serrano chiles, lime wedges, and Abuelita's fresh salsa.

She doctored her soup with lime, chiles, and a big dollop of salsa before tasting. "Wow. That's so good. Meaty and delicious."

His cock jerked in his jeans.

"I meant the soup, horny man." Giggling she dug into a fat meatball.

He enfolded her free hand in his. "Listen, angel, I'd love to strip that sweater and jeans off your luscious body and make delicious, meaty love all afternoon—but you wanted to talk, right?" He dug into his bowl. "When you're ready, I'm listening."

Anna's shoulders slumped as she stared into her bowl. "It's just—the Brock mess, getting chewed out by my dad, and then getting dumped by Elena. It's a lot, you know?"

He scooted his chair closer and hooked his leg around hers. "Must be hard, seeing her at work every day." His sister had been particularly frosty toward him at family gatherings lately, and she flatly refused to discuss Anna. She kept just as mum about her own recent breakup, too. This stony-face act wasn't like her, and it worried him.

Anna leaned onto her elbow. "Yesterday at work we had cupcakes for someone's birthday, and Elena froze me out. Everyone noticed, though they all pretended not to." She raised her watery gaze to his. "I miss her, you know? The other nurses are nice, but they can't replace my best friend."

What a shitty way to treat a friend. Maybe there was nothing he could do to break through Elena's stubborn block, but he'd damn well try.

Anna set her spoon down with a sigh. "First Elena, then Brock—being with me has brought you nothing but trouble."

He clasped her hand and waited until she raised her watery eyes to his. "Don't let the doubters get to you. Their minds don't stretch wide enough to imagine a relationship like ours. Nothing they can do will make me stop wanting to be with you. And I'll still want you when you're bigger. And when Turnip is born. And when she's colicky and cranky. I'm in this for the long haul."

She gave him a weak smile. "I really want to believe you."

Goose bumps prickled his skin as he realized just how precarious his hold on her really was. Any minute now, she might decide being with him was too much trouble. The pressure from friends and family would only grow stronger. All he could do was stick by her and pray she didn't change her mind.

They finished their meal in silence. It did his heart good to see her eat up every bite, despite her weepy state. Turnip needed fuel to grow, and he loved knowing he was contributing, even if it was only a few meatballs.

Finally, Anna pushed her empty bowl away. "That was amazing. Thank you."

"Thanks for seeing me." He reached for her hand. "So, what did you want to talk about? Besides how everyone wants us to split up, I mean."

She sucked in a breath. "I think we should talk about expectations."

Despite his churning gut, he arranged his face in a mask of calm understanding. "Okay. Tell me what you mean."

The ticking of the wall clock echoed in the stillness while Anna chewed her lip. Finally, she huffed, "Okay. I think we shouldn't get carried away. We're..." She pointed from his chest to her own. "Friends, right? With benefits, but still—" She dragged a fingertip through a drop of spilled tomato broth, leaving a scarlet smear. "It's foolish of me to depend on you. And it's unfair. You've got your own life. Being with me will just drag you down, not to mention causing strife in your family."

Time to release the truth before it tore him open and splattered the remnants of his heart all over her pretty little kitchen. He took her hand in both of his and pressed it to his heart.

"Listen, Anna, I can't speak for you, but I know what I'm feeling is more than friendship. A lot more. And I don't want to pressure you, especially when everyone else is piling on, but please know I'm—"

"Oh, God." Her eyebrows shot up, and her fingers tightened on his with surprising strength.

He bolted to his feet. "What is it? Are you hurt? Should I take you to the hospital?"

Her bug-eyed expression melted into a wide smile. "The baby's moving." She placed his hand beside her navel. "There, feel it?"

Something fluttered beneath his palm. "I feel it. Amazing."

Anna tugged her sweater up and pressed his hand to her warm, bare skin. "She's dancing. It must be your soup."

The flutters continued, a syncopated rhythm of starts and stops.

Kneeling, he pressed his cheek to the spot. "Hi there, baby. I'm your Uncle Diego. Did you like the albóndigas?"

A movement whispered against his cheek, a tiny caress. Tears of wonder sprang to his eyes, and when he looked up at Anna, her eyes glistened too.

She stroked his hair. "She likes you."

Taking her hand, he pressed a kiss into her palm. "Does her mama like me enough to stick around despite all the trouble I've brought into her life?"

She made a sound halfway between a giggle and a hiccup. "Oh, Diego, I don't want to push you away. None of this is your fault."

He pulled her to her feet, then into his arms. Her warm, soft body molded to his, easy, effortless, perfect. "Then stay with me," he murmured into the silky mass of her hair. "We have the chance to be really happy together. Let's grab that chance and hold on tight."

She didn't answer, but she wrapped her arms around his middle and squeezed. And that was enough.

Chapter Nineteen: Betrayal Served Hot and Cold

♥

Jiggling in her seat, Anna glanced again at the slow-motion clock in the divorce mediator's waiting room. The receptionist looked up with a bland smile. "We're ready for you as soon as your husband arrives."

Brock was already ten minutes late. Since his stupid stunt on Saint Patrick's Day, his insincere apologies had dried up, replaced by passive-aggressive bull dookie like this. Would he even show up this time? He'd cancelled their first scheduled appointment at the last minute, costing her time off from work. The next available appointment was today, April Fool's Day. Surely, that had to be a bad omen.

So here she sat in a beige-on-beige waiting room, hoping they could work out a plan like two reasonable adults. Not freakin' likely.

The front door whooshed open, letting in a blast of rainy wind as her ex stepped through, eyes narrowed, back ramrod straight. Everything about him looked crisp to the point of brittleness—sharp creases in his khaki pants, starched dress shirt in a goose shit green, stiffly gelled blond hair. Even the blade of his nose looked sharper.

"Ow." Charlie pried Anna's tightly clamped fingers from her wrist.

"Sorry," Anna whispered.

Brock stepped aside to reveal his equally pointy mother, who regarded Anna with a disdainful sniff. Neither of them carried the documents the mediator had requested, as far as Anna could tell. Perhaps Deborah had stuffed them into her designer handbag, along with snacks for her poor snookums.

Anna focused on the manila envelope in her lap—insurance forms, tax returns, bank statements. Solid stuff she could wrap her beleaguered brain around, unlike the nebulous future of their unborn child.

Deborah sat on the sofa opposite them and whispered to her son, shooting squinty glares at Anna and Charlie.

"Ignore them," Charlie murmured. "You're a strong, smart woman. You know what you want. Don't let them sway you."

I want Diego here holding my hand. She batted away that unhelpful thought and counted her breaths—in for a count of four, hold for seven, out for eight...

A door opened behind the receptionist's desk, and a tall, silver-haired woman stepped through. "Mr. Spencer? Ms. Khoury?"

Deborah sucked her teeth, just like she did every time someone said Anna's last name. Now, more than ever, Anna was glad she'd stuck to her guns on that point. At least she wouldn't have to change her name when the divorce went through. One less knot of red tape.

Brock rose and smeared on the same phony smile he gave his customers at Furniture World. "Hello, Ms. Jefferson. I'm Brock. Thanks for meeting with us today."

Suck-up. I'm the one who set this up. Anna stepped forward. So did Deborah.

The mediator tilted her head. "Are you Mr. Spencer's attorney?"

She squared her shoulders. "I'm his mother."

"I see." Ms. Jefferson bit her lip as if restraining a smile. "Nice of you to offer support, but I'll only be speaking with the parties involved."

"But she's here." Deborah pointed at Charlie, who calmly pulled a tablet from her messenger bag.

"Take your time, Anna. I've got plenty of work to do." The smile she shot Deborah oozed snark.

Inside the mediator's office, Anna sank into a cushy leather armchair facing the broad oak desk. Brock took the other chair, draped one arm over the back, and spread his knees wide.

The mediator took her seat and folded her hands atop a legal pad. "Now then, why don't you call me Pamela? I'm a retired family court judge, and I'm here to help you reach a fair division of your property and a custody arrangement for your child." Her smile grew warmer. "Congratulations, by the way."

Anna liked her immediately. She projected the same no-nonsense attitude tempered with kindness as her own Aunt Hala, and perhaps Diego's Abuelita.

Pamela uncapped an expensive-looking pen. "Did you bring the documents I requested?"

Anna set her envelope on the desk.

Brock folded his arms. "I thought we were just here to talk."

The older woman lifted her chin and stared down her broad nose at Brock. "Our goal today is to set a framework for reaching a fair decision. That will go best for you both if you cooperate, Mr. Spencer." Easy to picture her with judicial robes and a gavel—the perfect tool for smacking some sense into her obstinate ex.

Brock glared at Anna. "Well, I don't want this divorce."

Pamela sighed. "Mr. Spenser, Washington is a no-fault divorce state. Your agreement is not necessary for the divorce to go forward. If your wife—may I call you Anna, dear?"

"Yes, ma'am."

"If Anna wants a divorce, she'll get one. You can work out your differences or not, but as a mother and a grandmother, let me impress upon you that a contentious attitude will harm your child. Is that what you want?" Her laser-sharp stare pushed him back into his seat.

"I guess not. But she's got a boyfriend too. She's got no right to judge me."

A wave of icy heaviness pressed Anna down. Stupid of her to let Diego serve the divorce papers on Brock. If she'd been patient and hired a professional, Brock might not even know of Diego's existence.

"Young man, you are trying my patience." Pamela crossed her arms over her impressive bosom. "You are not here to play the blame game, and I'm not here to listen to you squabble. Are we clear?"

"Yes, but—"

Planting her hands on the desk, the judge rose and loomed over them both. "I don't take kindly to having my time wasted—time for which you are paying, by the way." She pointed a long finger at his chest. "And do not mistake me, Brock. Solving your differences through mediation is far less expensive than a contested divorce, which is much more likely to go in Anna's favor. If my son were in your shoes, I'd advise him to pull up his big boy pants and get with the program."

"Fine. Okay. I'm listening," Brock grumbled into his lap.

"Good." Pamela sat and rolled her shoulders. "Now, the usual arrangement in this situation is to provide for frequent short visits with the non-custodial parent in order to facilitate bonding with the child. A few hours a day, usually."

Anna released in involuntary squawk.

"What's that, dear?"

"Sorry. Something caught in my throat." And in her stomach, which curdled at the idea of seeing Brock a few hours each day. Or worse, handing their child over to him for a visit. What if he snatched the baby and ran?

Pamela continued, "When the child is older, the usual arrangement is for the child to stay with the non-custodial parent every other weekend, plus a mid-week evening visit, and for the parents to split vacation time. Lately, courts are amendable to longer visits for the non-custodial parent, such as week on, week off during the summer."

Brock shot Anna a sour look. "Why can't it be week on week off all year long?"

"Children need a home base—at least, that's the current thinking in most cases."

"But Anna works."

"So do you," Anna snapped back. "What's your point?"

His lip curled. "Who's gonna watch the baby? That's why we're here, right? To do what's best for the baby." His stare froze Anna's blood. "My mom's home all day. She could watch the baby until I find a new wife—one who puts family first."

Anna's heart halted. Her throat closed. Was he serious, or just spouting bull crap to harass her?

Pamela closed her eyes and massaged the bridge of her nose. "If you're suggesting Anna's status as a working mother makes her unfit, let me remind you we're living in the twenty-first century. You won't find a judge who'll award you primary custody on those grounds."

"Primary custody?" Anna bolted to her feet. "Are you seriously thinking I'd surrender custody to your cheating a—" Feeling the sharpness of Pamela's stare, she sank back into her seat. "Apologies, ma'am."

Truth be told, beyond signing up for the hospital's daycare program, she hadn't yet put much thought into what her daily routine would look like once the baby came.

Pamela rose, her expression stern. "I believe we've come as far as we can today. Before you schedule your next appointment, make sure I have all your paperwork." She shot Brock a pointed look. "And bring your attorneys next time."

"Yes ma'am." Brock's tone dripped scorn, as did the glare he gave Anna.

His all-out attack left her struggling for breath. She figured they'd squabble for a while, then come to terms. Now, it looked like he was hatching some evil plan to grab custody of Mango.

Her hand strayed to her belly as Brock stalked from the room.

She turned to the mediator. "Ma'am, do you think he could actually get primary custody?"

Pamela's expression softened. "To do that, he'd have to prove you an unfit mother. You got a drug habit? A criminal record? A brothel in your basement?"

"No, ma'am."

"Then he's highly unlikely to succeed. That sexist bullshit about working moms being unfit won't fly in today's system."

Pamela moved around the desk and rested a hand on Anna's shoulder. "Here's my advice. While you're pregnant, give your ex the chance to be involved, and keep written track of his contribution. Don't give him ammunition to prove you're shutting him out of his child's life. Let him know about medical appointments, birth classes, all that stuff. Discussion of baby names, items he buys for the nursery, write it all down. That way, if custody becomes contested, you'll be prepared."

"Do I need witnesses?"

"Not a bad idea." She gave Anna's shoulder a gentle squeeze. "And try not to worry too much. Most couples start out acrimonious, but they usually end up doing what's right for the kids."

The kindness in the older woman's eyes eased some of the tension from Anna's rigid muscles. "I hope you're right. And thank you."

Back in the waiting room, Charlie enfolded her in a tight hug. "Okay then, you got through the first step, and you're still standing."

"Barely." She sniffed and gave her sister a watery smile. "Can we stop on the way home? I need a notebook."

After leaving Abuelita in the foyer to greet her great-grandkids, Diego stepped into his parents' kitchen and slid his tray of empanadas into the oven to keep warm. Today's contribution to the Vargas Sunday dinner was Anna-inspired, though he wouldn't admit it to his family. He'd adapted a recipe for sfeehas, Lebanese meat pies filled with ground lamb cooked in ghee with onion, tomato, and rich spices, plus tahini for creaminess and pomegranate molasses for tang. The scent wafting from the oven made his stomach rumble. He couldn't wait to get Anna's take on these beauties.

Feminine voices in the hallway drew nearer.

"You get in here, missy. I want to talk to you." Scowling like thunder, his grandmother marched into the kitchen dragging Elena by her sleeve.

Oh no! Not here, not now. But it was too late—Abuelita was in full-on scolding mode. "Teaching," she liked to call it, and it was Elena's turn for a lesson.

This morning, while he tinkered with his recipe, Abuelita had peppered him with questions about Anna—was she showing yet? Did she know the baby's sex? Was he really ready to become a stepfather? What did Elena think of all this?

Lying to Abuelita was an exercise in futility since she always saw right through him. So he told the truth—their romance had ended Anna and Elena's friendship, and Anna was heartbroken over the loss. Abuelita went quiet then, glowering under painted-on brows as she banged pots and pans. Her only comment, "I will pray for you. All three of you."

And she did, muttering under her breath throughout mass. Now, she was ready to unload whatever wisdom the angels had leant her.

Abuelita pushed Elena into a chair. "You. Sit." She pointed to Diego. "You too."

Feeling about three feet tall, he complied.

"Now, Gordita, I wanna hear why you're causing your brother and your friend so much grief."

Elena blanched and opened her mouth to respond, but Abuelita cut her off.

"You are hurting people you are supposed to love. People who stood by you in your time of need."

"I just—"

"No excuses." She waggled a finger under Elena's nose. "Took me a while to remember where I'd met Anna before. It was your baby shower. That girl rushed around all afternoon, making sure everything was perfect. You told me she was like a sister to you. And now, when she needs your support, you abandon her because she likes your brother." She waved a hand at Diego. "What's wrong with him, huh? Not good enough for your friend?"

Elena tilted her head back and blinked at the ceiling. "'Lita, she's still married."

"Did your divorce happen overnight? Eh?"

Diego bit back a snarky grin as their grandmother rack up point after point.

"And she's pregnant."

'Lita screwed up her face, and for a moment Diego thought she was about to spit on the floor. But she settled for a disgusted tisk. "Hypocrite."

"Me?"

"You haven't been living like a nun. The whole family knows." At Elena's gasp, she added, "Or suspects, anyway. But you're a grown woman, and your business is your business."

A whoop sounded in the hall, and Elena's son bolted into the kitchen, his two cousins hot on his heels. "Tío D is base!" he shrieked and clambered into Diego's lap, his bony little knee landing perilously close to sensitive territory.

"No fair!" Anita wailed, stomping her foot.

Abuelita rounded on them. "You kids get outta here. We're having a serious grown-up talk."

"Grown-up talk about what?" Dad asked, ambling into the kitchen. He sniffed, then went to the oven and peeked inside. "Smells good, son. What's the empanada del día?"

"Lamb with Lebanese spices," he grumbled. Elena shot him a barbed glance, but she held her tongue, thank God. How long she'd continue was anyone's guess.

"I want a hot pocket!" Oscar declared.

Diego stood. "And you'll have one when we sit down to dinner. Now scoot so we can finish getting ready." He moved to the counter to stir the tahini-lemon sauce and prayed everyone but Elena would vacate the kitchen. He should've confronted his sister long ago, instead of hoping time would loosen her grudge. Now, it seemed, Abuelita was forcing their hand.

But no such luck. Mom bustled in, issuing orders. "Papa, come carve this ham. Jorge, you and Linda get the kids to the table. Elena, take the green beans."

And so they all settled in their customary places around the dining table, with Diego between the kids and Abuelita.

Tension from their argument lingered as Diego passed the empanadas. Elena, still red-face, kept her eyes on her plate.

Oscar took a bite of his pastry and wrinkled his nose. "This tastes funny."

"It's Lebanese," Diego told him.

"Where's that?" little Anita demanded.

"In the Middle East," her mother said.

"Like Egypt?" Anita dribbled tahini sauce onto her plate. "Do they walk sideways too?"

Linda chuckled. "We got a book about King Tut. She's been posing like tomb art all week."

Elena made a strangled sound, somewhere between a cough and a growl.

"You okay, Mama?" Oscar popped out of his chair. "I can do the Heimling on you. I'm super strong."

"Sit." She barked, then turned to Diego with an air of icy calm. "Actually, 'Nita, your tío got this recipe from his girlfriend. His pregnant girlfriend."

The room went silent. All around the table, forks froze halfway to mouths. Then Oscar piped up. "Cool! Am I gonna have a brother or a sister?"

"Neither, Corazón." Elena's smile dripped poison. "You see, Diego's not the baby's father."

That opened the floodgates. Everyone shouted at once, a chorus of "Are you crazy?" and "Not in front of the kids" and a few Spanish phrases Diego was pretty sure he'd never heard before. He sank lower in his seat as the verbal volleys flew.

"Come on, kids." Linda used her sing-song teacher voice. "Let's take our empanadas into the living room."

"Can we watch Sponge Bob?" Oscar bounced on his toes, oblivious to the chaos.

"You bet." She shepherded the littles out of the room. A moment later, the TV blared loud enough to cover the hissed conversation in the dining room.

Diego sent up a silent prayer of thanks for his level-headed sister-in-law. Jorge didn't deserve her.

Dad's deep voice cut off the others. "Hijo, explain yourself."

Abuelita set down her silverware with a clang. "Anna is a nice girl. It's not her fault her husband was a cheating bastard."

Diego cringed. She meant well, but she was not helping.

It had been years since Diego heard his father's voice this tight. "I didn't ask you, Mama. I asked Diego."

Baffled by his grandmother's sudden change of heart about Anna, Diego glanced around the table at the rest of the family. Dad's jowly face flushed a deep shade of maroon. Mama's was bright pink. Jorge looked smug—nothing new there. Luisita shot him a look of sympathy. And Elena hunched over her plate, her stony expression hard to read. They'd always been close, the youngest and oldest siblings. Why would she turn on him like this? Was it Anna's happiness she wanted to ruin?

He straightened in his seat, pushed his plate back, and folded his hands on the table. "Okay. What Elena says is true. I've been seeing her friend Anna." He gave the word friend extra punch and had the satisfaction of seeing Elena flinch.

"We met back in December, shortly after she left her husband, who cheated on her. And yes, she's pregnant with his child. But they're getting a divorce."

Dad's nostrils flared on a deep inhale. Mama touched Dad's forearm, but he ignored her, his gaze boring holes into Diego's skull. "And you've inserted yourself into their mess?"

"Yes. I care for her. Very much."

"But baby." Mama's voice quavered. "If you weren't in the middle of this, she might decide to work things out for the baby's sake."

And maybe cows will fly over Tacoma. It was long past time to assert himself with the family. He was a grown-ass man who knew his own mind—and his own heart. He forced his voice and gaze to remain steady. "Mama, would you advise your daughter to go back to a man who cheated on her?"

She sighed and dropped her gaze.

He shot Elena a sharp glance. Cheating had been part of the reason she left her horrible husband. She had other reasons too, and leaving him was absolutely the right decision. He addressed his next comment to her. "Anna doesn't want her ex back. But if she changes her mind, I'll step aside."

Luisita spoke up, a rare occurrence at the Vargas table. "Are you in love with her?"

He raised his gaze to the ceiling. No guiding angels up there, but the twinkle of the chandelier crystals gave him something to focus on while he searched his heart. It didn't seem right to say the words to his family before saying them to Anna, but maybe if they understood, they'd accept her. More than anything, he wanted to build a future with Anna—married, or just sharing a home. Or even living apart if that's what she needed. No matter how things shook out, no matter who else was involved, he and Anna should be family.

It started with a bolt out of the blue that shocked him to the marrow of his bones. But now, four months in, he and Anna shared so much more than mere physical passion. And there was so much about her to love—her generous laughter, her determination, her gentle way with Abuelita, her strength. Facing the toughest challenge a woman could, she stepped forward every day into an uncertain future. She was going to be an amazing mom, and the thought of meeting little Mango filled him with joy. Already, he felt connected to the little squirt. The child wasn't his, but she was Anna's, and that was all that mattered.

Smiling again, he faced his younger sister. "Yes. I'm in love with Anna. And she loves me." Okay, she hadn't told him explicitly, but he saw the truth in her eyes, in her touch, in the way she listened and shared and opened her heart to him. He didn't need the words, he just needed Anna.

Dad leaned back in his chair, smacked his forehead, and groaned. "Still as flakey as ever."

And there it was, the hated family label he'd never shake off. Why did he even try?

Abuelita pushed back from the table and glared at her oldest son. "Hijo, you disappoint me."

"Me?" Dad pointed at his chest, then at Diego. "This one poaches a pregnant woman and you're disappointed in me?" He shook his head. "I expect such foolishness from Diego, but from you, Mama?"

Abuelita stuck out her chin. "I've met the girl. She's a nurse like Elena. She's respectful and polite, and she looks at Diego like he hung the moon and stars. If she weren't pregnant, you'd be glad to welcome her into the family."

Diego's eyes prickled with tears. All this time, he thought Abuelita barely tolerated Anna for his sake—and here she was defending their love.

Dad shook his head. "My brothers were right."

"About what, Antonio?" Abuelita asked.

"We've been talking for some time now. We hate to worry about you, and this—" He waved a dismissive hand toward Diego. "This proves we can't trust Diego's judgment. We need someone more responsible looking after you."

Diego's heart sank like a runaway elevator. His romance drama was going to cost Abuelita her freedom. He should've lied, should've told the family Elena was wrong, and Anna was just a friend. But Dad and the tíos had been looking to send Abuelita away for years. If this mess hadn't given the excuse they needed, they would've found another. He had to protect her somehow.

Abuelita folded her arms. "I trust Diego. And so should you."

Mama patted Abuelita's arm. "We know you've been sleepwalking."

Diego's breath froze in his throat. Elena was the only person he'd told about 'Lita's nighttime rambles since she was a medical professional and might know how to help. And she'd sworn not to tell the family. Was there no end to her hatefulness?

He glared across the table, and she cringed like a dog caught chewing the sofa cushions.

Dad stood and smoothed his sauce-speckled shirt. "Mama, it's time we found you an assisted living facility. You'll be safe, and Diego can chase whatever crazy scheme his heart desires."

"Stop right there." Diego had never heard his grandmother speak so sharply. She rose unsteadily to her feet and glared at his parents. "You are in for a fight, Antonio, if you think you can force me from my home. I know my rights. Diego, darling, I would like to go home now. All this betrayal has spoiled my appetite."

A high-pitched whimper yanked their focus to the doorway. Oscar stood there clutching his stuffed tiger. "Are you sending Abuelita to jail?"

Elena folded her son tight against her side, stroking his hair.

Diego followed Abuelita into the hallway. Dad trotted up behind them, huffing and puffing. "Mama, you have to listen to reason. We love you. We only want what's best for you."

"That's not for you to decide." She slid into the coat Diego held for her. "And until you can treat me with the respect I deserve, I don't want to talk to you. Let's go, Diego."

His heart in ashes, he followed her out the door. But he threw a final backward glance at his family home, a place he'd always felt, if not respected, at least welcome. But today's debacle had revealed ugly cracks in the foundation of his life. Home would never look the same again.

Chapter Twenty: Love, Interrupted

♥

Anna wove her fingers through Diego's and shifted uncomfortably on her hard plastic seat in the imaging center's waiting room. She knew it helped the ultrasound tech get a clearer image of the baby, but this full-bladder torture made it hard to concentrate on what he was saying.

"If he shows up, I'll leave, okay? I don't want to make a scene." Diego's eyes shone huge and dark and earnest.

She squeezed his hand. "We're already half an hour past my appointment time. If Brock hasn't shown up by now, he's not going to." Following the divorce mediator's suggestion, she made a note in her phone: 4/12, ultrasound, Brock no-show. So much for his claims about wanting to be a family again. Jerk face. Little Carrot deserved better, someone excited to see her grow and change—someone like Diego?

He scooted a little closer, the scrape of his chair loud in the little room. The receptionist glanced up with a bland smile. "Just a few more minutes, guys."

"Listen." He squeezed her hand. "I'm gonna ask you something, and if the answer is 'none of your business,' that's a hundred percent okay." The intensity in his gaze kicked her pulse up a notch.

"Okay. Go ahead."

"How are you and Brock going to handle all this?" His wave took in the waiting room filled with bland abstract art and restless-looking pregnant women. "I mean, what kind of relationship do you want with him?"

Damn good question. "Tala, my friend from work, has an amicable relationship with her ex. They meet up for ball games, birthdays, all the important kid stuff. When it really counts, their daughter can look into the crowd and see both parents cheering her on. It's nice. Civilized. I'd like something like that with Brock, but I doubt it'll ever happen."

Holding her gaze, he nodded slowly. This must be so hard on him, figuring out where he fit into this mess. That he was even trying was a miracle.

She gave his hand another squeeze. "Thanks for coming."

His smile bloomed wider. "Thanks for letting me."

A door beside the receptionist's desk opened. "Anna?

Anna rose. So did Diego, then half-sat again.

"You too, Dad." The gray-haired tech beckoned. "You'll want to see this."

Anna opened her mouth to correct her, then thought better of it. Too complicated to explain, and why not let Diego meet the baby properly?

The ultrasound tech got Anna situated on the table and Diego on a stool beside her, then squirted cold gel onto Anna's bare tummy. Grinning like a kid about to watch his favorite movie, Diego stroked Anna's shoulder and stared at the screen.

The tech lifted her transducer. "Okay, lovebirds, we're checking your baby's anatomy to make sure everything's in the right place."

On the screen, various blobs swam into focus. The tech hummed as she rolled the scanner across Anna's belly, pressing gently. "Liver looks good, kidneys, lungs. And this —" She shifted the instrument again— "is your baby's heart. A good, strong one."

Awestruck, Anna gaped at the tiny, fluttering spot on the screen. She'd learned in nursing school how the gel helped the transducer see through muscle and tissue into the developing baby's hidden world, but experiencing this view first-hand stole her breath. There she—well, it—was. A tiny person growing inside her. A miracle.

She turned to Diego. "Isn't she amazing?"

Eyes glistening, he stroked her cheek. "She's beautiful. I think she has your nose."

The tech chuckled as she slid her transducer into a new position. "So, you already know the sex?"

"Oh. No, actually. It's just a feeling."

"Well, the baby's limbs look good, so does the spine. Do you want to know the sex, or would you rather be surprised?"

Anna held Diego's gaze. "You know, naming a baby is a huge responsibility. I'll need time to find a good one."

His grin widened.

"You concur, Dad?" the tech asked.

"Oh, I—" He chewed his lip and searched Anna's face for the right answer.

What was the harm in sharing this magical moment with the guy she adored? Other moms got the support of a devoted partner—why shouldn't she? She took Diego's hand and nodded.

"Yeah." Holding Anna's gaze, he said, "Let's find out."

"All righty." More gentle prodding. "Drat, she's hunched over. Roll onto your left side, hon'."

Anna shifted, and so did the baby, apparently.

"Come on, little one," the tech muttered. "Show Aunt Tessa what you've got between those perfect legs." With a wide smile, she looked up. "Congratulations. You're having a girl."

"Really?" Anna reached for Diego, her heart so full it might burst from her chest and fly around the room.

His smile could've lit the whole hospital. While the tech peeled off her gloves and washed up, he scooped Anna into a tight hug. "You were right," he whispered into her ear. "We're having a girl. I mean, you are." He stroked her cheek with his finger. "You're amazing, Anna."

"I can't wait for you to meet her." She rubbed her goopy tummy. "Carrot, your Uncle Diego is the most wonderful man."

Maybe it was the pregnancy hormones making her blood fizz like champagne, maybe it was his impossible sweetness, but she had to kiss him right now or she'd float off the table. So she did, smearing his shirt with ultrasound gel as she laughed against his lips. "A girl. Carrot's a girl."

Returning with a handful of paper towels, the tech beamed. "I swear, you two are the cutest couple I've seen all week. Your baby is lucky to have such loving parents."

What was the harm in pretending? Just for this moment, Anna let herself imagine a future where she and Diego raised this baby, this badly timed blessing, and no one challenged their love. A happy little family. Why not? There must be a reason why Diego entered her life when he did. Like they say, love works in mysterious ways.

After her ultrasound appointment, Anna had to go back to work, where she drifted a foot off the ground for the rest of her shift. Not only did she have the best news and a new photo for her baby album, but Diego had taken the night off and promised her a special surprise. Her mouth watered at the prospect—and other parts further south tingled in anticipation. Though worries about his grandmother still sent him home well before dawn, he'd been stretching their time together a bit longer. It wasn't her place to push, but she hoped he'd soon work out a way to spend the whole night in her arms. She craved waking up to his sleepy-soft body almost as much as she craved his cooking.

She'd just finished freshening her room when Charlie and River left for work. "Have fun tonight," River called down the hallway. "Don't do anything we wouldn't do."

Well, that didn't leave much territory. River had been sharing Charlie's room for three months now, and Anna still cringed whenever their noisy lovemaking echoed down the hall. Before she and Diego got down to amorous business, Anna always put on some music to dampen the sounds. She wished Charlie and River would do the same.

She got to work setting the table in the dining room. Today's shared joy at the hospital made tonight feel like a special occasion, so she set out silver candlesticks and their grandmother's good china. The doorbell rang, and she dashed to answer.

"Evening, angel." His curls damp from the spring drizzle, he cradled a crock pot in his arms. A plastic shopping tote hung from his shoulder, and a shiny gift bag dangled from his wrist.

"Aww, Diego, you didn't have to—"

Sliding past her, he smooched her cheek on the way to the kitchen. "Just a little something to mark a special night."

"Special day, you mean?" She followed, sniffing the savory steam wafting from beneath the glass lid.

"Both." He set the dish on the counter, then lifted her in a movie-worthy twirl before setting her down and kissing her breathless. Then he dropped to one knee, lifted her top, and smooched her belly. "Evening, Miss Carrot."

Silly, the way a shiver raced up her spine at the sight of him kneeling before her. But he popped back up, dashed to the counter, and whisked the lid off the slow cooker. "Braised pork spareribs with poblanos, corn, and zucchini." From the shopping bag, he pulled foil-wrapped tortillas, a glass bowl of salad, and a tiny dish of crumbled cheese. "Cotija," he told her as he pried off the lid. "To sprinkle on the meat, or the salad." He waggled his eyebrows. "Or your boyfriend. Wherever you like."

He dished up their plates and carried them to the dining room. Suddenly starving, she attacked her portion of falling-off-the-bone meat, sopping up the rich, tomatoey sauce with tortillas. When she looked up, she found him grinning, his chin propped on his palm.

"I love watching you eat."

She grunted and blotted her sauce-stained face. "Ugh. I'm a pig."

"You're a sexy siren." With his napkin, he wiped a spot of sauce from the corner of her mouth.

Crossing her arms over her growing belly, she pursed her lips. "You know, everyone says you shouldn't find me attractive. I'm getting thicker and thicker, and—" The thought pricked her with alarm. "You've seen my stretch marks." Just last week she'd noticed the first shiny pink lightning bolts on her lower belly.

His smile slid toward feral. "Tiger stripes, angel. Signs of your wild side."

She stared for a moment. Was he for real?

He hooked his hands into claws and growled before launching from his seat and burying his face in the crook of her neck. "Nom, nom, nom."

"Stop, you goof!" She smacked him with her napkin. "You'll get sauce on my shirt."

"I'll wash it." He nibbled his way up her neck, licked behind her ear, then took her lobe between his teeth and applied just enough pressure to make her moan.

She let her head loll back, inviting more intoxicating kisses. "We're done with dinner, then?"

"I'm hungrier for you." His laugh rumbled against her skin. "Cheesy, but true."

"Fine by me." She grasped his hand and sucked his fingers clean, one by one.

"Okay, okay. Wait." Gulping a breath, he pushed back from the table. "Time for your first surprise. Why don't I clean up the table while you go get naked?"

Giggling, she complied. While he rattled dishes in the kitchen, she brushed her teeth, lit candles in the bedroom and pulled up a sexy R & B playlist before shedding her clothes and gliding between the sheets. She heard water running in the bathroom—he'd taken to leaving a toothbrush and shower things here. While she waited, she tried pose after pose, searching for the most flattering view of her decidedly round belly.

He appeared in the doorway, barefoot, wearing only jeans and a shirt open over golden skin. Dark hair dusted his sculpted torso, and her fingers itched to trace those hypnotic whorls.

Banked fire glimmered in his ebony eyes. "Look at you," he rasped, stepping nearer.

Delicious shivers danced over her skin. Wonderous, the way he could make her feel like a lush goddess with just a hungry glance, a few whispered words.

"Surprise number one." He held up the gift bag she hadn't noticed him carrying—too focused on the shifting of his muscles as he prowled toward her.

He placed the package before her, then knelt beside the bed and ran his fingertips over her flank, down her thigh, back to the dip of her waist...

"Aren't you going to open it?"

"Huh?" She tore her gaze from his face to the package before her. "Oh."

Inside, beneath lavender-scented tissue paper, she found a large jar printed with vines and flowers. "Earth Mama Stretch Mark Balm," she read aloud. Horror curled her bare toes. "They're that noticeable?"

Eyes wide, he pried the jar from her hands. "No, no, no. See, I was at the natural food store looking for poblanos, and there was a demo of lotions and stuff." He pried the jar open. "The woman rubbed some of this on my arm."

I'll bet she did. Anna felt her lips curl into a scowl.

He held it to her nose, "It smells really good, and it's supposed to be good for your skin." He scooped up a generous dollop. "It felt so silky, all I could think of was massaging some into your bare skin." He stroked the cream around the curve of her belly, a cool, satin glide. "The thought made me hard, right there in the toiletries aisle. Pretty embarrassing."

Round and round his fingers glided, smoothing, soothing...and somehow, she forgot to feel jealous of the saleswoman or irritated with Diego for letting himself be fondled in public. Because he was here with her, warming her skin with his broad palms, his tousled head dropping lower, lower, until the tip of his tongue swirled over her breast in a dizzying spiral.

She stretched like a spoiled Persian cat and gave him her other side to caress. And he did a wonderful job, lubing her skin with the rich cream that smelled like a summer garden.

"What's in this stuff, magic fairy dust?" she muttered into the pillow.

He glanced at the label. "Organic olive oil, argan oil, shea butter, coconut oil, avocado oil, rosewater, vitamin E."

"Sounds like one of your delicious dishes." She arched her back on a hiss. "Yes, please. More there."

While he kneaded her breasts, he moved over her, his muscular thigh settling between her legs, course hair tickling her sensitive folds. Where did his pants go? Clever boy, he'd shed his clothing somewhere along the way. The hot length of his shaft pressed rhythmically against her hip.

She reached for him, but he gently shoved her hand away. "Just relax, angel. Let me make you feel good."

"You are. You always do."

His low laughter rumbled against her ribs as he spread more cream over the sensitive skin of her inner thighs. Whimpering, she opened to him. He shifted to lie on his side, his warm body pressed against her from shoulder to hip. Lifting her thigh, he danced feathery strokes over her folds, his hips rocking in counterpoint to his teasing caresses. "Angel," he muttered into her hair. "You make me burn in the most delicious way." His shaft glided over her pussy, sliding in the slickness.

Aching, desperate for more friction, she grasped his cock and pressed it firmly against her clit. He thrust faster, his heated shaft tantalizing her nerve endings with each pass. Her muscles quaked as heavenly pressure built, achingly delicious but not quite enough.

"Please, Diego. Give me what I need."

"That's all I want to do, angel." His fingers teased her clit in swift, tight circles while the fat head of his cock nudged, pushed, glided deep inside. One thrust, two, and a bolt of bliss sent her body soaring.

Gripping her hips, Diego pummeled her until, with a harsh cry, he froze, his only movement the pulsing of his cock deep inside her.

Slowly, the heaving of his chest subsided into a chuckle. He nuzzled her bed-snarled hair. "That was—wow."

"It always is, with you." She nestled into his encircling arms, but the sweet afterglow wasn't enough to erase the bittersweet pang that always followed their joining. "I wish you could stay."

He pushed onto his elbow. "No fair. You guessed my second surprise."

"Huh?" She rolled to face him.

"Abuelita's friend is spending the night. They're having a pajama party."

"You mean it?"

Ginning, he nodded. "It started as a joke, but she went and arranged it all—stockpiled snacks, borrowed a huge stack of DVDs from the library. That's all the tech she can handle. Anyway." He kissed her temple. "If it's all right with you, I'd like to spend the night."

She wove her fingers into his silky hair and pressed her forehead to his. "Nothing could make me happier."

A wiggle in her belly made her gasp. Another followed, and another. She grabbed Diego's hand. "Baby Carrot is happy too. She wants you to stay, don't you, little one?"

He slid down the mattress and pressed a kiss over the dancing baby. "You are amazing, Miss Carrot. And so is your mama."

Anna's fingers moved through his hair, and the words just tumbled out, as impossible to stop as time. "I love you, Diego."

He popped up to his knees, eyes wide, mouth open, cock still half-hard. "You do?"

She pressed kiss to his palm. "I do."

With a boyish whoop, he scooped her into his arms and rolled her atop him. Cupping her cheeks, he gazed at her through joy-crinkled eyes. "Nothing in the world could make me happier. I love you too. I want to be with you, now and tomorrow and always."

The baby kicked again. Giggling, Anna pressed Diego's palm over the spot. "That's a yes vote from Carrot, I think."

"And from you?"

Straddling him, she rocked her still-tingling pussy against his firm cock. "Well, it's going to be a long, rocky struggle until I'm free to promise you always, so let's start with today."

He gripped her hips and ground against her. "And tomorrow?"

"Tomorrow too." She leaned forward to kiss him, her hair falling like a curtain that shut out the world and hid any obstacles from view. For now, it was just the two of them, together in sweet peace.

And then, from somewhere near the foot of the bed, his phone shrilled.

Chapter Twenty-One: Abuelita Up and Down

♥

Hopping on one foot, halfway into his jeans, Diego held the phone to his ear, barely able to understand the old lady over the hammering of his heart and Anna's insistent cries of "What is it? What's wrong?"

"Okay. Right. I'm on my way." He dropped the phone and tugged on the rest of his clothing.

Still in bed, Anna clutched the covers to her chest, her lovely face sharp and pale.

"Abuelita fell," he told her. "Where the hell did I leave my shoes?"

"Bathroom?" She sprang from the bed and threw open a drawer. "I'm coming with you."

"No, you can't."

She flinched at his sharp tone.

"Shit, I'm sorry." He swiped a sweaty palm down his face. "It's just, 'Lita's friend already called Elena."

"Oh, okay." Clutching a T-shirt, she stared at her bare toes.

"Please understand, angel." He raised his hands and let them drop. "I should've been there. What was I thinking, leaving her in the hands of another old lady?"

Anna's face crumpled, but she didn't cry. "It wasn't your fault. Now go."

Throwing his arms around her, he squeezed her tight. His voice broke as he murmured, "I love you."

"Yeah, me too. Call me when you know something."

He dashed out the door, cranked his pick-up's engine, and tore across town. He threw open Abuelita's door expecting to find bloody mayhem, but all he saw was three non-bleeding women: Abuelita sprawled on the couch with her bare foot propped on pillows, Elena kneeling beside her, and Mrs. Reyes from church, pacing and chewing her knuckle.

"Too tight. Are you trying to rip my foot off?"

"For God's sake, 'Lita." Dressed in pajama pants and an oversize hoodie, Elena rocked back onto her heels and pushed her messy hair from her face. "You've got a bad sprain. If we don't compress it, it's gonna swell even more. Mrs. Reyes, where's that ice pack?"

"Sorry, dear," the other woman spluttered. "I'll just—"

"I'll get it." Diego strode past them, into the kitchen where he fetched the cold pack they kept behind the frozen peas. This is how his perfect evening ended? A family squabble over a sprained ankle? He glared up at the shelf of angel figurines. "Where were you guys when I needed you?"

He returned to the kitchen and handed Elena the ice pack. "Where's Oscar?"

"With my neighbor. Her son is Oscar's best friend." The glance she shot him reminded him of a dog caught chewing the sofa cushions. What the hell was she feeling guilty about? It's not like she pushed Abuelita off the— He groaned.

"'Lita, were you climbing on the stepstool again?"

She huffed. "We wanted the good cookies, the ones I keep for special occasions."

"Right. In the tin above the fridge." He glared at her, then at her friend, who cringed.

Elena set the ice pack atop Abuelita's ankle. Even wrapped in an ace bandage, the purple tinge was visible, climbing up her shin and down toward her toes.

"How bad is it?" he asked his sister.

"No obvious break, but she should go to the emergency room and get an X-ray, just in case. At her age, even a small fracture can be quite serious."

"No." 'Lita crossed her arms. "Your papa is trying to lock me up in a home. This will just prove his point."

Diego stabbed a finger toward his sister. "Then why did you call Elena? She'll just tell Dad."

"I won't!" Elena's voice broke as tears dribbled down her flushed cheeks. "I never meant to hurt 'Lita." She raised her watery eyes to his. "Or you."

"Oh really? Sure looked like you were enjoying it when you told the fam about Anna."

She hunched as if he'd punched her. Her shoulders shook with silent sobs.

Abuelita's voice came soft but firm. "Diego, that's enough." She turned to her friend. "Thank you, Joyce. I'm sorry our sleepover didn't work out. Another time?"

"Sure." With a wobbly smile, Mrs. Reyes collected her things and headed out.

"Now then." 'Lita wiggled her butt deeper into the couch cushions. "Time for you two to talk this out."

Diego's head throbbed. Too much emotion in one night, ripped from the highest peak to the lowest swamp. It was exhausting. But Elena's inexplicable hatred was a barrier between him and Anna. He owed it to her, and to Baby Carrot, to at least try to breach this wall.

He straightened his shoulders. "Okay, 'Lena. I'm listening. Why do you hate Anna and me so much?"

She hugged her knees to her chest and rested her chin on them. "I don't hate either of you. I just want to protect you from pain."

"By causing more pain? For Abuelita too?"

"That's not what I wanted." She shoved a hand through her hair. "I can't believe Dad's actually talking to a lawyer about getting 'Lita declared incompetent. It's her life. She deserves to make her own decisions."

"Damn right I do," Abuelita grumbled.

"And Anna doesn't?" Diego wheeled on his sister. "Or me?"

Elena threw up her hands. "You just don't understand the pain you're setting yourself up for. Yes, okay, I overreacted because I was hurting. I should've handled this better, but damn!" She smacked the floor with her palm. "It's exhausting holding in my feelings all the time. It's so hard to always be a responsible grown-up and do the sensible thing—like forgetting about Justin." Her voice rose to a tearful squeak. "I thought I'd found the one, you know? I thought I wouldn't have to be alone anymore, and it just hurts so damn much." She swiped her streaming eyes with her sleeve. "And then I see you and Anna heading for the same heartache. I love you both. I wanted to spare you the pain because it'll never work out. Don't you see?"

"How do you know?" Abuelita interjected.

"Diego's too tender-hearted. He rushes into things. And Anna's so practical and strong. When Brock makes enough trouble, and he will, she'll end things with Diego to keep the peace. And he'll be crushed."

A chill prickled his skin. Elena had been Anna's friend for years. Surely, she knew Anna better than he did. Was she right? Would Anna set him aside when things got rough?

Abuelita spoke up. "Seems to me, carina, you're forgetting something important."

Elena sat up straighter. "What's that?"

"People change. They grow. They learn. You're not the same helpless girl who couldn't get out of bed when she caught her husband cheating and stealing her money, right? Look at you!" She chuckled. "Okay, maybe not right now, but in general, you're a bad-ass girl boss."

"'Lita!" Diego and Elena chorused.

"That's right, I can learn too. From the Facebook and the Instant Gram." She giggled. "My senior group, we're going to make a dance for the Ticky Tock to advertise the Saint Anthony's Festival. Father Polanski will film it."

Diego caught his sister's eye. She was biting her lip. Hard.

"My point is," Abuelita continued, "Diego's smarter than you give him credit for. And more mature. I've watched him plan this food truck step by step. He researches everything. No more leaping before he looks. And I've met Miss Anna. She's in love with your brother. Real love, not like your trifling boyfriend. It's a shame you can't see that."

Subdued, Elena stared at the floor. After several long, silent moments, she sniffled. "I'll think about it. In the meantime, maybe Oscar and I should move in here with you."

"With me? Why? Don't you like your apartment?"

"We like it fine. But Mom and Dad are right about one thing. It's not fair Diego has to watch you all the time."

Abuelita spluttered. "He doesn't have to watch me. I can handle my business, thank you very much."

Now it was his turn to splutter. "By falling off ladders? 'Lita, you could have broken a hip."

"And then you would be in a nursing home for sure," Elena added.

Diego shot her half a smile. Nice to be on the same side of an argument again.

"Okay, okay. Maybe I need more help." She pointed a crooked finger at each of them in turn. "But not at the expense of your sex lives."

Diego muttered out of the side of his mouth, "I can't believe she went there."

Elena giggled.

"Tell you what. Tomorrow, I will talk to Father Polanski. He has lots of good ideas."

"After you go to the urgent care clinic," Diego said. "I'll take you in the morning."

"Yeah, yeah." She subsided with a huff and closed her eyes. "All this arguing wears me out. Think I'll sleep here tonight."

Diego walked Elena to her car. Before dropping onto her seat, she darted forward and wrapped him in a tight hug. "I'm sorry, Gogo. I still think you and Anna is a terrible idea, but I'll keep out of it."

"Good." He watched her drive off, then turned back and climbed the stairs. Leaning on a porch pillar, he stared up at the stars. "But the damage is done, isn't it?" he asked whichever angels might be listening. "I have to choose— protect Abuelita or be with Anna. There's no way this ends well."

Two weeks later, Diego was relieved to see Abuelita back to her usual cheerful self, shuffling from her back porch to the Airstream with snacks and refrescos, her scary purple bruises hidden beneath pale pink slacks. She seemed to get such a kick out of the work party going on in her backyard, fussing over his friends from Bangers as if they were her own grandkids.

One good outcome from her accident—Abuelita finally relented and agreed to let Anna spend the night. Last night had been their third night together in his narrow bed —hardly ideal sleeping conditions. But waking up with his face mushed in Anna's hair, his arms around her cozy warmth, his happy dick nestled against the softness of her ass—that was heaven. Even if pregnancy did send her to the bathroom every two hours, he'd take sleeping with Anna over sleeping alone anytime.

"Diego," Rosie hollered from the other side of the Airstream. "Which color you want for the Angel's halo?" She and River, Bangers' window-mural artists, were painting the Empanada Angel's namesake beside the service window, along with his handle for the social media accounts Lana set up for his food truck.

He opened the window and leaned out. "I dunno, gold?"

"Yeah, but which one?" She held up two cans of paint.

"You're the artist. You pick." While he was grateful for their help, he was more concerned with being ready for Bangers' Cinco de Mayo bash than with picky details like halo colors. It was very generous of Dawn to let him replace last year's popular taco truck in the parking-lot beer garden. There were still so many details to arrange: food safety training for Anna, tax forms for his friend Milo from culinary school who'd agreed to help out, and his Health Department inspection on Monday. Plus, he'd have to scrape together a nauseating amount of money for licensing and registration fees. The new generator wiped out the last of his renovation fund.

Before meeting Anna, he might have humbled himself and asked his parents for a loan. But now, there was no way in heaven or hell they'd ever fork over the money. Thank God they hadn't caught wind of Abuelita's fall.

Anna and Charlie returned from the house with buckets of soapy water and spray cans of disinfectant. Giggling, they splashed each other as they scrubbed the interior. A moment later, Eddie poked his head inside, a tablet in his hand. "Okay, man. I got the total picture. It ain't pretty, I'm afraid."

Anna looked up, alarm written all over her beautiful face.

He smooched her cheek on his way out to confab with his volunteer bookkeeper. "It's nothing, angel. Just paperwork and red tape." And a hole in my bank account.

Diego sat beside Eddie at the picnic table. "Okay, hit me."

Eddie pinched the bridge of his nose with one hand and tapped the screen with the other. "It's tight, my friend. Like, squeaky tight. If you make your projected sales for Cinco de Mayo, you'll have enough to pay your helpers minimum wage for your next gig, but you're gonna have to rein in food costs." He hooked a thumb over his shoulder. "And if anything else breaks in that money pit, you're screwed."

"Ugh." Diego folded over and rested his head on the table. He'd budgeted for unexpected expenses, but he hadn't counted on there being so damn many of them.

A soft hand fell on his shoulder. "I'll give you what I can, love."

"No." He bolted upright and fixed her with a stern look. "Absolutely not. Your money is for you and the baby."

Abuelita tottered up with a tray of cookies and pastries. Of course, her sharp ears had caught the whole exchange. Why couldn't she be hard of hearing, like other old people?

"I told you, Corazón, I'll give you a loan."

"Nope." He flipped Eddie's tablet face down. "You've done more than enough to help. This is my project, and I'll find a way to make it work." Or die trying, which was beginning to feel like a very real possibility.

Besides, his dad had some kind of financial power of attorney. No doubt he was checking up on his mother's account. The disappearance of a large sum would provide more ammunition in his campaign to have 'Lita sent away. And it would be further proof of Diego's flakiness, a label he couldn't seem to shake no matter how well he planned and researched. It was like he was born under an unlucky star.

He pasted on a phony smile. "I've applied for a small-business loan. I'll hear soon. In the meantime, I'll just put the fees on my credit card and pay it off bit by bit." He had to prove to the family and to himself that he could handle this project on his own.

Abuelita raised her chin and sniffed. "I see. You'll take help from your friends but not from me"

Eddie raised an eyebrow, waiting for an answer.

"That's different," Diego protested. "They're giving me help, not money. And I'm paying them."

River called out, "Not taking your money, dude."

Eddie met Abuelita's stare with a grin. "And I'm working for cookies. These are delicious, Mrs. Vargas."

Abuelita sniffed again. "Looks like family to me."

After an awkward silence where Diego failed to give her the reaction she was looking for, she retreated to the house, grumbling all the way.

"Where are you going, 'Lita?" he called.

"Senior Club meeting at church." She shot him a final glare. "While I'm there, I'll pray for you. Maybe God will pound some sense into your stubborn head."

Eddie chuckled. "Grandmas. Can't tell 'em anything."

Diego massaged his aching forehead. "Yeah. Because they're usually right."

Chapter Twenty-Two: Sweet Success and Dirty Tricks

♥

"Coming right up. And don't forget, everyone who posts with our hashtag tonight is entered in a drawing for an Empanada Angel hoodie." Anna jotted the customer's order, then poked her head through the Airstream's door, shouting to be heard over the roaring generator and the salsa music blasting from the food truck's speakers. "Two vegan peccadillo empanadas with chimichurri sauce, One chorizo-queso with avocado salsa, and three dulce de leche."

Milo, Diego's culinary school friend and copilot for Empanada Angel's debut, snatched it. "Thanks, pretty mama."

Dancing at the fryer station, Diego stopped swiveling his hips long enough to blow her a kiss. "How you holding up, angel?"

She wiped her damp forehead with her apron, emblazoned with the same grinning angel that graced the Airstream itself. "Kinda dizzy, to tell the truth."

He bolted to her side. "You okay? You want to sit down?"

"No, no, no. I'm fine." She patted her baby bump. "So is Pomegranate. I've just never had to think this fast before. How do you do it?"

"Passion, my love." He gave her a quick smooch. "That, and a lot of coffee. Go get us another tray of dessert empanadas, would you?"

Anna adjusted her paper-flower headband as she trotted toward Bangers' back door. Not since her nursing-school stint in the Emergency Department had she had to hustle this fast. And so far, Diego had not screwed up one order! Every paper dish that passed through the service window was filled with piping-hot pastries and jewel-bright dipping salsas. A line of hungry customers stretched across the parking lot, transformed for Cinco de Mayo into a beer garden where Kiara, cute as pie in her off-the-shoulder Mexican blouse, poured cervezas and margaritas. Colorful papel picado banners fluttered overhead. Sporting a campy sombrero, Jojo checked IDs and guarded the fence line.

As she entered Bangers' back hallway, Anna heard Lana bellowing from the stage. "La Estrella"

"What does that mean?" someone called.

"Your mama," a customer hollered.

Ignoring them, Lana plowed on. "La Escalera."

"Bingo!"

"You gotta say Lotería, dumb shit," some dude said with a loud guffaw.

Who knew a picture bingo came could get so competitive? Dawn must be offering killer prizes tonight.

She pushed through the swinging doors into the kitchen and found Shelby perched on a stool playing with her phone. Alice, the grumpy lunch shift cook, could not have looked more bored as she flipped a single burger. She shot Anna a weary glance. "More empanadas? Hmph. Don't know why Dawn's wasting our time tonight. Shoulda just shut the kitchen down."

"Ignore her." Shelby tilted her chin toward the older. "Alice just hates staying up past her bedtime."

Alice swatted her with a spatula. "None of your sass, sprout."

From the cooler Anna grabbed a tray of chocolate-pastry empanadas filled with gooey dulce de leche, ready for the Airstream's deep fryer. Tipsy customers waiting for the restroom blocked her path to the back door, so she headed through the bar and waved at Eddie, busy stringing up the next piñata. Dawn's laughter rang out from the tarp-covered pool tables where customers crafted Mexican-style tissue paper flowers. Dawn waved as Anna passed. "I love this artsy-crafty shit."

Come to think of it, with her multi-tasking skills and earthy humor, Charlie's boss would've made an excellent nurse.

Anna ducked back into the trailer, set the tray on the counter, then pulled her order pad from her apron pocket. "Next customer, please." She scribbled orders as fast as she could write and handed them through the service window.

Diego leaned out, a paper tray in his hand. "Two chicken chipotles for Lucy."

A tall redhead sauntered to the counter, hips swaying to the music. "Thanks, Señor Hottie. How about your number?" Holding up her phone, she snapped his picture.

Behind her, a cluster of young, skinny, not-pregnant cuties giggled and hooted.

"Me too!"

"We can share."

"Muy caliente!"

Diego shook his head. "Sorry, ladies. My heart belongs to another. All I can give you is empanadas."

"Aww, boo." The girls moved off to wait for their orders.

Take that, horny hotties. Grinning, Anna returned to her volunteer duties. Despite Diego's repeated urgings, there was no way she was going to accept payment for helping him tonight. He was family. Well, family-ish. As she took orders and served empanadas, she let her imagination wander. What would it be like to be a chef's wife? Her childhood friend Josie grew up in a restaurant family. Anna loved hanging out with her after school to do homework in a back booth of Samurai Hibachi and sneak fried gyoza from the kitchen. Josie's dad would wave his cleaver in mock menace, but he always handed over their study snacks. And Josie's mom showed her how to fold linen napkins into ornate shapes—Anna's only impressive kitchen skill to date. At the time, Anna thought Josie was the luckiest kid she knew. Would Diego have his brick-and-mortar restaurant by the time little Pomegranate was old enough to have homework?

Diego stepped through the Airstream door. "How's it going, Anna? You want a stool?"

She rubbed her lower back, aching after a long day on her feet in the clinic followed by three hours here. "I wouldn't mind, to be honest."

"Jojo," Diego bellowed. "Anna needs a stool."

"I'll get you one." Lana trotted up, holding her phone out. She grabbed Diego's shoulder and Anna's, pulling them into a tight huddle. "Bad news, guys. I've been watching your social media. Lots of positive feedback, but this asshole is on a rampage."

She showed them a photo—a paper plate holding an empanada cut open to reveal a fuzzy gray lump. The text: **@EmpanadaAngel serving rotten food @BangersTavernTacoma tonight. Made me puke. Eaters beware. #EmpanadaAngel #FoodPoisoning #Gross**

Diego's face blanched. "That's not my food. We're using paper trays, not paper plates, and the shape's all wrong. Looks like a kindergartener made it out of clay." He squinted at the screen. "Who wrote this?"

"@FurnitureDude" Anna read. "Well, fuck me sideways."

Diego jolted at her uncharacteristic language. But damn it to where Brock belonged, when was he going to quit with his juvenile harassment?

"That's my ex-husband. He's trying to make trouble for Diego."

Lana tisked. "Well, he's succeeding. Look at all these comments."

Diego's wide-eyed gaze darted from the phone to Anna's face, then to the truck behind him. "This is my freakin' debut. He's gonna drive away all the customers. What do we do?"

Sure enough, a glance around the beer garden showed customers squinting at their phones. A sour taste filled Anna's mouth. All night long she'd been encouraging customers to post on social media, thus fanning the flames of Brock's dirty trick.

"I'll tell you what we'll do—time to fight fire with fire." She popped into the trailer and told Milo to kill the music, then stuck two fingers into her mouth and let fly an ear-piercing whistle. "Excuse me. I have an important announcement."

Customers looked up.

"I don't usually share my personal business like this, but I want you to know that Diego"—she pointed— "is my boyfriend. And this bozo posting about moldy empanadas"—she held up Lana's phone— "is my ex-husband. He hasn't set foot here all night. This is the second time he's tried a stunt like this."

Raucous laughter rang out nearby. "Dude, was he the one with the plastic cockroach?"

"The very same. He's jealous, so he's trash-talking our empanadas."

"What a douche canoe," someone called.

Diego's hand closed on her shoulder. He pulled her tight to his side and raised his voice. "We're just a small business trying to make a living, and we need your help. If you liked the food tonight, would you call out this guy's lies?"

"Of course, doll," the flirty redhead called. She and her girl squad bent over their phones.

Anger burned hot in Anna's chest as she added, "His name is Brock, and he works at Furniture World."

"Hey now." Diego squeezed her shoulder and lowered his voice. "No need to pour gasoline on the fire."

She glared up at him. "That butt-munch is trying to ruin our business."

The corners of Diego's mouth crept up. "Our business?"

"Sorry. I mean yours, of course."

"Nah, you had it right the first time." He pressed a kiss to her temple. "Thanks, Anna."

He returned to the trailer and cranked up the music again. For a few, fingernail-chewing minutes, no one approached to order food. But soon, a few customers trickled up to the window, and within twenty minutes, they were back to cranking out orders at full speed.

Anna kept up her duties, taking and delivering orders, though she twinged each time she pointed to Diego's Twitter handle painted beside the beaming cartoon angel. Social media was so important to a food truck's success, and Brock was smart enough to weaponize that knowledge. How could she ever protect Diego from Brock's venom?

Since Cinco de May fell on a Wednesday this year, the party wound down around eleven. Perched on her stool, Anna kicked off her nurse clogs and massaged her aching feet. Tomorrow's shift at the clinic was going to be rough after this late night, but helping Diego with his launch was worth the aches and fatigue. It would've been a perfect night if it weren't for Brock's asshattery.

Diego climbed down the stairs, wrapped his arms around her shoulders from behind, and pressed his cheek against hers as he surveyed the nearly empty beer garden, now littered with salsa-smeared paper dishes and empty plastic cups. "Thank you, angel. I never expected—well, all of this. Couldn't have done it without you."

She kissed his knuckles. His hands smelled of disinfectant soap, but the scent of fried pastry clung to his hair and clothes. It was a pleasant combination, one she could get used to. "If only Brock hadn't taken a dump on your social media, it might've been even better."

Diego's sigh stirred her hair. "How are you two ever gonna coparent if he's always pulling this kind of hateful shit?"

"It's gonna take a lot of counseling." She nestled into his embrace. "I'll talk to him."

"No, I will." Diego's voice took on a heavy note, as if resigning himself to bad news. "If it weren't for me, you two wouldn't be battling like this."

Anna spun to face him. "That's not true. He hates me for taking away his comfortable little life." She cupped his cheek. "I don't regret one second of the time we've spent together. And I won't let Brock ruin your food truck's reputation."

His laugh rang dry as old bones. "You're more important to me than this project. If you need me to step away for a while, I'll do it."

Her heart shriveled. "Listen to me." She gripped his slumped shoulders. "That's not what I want. Not at all. Okay?"

His chest rose and fell. Finally, he pressed a kiss to her forehead. "I'm exhausted. Will you be mad if I just crash at home tonight?"

"Not at all," she lied. After tonight's drama, she craved his arms around her, even if it meant squishing together in his narrow, lumpy bed. But she'd cause him enough hassle for one night. And she needed her own rest, for the baby's sake. So she wound her arms around him for a lingering hug before trailing back to her car.

"I can't be the reason he fails," she muttered as she cranked the ignition. "I've got to fix this."

Chapter Twenty-Three: Make Up, Lock Up

♥

Aunt Hala pulled into her driveway and turned to Anna. "Come in for just a moment, hon.' I want to show you this cute website I found for new parents."

Anna let her head thunk back against the headrest. Though the baby was only as big as an acorn squash, after a full morning of comparison shopping for baby furniture, the little squirt felt as heavy as a sixpack of bowling balls. Her feet were swollen, her back hurt, and her wallet stung. How could something as small as a baby's crib cost as much as a freakin' sofa?

For some weird reason, Hala had insisted they get an early start, then dawdled in a café over tea, pastries, and stories of when her own three kids were small. Funny stuff, for sure, but why pull Anna out of bed so early to hear family stories she'd already heard a hundred times? And why rush her home before they actually bought anything?

The lingering Brock drama didn't improve Anna's mood. At one of the baby goods stores, a shopper recognized her—again. Someone at Bangers' Cinco de Mayo party posted her rant on social media, so now half of Tacoma was chuckling over her red-faced outburst. Brock even had his own hashtag now, #FurnitureDouche. Three weeks after that fiasco, people still tagged Empanada Angel, too. People don't read carefully while scrolling through social media. What if all they remembered was a moldy empanada?

As much as she'd like to chew Brock a new one, her lawyer cautioned her not to engage online or in real life. "Don't give him more ammunition, dear."

The prospect of a protracted court battle made her stomach hurt. Or maybe it was just little Squash, practicing her clogging in there. The kid was extra restless today. Maybe a snack would put her to sleep.

"Come on, slowpoke." Already out of the car, Hala beckoned. "Just a few minutes, I promise. You're going to love this."

"All right, all right." Anna heaved herself to her feet and followed her aunt up the porch steps.

Someone flung the door open.

"Surprise!" The shouted chorus nearly knocked her onto her behind.

Pink balloons floated everywhere. Pastel streamers crisscrossed the living room and dining room. It's a girl! proclaimed a banner above a mountain of wrapped gifts.

So many guests! With Elena out of the picture, she hadn't expected much of a baby shower, maybe a small family gathering, perhaps cupcakes and a few gifts at the clinic. But stuffed into the living room were most of her female coworkers, including Dr. Zakariya, plus her new friends from the single parents' group, all the Bangers girls, and Hala's two daughters, down from Seattle.

She clapped her hands over her mouth as her eyes welled with tears. "You guys! This is too much."

"More like too little, too late." The crowd parted, and Elena stepped forward clutching a huge basket wrapped in pink cellophane and tied with a froth of ribbon.

Anna stared, slack jawed. Elena hadn't spoken to her since that horrible argument on Valentine's Day—and now she was here?

Charlie slung her arm over Elena's shoulder. "Your friend wanted to make sure you had an excellent baby shower."

Elena winced a little on the word friend.

Her rupture with Anna was no secret to their coworkers. Judging by the avid stares from the Bangers crew, Charlie had filled them in too. Just what she needed—more drama for public consumption.

Elena set her basket on the coffee table and spent an awkward moment examining her shoes. "So, uh, I want to apologize."

Charlie stepped in between them. "Why don't you two go chat in the kitchen? We'll set up the first game." When neither budged, she tugged them through the door and left them face to face among the foil-covered dishes and cupcake trays.

Anna's stomach squirmed. Ever since their fallout, she'd longed for this moment, imagined what Elena might say. But releasing the ache of betrayal wasn't so simple. She needed to understand why her best friend would inflict so much pain.

Elena clasped her hands at her chest and sucked in a deep breath. "Let me get this out before I forget everything I wanted to say, okay?"

Heart fluttering, Anna nodded.

"First of all, I've been acting like a frustrated toddler. I hurt my best friend, my brother, and my grandmother." She raised her tear-bright eyes. "I hope it's not too late to make it up to you."

Even after all the pain Elena inflicted, Anna fought the urge to hug her. But first, they had to get through the hard part.

"Why did you do it?"

Elena's lips compressed in a tight line. "Funny how, when you're hurting, you rationalize stupid shit. I told myself I was protecting my little brother and saving you both from pain. But deep down, I was jealous. It didn't seem fair that he loves you despite your baby when my baby cost me Justin's love." She jutted her chin. "And it isn't. Fair, I mean. But so what? Your happiness doesn't take away from mine. You dumped a loser and moved on. I got dumped by a loser and got stuck in my bitterness." She reached for Anna's hand. "I want to learn from you how to be stronger. How not to give up."

Anna's throat tightened, and tears spilled down her cheeks as she squeezed Elena's hand. "And I want to learn from you how to do this whole single mom deal."

With a sob, Elena squished her in a tight hug. "I don't think you're gonna be single for long. And I'm so, so sorry."

"I missed you so damn much, 'Lena." She rocked her friend as their tears washed away months of hurt.

Finally, a discreet throat-clearing pulled Anna's attention to the doorway. "You two about done?" Charlie asked. "The guests are hungry."

Anna mussed Elena's short curls. "Let's get this party started."

And what a party! Sweet and savory snacks covered the dining table and sideboard. Hala guided Anna to the wingback chair near the fireplace while her cousin Miriam fetched her a plate brimming with felafel, chicken satay skewers, mini meatballs, tiny quiches, pulled pork sliders, pasta salad, fruit salad, corn salad, green salad...

"Where am I going to put all this?" Anna protested.

"You're eating for two." Miriam patted Anna's belly. "By six months, I was way bigger than you, so eat up! My boys need a sturdy cousin to play with."

Charlie's friend Lana skipped around the room fastening clothes pins to everyone's clothes. "If anyone says the word 'baby,' snatch their pin. Big prize for the person with the most clothes pins at the end of the party."

While her friends and family peppered her with questions, Anna stuffed her face with delicious goodies.

"How far along now?"

"Twenty-seven weeks. The baby's as big as an acorn squash."

"Gotcha!" Rosie snatched the clothespin from Anna's collar.

"Are you taking birthing classes?" Shelby asked. "At my cousin's class they showed us this movie where the lady screamed like a banshee." She chomped into a crisp lumpia, then licked crumbs from her fingers. "I ain't never having kids."

Anna hid her grimace behind her napkin.

Kiara smacked Shelby across the top of her spiky head. "Stop with the damn horror stories."

This wasn't the first time someone had regaled Anna with tales of birthing terror. Now that her baby bump was visible to all, perfect strangers showered her with un-asked-for advice and stories of their own birth experiences, or their sister's, or their friend's, or their neighbor's...

Dr. Zakariya pulled up a chair beside Anna. "You look marvelous, dear." She lifted a samosa to her lips. "When I was pregnant, fried goodies like this made me belch like a foghorn."

Charlie set up a portable screen in front of the fireplace. Lana followed with a small projector, while Rosie handed each guest a slip of paper.

Charlie clapped her hands. "This game is called 'Guess Anna's age.' Write down your best guess for each photo."

Anna groaned and sank deeper into her seat. Even today, she had a hard time smiling for the camera. In childhood photos she grimaced like she'd been pinched.

"Aww," the guests chorused as the first photo filled the screen—naked baby Anna, her pudgy butt dusted with powder, a spit bubble clinging to her lips.

"You were so cute!" Charlie's boss cooed.

I was cross-eyed. Anna squirmed in her seat as everyone scribbled numbers on their papers. Hopefully Squash would take after her father in that respect—Brock's baby pictures were child-model perfect.

The next photo showed toddler Anna and gap-toothed Charlie grinning in front of a shiny aluminum Christmas tree. Behind them stood Mom, a fond smile on her apple-cheeked face as she gazed down at her daughters.

Anna's chest tightened. Oh God no, please don't let me cry in front of everyone.

Even before pregnancy magnified her emotions, photos of happy, smiling Mom sharpened memories of the awful last year when cancer drained the color from her cheeks and the music from her laugh. Mom would have showered so much love on her granddaughter. The reminder ripped a fresh hole in Anna's heart.

She mentally limped through the rest of the party games. Rosie collected her prize for snatching the most clothespins, and then it was time for cake and presents.

Charlie armed herself with a notepad to record who gave which gift, and the great unwrapping began. Touched to tears by her friends' and family's generosity, Anna opened a treasure trove of toys, picture books, a baby carrier, impossibly tiny outfits, electronic gadgets to soothe the baby with white noise or music, a nightlight that projected stars onto the nursery ceiling, and from her family, a beautiful wooden crib that converted to a toddler bed.

She was emptying a gift bag of animal-shaped teething toys when the doorbell rang.

Charlie popped to her feet and trotted to the door.

"Am I too late?" a familiar, scratchy voice asked.

"We're just opening presents. Come in, Mrs.—"

"Maricela!" Anna sprang from her chair to greet Diego's grandmother, wrapped up in a fuzzy pink cardigan, a felt beret atop her snowy hair.

"Sorry I'm late. Our senior group meeting ran long." She tottered in and set a large paper gift bag at Anna's feet, then shot a sharp look at Elena.

"It's okay," Anna whispered. "We made up."

"Good." The old lady gave a crisp nod. "Any food left? Those church donuts are always stale."

Elena rose to find her grandmother a seat and fix her a plate. Once Maricela was situated, Anna dug into the huge gift bag, discarding handfuls of pink tissue paper until her fingers sank into something soft as kitten fur. She pulled out a baby blanket the shade of a baby bunny's ear. Woven into the design, the silhouette of an angel in a contrasting shade of pink.

Anna rubbed the downy blanket against her cheek. "Oh, Maricela. It's so soft. Did you make this yourself?"

"Of course. Every little girl needs her guardian angel."

A cozy warmth filled Anna's chest. Even though Squash would never know her maternal grandmother, she'd have plenty of surrogate grandmas—Aunt Hala, Mom's sister Molly, Dr. Z, and Diego's abuelita.

Overcome with fondness for the sweet old woman, Anna launched from her chair and bent to give her a gentle hug. "I'll treasure this. Thank you so much."

Holding her close with a surprisingly strong grip, Abuelita whispered, "Bienvenida a la familia."

Anna straightened, wiped her tear-blurred eyes, and addressed the group. "I can't tell you all how grateful and touched I am. This is—" Her voice cracked as she swept a hand over the pile of gifts. "So much more than I hoped for. Thank you." She snuffled into a paper napkin. "Dang it. I hate crying in front of people."

Aunt Hala wrapped her arm around Anna's shoulders. "It's okay, honey. Pregnancy is an emotional time. You're about to experience the biggest change of your life."

And because no perfect moment can last, the doorbell rang again. This time, Charlie opened the door to reveal a UPS delivery dude. "Got a package for Mrs. Anna Spencer."

Anna's fluffy, happy cloud evaporated, plummeting her to hard, cold reality.

The delivery guy held out an electronic tablet. "I need a signature."

Anna smoothed her blouse over her suddenly tight belly. Even Squash wanted nothing to do with this bullshit. "Who's it from?"

He consulted his tablet. "Deborah Spencer."

Anna's hands fisted at her sides. "Tell Mrs. Spencer to shove—"

With impressive swiftness, Aunt Hala darted to the door and took the tablet. "Now, now. Let's just see what it is." She nudged the device into Anna's hand and murmured. "We can sort this out later. You don't want to make a scene."

"How did she know?" Anna hissed.

"No idea. I sure as hell didn't invite her. Just sign."

Anna scribbled, and Hala returned the tablet to the confused delivery dude who wheeled in an enormous box wrapped in teddy bear paper and topped with a blue bow.

"Lord," Kiara called out, "who wraps a package this big?"

"Aren't you gonna open it?" Rosie asked.

"Go ahead, if you're curious." Anna knew there was nothing but bad news under that shiny paper.

Aunt Hala thanked the deliveryman while Charlie and her Bangers friends tore the wrapping paper from the box.

"Ooooh," one of the nurses cooed. "I've seen these cribs online. They work off an app. You can rock the baby without getting out of bed."

Charlie plucked an envelope from the wrappings and handed it to Anna, who ripped it savagely and read

Deborah's prissy cursive. "For my grandson. Sweet dreams, little one. Love, Grandmama."

She tossed the card to the floor.

"Anna," Hala scolded, her brow rumpled.

"I don't want this. I have a crib."

A pall fell over the guests as they watched the tense exchange.

Charlie stepped in, wrapping her arm around Anna's shoulders. "Let it go. Don't spoil the party."

But Deborah had already done that. Anna knew she was being childish, but she couldn't shake her disgust at the way Brock's mother poked her ostentatious nose into their celebration. And she'd keep on poking for the next eighteen years, probably longer. This gift was a shot across the bow.

I'm here. I'll let you know if I need backup.

Diego slid his phone into his jeans pocket. Anna's baby shower was girls-only, according to Charlie. Seems their Aunt Hala had traditional ideas about such things. He'd love to be there to watch Anna open her presents, but at least Elena was attending the party—a huge step, and he needed to give them space to talk it out. Meanwhile, this gave him the perfect chance to work on his gift to Anna and the baby—making peace with Brock.

Anna had reluctantly given him Brock's number and made him promise to bring back-up to any face-to-face confrontation. But Diego knew more about the male mind than Anna, especially about the dynamics of pissing contests like this one. If he showed up with River and Jojo, Brock would never lower his shields. So he had both guys on standby, ready to charge into Furniture World's employee parking lot if things got out of hand.

Now came the nauseating part: humbling himself to Anna's ex. But it was his only chance at breaking this cycle of malice and retaliation. Anna and her baby deserved a break. And Elena was right: if this bullshit didn't let up soon, Anna would get exhausted enough to break things off with him for the baby's sake.

Leaning against his pickup, Diego mentally rehearsed the lines he'd practiced all night. Brock had agreed to meet him here during his four o'clock break. Would the asshole even show? Already, he was ten minutes late.

The store's employee entrance door swung open, and Brock stepped out, shielding his eyes against the brilliant sunlight. Diego's whole body tightened, but he forced a relaxed expression and raised a hand in greeting.

Brock smoothed his crisp dress shirt, squared his shoulders, and strode toward Diego in comically large strides—stomp, stomp, stomp. As if that's gonna make a sound on asphalt, you douche.

Diego drew deep, calming breaths and focused on putting himself in Brock's shoes. Everyone needs a way to save face, especially after they get caught doing something asinine. His best chance at a happy future was placating this numbnuts.

Brock stepped right into Diego's space, crossed his arms, and took a wide stance. "What the fuck do you want?"

This is for you, Anna. "I want to make peace." He pointed from his chest to Brock's. "This shit is hurting Anna. The baby too."

Brock snorted.

Yeah, you're gonna be a great dad.

"Look, man," he continued. "I'm not trying to replace you, okay? You're the baby's father, and you'll be the number one man in her life. I respect that, and I'm not going to be a wedge between you and your daughter."

Another snort, but softer this time.

"But Anna and I are in love, and we're gonna build a life together. That means I'll be a part of the baby's life too."

"The hell you will." Brock stiffened and rose to his full height. Just a few inches taller than Diego with a physique like a well-dressed string bean, he hardly inspired fear. "You care about Anna and the baby? Prove it. Step aside."

Diego felt the hairs on his neck bristle. He should've known better. Trying to reason with this asshole was a waste of time. "I'm not gonna do that."

"Motherfucker, you can't have my woman. She might be a cheating whore, but she's mine." Telegraphing his intentions with comic ineptitude, Brock drew back his fist and threw a punch.

Diego ducked it easily. "Come on, man. That's not gonna help anything."

Snarling, Brock swung with his left, connecting with Diego's shoulder.

Red-hot rage drove Diego's fist right into the asshole's face with a satisfying crunch. Blood flew, splattering Brock's pristine shirt.

Oh shit. I'm gonna pay for that.

Staggering backward, Brock clapped his hands to his face, then pulled them away and gawked at his bloody palms. "You broke my nose! I'll sue your ass. I swear, you'll never get near Anna again."

The rest happened so fast, like a jerky amateur film, the dialogue drowned out by the thundering of Diego's heart. Someone came running across the parking lot. The cops arrived and handcuffed Diego. On the ride to the police station, a single thought rattled his aching skull, over and over.

I've ruined everything.

Chapter Twenty-Four: Diego on Ice

♥

Anna and Charlie were cramming the last gifts into the back seat of Charlie's Subaru when Elena burst through Hala's front door, waving her phone overhead.

"Diego's in jail!"

For an ice-cold moment, Anna's mind went blank. Certain words just didn't go together, like "Diego" and "jail." Sweet, polite, good-natured Diego arrested? Even when faced with Brock's worst stupidity, he'd kept his cool. This had to be a mistake.

She slammed the SUV's rear hatch and grabbed Elena's arm. "Let's go." But Charlie's car was too full for a third passenger.

"Let's take mine." Elena pulled out her keys and dashed to the curb.

With Elena behind the wheel, they tore through the streets of Tacoma, heading for the police station where Diego was unjustly imprisoned. In the front passenger seat, Anna clutched her bag with a white-knuckled death grip while in the back, Charlie called their Aunt Molly, a lawyer who lived in the Old Town neighborhood just minutes away.

Charlie ended the call. "She's on her way. Thank God she was home."

On the verge of hyperventilating, Anna forced her breath to slow. "Isn't she a tax attorney?"

"Any port in a storm, right?"

Elena's voice shook as she rounded the corner and turned into the station's parking lot. "If our parents find out, they'll use this against him and Abuelita."

"Good luck keeping it secret," Charlie grumbled. "Your asshole ex will probably blast it across social media. Hell, he'll take out an ad in the paper."

As soon as Elena's car came to a stop, Anna popped from her seat and sprinted to the station entrance, Charlie and Elena hot on her heels.

Inside they faced a gray, cement-brick lobby. At the chest-high counter, a stern-looking lady cop with a bosom the size of Minnesota cocked an eyebrow. "Can I help you ladies?"

Panting, Anna clutched the counter. "We're here for Diego Vargas."

"Family?"

She nodded. Hopefully, that lie wouldn't come back to bite her behind.

The cop tapped a button on an office phone thingy. "Yo, Reyes. Your customer's got visitors."

"Have a seat, ladies. Sergeant Reyes will be out in a minute."

There weren't three seats together in the rows of molded plastic chairs lining the lobby, so Anna perched between a disgruntled-looking old guy mumbling in a language she couldn't identify and a thin-lipped woman with teary eyes.

A few endless, gut-churning minutes later, a short, stocky cop stepped through the swinging half-door at the end of the counter. "Someone here to see Diego Vargas?"

Anna bolted to her feet. So did Elena.

"I can only take one of you."

After a long, fraught stare, Elena sighed. "Go ahead."

Unsure she could've been so generous in Elena's shoes, Anna hugged her friend tight then followed the policeman through a warren of desks and file cabinets.

"Officer?" she asked in a quavering voice. "What's Diego charged with?"

"Assault."

Her vision began to blur around the edges as a wave of cold washed over her. Diego? Assault? There was only possible explanation—Brock.

An ugly thought wormed through her brain. She was her child's protector. Anyone she let into her inner circle had to be completely trustworthy. Had her attraction to Diego blinded her to his faults?

She shuddered. Don't react out of fear. Listen to his story before you make a rash decision.

They rounded a partition, and there he was, pale and slumped in a plastic chair, a scarlet smear across his T-shirt.

Her heart stopped. "You're hurt!"

Diego's head jerked up. "Anna!" He lurched forward, but his hands were cuffed behind him.

Anna whirled on the cop. In a voice she didn't recognize as her own, she barked, "He's bleeding. You uncuff him right now."

The cop chuckled. "Take it easy, little mama. That's not his blood."

Head spinning, she turned back to Diego. "Then whose?"

He ducked his head. "Brock's."

She clutched the edge of the desk. "I think I need to sit down."

Reyes pulled up a seat, then someone across the room called his name. "I'll give you two a moment."

Anna scooted her seat forward until their knees touched. "Tell me."

His eyes downcast, Diego shook his head. "I just wanted to bury the hatchet." He winced. "Sorry, bad word choice. I wanted to make peace with your ex so he'd stop hassling you."

"Oh, Diego." She cupped his cheek and waited until he met her gaze. "That was a sweet thought, but there's no way it could work. Brock's completely—"

"I know. It was stupid. I'm so sorry, angel."

"You hit him?"

"He hit me first. Tried to, anyway. He kept coming at me and saying ugly things about you and"—he sighed— "I just lost it. Kapow. Blood everywhere."

Shame flooded her, tinged with perverse glee. How could she doubt Diego when she'd wanted to punch

Brock's smarmy face so many times? If he'd ever laid hands on her in anger, her knee would have launched his balls to the moon.

A familiar voice behind them jerked her attention from Diego's sad-puppy face.

A large, gray-haired cop was leading an uncuffed Brock across the room. Both Brock's eyes were purple and swollen, and something resembling tampons protruded from his nostrils.

"That's him," he yelled, his voice tight and shrill. "That's the thug who assaulted me."

Anna popped from her seat and glared.

The cop holding Brock's arm thrust him into a seat two desks away. "Save it for your statement, son."

Brock glared back at Anna and Diego. "Here's my statement. He hit me."

"Are you saying he threw the first punch?"

Brock held Anna's gaze. His mouth twisted in a smirk. "That's right."

Anna spluttered. "You lying, scum-sucking snake."

"Take it easy, Anna." Aunt Molly, their mother's sister, strode up to Anna's side. Dressed in a matching blazer and pencil skirt, she looked every inch the legal eagle. "Sorry I'm late," she whispered into Anna's ear. "Had to dig out my court suit. Hardly ever get the chance to wear it." She faced the police officer. "What is my client charged with?"

Diego's confused gaze darted from Anna to Molly.

Sergeant Reyes called to his colleague, "Hey Duffy. Is the guy's nose broken?"

"Nope. Just bruised."

"Just simple assault, then." Reyes hooked his thumb toward Brock. "Same as the other guy."

Brock shot to his feet. "What are you talking about?" The other cop pushed him back into his seat.

"Rude little shit, ain't he?" Reyes turned back to Diego. "Here's how it works, son. We take your statement. You get a case number. If your pal over there wants to press charges, it's up to him to pursue it with the city prosecutor."

"But he threw the first punch," Brock bellowed.

Officer Duffy shook his head. "You pipe down, or I'm gonna throw you in a holding cell."

Aunt Molly crossed her arms. "Any witnesses, officer?"

"No, ma'am."

"Security camera?"

"Duffy? Camera in that back lot?"

Officer Duffy checked his notes. "Affirmative."

"Shit," Brock hissed.

Anna sat and squeezed Diego's knee. "So, if Diego's telling the truth and Brock is lying like the lying liar he is, what happens then?"

Aunt Molly spoke up. "The city prosecutor's going to ask, what's a reasonable reaction in these circumstances?"

Brock gestured to his bloody shirt. "Does this look like a reasonable reaction to you?"

Molly raised an eyebrow. "Depends on what we see on the security tape. If that young man threw the first punch, my client is entitled to defend himself."

"Your client?" Diego wobbled in his seat.

Poor love, so discombobulated by all this. Anna wanted to throw her arms around him, but that would just add fuel to Brock's fire. "Diego, meet my aunt, Molly Eisinger. She's an attorney."

"Pleased to meet you, hon'." Molly extended her hand, then frowned. "Sergeant, are these cuffs really necessary?"

Reyes shrugged, then uncuffed Diego. "Sorry, kid. With the blood and all, we had to be sure."

Diego rose unsteadily to his feet and fixed Anna with a baleful glance that pierced her heart.

He thinks we're over.

He turned to Molly. "Thank you, ma'am. I'm grateful."

Molly patted his shoulder. "Never did like Brock. You ask me, he's not good enough for our Anna."

Judging by Diego's shattered expression, he didn't think he was good enough either.

Anna straightened her shoulders. "Sergeant Reyes, could I have a moment alone with Brock?"

Reyes scratched his temple. "Why would you want—"

"It's okay, Officer." Brock puffed out his skinny chest. "She's my wife."

"Ex-wife," she snapped.

Reyes exchanged a look with Duffy, who pointed. "Interrogation room three's open."

"Suit yourself, then." Reyes beckoned. "This way." He led her to a small room just like in the movies—cement brick walls painted gray, simple table and chairs, and a one-way mirror. Good. Let the cops watch in case he tried anything funny. She sat.

Brock pulled the other chair toward her. "Listen, Anna."

"Over there." She pointed to the other side of the table. She needed space between them, or she just might throw a punch of her own.

"I can explain," he started.

"No. We start with this." Summoning her inner bad cop, she leaned onto her elbows and narrowed her eyes. "I am not your wife. You want a wife, ask Kristi."

Brock's gaze fell to his lap. In a voice emptied of all bravado, he muttered, "When she found out you're pregnant, she dumped me."

So, Kristi did have a conscience. A tardy one, but still.

He raked his fingers into his shiny hair. "I've lost both women in my life. Seeing you with that low-life cook, it's just—"

She smacked the table with her palm, the sound echoing in the spartan room. "Enough with your hateful bullshit. Enough with the excuses. You made your choice. There's no going back. The only question now is how to go forward. Do you really want to center your life around making me and Diego unhappy?"

He slumped in his chair like a rag doll, all the fight gone out of him.

Anna softened her tone. "We're having a child together, Brock. Both of us will play an important part in our daughter's life. If we're always sniping, she'll suffer."

Heaving a huge sigh, he gave the tiniest nod.

She reached across the table and set her hand on his. "Someday you're going to find someone you want to build a future with, and she'll be part of the baby's life too. Modern families are complicated, but if we do it right, our child will have a big, strong net of loving support. Or she can grow up in a battle zone. But I'm telling you, if you take that path, I'll sue for full custody."

Brock looked up with an expression she'd never seen on him. The scorn was gone, replaced by a look of such hopelessness she almost felt sorry for him.

"It was just one mistake, Anna. Everyone makes mistakes. Why should it cost me everything?"

Her ribs ached with the effort of holding back a torrent of accusations and recriminations, an inventory of Brock's every fault and failure as a husband, a lover, a friend. He deserved every scathing word, every verbal stab.

But ultimately, what would that accomplish? Hating Brock was a self-inflicted wound that would fester, infecting the best parts of her. And their child would grow up treading water in a lake of venom. Brock would never take responsibility for destroying their marriage. He didn't know how. The only way to save herself was to forgive him —not for his sake, but for hers.

She reached across the table and squeezed his hand. "You don't love me, Brock. Whether you admit it or not, we both know it's true."

Silent, his jaw working, he held her gaze.

"And now I'm in love with Diego. Nothing you can do will change that."

She almost had him. She could see the wheels turning behind his smooth, tanned forehead. Somewhere under that polished façade, he still had a conscience. Maybe even a heart.

The door banged open, making them both jolt upright as Deborah Spenser barreled in, tugging a suited man behind her.

"What the hell do you think you're doing, Anna?" she snarled.

But Anna had had a thousand percent enough of the Dragon Lady. Keeping her voice low and even, she stabbed a finger toward her soon-to-be-ex mother-in-law. "And tell your mom to quit interfering."

"Gah." Brock rolled his eyes. "What did she do now?"

"She had a space-shuttle crib delivered to my surprise baby shower." She turned to Deborah. "How did you even know about the party?"

She sniffed. "I have my sources."

"Mom?" Brock's eyes bugged out.

"Okay, okay. I was at the bakery when your friend ordered the cake. She gave the address and the date and told the baker to write 'Congratulations, Anna'."

Brock massaged his forehead. "You said that crib was for the baby's room at your house."

Deborah poked her own chest with a pointy-nailed finger. "I'm the child's only grandmother." Her voice cracked. "I should have been invited to the party."

Diego stepped into the open doorway. "After the way you treated Anna? Saying her happiness doesn't matter?"

Deborah stomped her foot. "Well, it doesn't."

"Mom, stop." With the shakiness of a much older man, Brock pushed to his feet and faced Diego. "You and me, we're not finished. But I'm not pressing charges. Let's all just go home."

Anna released a pent-up breath. This was as close to an apology as she and Diego were likely to get. But it was a start.

Diego clasped Anna's hand as her aunt drove them back to his truck, still parked behind Furniture World. Molly absolutely refused any payment for helping him, but finally agreed to let him cater her next office party. And so, he and Anna found themselves alone in his truck's cab, staring into the darkness, the only sound the soft whoosh of traffic and the pounding of his pulse at his temples.

This was it. She was going to break things off. She had every right, after his stupid stunt. Hell, he couldn't even look her in the eye. He didn't deserve to.

"Anna," he croaked, "I don't have words for how sorry I am."

He glanced at her hands, tightly clasped in her lap. Reaching out, he brushed her knuckles with his fingertip. "Are you okay?"

She inhaled, then released a sigh that went on and on. "I'm exhausted. All of me—my body, my brain, my heart." She didn't cry, but she didn't look up either, didn't touch him. Just trailed off, her voice flat and lifeless.

This was his fault. His foolish interference had extinguished her love for him. Time to abandon his stupid hopes and let her rebuild her life. But first, he'd allow himself one last touch.

With aching tenderness, he coaxed her hand open and laced their fingers together. "I wanted this to be my baby gift to you—making peace with Brock. But I only hurt you. No matter how much I love you, Anna. I have to let you go."

Every nerve taut, he counted his heartbeats until good-bye. Lub dub, lub dub...

She slid her hand from his and clawed into her hair, pulling the glossy strands tight. "It seems like we just can't win."

"Maybe we were stupid to try." With a bone-dry chuckle, he thunked his chest. "That's me, the flakey one. Guess I lured you in with another one of my stupid schemes."

He had just enough strength left to do the right thing, but he couldn't bear to look at her beautiful face as he did it. "You need to work things out with Brock, and that'll never happen if I'm around. I'll step aside."

Anna stared into the gathering twilight. The sky had reached a heavy indigo shade, like a velvet curtain closing out the light. The air around them felt heavy, still.

Finally, she broke the silence. "You're not the only one who acted without thinking. I gave you Brock's number because"—another shaky sigh— "deep down, I wanted him to get his comeuppance, you know? I wanted him to admit he was wrong." She closed her eyes and massaged her temples. "That's never going to happen. And that stupid desire brought you nothing but trouble."

She turned to him, her eyes brimming with tears. "Your family will find out about tonight, and Maricela will pay the price. I did that." She rapped her chest with her fist. "Everyone warned me, but I thought I knew better. I thought I could handle my divorce and love you at the same time."

"Listen." He enfolded her trembling hands in his and pressed them to his lips. "My family's been gunning for Abuelita's freedom ever since Abuelo died. Maybe this thing between us was a trigger, but if I'd never met you, they'd have found another excuse. And I'm not giving up on her. I promise you that."

"Why can't they just let her be?"

He shrugged. "They think they're protecting her. Sometimes, love makes people stupid."

"Like us?" Though a tear dribbled down her cheek, the shadow of a smile flickered across her lips. "You tried to make things right with Brock. I wish you hadn't approached him without warning me, but it's not your fault he's a stupid ass."

And then, miracle of miracles, she leaned onto his arm. The warmth of her body loosened dread's hold, just a tiny bit. Just enough for hope to slip through.

She nuzzled her head under his chin. "In one of those sappy TV movies, this would be the part where the couple breaks up."

He pressed a kiss to her hair. "When I met you, I thought I knew what I was getting into, but I had no idea. Cupid's arrow hit me right in the brain."

She sighed again. "Being with me has cost you too much. Brock's still trying to ruin your business. I can't help feeling you'd be better off without me."

That's the cruel thing about hope. It opens you up, only to slide the blade in deeper. Holding his breath, he braced himself for the killing blow.

"But here's the thing." She pressed her palm to his cheek and turned him to face her tear-bright gaze. "I've had enough heartbreak for one year. Being with you makes me happy. And I don't care who thinks we're a bad match— my family, your family, our friends." The corner of her mouth quirked up. "Let's just skip those pages in the script and get to the happily-ever-after part."

Afraid to breathe too deeply, he traced the delicate angle of her jaw. "It's not gonna be easy, with your crazy ex making trouble for us both."

She huffed a low laugh. "Even if you and Brock become best buddies, our lives won't be easy. But I'd rather face the hard stuff with you at my side."

"Oh, Anna." If he were a poet, he'd craft the perfect words to capture the joy lighting up his battered heart. But all he could manage was her name, murmured like a prayer of thanks as his fingertips skimmed over her face, her hair. "I promise you, I'll be there for every moment, easy or hard. I love you so much."

Her voice broke on a squeak. "I love you too." She kissed him, a soft press that meant so much more than any passionate dance of tongues ever could. Her kiss held sweet welcome and total acceptance. Two imperfect people, two messed-up lives that somehow fit perfectly together.

She pulled back and licked her lips, a mischievous twinkle in her eye. "Do you want to come to my place and see all the baby shower loot? Your Abuelita knit us the most beautiful blanket with a guardian angel."

He slid his hand down her side and over her hip. "Absolutely. Afterward, maybe we could go back to my place and thank Abuelita in person."

"Won't she be asleep?"

"If we're lucky." Grinning like the lovestruck fool he was, he steered toward home.

Chapter Twenty-Five: Lost and Found

♥

"Last order," Abuelita barked from her stool outside Empanada Angel's service window. "I got two more cheeseburger empanadas. Who wants 'em?"

Diego peered through the window to see if she'd get any takers. If not, he'd eat them himself. Ten hours of slinging empanadas to the Fourth of July crowd left him achy and light-headed. When had he last eaten? Probably dehydrated, too, from working in the overheated Airstream.

"Yo," a gangly dude rose from one of the raucous beer garden's picnic tables and wobbled up to the window, sloshing his beer. "Hook me up, Señorita."

Giggling, Abuelita adjusted her floral headband and patted their last customer's arm. "You won't be sorry, hon'. These are deeelish."

The Americana-themed empanadas were Abuelita's idea. "It's the fourth of July," she insisted. "You'll sell more if you keep it traditional." Not that there was anything traditional about empanadas filled with cheeseburger, pulled pork, mac and cheese, or apple pie filling, but with three hours to go before the fireworks, they were well and truly sold out. From now on, Abuelita was his number one menu advisor.

Winning this slot at the Freedom Fair's beer garden was an enormous stroke of luck—or maybe his grandmother's angel brigade had something to do with it. Tons of competition, but with most of Tacoma strolling or staggering along the waterfront and hungry for tasty treats, there was plenty of business to go around.

He plated the last two savory empanadas, slid them across the counter, and wished his customer a happy Fourth. Then he flipped his window sign to Closed before plunged his final batch into the fryer. Five minutes later, he carried a tray outside to Anna, seated like the queen she was in a folding camp chair, an embroidered Mexican scarf draped over her shoulders to keep off the sun. Even with swollen ankles and a substantial baby bump, the sight of her filled Diego with a happy glow.

"Would you and Butternut care for dessert?" He bowed and offered her the tray.

"Are you kidding?" Anna's smile twinkled under the multicolored fairy lights. She patted her belly. "This big ol' squash is always hungry. And that cinnamon dulce de leche sauce? I want to be buried in a vat of that stuff."

He leaned over to murmur in her ear. "How about I just drizzle some over you tonight?"

With a smile that promised wicked fun, she whispered, "How about we dip Mr. Happy in some and let me lick it off?"

Abuelita's voice broke through their sexy bubble. "You two work well together, don't they, Hala?"

Anna's aunt huffed a laugh. "I didn't want to admit it at first, but she's right. You make a good team." She dusted her hands on her apron. "This restaurant biz is hard work. Glad I don't have to do this full-time." She fixed him with a squinty gaze. "You sure this is what you want, Diego?"

"More than anything." He gave Anna a fond smile. "Well, more than anything except your niece. Thanks so much for helping today, Hala." When his scheduled help begged off with a hangover, Hala showed up, her food-safety training certificate in her purse, "just to get you through the lunch rush," and ended up playing sous-chef all day.

"It was my pleasure." Hala hooked a thumb over her shoulder at Anna and stage whispered. "And I wanted to make sure this one stayed off her feet."

"I promised, didn't I?" Anna indicated the seat where she rang up orders on her tablet. "Haven't budged from this spot except to go pee." She giggled. "About twenty thousand times."

"But now, it's time for this old lady to hobble back to her car." Hala kissed both his cheeks, then Anna's, then Abuelita's. "And you, Maricela, are an absolute hoot. Let's get together again soon."

He waved as she left, then turned back to Anna. "How'd we do, boss?"

She tapped her tablet. "Three thousand, five hundred, seventy-two dollars and fifty-nine cents. Is that enough?"

He did a rough mental calculation. "Not quite." The entry fee for next month's Food Truck Derby at the Tacoma Dome was damn steep, and to have a shot at the big prize, he'd need to offer his most original recipes with ingredients that didn't come cheap.

"Maybe I can work some extra shifts at Bangers." Despite an increasing number of gigs for Empanada Angel, he still couldn't bring in enough profit to quit his night job. It was damn disheartening. As usual, he'd painted too rosy a picture in his mind, and success shimmered just out of reach.

"Help me down, Gogo," Abuelita called.

He lifted his grandmother from her stool and set her on her Huaraches. She smoothed her full skirt—she'd gone all out with the Mexican finery for the occasion—and faced him with a saucy smile. She was up to something.

"This is for you." From her pocket, she pulled an envelope and pressed it into his hand. "Go on, open it."

He did, and pulled out a check with a lot of zeros. His heart stuttered, then sped.

"'Lita, I told you I can't take your money."

"It's not my money. It's a—Whataya call it? A consortium of investors."

"Investors?"

"You heard me." Shaking her head, she turned to Anna. "This one needs to work on his vocabulary."

Diego huffed. "I know what investors are, but how? Who?"

"You remember Morty at my Senior group? He's real good with technology. Used to teach computers at UW. He helped me set up one of those Quickstarters. This is seed money to get your business started." Her smile widened, pleating her papery cheeks. "We all chipped in. Even Father Polanski and Sister Ursula."

Diego shook his spinning head. "I can't take charity from a bunch of seniors."

Anna grasped his arm. "Diego—"

Abuelita cut her off. "It's not charity. We expect you to pay us back, eventually. And we have conditions."

He exchanged a wary glance with Anna. "Conditions?"

"You bring your food truck to the Church Harvest Festival in October, and you cater our Christmas ball. At cost."

Anna's smile shone brighter than fireworks. Holding his gaze, she nodded.

"Okay," he told Abuelita. "I'll do it."

She clapped her hands. "Wonderful. But I have one more condition. I'm kicking you out."

The country music blasting from the beer garden's stage was so loud, he must not have heard her right. "'Lita, you can't."

She raised her chin and fixed him with a sharp look. "As long as you stay with me, your Papa's gonna make trouble for us both. So I got a roommate. Two, actually. Alma is sixty-seven." She winked at Anna. "Just a kid. She got divorced and wants to leave her old neighborhood. And Monty is seventy-five. He's a widower and misses having a woman around the house."

"So he's your—" Diego gulped— "Your boyfriend?"

Abuelita flapped her hand. "No, silly. He's not my type. It's called co-housing. Father Polanski is working on some pilot program with the city. Alma will get your room, and Monty can have my sewing room. Haven't used it in years. You can help me clean it out."

"Um, I mean—"

Ignoring him, she turned to Anna. "Part of the program is a visiting nurse. That would be a nice job for you when the baby comes. Old people love babies."

He spluttered, "But you—"

"Between the three of us and our friends and family, we'll have plenty of company and help. And we get to keep our independence." She grasped his hand. "You can't imagine, at your age, how much that means to someone like me."

"But I'll worry about you all the time."

She patted his cheek. "Dear heart, I never wanted you to put your life on hold to take care of me."

Even though she was dangling the key to happiness under his nose, he couldn't quite force himself to grasp it. "You took care of me all those years. You taught me how to cook."

"And I look forward to teaching your children too." She patted Anna's tummy. "Starting with this one. But I'll be fine." She moved between them, winding one arm through Diego's and the other through Anna's. "You know, sometimes true strength is knowing when to ask for help, when to accept it, and when to change course. You two are putting together the ingredients for a wonderful life. I can't wait to see what you cook up together. Now, talk it over. I need a cerveza." Releasing them, she toddled off toward the beer line.

Diego swiped at his leaky eyes. "What do you say, Anna? Are you ready for a roommate?"

Beaming, she gazed at him with teary eyes. "It's gonna be tight with you and me and Charlie and River."

"And the baby," he added, pressing a kiss to her forehead.

She clasped his neck and held him close. "But waking up next to you every morning will be worth it. You ready to live with a noisy, stinky little roommate?"

Joy suffused his body, nearly lifting him off the ground. "I can't wait."

Anna sighed with contentment and surveyed the mess on their patio table. Somehow, during the long day of transporting Diego's stuff from Maricela's house, he'd snuck off to the kitchen to prepare a family feast, the first of many for the four of them. Smiling, she rubbed her round belly. Soon to be five.

River pushed away his sauce-smeared bowl and burped into his fist. "Fantastic grub, Diego. Glad you're joining our little family."

Charlie smacked his arm. "Rude boy." Then she grinned at Anna. "Good job, falling for a chef."

Anna wiped chile-tomato sauce from her chin. "It's a sacrifice, but I do it for you two."

Diego's eyes held a devilish gleam as he wiped his index finger around his empty bowl, then—holding her gaze—licked the sauce off.

"Yum," Anna purred.

Charlie groaned and tossed her napkin at his head. "You two are gross. C'mon, River. We need to get to work."

"I got the dishes." River stacked the bowls and silverware. "Maci's first solo shift tonight. You think she's ready, Chef D?"

"Are you kidding? She was sous-chef in a huge restaurant kitchen. I'm amazed she took the job at Bangers. Said she wanted some down time to figure out her next move."

"As long as it's not an empanada wagon." Anna hadn't yet met Diego's replacement. "What's her specialty?"

"Caribbean-French fusion." Diego's gaze took on a dreamy cast. Must be cooking up a new recipe.

"So, jerk chicken tots?" Charlie asked.

"Why not? Bangers' customers will eat anything if you dump it on tater tots."

River scrunched his lips in a thoughtful expression. "We'll need more rum drinks on the weekly specials. Have a good night, you two." He waggled his eyebrows. "Enjoy your privacy while you still can."

"Eew, Riv, don't make dirty jokes about my baby sister." Charlie hefted the slow cooker, still half-full of Birria, and followed him into the house.

Diego refilled Anna's glass with cucumber and mint infused water. "You comfortable, angel?"

Comfortable wasn't the word Anna would use to describe this scene. More like paradise. They'd finally reached the full glory of a Pacific Northwest summer, when twilight stretched on and on. An evening breeze cooled the mid-July heat to the perfect temperature for outdoor dining. Like most Tacoma houses, their rented bungalow didn't have air conditioning, but out here the low sun gilded every leaf, from the monster fig tree in the corner of the yard to the Japanese maple fluttering its lacy leaves over the patio.

The fairy lights overhead flickered to life. Swallows swooped low over the lawn in acrobatic loops and dives. The jasmine climbing the fence wafted its sweet perfume. And Diego sat beside her, his hands laced behind his head, watching her with a heavy-lidded gaze. Tonight he'd finally spend the whole night. And tomorrow night, and the next, and the next...

She reached out a finger and traced the muscular curve of his shoulder. "What has you looking so dreamy?"

"This." He waved a hand, taking in the pretty little backyard, the cornflower blue sky dotted with blushing clouds, and Empanada Angel, parked beside the detached garage. "You." He pulled her hand to his lips and kissed it. "Us." Turning it over, he kissed her palm. "I could not imagine a more perfect first day of living together."

She giggled at the tickle of his short beard against her skin. Now well into her third trimester, every nerve seemed extra sensitive. Even the slightest touch on her tightly stretched skin drew shivers. And when that touch was Diego's, the shivers were the delicious kind. Her OB-GYN doc had warned her many women lost their libido in this phase of pregnancy. Thank God she wasn't one of them.

"Our first night together." She sighed. "At least, our first uninterrupted one. Remind me to send Father Polanski a thank-you note for helping Abuelita find roommates." She rubbed her belly, and Baby Pineapple responded with a sturdy kick. "I'm afraid you're going to feel awfully cramped once the baby's here."

"Are you kidding? There's plenty of room. And if I ever feel claustrophobic, I can hide out in the Airstream. Besides, the most important thing is having you near." He laid his hand beside hers. "Ooh! Good strong kick, kiddo. Better sign her up for soccer."

She laced her fingers through his. "We only have seven more weeks before we add another roommate, so we might as well enjoy the quiet."

"Starting now." Tapping his phone, he found a slow, smokey jazz tune, then pulled to her feet and into his arms. "Dance with me, Anna."

But with her bulging belly in the way, she couldn't find a comfortable fit.

"How about this?" She pivoted so her upper back rested against his chest.

"Very nice." His hands slid down to rest on her hips as they swayed to the saxophone's sexy wails. Diego hummed softly in her ear, the rumble of his voice setting up sympathetic vibrations that danced across her skin and pulsed in her bones. Her muscles softened, relaxing into his hold.

"Anna," he whispered, his warm breath a delicious counterpoint to the breeze cooling her front. He slid one hand up to gently cup her breast while the other gripped her hip and snugged her against firm muscle and the hot, hard ridge of his cock. "So lush and soft and mine." When he swept her hair aside and pressed his open mouth just below her ear, her knees turned to jelly.

Just then, a shriek of laughter rang out, and the neighbor kids' basketball flew over the fence to land at their feet.

Chuckling, Diego scooped up the ball and launched it back across the fence. "Inside?"

"Yes, please."

Hands linked, they ambled up the steps, stopping for more languid kisses, more lazy caresses. Before, Diego's tight schedule always lent an urgency to moments like this. But from this day forward, they had all the time in the world.

Well, until the baby came. But she'd think about that later. Right now, she had her favorite warm, horny man wrapped around her, and she was going to enjoy every delicious minute until he wore her out.

And then she'd sleep peacefully in his arms until, rested and ready, he woke her with more kisses.

Swaying to music from the phone in his hip pocket, they slow-danced into the bedroom. Diego lowered her onto the bed, now covered with his colorful woven bedspread.

Hips swaying to the music, he stripped off his shirt, then unfastened his jeans and let them fall to the floor. With a flirtatious grin, he hooked his thumb in the elastic of his tight boxer briefs and inched the thin fabric down until his cock's ruddy crown peaked out.

"Yes, please." She reached for him, but he gently gripped her wrists.

"Nuh-uh. First, this." He sat beside her and, with amazing dexterity, unbuttoned her loose hippie blouse while his other hand wove into her hair, tugging gently in some magical way that made her nipples pucker and her clit throb.

He released her breasts from her sturdy bra. Heavier now, exquisitely sensitive, they could only stand the lightest touch, and that's exactly what he gave her, his fingertips skating in ever-tightening circles.

"So nice," she purred.

"Not too much?" he murmured into the crook of her neck.

"Perfect." She arched into his caress, but his hands were on the move again, gliding down her sides to grip the waistband of her yoga pants and pulled them over her hips.

She flopped onto her side with a happy sigh. She'd long ago given up on arranging her swollen body into a seductive pose. Her rear was wider now, her thighs heavier, and her belly round and firm. But Diego's avid touch and the glittering hunger in his eyes calmed her insecurity and let her relax into their slow, lazy lovemaking.

He nudged her into the center of the bed, then opened the nightstand drawer. "Let's start with this." Having used up the stretchmark cream, he'd arrived today with a new jar of body butter, rich and thick, scented with mango and coconut. He spread a generous scoop over her flank, then stroked it down her thigh. "Your skin is like satin."

"Mmm." She stretched in bliss as he kneaded her calf muscles, then her swollen feet. "I am the luckiest preggo on the planet."

"You are the most beautiful." His intense gaze followed his hands as they worked back up her side, then gently turned her to give her other hip and leg the same slow pampering. By the time he worked his way to her inner thighs, her breath came fast and hard.

The drawer opened again, then the mattress dipped as his warm body pressed against her back from shoulder to knees. His hand snaked around the front, holding a tube. "Thought we could try this."

She took it from him and read the label. "All-natural love lube, one hundred percent organic ingredients. Honestly, what must they think of you at the natural foods store?" Giggling, she nestled her hips against his erection, loving the way his breath caught.

"They probably think I'm crazy in love with a pregnant woman. Which I am." His tongue traced the shell of her ear while his fingers slicked lube over her tingling folds. His shaft slid over her swollen pussy in a slow, steady rhythm. "Does this feel good?"

She moaned and reached down to press him more tightly against her aching clit. He gasped when her fingers brushed his swollen crown.

Again and again he pushed, each thrust dragging over her clit in the most delicious way. His cock grew even harder beneath her hand, his breathing shallow and rapid. "Anna, please."

Shifting her hips, she guided him inside. Her pussy felt swollen, impossibly full, but in this position she could control the angle so each short dig of his cock sparked pleasure that built higher and higher.

Grunting now with each thrust, he stroked her clit. Sharp bliss tightened her muscles and set her nerves alight. Just a little more...she squeezed her eyes shut and reached for the climax shimmering just out of reach.

"Oh God, Anna, I can't—" His fingers dug into her thigh as his body went rigid, then shuddered. The warm pulse of him sent her free-falling into a climax that flowed on and on...

"Oh, wow—" Still panting, she grabbed Diego's hand and pressed it to her suddenly rigid belly.

"Shit!" In a split-second, he was up on his knees, staring down at her in horror. "I hurt you."

"No, no." She grasped his arm and tugged him back onto the mattress. "It doesn't hurt. Just feels weird, kinda tight. These Braxton-Hicks contractions don't harm the baby. Look." She placed his palm on her belly. "Pineapple's fine." In fact, their lovemaking seemed to wake the baby, because she pushed with a knee or foot hard enough to make a visible bulge.

"See? You can push back." She pressed his hand against the little one's protruding limb, and the baby withdrew, only to nudge hard on the other side of Anna's belly.

With a laugh, he gently prodded back. "It's like playing Whack a Mole."

"Exactly." She relaxed onto her side and nuzzled her butt against him. "You're bonding already. She likes you."

"Amazing." He sighed into her hair. "Like her mama."

Chuckling softly, he pulled the covers over both of them. Spooned against him, her fingers interlaced with his, she drifted off to the sweet sound of Diego crooning to the baby.

Chapter Twenty-Six: Almost Sorry

♥

"Brock wants what?" Charlie squawked.

Anna blinked at her phone screen. Her almost-ex-husband's words were clear enough, and yet they made no freakin' sense.

"He wants to come to my next prenatal appointment."

"After eight months of ignoring your invitations, now he wants to come?" Charlie's lip curled. "I smell a rat."

Anna's thumbs flew over the screen. "Don't worry. When I tell him we're on our way to the clinic now, he'll back out." She texted him her appointment time and address.

Three dots pulsed in a text bubble, and pulsed, and pulsed…

See you there.

Anna sank into a chair.

"Lemme see." Charlie darted to her side and snatched the phone. "Holy jalapeños."

"Good one." In preparation for the baby's arrival, Charlie was trying to train away her potty mouth tendencies. They didn't want the baby's first words to be one of her auntie's creative curses.

Charlie sat beside her. "You want me to call Diego?"

"No way. He's meeting with that wedding planner this morning. It's a huge gig. Besides"—she gently pried the phone from Charlie's hand— "I'll have my birthing coach to defend me."

"Damn straight." Charlie had been an absolute champ, studying her birthing partner duties like she was prepping for the bar exam. Diego understood when Anna explained that she'd promised this job to Charlie early on. All the same, after each birthing class she caught him curled up on the couch with Charlie's notes. "Just in case, angel. Besides, this is interesting. Want to practice your breathing?"

Oh, but what if Brock wanted in on the action? The very idea of him in the delivery room turned Anna's stomach. And Papaya's too, apparently, because she pummeled Anna's ribs with kung fu kicks.

She rubbed soothing circles on her belly. "Hang in there, kiddo. We won't let Daddy spoil our day." With a grunt, she pushed up from her chair and grabbed her purse. "Let's go, Char. If we're lucky, Dr. Tanaka will be early, and Brock will be late."

They weren't lucky.

When they arrived at her OB-GYN doctor's waiting room, there sat Brock, his hands clasped in his lap like a kid waiting to be called into the principal's office.

"Uh, hi." He flashed a wan smile and lifted a leather-bound notebook. "Ready to learn about this birthing business."

Charlie flushed maroon. "If you think for one minute you're going to—"

"Easy." Anna grasped her sister's arm. "Not in front of the kids."

A trio of littles stared bug-eyed from the kids' corner beside the fish tank, their block tower forgotten. An angel-faced, tow-headed boy took advantage of the distraction to sidle up and kick their building down.

I'll bet Brock was just like him. Anna sucked in a steadying breath, pasted on a smile, and faced Charlie. "Would you mind getting me a coffee from the cafeteria?"

Brock shot her a sour look. "Won't that stunt the baby's growth?"

"She drinks decaf, numbnuts," Charlie snarled and stalked out of the room.

"Nice talk, Aunt Charlie."

"Shut up, Brock."

A tiny girl with a mop of dark curls tugged on Anna's pants leg. "You're not supposed to say shut up. Say 'Be quiet, please.'"

Anna raised her eyes heavenward. God, give me strength. "Sorry, honey," she told the tot. "I'll do better next time." She lowered herself into the seat beside Brock's. "Why are you here?"

His gaze slid to the side, a sure sign of an impending lie.

"My therapist said I should come."

She blinked rapidly. "Sorry, I thought you said therapist."

"I did." He slumped in his seat. "After your boyfriend attacked me, my boss gave me an ultimatum—get help for anger management or find a new job."

"Bull poop." She glanced at the kids in the corner. "Diego didn't attack you."

Brock crossed his arms and pouted, but he didn't contradict her.

"I don't want you in the delivery room, Brock."

"I'm the baby's father." His lip protruded further. "I'll be there if I want to."

Anna fisted a handful of his shirt and yanked him close. "Listen to me," she hissed through clenched jaws. "I know my rights, and you will absolutely not—"

"Anna?" Sherri, Dr. Tanaka's nurse, stood in the doorway, file in hand.

Of all the days for her doc to be running early. Anna rose, and so did Brock. He followed her down the hallway and stood silently while Sherri took Anna's blood pressure and weight. "A hundred fifty-seven. Right where you should be."

Brock snorted.

Sherri's smile flattened. "Who is this bozo?"

"My ex-husband."

"Eew." She leaned in and whispered. "You want me to call security?"

For a moment, Anna let herself imagine one of the burly guards tossing Brock out on his skinny behind. Then Papaya gave a sharp kick, bringing her back to reality. Both her lawyer and their divorce mediator advised her to avoid any appearance of alienating Brock from his child, which meant if he wanted to sit in on her exam, she'd better let him. Until they got to the pants-off part.

"Just ignore him," she said with a sigh.

"Right. You're in exam room three. This way." Sherri shot a wary glance at Brock, who trooped after them with no further snark.

"Just hop onto the table, Anna. Dr. T will be with you in a moment." With one more pointed look at Brock, she left them alone.

"Okay, out with it."

With an eye roll worthy an aggrieved teen, Brock sank into a seat. "Why can't you believe I'm interested in the welfare of our child?"

"Because you've shown zero interest so far, except when it gave you a chance to hassle me."

He huffed a sigh. "You're merciless, you know that? Someday, our kid is going to disappoint you too. Is this how you'll treat her?"

Ouch. He did have a point—or perhaps a tiny fraction of a point.

She squirmed on the exam table, making the paper covering crackle. "I'll love our daughter always, though she may need tough love someday."

"Tough love. Hmmph." His gaze roamed the room. "You must be pretty sick of all these appointments."

She shrugged. "It makes me feel better knowing the baby's growing as expected."

"Must be pretty uncomfortable, now that you're all..." He waved his hand toward her middle.

Choose your words carefully, Brock.

His eyes narrowed as he gave her a head-to-toe inspection. "Does it hurt, carrying all that weight?"

She scanned the room for something to bash him with.

He lifted his palms. "Look, I'm trying to show an interest here. The baby's due in, what, five weeks?"

"One month from today."

"Holy shit." He ran a hand through his hair, mussing it in a most un-Brock-like way. "One month more, and I'm gonna be a dad. It's really starting to sink in. At first, I couldn't picture myself with a kid. But there she is, a tiny person." He gave a wobbly smile. "Hope she gets your nose."

Anna chuckled. "I hope she gets your height."

He laced his fingers together between his knees. "Do you think she'll like me?"

The vulnerability in his gaze touched her—a tiny glimpse of the Brock she fell for years ago, the one with a sense of humor and a heart. It was too late to repair what they'd broken, but maybe they could work out this coparenting business after all.

Dr. Tanaka bustled in, all brisk efficiency and wide smiles. "Anna, dear. Good to see you. Oh." She started at the sight of Brock. "And you are?"

He rose and extended his hand. "Brock Spenser, ma'am. I'm the baby's father."

"Ah, the ex-husband." Dr. T's nose wrinkled. "And you're here...why?"

Anna hid her grin behind her hand. I love you, Dr. T.

"Well, it's my kid too. Why shouldn't I be here?"

Ignoring him, Dr. T sat on her rolling stool and prodded Anna's abdomen. "Baby's movements still vigorous?"

"Very." Anna patted her belly. "She's a little judo champ."

"Good. How's your energy?"

A knock on the door, and Charlie entered carrying two coffees. "Hi, Dr. T."

"Charlie, good to see you. How are the birthing classes? Any questions for me?"

Brock raised a finger. "Actually, I was wondering—"

All three women stared at him.

His voice wavered. "Is it too late for me to, you know, help out?"

Anna's stomach plummeted. Dr. Tanaka must've noticed, because she rose from her stool and pressed her hand to Anna's forehead. "Deep breaths, hon."

Brock spread his hands wide. "Look, I'm not trying to upset Anna. I just want to be a part of this experience, you know? I want my daughter to know I'm her dad."

Dr. T faced him, her expression stern. "That's entirely up to Anna. But in my professional opinion, it's best for a laboring mother to keep stress to a minimum. Anna?"

Why did he have to insert himself now? Why couldn't he just stay on the sidelines like he had for the past eight months?

She straightened her spine. "I'm sorry, Brock. Charlie is my birth coach. You'll have to wait until the baby is born."

"Oh." His face fell. "If that's what you want."

"It is." She reached out her hand. "But Charlie will text you when I'm in labor. You can meet our daughter as soon as the doctor says it's okay."

Charlie scowled but nodded.

"Yeah, okay. That's fair." Brock raised his finger again. "So, I've definitely got another month?"

"In general, due dates are give or take a few weeks," Dr. Tanaka said, "but first babies tend to be late rather than early."

"Good." He rose. "There's a golf tournament in Bellingham on the weekend before." He answered Charlie's incredulous scowl with a shrug. "It's kind of my last hurrah. Pretty soon I'll be busy with dad stuff."

Charlie snorted. "You'd risk missing your kid's birth for golf?"

Anna gripped her sister's arm. "It's fine, Brock. Go. Enjoy yourself." Secretly, she hoped he'd miss the birth entirely, giving her, Diego, and the baby time to bond without his interference.

"Well, that's settled." Dr. Tanaka stepped to the counter and pulled on a pair of rubber gloves. "Now, if you'll excuse us, I need to examine Anna's cervix.

Brock's gaze darted from Anna to the door, and for a sickening moment, she thought he'd ask to stay for that bit too. But Charlie gave him a shove. "Let's go, Daddy."

Dr. Tanaka chuckled as she extended the stirrups on the exam table. "Looks like your ex is trying to make up for lost time."

Anna lay back, spread her knees, and sighed. Brock would always be a pain in her behind, but she was stuck with him. Today's encounter might be a fluke, an act designed to lower her defenses. On the other hand, maybe there was hope yet for an amicable partnership for the baby's sake. As much as she hated the idea, she had to give Brock a chance.

Chapter Twenty-Seven: Empanada Angel

♥

Carrying an offering of her favorite dessert empanada, apple-marionberry, Diego popped out of the Airstream for the hundredth time to check on Anna. No change—she sat under her golf umbrella, her feet propped up, a tinsel halo perched on her head and an Empanada Angel apron draped over her huge baby bump, yelling like a 1920s newsboy.

"Empanaaaadas. Hot and spicy. Get your empanaaaadas."

He handed her the pastry. "Sure you don't want to go home? It's gotta be cooler than here."

The Tacoma Dome parking lot shimmered in the August heat, and the huge crowd attending this Food Truck Derby just added more noise and heat. She couldn't be comfortable here, but she'd insisted on helping, and telling Anna no didn't come easy.

"Pssht." She waved away his concern. "The baby's not due for another week, and first babies are usually late. Waiting alone at home would drive me buggy." Grabbing his apron, she pulled him down for a smooch. "Besides, I want to support you, and this is entertaining."

Their spot on the lot's upper slope offered prime people-watching. The tepid breeze stirred cooking smells from the twenty-five food trucks into a heady stew of spicy, greasy, meaty, cheesy, sugary temptation. On the beer garden stage, a nineties cover band gyrated in perfect boy-band unison.

Anna lifted her water flask. "Quit worrying about me, okay? I'm hydrated, I've got shade, and the Porta-Potty isn't too gross. Hey, is Abuelita coming out to dance with Monty again? That was a hoot."

Milo wasn't available this weekend, and Diego flat-out refused to let Anna work inside the truck, so today's crew consisted of his grandmother and her two housemates, who all got their food-service licenses for the occasion. With the two grandmas taking orders and ex-army cook Monty manning the fryer, empanadas flew out the service window.

Winning today's competition, or even placing, would be a huge boost to his career. Already, reporters from three different foodie websites had stopped by to interview him. Abuelita's salsa dancing skills probably had something to do with that. For a lady pushing ninety, she still had impressive moves.

Among the crowd waiting for their empanadas, a little boy of maybe three or four pointed at Anna and shouted, "Does that lady have a baby in her tummy?"

His mother mouthed, "Sorry," but Anna didn't seem to mind.

"I sure do." She beckoned. "Want to say hi to her?"

The kid ran to her side.

"She's kicking a lot today. See?" She pressed his hand to her belly. The little guy stilled for a moment of intense concentration, then squealed and bounced. His infectious laughter brought a smile to Diego's lips. Soon, their home would ring with the same joyful sound.

On his next check-in, Diego found Elena seated across from Anna, massaging her feet. Anna turned down the chicken pot pie empanada he offered, but Elena snatched it up.

"Can you believe it?" she said between bites. "This close to the birth of his kid, Douchewaffle goes on a golf trip."

"No big deal." Anna squirmed in her seat. "If he were here, he'd just make a pest of himself. Hey, 'Lena, come to the restroom with me? This kid is dancing on my bladder."

Diego took one hand, Elena took the other, and they heaved Anna to her feet. She clutched her belly for a moment.

Alarm prickled his skin. "Something wrong?"

"Just another Braxton-Hicks contraction." She blew out a breath through pursed lips. "That was a good one." Her over-bright smile didn't soothe his nerves one tiny bit. "All done. Off we go."

"Watch her," he whispered to his sister.

"Yeah, yeah." She tapped her sternum. "Medical professional, remember?"

Nibbling his lip, he watched until the crowd swallowed them up.

About twenty minutes later, Abuelita's yelp jerked his attention from the salad bin.

"What is it, 'Lita? Did you hurt yourself?"

"Outside, now." She gave him a hearty shove.

He nearly tripped down the stairs in his haste. He found Anna bent over, hands on her knees, puffing hard. Elena clutched her phone. "That's seven minutes."

"Is it time?" He could hardly force the words out his tight throat.

"Can't be," Anna said with a grunt. "Doc says next week."

Abuelita stepped between them and rubbed Anna's back. She and Elena exchanged a knowing look. "Anna." Elena cupped her face. "Does this contraction feel like the other ones?"

"Hurts a little more, but that's normal, right?" Anna straightened and gave Diego a tense smile. "Maybe I will go home. If I just lie down—" She gasped and clutched her apron. "Oh, shit."

He followed her downward glance to the puddle growing at her feet. "Is that...Are you...?"

Like a brisk little general, Abuelita grabbed the reins. "Go now, Gogo. Get her things from the house—"

Anna clutched his arm with painfully surprising strength. "My go bag's in my trunk."

"Straight to the hospital, then." Abuelita smacked his arm hard. "What are you waiting for?"

"But the food truck," Anna protested.

"We got this," Elena said in a tone that brooked no argument. "I'll call Charlie and let her know you're on your way. Now go."

Somehow, Diego unglued his feet from the pavement and wound his arm around Anna's shoulder. "Make way. Coming through. We're having a baby."

They stopped twice for Anna to breathe through contractions, but finally made it to her car. Saturday afternoon traffic was fierce, and people must've wondered why the lunatic behind them kept blaring his horn and why his passenger was wearing a halo. As they neared the hospital, her grunts morphed into long groans that tore at his guts. Nearly side-swiping a delivery truck, he peeled into the emergency room lot, then bolted from his car and dashed into the lobby. "Hey. Somebody. We're having a baby."

A plump nurse stepped around the counter far too slowly. "Take it easy, Dad. Where's your wife?"

"Shit!" He dashed back to the car, flung open Anna's door, and helped her to her feet.

A guy in scrubs pushed a wheelchair into place, and together they lowered Anna into it. "Who's your doc, hon'?" he asked.

"Dr. Tanaka," Diego barked. Charlie was Anna's birth coach, but he'd memorized all the pertinent details. "Fourth floor. Let's go." Pulse racing, he pivoted Anna's chair toward the entrance.

"Easy now, Mario Andretti." Chuckling, Scrubs Guy nudged Diego aside and gripped the handles. "Follow me."

The elevator ride took for-freakin' ever, especially with Anna's grunts of pain. How long since her last contraction? It couldn't have been more than five minutes.

Up in the maternity ward, nurses bustled around Anna as they helped her into a hospital gown, hooked up an IV line, and attached monitor wires.

A nurse grabbed his shoulder. "Booties on your shoes, Charlie, then wash your hands and put on this gown." She steered him toward a sink.

"Oh, I'm not—"

"Hurry up, son. This baby's coming fast." The nurse patted Anna's arm. "Lucky girl. My first labor lasted two days."

"Mine lasted three," another chirped. "Then I ended up having a C-section. I was so pissed."

"Enough with the horror stories." Oops. Hadn't meant to bark at them. He lowered his voice. "Can we focus on Anna?"

"Ow, ow, ow!" Anna hollered, her head thrashing from side to side. "Is it supposed to hurt this much?"

Dr. Tanaka strode in. "Big day at last. You ready, Anna?"

"Diego," she growled through clenched teeth, her face contorted in a grimace.

He darted to her side and took her clammy hand.

What do I do? He hadn't attended any of Anna's birthing classes since that was Charlie's job. But right now, he was all Anna had. He couldn't fall apart. Shutting his eyes tight, he forced his breath to slow and pushed his own fears aside.

"You got this, love. I'm right here. Whatever you need, just tell me." He smoothed her hair from her damp forehead.

Holding his gaze, she pressed her lips into a tight line and nodded.

The doctor tapped her tablet. "Where's your sister?"

"Coming." Anna grunted again, the let fly a howl. "Motherfucker, that hurts."

Chuckling, he pressed a kiss to her forehead. "Listen to you, Miss Potty-Mouth. I knew you had it in you."

"Sorry," she muttered between panting breaths. "Bad example for the baby."

Dr. Tanaka pulled a rolling stool between Anna's legs. "Go ahead and curse if it helps, dear. We've heard it all."

While the doc checked down below, Anna puffed, and growled, and flung curses that would make a gangbanger blush.

"Where the ever-lovin' fuck is my sister?" She asked with a moan.

Diego tapped his phone screen and found a text from Charlie. Shitshitshit. An accident on the Tacoma Narrows Bridge had her stuck in traffic with no way to turn around. He composed a quick text to reassure her, then turned back to Anna. "On her way. Want me to rub your back?"

"Please."

A moment later, a nurse poked her head through the door. "Family's here, Anna. Your dad, your aunt and uncle, and your sister Elena."

Dr. Tanaka looked up from between Anna's knees. "We're almost there. They'll have to wait. Don't push yet, Anna."

"Gotta push," she growled and squeezed Diego's hand so hard his bones crunched.

"You're almost at ten centimeters. Just a few more minutes, hon'." Her face a mask of impenetrable calm, the doc turned away to check the monitors.

How did she do it? Didn't she know Anna was in freakin' pain? It took every atom of self-control Diego had not to howl along with her.

Keep your shit together, idiot. He leaned his cheek against Anna's. "You're so strong, angel. I'm so proud of you."

"Hold my hand," she hissed. "Baby's coming."

"Yes, she is." The doctor beamed. "Okay, Anna, on the next contraction, I want you to push with all you've got."

Anna gulped air like a drowning woman, then curled up off the pillow as the next contraction hit her. The scream that tore from her throat shredded him, but he held on tight, supporting her shoulders with his free arm.

"Good girl." The doc patted Anna's thigh. "Another couple of pushes and you'll be there. Ready?"

"Fuuuuuuck me sideways with a motherfuckin' briiiiick," Anna roared. Sweat beaded her forehead and soaked her hair.

The nurses called out encouragement, and Diego joined the chorus. "You're amazing, Anna. Keep going. Almost there. I love you so much."

She grunted, and pushed, and—

A thin wail rang out.

Anna's grimace relaxed into a happy sob. "Hold me up. Let me see her."

The doc held up a purple, splotchy, squirming miracle.

Eyes shut tight, tiny fists clenched, the baby howled so loudly her whole body vibrated.

Anna's eyes met Diego's with a joyful gaze he'd remember to his dying day. "We did it."

"You did it, angel." His arm still around her shoulders, he watched the doc lift Anna's gown and place the baby against her bare tummy. The little one calmed at once, waving her limbs like a clumsy swimmer.

"Hey, baby," Anna sobbed and caressed her daughter's damp head. "Welcome to the world."

The baby's eyes opened, just a slit, as she took her first look at her mom and her—uncle? Stepdad to be? Who cares what people called him? He would love this child and her brave, beautiful mother forever.

The next morning, Anna woke to something stroking her cheek. She opened her eyes to find Diego bent over her bed, his dark eyes sparkling with tenderness.

"Sleep well?"

"Diego, hey." She stretched and reached for him, then winced as her sore muscles protested. Fondness overwhelmed her as she held his gaze. How could she ever have made it through that rollercoaster birth without his strong arms holding her? "Thank you, love. You're my rock." She glanced at the little sofa beneath the window. "Did you sleep there all night?"

"Hey, if you can push a person out of your body, I can sleep on a couch." He stroked her hair. "I've never been more impressed with anyone, ever. You're a warrior, Anna."

"A sticky one. Wonder when they'll let me take a shower. She pushed up on her elbow. "Baby?"

He pointed to the bassinet beside her bed. "Snoozing again. Have you decided on a name?"

"Let me think on it some more over breakfast. After all, I've only just met her." In truth, she was still somewhat ill at ease with her choice of a middle name and wanted to see Brock before deciding.

A raspy squeak from the bassinet jerked her attention to the baby.

"Here you go, squirt." Diego rolled the crib closer, and Anna gingerly lifted the little one to her chest.

"Hungry again? Good thing your Abbi is a chef." She opened her gown, and the baby latched onto Anna's nipple right away, grunting like an adorable piglet. The gentle tug on her breast unleashed a sweet sense of relaxation and primal connection.

"Abbi?" Diego toyed with the baby's fingers as she gobbled her breakfast.

"Means Daddy in Arabic. It's what I called my dad when I was little." She felt herself blushing. "If you don't like it, you can pick another nickname."

"Abbi. I like that." He pressed a kiss to Anna's temple, then gave a little gasp. "Look, she's got my finger."

"You amazing little person," Anna cooed, stroking the baby's downy dark hair. "I'm going to take good care of you, and protect you, and teach you to ride a bike, and Uncle Diego will teach you how to cook because I'm horrible at that, sorry. But we'll have so much fun together." The baby let go and urped up a bit of milk.

"All done?" She kissed her daughter's and inhaled her milky baby scent. Powerful stuff that made her heart squeeze in the nicest way.

"Gotta do both breasts, honey," said the nurse Anna hadn't noticed enter the room. "Your family is here whenever you're ready."

"Oh, I, uh—" She gestured to her bare breast. Charlie and Aunt Hala were no problem, but she wasn't quite ready to flash her swollen boobs and Dad and Uncle Fred.

"Just buzz when you're ready." The nurse nudged the call button thingy closer. "Such a pretty baby."

When the door closed, Diego's misty smile faltered. "There's someone else here to see you."

She blinked for a moment, baffled at who could make him look so solemn.

Oh.

"Yeah. Raced back from his golf thing. To his credit, when the nurse told him you were sleeping, he actually planted his ass in the waiting room like a reasonable person."

Anna chuckled. "Miracles do happen, I guess. Go ahead and send him in."

Looking slightly horrified, Diego glanced at her bare breast. "You want me to stay?"

She shook her head. "We have to work this out. Might as well start now." To placate him, she drew the receiving blanket over her bare breast.

"As you wish. But if he gives you any shit, just yell. I'll be right outside."

A moment later, Brock pushed the door open and hovered in the doorway clutching a bouquet of pink and white roses.

"Hey, Anna." He shuffled one foot on the linoleum. "You okay?"

"Sore, but yeah. I'll be fine."

"Listen." He stepped into the room and raised his gaze to hers. He looked different, rumpled and unguarded. "I'm sorry I wasn't here. I should've been."

I'm so glad you weren't. Brock might come to love the baby in time, but he didn't love Anna, and his presence at such a vulnerable moment would only bring pain.

His pointy chin trembled, just a bit. "I missed my kid's birth because of a stupid golf tournament. It's a moment I can never get back." He reached out his hand. "I promise you, I'll never miss another of our daughter's important moments. Never." He sniffed hard and pressed his lips into a tight line.

She took his hand and gazed at those long fingers wrapped around hers. She'd never love him as she once did, but they were partners of a sort, and undeniably family. This was their chance to heal the breech.

"I'll hold you to that."

"How's our little angel?" The nurse sing-songed as carried in Anna's breakfast tray. "Oh." She looked Brock up and down. "You must be Anna's...?"

He blushed bright red.

Gonna spend the rest of my life explaining this. "Brock is the baby's father. Diego is my boyfriend."

The nurse shrugged. "Modern families, eh?" Leaning over the hospital bed, she cooed, "You 'bout done with your breakfast, cutie? Your mama needs hers."

"Here you go." Anna rearranged the baby's swaddling blanket and set her in the bassinet.

"Can I hold her?" Brock asked in a tremulous voice.

"Oh. Of course." Her stomach tightened as she watched him gingerly lift their newborn daughter. "Support her head."

"I know. My mom's been drilling me on new-baby care." Awe softened the sharpness of his face as he folded his sleeping daughter against his chest. "She's so beautiful. We did this?"

"Well, your part in the endeavor was pretty small."

He flinched, and she instantly regretted her snark. He deserved a chance to get to know his daughter too.

"But yeah, she's yours. See those dark-blue eyes?"

"What's her name?" he whispered as he traced her tiny cheek with his fingertip.

Okay then. A peace gesture. She'd first thought to call the baby Elizabeth Hala, but...

"Elizabeth Rose."

When he looked up, his eyes sparkled with tears. "Rose for my grandma?"

"Yeah." Brock's maternal grandmother was the only member of the Spencer clan she liked. "And Elizabeth for my mom."

"That's perfect." Snuffling, he hunched over the baby and cooed nonsense, rocking her slowly.

The door banged open, and Brock's mother strode in. "Is that her? Is that my precious angel?"

Brock whirled on her. "Mom, keep it down. You'll wake the baby."

"Can I hold her?" Deborah asked her son, not Anna.

Brock shot Anna a grin tinged with embarrassment.

This moment would set the tone going forward. Anna lifted her chin and stared at Deborah until the older woman acknowledged her.

"Of course you can hold your granddaughter." Taking the high road didn't hurt quite as badly as she feared. "But I expect all this hostility to stop, Deborah. For Elizabeth Rose's sake."

"You named her after my mother?" The Dragon Lady's voice wobbled.

Anna allowed herself the tiniest smirk.

Brock carefully laid the baby in Deborah's arms, then turned to Anna. "I'll sign the parenting plan. There's no need to go to court."

Deborah squawked, but Brock shut her down. "She's my daughter. It's my job to give her the best life I can. Fighting with Anna won't help."

With a huge sigh, Anna sank into her pillows. Time would tell, but for now it looked like little Lizzie just might grow up in a big, loving family. Lizzie? Liza? Eliza? Beth?

With a blast of too-loud talk, the Khoury clan spilled into the room, followed by the shift nurse. "Now hold on," she admonished the crowd. "Too many visitors. Someone's got to go."

"We were just leaving." Brock pried the baby from Deborah's arms, kissed her forehead, and placed her back in her crib. "See you soon, Anna."

Deborah pointed a stabby finger at Diego. "How come he gets to stay?"

"He's Anna's boyfriend. Partner. Whatever." As he passed, Brock clapped Diego on the shoulder. "Thanks for being there for Anna."

Anna chuckled at Deborah's slack-jawed reaction, then turned to her family. "Guys, meet Elizabeth Rose Spenser-Khoury."

Epilogue: Ellie's Debut

♥

"Feels weird, bringing a baby to a bar." Anna giggled as she pushed Ellie's carriage toward Bangers Tavern.

Diego held the door and waved her through with a flourish. "Not when she's the guest of honor."

"Pretty sure that's you, love." Anna pecked his cheek as she passed.

"Babeeee!" Squeeing like tweens at a K-Pop concert, Rosie and Lana rushed forward.

"Easy now." Diego stepped between his former coworkers and Ellie. "Don't scare her. Or Anna, for that matter."

Anna unwound Ellie from her blankets and lifted her from her carriage. "Up you go, Peanut. Say hi to your aunties."

"How old is she now?" Rosie asked, her hands clasped to her heart.

"Five weeks. Careful, she's got grabby hands." Sure enough, Ellie's tiny fist reached for Rosie's bright blue curls.

Cradling Ellie's head, Anna rested the baby against her shoulder to give her a good view of her Abbi's farewell party. Not that he was going very far, but with Maci settled into the Bangers kitchen, Diego was officially passing the baton.

Anna giggled. Passing the spatula? The fryer basket?

In any case, Diego's nights of slinging tater tots were over, and Dawn insisted on an official farewell party now that Ellie was old enough to attend.

"How's my favorite cutie pie?" Jojo strode up and reached out a finger. Ellie examined it with wobbly intensity, then grasped it tight.

"That's right. I'm your Uncle Jojo. Can you say Jojo?"

Ellie grunted and blew a spit bubble.

"Close enough." Jojo beamed. "See, the ladies can't resist me."

"Such an ego." Lana swatted his massive arm, but Anna spotted a glimmer of fondness behind her smirk. And really, what was cuter than a grown man playing with a baby? She never got tired of watching Diego and Ellie babble back and forth. Well, Ellie babbled, and Diego interpreted.

Like right now. "What's that, mijita? You want to say hi to Mama Dawn? Let's go find her." He pried Ellie's tiny fingers from Jojo's giant one and danced her toward the bar.

Lana followed him with her gaze and sighed. "You're a lucky girl, Anna. You landed a good one."

"Amen." She nudged her with her elbow. "You've got a good one too."

"What do you mean?" Lana's wrinkled nose didn't fool Anna for a minute. She knew darn well Jojo was gaga for her.

While Diego made the rounds with Ellie, Anna eased into a booth and propped up her feet. Five weeks into this motherhood adventure, she was still bloated, usually exhausted, and absolutely blown away with love for her noisy, drooly, gassy little angel. The whole world was brand-new to Ellie, and her comical expressions as she took it all in kept Anna and Diego laughing—especially when she pooped. And now that he no longer worked nights, Diego was a champ about soothing Ellie's nighttime fussiness so Anna could sleep.

Charlie joined her in the booth and slid Anna a tall, frosted glass. "Spiced apple sparkler, mocktail o' the day." She chuckled. "Ellie's a charmer. You're gonna give everyone in here baby fever."

"You and River would make pretty babies," she teased.

Charlie made a stink face. "Me? A mom? When donkeys fly."

"Uh-huh." Anna glanced at the bar, where River babbled gibberish at the baby. "Look at that sappy grin. I give you guys two, three years tops before Ellie has a little cousin."

"Hmph. How'd it go with Brock yesterday?"

"Better than I expected." She'd been a nervous wreck for all four hours Brock had the baby, despite the flurry of videos he sent—Ellie in the park, Ellie in the toy store, Ellie spitting up on her Grandmama Deborah's fancy couch. And he delivered her back home exactly on time, expertly extracting her from the fanciest car seat Anna had ever seen. "It's got an app, see?" he explained. "Monitors her temperature and alerts if her harness comes loose." He handed over a paper sack of picture books. "Got you extra copies of her favorites. Never too early to start reading."

Who'd a thunk it? Brock was really into his new role. She hoped his enthusiasm would last.

Anna fished her phone from her bag and showed Charlie the videos Brock sent. "Next Sunday comes another milestone—we're taking Ellie to Diego's parents for Sunday dinner."

"You worried?"

"Terrified. But Diego's confident she'll win them over, and Elena's little Oscar wants to meet his new cousin."

Dawn rang the ship's bell behind the bar. "Settle down, kiddos. Let's get this party started. Those karaoke nuts will get ugly if I don't open by seven."

Diego brought Ellie back to the booth and sat beside Anna, cradling the sleeping baby to his chest.

"Okay, Shelby," Dawn called.

A buzzing, tinny sound drifted from the hallway, getting louder as it approached. "What on earth?" When she saw the source, she nearly sprayed her drink across the table. Shelby and Maci came dancing from the kitchen, each with a kazoo in her mouth. Shelby held a sparkler-decked cake, and Maci carried a platter of chicken wings.

Clapping and dancing, the rest of the Bangers crew fell in line, singing, "Na na na na, na na na na, Dee-Ay-Go, good-bye."

Diego laughed so hard she worried he might piss himself.

Dawn beckoned. "Get up here, you two."

He pulled Anna to her feet, and off they went to join the dance party. Diego's bouncing steps woke the baby, who urped on his shoulder. Still chuckling, he handed her off to Anna and wiped up the mess.

"Speech, speech!" Shelby called.

Diego blotted his streaming eyes with his sleeve and raised his hand until the chanting and singing quieted. "Guys, this is too much."

"I'd say it's not enough," Dawn corrected him, her eyes misty. "You've been great for Bangers, kiddo. Your creative tots drew customers from all over Tacoma, and your smile lit up the place." Her voice wobbled. "Now you're going out on your own. And I couldn't be prouder."

Anna's heart swelled with love and pride for her sweet, smart, generous partner. Their near disaster at the food truck festival gave the Empanada Angel a huge boost, but Diego's hard work is what pushed his business into the black. Between social media coverage of her water breaking and the Tacoma News Tribune's story on the aftermath, Diego had more bookings than he could handle —farmers markets, street fairs, private parties, and Bangers' Halloween Bash. And whenever she stopped by with Ellie, the lines for empanadas got even longer. Funny, she always spotted a few heavily pregnant women in line. Rumor had Diego's pastries could speed a late delivery.

Who knows? Maybe they could. There was magic in Diego's cooking—of that she had no doubt. He poured so much love into his food and made Empanada Angel's every gig a fun party with salsa music, campy beach umbrellas, and—if customers pestered him enough—he'd pop out from the Airstream to dance with them.

Yeah, luck got him started, but his huge, generous heart made him a success.

Diego's voice broke as he addressed his chosen family. "Bangers has been my home for five years. You all have become my family." He threw his arm around Anna's shoulders and squeezed her tight against his side. "I met the love of my life here. But hey, this isn't good-bye. Look for me parked outside Anna's hospital selling breakfast empanadas Monday through Friday." He smooched her temple. "That way, when she goes back to work, I can be sure she's well fed."

Ellie chose that moment give a loud yawn.

"Aww," everyone chorused and closed in for teary hugs.

Anna retreated with the baby and a piece of cake while the others oohed and aahed over Maci's jerk chicken wings. Tears pricked her eyes as she watched Shelby squeeze Diego tight, her spiky head tucked under his chin. "Gonna miss you, man," she muttered into his chest.

"Naw." He ruffled her hair. "I'll visit so often you'll be sick of me."

River poured drinks all around. Everyone toasted Diego's new beginning, Ellie's health, and Anna, the newest member of the Bangers family.

At last, Diego returned to her side and pressed a teary kiss to her temple, then another to the top of Ellie's fuzzy head before tucking the sleeping baby into her carriage. "Well," he said with a sniffle, "that's that. The end of an era."

She leaned onto his shoulder. "Are you sad?"

"A little. But also very, very happy." His dark eyes sparkled. "Those guardian angels Abuelita sent our way? They know what they're doing, eh?"

"Yeah." She lifted her drink. "Here's to angels."

He raised his glass. "To you, angel. You believed in me, and you made me believe in myself."

They clinked.

"I've got one," Anna added. "Here's to the man who refused to give up on us. He's the best man I know."

His gaze softened, his lips parted, and he took her mouth in a slow, sweet kiss that went on and on. They were still kissing when the karaoke D.J. started his sound check. And when Dawn finally stepped up to their booth. "Uh, guys. Babies aren't allowed in the bar once it's open."

Grinning, Diego pulled Anna to her feet. "Let's go home, my lovelies. Thanks a million, Dawn, for everything."

On their way out, he took a last, wistful look around Bangers. From now on, he'd be a visitor, not a member of the team. But the wonderful people who worked here would always be family.

Arm in arm, they walked into the crisp autumn night, toward a lifetime of shared tomorrows.

Thanks for reading Anna and Diego's story! Want a little more of their love story? Click here for a bonus epilogue with Anna and Diego's wedding in Tacoma's Point Defiance Park. You'll also get Cupid's Silver Spark: A Bangers Tavern Romance Novella, yours free for joining my monthly reader newsletter.

If you enjoyed Delicious Heat, please consider leaving a review on your favorite eBook retailer or review site.

Read on for cocktail recipes from Delicious Heat.

♥

Boozy Emerald Shake

River makes this with marshmallow-flavored vodka, but whipped cream flavor or vanilla flavor work just as well. For each milkshake, combine in a blender 2 scoops of vanilla ice cream, ¼ cup milk, an ounce of crème de menthe, a shot of flavored vodka, and a few drops of green food coloring. Whirl it up, add more green if needed, pour into a tall glass, and garnish with whipped cream and rainbow sprinkles. Not the tiniest bit Irish, but delish!

Irish Mule

Fill a copper mug with ice—or use any substantial mug or glass. I won't tell! Pour in a generous shot of your favorite Irish whiskey. Kiara prefers Tullamore D.E.W., but you do you! Add the juice of half a lime, then top with a bit of good ginger beer. Stir and taste. Maybe you want more ginger beer, maybe you want more whiskey. At Bangers, we don't judge. Garnish with thinly sliced lime and a sprig of fresh mint. Sláinte!

Baileys Mint Martini

Fill a cocktail shaker with ice. Dump in one ounce each of Baileys Irish Cream, Crème de Menthe, vodka, and heavy cream or half and half. Shake it up good, then strain into a martini glass. Have fun with garnishes: shaved chocolate, whipped cream, fresh mint? It's magically delicious!

Acknowledgments

♥

One of the many things I love about writing fiction is the chance to try out (virtually) the many careers I never got a chance to pursue in real life. So far, I've written about running a bookshop (Through the Red Door), an ice cream shop (Gelato Surprise), being a photographer (Runaway Love Story), a graphics artist, a potter (Love, Art, and Other Obstacles), a tattoo artist (Opposites Ignite) a bar owner, and now a food-truck chef!

I owe a huge thanks to the many professionals who answer my pesky questions. Thanks to Michael Graham from KKWT Process Server in Tacoma for his lesson on serving divorce papers, and to Officer J. Mortensen of the Salt Lake City P.D. for his advice on Diego's arrest.

Thanks to my beta readers Laurie Ryan, Cari Davis, and Marie Tuhart for untangling my plot knots. A huge smooch to my editor Judi Mobley, AKA Music City Freelance Editor. Another smooch for Dar Albert of Wicked Smart Designs for her lovely cover.

And most of all, thanks to my husband for supporting me in my writing journey. You're the BHE!

jump-start their careers. Their surprise connection sizzles, but can he battle past her defenses and prove he loves her as she is? Rivals to lovers, bisexual heroine, grumpy/sunshine.

Gelato Surprise, a standalone beach romance novella
When her dastardly ex spoils their family vacation, Danielle heads to the beach alone to lick her wounds. Dashing young gelato vendor Matteo is too delicious to resist. He's determined to make their vacation fling last beyond summer, but convincing her he can fit into her life will take much more than sweet treats and summer kisses. Older woman/younger man, divorced heroine, summer fling.

The Bangers Tavern Romance Series

Sizzling contemporary romance set in neighborhood bar in Tacoma, Washington. Found family, all the feels, and the best tater tots in town!

Christmas Rekindled: Bangers Tavern Romance One
Bangers' bartender River has a damn good reason for hating Christmas, and an equally good reason for resenting new server Charlie—until a kiss under the mistletoe flares hot enough to melt the North Pole. To save the bar they love, these two Scrooges must put aside their enmity and find the good in each other. Enemies to lovers, fake dating, workplace romance.

Opposites Ignite: Bangers Tavern Romance Two
A mismatch sparks the hottest flames! Bodacious, curvy, blue-haired, aspiring tattoo artist Rosie is too smart to fall

for her strait-laced coworker at Bangers Tavern. But his shy smile and quiet charm disarm her defenses just when she needs them most. Curvy heroine, shy hero, opposites attract.

Coming soon: Bangers Tavern 4, Jojo and Lana's story.

Pediatric phlebotomist by day and Bangers Tavern's hunky bouncer by night, Jojo Williams has been flirting with his coworker Lana Lopez for two years, but she never takes him seriously. Determined to convince her he's the one who belongs at her side, he plunges into the hot mess that keeps her from dating. If he screws this up, his heart and hers won't be the only ones broken.

Orphaned by a car wreck at twenty-two, Lana's sole focus is keeping her teen brothers on track and together in the home they grew up in. One more slip-up, and her interfering tías will separate the boys. The last thing Lana needs is a big goof like Jojo meddling with her fragile little family.

But when the boys' teen antics land them in trouble, Jojo may be the only person who can save them from the wrath of the tías. Her growing attraction to the gentle giant makes it harder and harder to shut him out, but loving him is a gamble that could cost her everything.

Exclusive to Sadira's newsletter subscribers!

Cupid's Silver Spark: A Bangers Tavern Romance Novella

Will Cupid's misfire cost her everything? Still stinging from a breakup, Carla Portofino wants nothing to do with Valentine's Day. When her bestie drags her to Bangers Tavern's Anti-Valentine's Bash, Cupid gifts her a swoonworthy silver fox. Maybe a no-strings fling is the remedy for her tattered heart? He seems perfect, until a greedy real estate development scheme tangles them in more string than either can handle. Seasoned romance, Valentine's Day, lovers to enemies to lovers.

To claim your copy, visit www.sadirastone.com and sign up for Sadira's monthly reader newsletter.